Praise for bestselling author
Cara Summers

"With exquisite flair, Ms. Summers thrills us
with her fresh, exciting voice, as well as
rich characterization and spicy adventure."
—*RT Book Reviews*

"A writer of incredible talent with a gift for emotional
stories laced with humor and passion."
—*Rendezvous*

"Ms. Summers weaves strong lovers and entertaining
secondary characters into a lush, suspenseful story."
—*RT Book Reviews* on *Intent to Seduce*

Praise for bestselling author
Debbi Rawlins

"When you combine two well-formed characters
with a romantic setting, loads of sexual tension,
a few laughs and a deft touch of realism,
you get a knockout story."
—*TheRomanceReader.com* on *If Wishes Were...Husbands*

"Rawlins's books are jam-packed
with witty dialogue, crazy situations,
excellent characters and a lot of laughs!"
—*Affaire de Coeur*

Was **CARA SUMMERS** born with the dream of becoming a published romance novelist? No. But now that she is, she still feels her dream has come true. She loves writing for the Harlequin Blaze line because it allows her to create strong, determined women and seriously sexy men who will risk everything to achieve *their* dreams.

Cara has written more than thirty books for Harlequin, and when she isn't working on new stories, she teaches in the writing program at Syracuse University and at a community college near her home.

DEBBI RAWLINS lives in central Utah, out in the country, surrounded by woods and deer and wild turkeys. It's quite a change for a city girl, who didn't even know where the state of Utah was until four years ago. Of course, unfamiliarity has never stopped her. Between her junior and senior years of college she spontaneously left her home in Hawaii and bummed around Europe for five weeks by herself. And much to her parents' delight, returned home with only a quarter in her wallet.

CARA SUMMERS

Intent to Seduce

DEBBI RAWLINS

A Glimpse of Fire

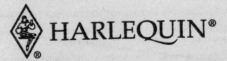

HARLEQUIN®

TORONTO • NEW YORK • LONDON
AMSTERDAM • PARIS • SYDNEY • HAMBURG
STOCKHOLM • ATHENS • TOKYO • MILAN • MADRID
PRAGUE • WARSAW • BUDAPEST • AUCKLAND

Recycling programs
for this product may
not exist in your area.

ISBN-13: 978-0-373-68816-6

INTENT TO SEDUCE & A GLIMPSE OF FIRE

Copyright © 2010 by Harlequin Books S.A.

The publisher acknowledges the copyright holder of the individual works as follows:

INTENT TO SEDUCE
Copyright © 2002 by Carolyn Hanlon

A GLIMPSE OF FIRE
Copyright © 2004 by Debbi Quattrone

This edition published by arrangement with Harlequin Books S.A.

For questions and comments about the quality of this book please contact us at Customer_eCare@Harlequin.ca.

www.eHarlequin.com

Printed in U.S.A.

CONTENTS

To my sister-in-law and friend, Julie Oliver Fulgenzi—the risk-taker who married my brother. Thanks for always being there and for being the voice of reason. I love you.

INTENT TO SEDUCE

Cara Summers

CHAPTER ONE

"LET ME GET THIS STRAIGHT," Sophie said. "You're planning to ask some man to offer himself up as a sex object so that you can practice on him?"

"*Sex object* isn't exactly the word I would have chosen." MacKenzie Lloyd kept her gaze locked on her best friend. Just as long as she didn't look down at the ground, the bubbles of panic rolling around in her stomach were going to subside. "I've conducted all these surveys on techniques and collected all this narrative data on male sexual fantasies. The next step is to test its validity in the field. What I need now is a research companion."

Sophie rolled her eyes. "Okay, nix *sex object*. We'll go with *research companion*. But I got the *practice* part right. You're not quibbling over semantics there."

Sophie was clearly upset. Mac could tell by the way she slapped her wineglass down and began to tap her fingers on the wide-planked floor of the tree house. They were seated just outside the doorway on a narrow platform. Only a small, flimsy railing separated them from a drop to the ground thirty feet below. If she let herself think about that...

Biting down on her lip, she fought against the sudden spin of dizziness that whipped through her. She would have been just fine if she hadn't glanced down on her climb-up-the-rope ladder. It had been the laughter from the tennis courts that had distracted her. The sound floated up again, bright, rich and infectious, but this time she resisted the temptation to look to her left beyond the hedge of forsythia bushes where four Wainrights were playing.

Tomorrow was Sophie Wainright's birthday, and the entire clan had gathered to celebrate it. Family was important to the Wainrights. It was something Mac had always admired about them—and envied.

What she intended to do was the best chance she had of creating and preserving that kind of family for herself.

"I know what I'm doing, Sophie."

"Do you?"

"I've been very thorough in my research, and I've learned so much."

Sophie rolled her eyes. "Some research. You've interviewed hookers and madams."

"Madame Gervais does not refer to herself as a madam. She runs a very exclusive finishing school for female companions. It's really more like a matchmaking service. Most of the girls she's trained have married the men she's introduced them to. They're really very bright women. The only difference between them and me is that they were very beautiful and very skilled at pleasuring a man in bed."

"And they shared all their secrets with you?"

Mac studied her friend. In addition to the worry in Sophie's eyes, she saw curiosity. Leaning a little closer, she said, "Pretty much. Did you know that if you wrap a string of pearls around a man's erection during fellatio, you can get amazing results?"

"Pearls?"

"You can use a silk tie—or better still, a wispy silk scarf—but pearls are the best. You wrap them around several times, then draw them slowly up the entire length, and then down again. Men love it."

"I don't doubt it. It's just that I…I don't like the idea of you wrapping your pearls around a stranger." Pausing, Sophie shook her head with a rueful sigh. "I should have known the minute you suggested coming up in this tree house that you were going to spring something on me. You dragged me up to the roof of my shop the night before you tried that last experiment in your lab—the one that gave you a breakthrough."

Mac tightened her grip on her knees and kept her eyes fixed on Sophie. "I figure if I can face my fear of heights, I can succeed at all the other things that scare me."

Sophie pointed a finger at her. "There. You *are* nervous about inviting some strange man to be your boy toy. And you should be." Then swearing softly, Sophie picked up Mac's wineglass and handed it to her. "Here. Take a drink of this. You're white as a sheet."

Mac took a careful sip.

"Why don't we get you out of here? I'll call Lucas. Between us, we can get you down the rope ladder."

"I'm fine."

Sophie studied her over the rim of her glass. "I wish I could be sure of that. This field-testing thing you're planning…it's not you."

"You're wrong. It *is* me. That's the beauty of it. I'm not good at dating or relationships, but I'm excellent at doing research and then devising a way to put the results to work. If I approach keeping a husband that way, I know I can do it."

"But you don't even have a husband yet. Shouldn't that be your first step?"

"That's the plan that most people follow and over fifty percent of all marriages fail. Research shows that the number one cause of divorce is infidelity. Usually it's the man who strays—just as soon as routine sets in. I saw that happen to my parents, and my plan is designed to prevent it."

Sophie gazed helplessly at Mac. "You're making it sound so logical, and it's not! Sex and relationships aren't something that you can map out and predict like something in your lab. Shit happens. Take it from someone who's been out there in the trenches."

Leaning forward, Mac took Sophie's hands in hers. "I'm sorry I'm laying all of this on you right now when you've just broken up with Bradley."

Sophie shrugged impatiently. "Bradley Davis is history. But he's a good example of what I'm talking about. When it comes to a relationship, there are no guarantees. And the only man I've ever been able to predict is my brother. He never gets involved emotionally in his relationships. He runs them the same way he runs Wainright Enterprises. And he thinks he has the right to run mine that way too."

Mac didn't say anything for a moment. Although more than a month had gone by, she knew Sophie still resented that Lucas had uncovered information on Bradley Davis that had caused her to break off her engagement. "The one thing that you can always depend on is that Lucas loves you, and he cares about what happens to you."

"He's smothering me. Ever since he took over Wainright Enterprises, he's decided that he can run all of our lives. He's even having me followed. But..." Sophie stopped, shook her head and then narrowed her eyes at Mac. "Oh no you don't. You're not going to change the subject. I want to know what I can say to convince you to drop this whole idea."

"Nothing."

Sophie slumped back against the wall of the tree house. "There's got to be something I can do."

"You don't have to worry. I've taken every possible safety precaution."

"I'd feel a lot happier about this if you were going to try out your research on someone you knew. What about that representative from the biotech company that's been wining and dining you lately?"

Mac made a face. "Vince Smith is panting over my research not me. All he talks about is how brilliant I am, what wonderful lab facilities they could provide for me if I would just sign over exclusive rights to anything I might discover."

Taking a sip of her wine, Mac pushed the thought of the man out of her mind. The truth was she wasn't good at dating. It probably had something to do with the fact that she'd started college at fourteen. The men she'd met had treated her like a kid sister. If they'd called her, it was to get help on some assignment they were having trouble with. And then, later, in graduate school, her two forays into the realm of romance had been disasters. "Men just don't seem to think of me in a sexual way."

"And they won't until you start to think of yourself that way."

"Now you sound just like Madame Gervais. In fact, she thinks field testing my research will increase my self-confidence."

Tilting her head to the side, Sophie studied Mac for a moment. "Maybe I'll have to revise my opinion of her. Is she the one who talked you into lightening your hair?"

Mac tucked a loose strand back into the bun she wore at the back of her neck. "Yes, and she took me shopping for a new wardrobe."

Sophie's eyes widened. "Why aren't you wearing it?"

"I bought most of the clothes for the field testing I'm going to do. I don't feel quite myself in them. When I put them on, I feel like I can do things Dr. MacKenzie Lloyd would never do."

Sophie paused with her wineglass halfway to her lips. "Oh? More stuff like the pearl trick?"

"Yes, and other kinds of things too. When Madame Gervais and I shopped for the clothes, we chose pieces that would facilitate some popular male fantasies."

Sophie studied her friend over the rim of her glass. "Okay, I'm hooked. How about filling me in a little more on the specifics of this research of yours?"

"I started out by reading a number of anthropological and sociological texts."

"Let's just fast-forward to the good stuff."

Mac grinned at her. "It's always good to have a sound theoretical background."

"Mac..."

"There's so much. You have no idea how many books have been written on sex. Or what's available online. There's this one woman who makes her living giving all-day seminars on how to...pleasure the penis."

Sophie choked on her wine. "All-day seminars?"

Mac nodded. "I went to one. We worked on plastic models."

"And you're actually going to field-test that on a complete stranger?"

"I'm trying to think of a fantasy I can fit it into."

Setting down her glass, Sophie said, "And these fantasies—what exactly are they like?"

"Well, there was one I found very interesting. It involved male bondage."

"Handcuffs, silk neckties—that kind of stuff?"

Mac shook her head. "Plastic wrap."

"Let me guess. You meet him at the door wearing nothing but?"

"Nope. It's the one where I wrap him up in it like a mummy. Of course, I would leave his nose free. And his toes." She smiled at Sophie. "And one other part."

"Something you could wrap your pearls around."

"Exactly. A blindfold is optional, but I've heard it doubles the pleasure."

"I'll bet. In these fantasies—is turnabout fair play?"

Mac blinked, then smiled slowly. "I think that depends on how well round one goes."

They were both laughing when the ringing of Sophie's cell phone interrupted them. Mac could tell by the expression on Sophie's face it was someone she was happy to hear from. When she moved inside the door of the tree house for privacy, Mac decided it was a new beau calling. Sophie just naturally attracted men.

Pressing her back against the wooden frame of the doorway, she reminded herself not to look down. Sophie's laugh drifted out to her, low and intimate. She was definitely talking to a new beau.

Very carefully, Mac shifted her gaze in the direction of the tennis courts. This time there was no onslaught of panic. Though her view was partially blocked by trees, she recognized Sophie's two stepbrothers, the "step-twins" as she called them. Nicholas and Nathaniel were both in college now. They lived with their Aunt Jan. The estate was their home, but it was owned by Sophie's older brother Lucas Wainright, the final member of the foursome.

Tall and lean, with a swimmer's athletic build, Lucas looked very much at ease as he rushed forward to the net and killed his stepbrother's serve. According to Sophie, Lucas was good at everything he put his hand to—sports, as well as the family business. Four years ago when his father had died, he'd taken over and ruthlessly dragged Wainright Enterprises back from the edge of bankruptcy.

The first and only time Mac had met him, he'd reminded her of a fallen angel, incredibly good-looking on the surface with danger lurking just beneath. But that first impression of danger had been softened somewhat by the fact that he'd spent most of the day hidden behind a camera snapping pictures of the grand opening of Sophie's antique shop.

According to Sophie, Lucas regarded his duties as the head of the Wainright family every bit as seriously as he took his financial obligations. As a result, he'd turned into a total dictator and an interfering ogre.

The man on the tennis court did not resemble an ogre. She let her gaze linger on the dark hair and the tanned skin stretched taut over what she was sure were hard muscles. His hand had certainly been hard when he'd shaken hers that day. She'd felt something too—a little jolt. Whatever it was, it had made her very aware of him for the rest of the party.

"Who's winning?" Sophie asked as she joined her on the edge of the platform.

"Looks like Lucas and your aunt."

"Who would have thought?" she muttered. "Not that I begrudge Aunt Jan the victory, but I would give a lot to see Lucas taken down a peg or two."

Mac turned to study Sophie. "You never told me what he did to make you break things off with Bradley."

"He had him followed. Turns out the man I thought was the love of my life was cheating on me. There were some very compromising photos, thanks to the Shadow."

"Shadow?"

"That's what I call the super spy who heads up Wainright

Enterprises' security. I managed to get a pretty good look at him once. But he doesn't like to be seen. He's there, and then he's not. Anyway, he checked into Bradley's finances. Lucas made me read the report so that I would have no doubt that old Brad was obviously only interested in me for my money."

Mac covered Sophie's hand with hers. "Lucas loves you, Soph."

"I love him, too, but he sees everyone I date, especially anyone I get serious about, as a threat to the company. The worst of it is he's probably right. I've decided that the next man I decide to go out with is not going to know that I'm a Wainright. And I'm going to make very sure that no one—not even the Shadow—knows who I'm seeing."

Mac put her arms around her friend and just held her. For a moment, neither of them said a word.

"Okay," Sophie said as she drew back. "Enough of my problems. I think we ought to come up with a solution for yours."

"You're not going to talk me out of it."

"I know better than to waste my breath. Besides, the more I think about it, the more I can see that this field-testing plan of yours might have some merit. In fact, it could even be fun if you did it with someone you could trust. There's got to be someone I know—"

"Hey, you two!"

The sudden shout had Mac glancing down through the branches before she could stop to think. Lucas was striding toward them across the lawn. "C'mon down out of that tree. Aunt Jan and I have defeated the step-twins and we're ready for our next challengers."

For just a moment, Mac's gaze locked with Lucas's, and she experienced that same instant jolt of awareness she'd felt before. Then a wave of dizziness slammed into her and she squeezed her eyes shut.

"That's it!" Sophie whispered in Mac's ear. "I don't know why I didn't think of it sooner. Lucas is the answer! You can practice your research on him!"

Lucas? No. Mac shook her head, and a second, more potent, wave of dizziness hit her. Her hand shot out to the railing. It gripped nothing but air.

As she pitched forward, fear fisted in her throat, leaves scraped her face, and one image formed in her mind—the earth below racing toward her. Then arms clamped around her like a steel vise, pressing her against something hard and solid and warm before she hit the ground and lost her breath in a whoosh.

"Mac!"

Sophie's voice was almost drowned out by the beating of her heart. As she struggled for breath, Mac became aware of the very male body beneath her.

"You can open your eyes now. You're safe."

The moment she did, she saw that Lucas's eyes were just as dark as she remembered—the deep blue of the sea.

"Are you all right?"

Mac said nothing. She couldn't. He was holding her so tightly, molding her body to his from breast to thigh. An icy flame was searing her nerve endings and sensitizing her body to every plane and angle of his. For the first time in her life, words, thoughts, logic, deserted her, washed away by a flood of sensations. The warmth of his breath on her lips. The pressure of each one of his fingers on her back. The swell of her hips. His body growing rock hard beneath her. She watched awareness fill his eyes as her body melted in reaction.

"Just what I've been waiting to see all my life—my

brother knocked off his feet by a woman! I think it's an omen of things to come."

Omen of things to come. Sophie's words and the memory of what she'd suggested—practicing her research on Lucas—penetrated the haze filling Mac's mind. She broke free of the paralysis that had gripped her, and shifting off Lucas, she scrambled to her feet.

Sophie grabbed her arm and pulled her toward the tennis courts as she tossed over her shoulder, "C'mon, bro. Prepare to meet your match…"

CHAPTER TWO

LUCAS LEANED BACK in his chair and listened to the steady ticking of his grandfather's clock. It was the only sound that marred the tense silence in the room as he studied the two men seated on the other side of his desk.

Both of them were self-contained. Both were very intelligent. And he wouldn't relish going up against either one of them in a dark alley.

It was ironic that in spite of their many similarities, the two men were the complete antithesis of each other.

The younger was his best friend, the man he'd recently hired to head up security at Wainright Enterprises. He'd known T. J. McGuire since they'd served together in the Gulf War. Tracker was the name the flight crew had given T.J. because he'd been a hell of a lot better at finding their targets than both the high-tech radar systems and so-called "smart" missiles.

It had taken Lucas four years to convince his friend to come and work for Wainright Enterprises. He'd needed someone he could trust, and Tracker was that kind of man. Beneath the black-Irish good looks and the accompanying charm lay the strength and the loyalty of a Celtic warrior. Lucas ranked loyalty right up there next to competence when it came to his employees—and his friends.

The older man with the mane of white wavy hair and the impeccably tailored suit was not a friend. Nor could he be trusted. Doing business with Vincent Falcone had been one of the biggest mistakes his father had made. It had taken Lucas four years to find the money and the right opportunity to buy Vincent Falcone out of Wainright Enterprises.

Still, he didn't want the man as an enemy.

A rustle of paper broke the silence as Vincent turned over the final page of the contract. Glancing up, he met Lucas's eyes squarely. "If I sign this, I will own Lansing Biotech outright. Wainright Enterprises gives up any right it may have had in the past to patents or future research results. You're being very generous."

"I want the break between us to be fair but clean. This deal severs all connections between your various other businesses and mine."

"Ah yes, there is that. And the fact that I will no longer sit on the board of Wainright Enterprises."

"That's correct."

The older man smiled slowly. "You've done a thorough job of systematically cutting me out for the past four years. I admire your technique. And today, inviting me here to your home to end our business relationship over a drink..." Pausing, he glanced around the room. "It's a nice touch. Very classy. Your grandfather would be proud of you."

Lucas was careful to keep his expression impassive. He hadn't wanted to invite Falcone to the Wainright estate. He'd never lived here himself. It was the place his father had lived with his last three wives. If it hadn't been for Sophie's birthday celebration, he would have worked as he usually did on the weekends and the contract would have been signed at his D.C. office.

"I would have enjoyed meeting your sister. I hear she is very beautiful."

Lucas didn't let his gaze waver, and for a moment neither man spoke.

With a slow smile, the older man raised a hand. "Another time perhaps. If I could borrow your pen?"

Lucas picked up a pen and handed it to him without a word.

Seconds later, Falcone rose and placed the signed contract on Lucas's desk. "It's a shame that you felt it necessary to terminate our business connections."

"You have certain interests that I do not want Wainright Enterprises involved in."

"Your father was not so particular."

Saying nothing, Lucas rose from his chair and, after a moment, Vincent Falcone continued, "The connection between our families is still close. Like this." Raising his hands, he clasped them together tightly. "For that reason, our paths will cross again."

"It's very unlikely," Lucas said as the man turned away and allowed Tracker to escort him from the room. The moment the door closed, he sat down in his chair. It had gone smoothly. Too smoothly, perhaps? Closing his eyes, he began to run the entire event over in his mind, turning over every word, every nuance in his mind. He stopped only when he heard Tracker reenter the room.

"Nice job, boss."

"It was too easy."

Tracker's eyebrows shot up. "The four years of work and sacrifices that went into accomplishing this weren't easy. And you chose the right time to make your move. Vincent Falcone has troubles of his own right now. There are factions in his other, less legitimate business interests who require his attention."

"I don't like that he mentioned Sophie's name. He's quite capable of exacting some kind of revenge for this on my family." Rising, Lucas moved to the window, but he didn't focus on the sweep of lawn that ended at the tennis courts. "I have a feeling that Falcone is plotting something."

When Tracker didn't reply, Lucas turned to face him. "You think I'm overreacting, don't you?"

Tracker grinned. "You're not going to get me to say that, boss. You're worried about your little sister. It could be because you've been going through a rough time with her. But in my experience, a man had better pay attention to his hunches or they'll come back to bite him."

"I don't like that you saw her with Falcone's son."

"Sophie only met Sonny once for a casual drink in a Georgetown watering hole. She hasn't seen him since."

Lucas shook his head. "She knows nothing about the Falcone family and certainly nothing about the fact that my father was doing business with them. But if I try to warn Sophie off, she might take it in her head to get really serious about him. She's in rebellion mode right now."

"And you even end up with a black eye this time," Tracker said.

Lucas rubbed his jaw, where his sister had landed him a pretty decent right cross. "You may be right about that. Sophie got past you last time."

"She's got some good moves. And she was pretty upset about that information you dug up on Bradley Davis." Tracker's grin widened as he moved to the small built-in refrigerator near the windows. Opening it, he took out two beers, twisted off the caps and handed one to Lucas. "She's smart too. I think she may suspect she's being followed. She tried some evasive tactics the other day when she left her shop."

"Did she lose the tail?" Lucas asked with a frown.

Tracker nodded. "For about a half hour. My man picked her up coming out of a restaurant. I have two men on her now. Another two are keeping tabs on Sonny Falcone."

"Good. I'll feel a lot better when she's down in the Keys with me. I'll send the plane for Sophie on Wednesday. She claims she can't get away before then. And I didn't want to push." He rubbed his jaw again. "Once you're sure she's on my plane, you can devote all your attention to both Falcones."

"You want me to continue to keep tabs on your aunt and stepbrothers?"

"For the time being." Lucas frowned as he turned and led the way through the open French doors to the balcony. Beyond a row of flowering shrubs, an Olympic-size pool gleamed in the late-afternoon sun. His younger siblings were engaged in an intense water-polo match with their aunt, and at the far end of the pool he spotted Sophie seated on the edge of a chaise lounge talking to Mac-Kenzie Lloyd.

"I think you ought to put someone on Dr. Lloyd. She's been Sophie's best friend for years. They live about three blocks apart in Georgetown. Falcone may try to use her to get to Sophie."

"I'll get right on it, boss. You want me to run a background check on Dr. Lloyd?"

Lucas considered for a moment. He'd been thinking of MacKenzie Lloyd off and on quite a bit in the last few hours. When she'd fallen out of that tree into his arms, she'd called up the memory he had of the little waif in jeans and a T-shirt whom he'd met at the opening of Sophie's shop two years ago.

There'd been something about her that day that had caught his attention. At first, he'd thought he'd imagined the tug of desire that he'd felt. But each time he'd found her framed in the viewfinder of his camera, the pull had grown stronger. Later, he'd studied the photos he'd taken, trying to put his finger on just what it was that had drawn him.

She wasn't anything like the women he usually dated. His taste ran to tall, leggy brunettes and blondes. She was small, and she wore her red hair pulled back into a bun. But her eyes... Even in the representation on film, they were the incredible color of golden amber.

Today her hair had seemed lighter and looser—a reddish-gold explosion of color as he'd stared up at her in the tree. His body had reacted to her the moment he'd seen her, hardening, tightening. And when she'd been lying on top of him...for a moment he'd forgotten everything—where they were, who was watching. If Sophie hadn't spoken, he might have rolled her beneath him and taken her right there beneath the branches of the elm tree. Frowning, he pushed away the image.

It had been years since he'd been tempted to be that reckless with a woman. He'd put it out of his mind during the tennis game, chalked it up to putting in too much overtime on the Falcone deal.

Then she'd beaten him.

Oh, Sophie had made some good plays, but Lucas was fully aware that it was Dr. Lloyd's careful, methodical style that had been his downfall. It was almost as though she could predict exactly what he would do next. And that was...he searched for a word...intriguing.

"Boss?" Tracker cleared his throat loudly.

"What?" Lucas asked, turning to him.

"Do you want me to run a background check on the doc?"

Once again, Lucas hesitated. On some gut level, he knew that he should steer clear of his sister's best friend. It wasn't merely the strength of the physical attraction he felt that had the warning bells going off in his mind. She was Sophie's friend. He kept his dating life separate from his family. To pursue a relationship with MacKenzie Lloyd would foster expectations that he would never fulfill.

Relationship? He frowned at the direction his thoughts had taken. Who was she that she could affect him this way?

Experience had taught him that ignorance was seldom bliss, and knowledge was always power. "Yeah. I want to know everything about her."

"MACKENZIE, you've got to listen to reason."

Mac opened a bag of carrots and for a moment allowed herself to picture dumping the whole bag over Gil Stafford's head. Then stifling the image, she selected one carrot and began to shred it on a grater. She hoped feeding Wilbur, her pet lab rat, would soothe her temper. Gil was her department chair and he had ten years' seniority on her. That and the fact that she worked in a lab that adjoined his had made him think he could give her advice.

"If you'd just listened to me earlier and signed a contract to turn the results of your research over to that biotech company, you would have prevented this break-in."

Mac shoved down the little skip of fear that she'd been experiencing ever since she'd arrived at the university and learned that her lab had been broken into sometime on Sunday. The intruder had gotten away, but not before he'd broken into her office safe.

"They would have made sure that there were better security measures taken around here. And I still don't understand why you turned down the money. Even if you don't want it for yourself, think of all the equipment it would have provided."

As Gil continued to pontificate, he strode toward the

window. Mac privately thought the man should have gone into politics instead of science. Not only could he talk nonstop, but he had the tall, rangy build of an athlete and a very photogenic face. With the sunlight turning his blond hair into a halo, he looked like one of the good archangels.

The antithesis of what Lucas looked like with his dark hair and those midnight-blue eyes.

Lucas again. She hadn't been able to block him out of her mind since Sophie had first suggested she use him for her research. The idea had been enough to put her off her serve in the first two sets of the tennis match. After that she'd focused all her concentration on the game. Beating Lucas had been a challenging and exhilarating experience. And the moment they'd won, Sophie had started making her case.

It was a good one. Everything that Sophie had said made perfect sense on a logical and theoretical level.

It was just that every time she thought of actually trying out her research on Lucas, she felt the same funny quaking in her stomach that she got whenever something was about to go wrong in her lab. No matter how hard she tried, she couldn't seem to forget what it had felt like to be pressed against him, to feel his body react to hers, especially a certain unmistakable part of his body. A vivid image slipped into her mind of looping a long strand of pearls around and around—

"Are you listening to anything I say?"

Mac dropped the grater as she struggled to gather her thoughts. "Gil, I know you mean well." She was almost sure of it. But he was giving her a headache. Glancing down at the carrots, she considered dumping them on his head, after all.

"Am I interrupting?"

Mac looked up in surprise to see Sophie hurrying toward her. "Who told you?"

"Who told me what?"

"Someone broke in here last night."

"They did? Are you all right?" Sophie enveloped Mac in a hug.

"I'm fine."

"What about Wilbur?" Sophie flicked a glance at the small white rat running circles in his cage.

Mac couldn't prevent a smile. "I thought you couldn't stand Wilbur."

Gil cleared his throat, and the moment Sophie turned, shot her his best smile. "I'm Gil Stafford. I'm the chair of the biology department and I work in the lab next to MacKenzie's."

"My friend, Sophie Wainright." Mac completed the introductions as the two shook hands.

"Perhaps you can talk some sense into her, Ms. Wainright," Gil said. "The research she's doing has been getting a lot of attention. It was only a matter of time until this happened."

Sophie turned to Mac with a frown. "Were they after your research?"

"The police certainly suspect it," Gil said as he glanced around the room "And it clearly wasn't vandals. Nothing's been touched except the safe."

"No harm's been done," Mac said as she watched Wilbur attack the grated carrots she'd shoved into his tray. "Wilbur's appetite hasn't been affected. And I don't keep any of my records here in the office anyway."

"I still don't like it." Turning, Sophie paced down the length of the lab and then whirled around. "Lucas could send the Shadow over. On a personal level, I can't stand him, but he's good at what he does."

"Not necessary," Mac said. "The university is going to install a high-tech security system. They've even given me a few days off while they work on it."

"That's wonderful. That means you can get started right away on your…" Sophie's voice trailed off as she glanced at Gil.

He was frowning at her. "The university doesn't have the funds to install a proper security system. And the research she's doing is much too valuable. I was just trying to explain that to MacKenzie."

Beaming a smile at him, Sophie moved toward him and placed a hand on his arm. "Would you mind terribly if Mac and I have some time alone? A little girl talk does wonders for the nerves."

"No. Of course not." A little uncertain, Gil glanced from one woman to the other. "I'll be right next door if you need me, MacKenzie."

Sophie waited until the door closed behind Gil Stafford. "*MacKenzie?* No one calls you that."

"He means well." Mac glanced at the bag of carrots again.

"You weren't thinking of asking him to be your research…guinea pig, were you?"

Mac stared at Sophie. "Gil?"

"Good. Because I've come here on a mission—to convince you that Lucas is your man."

Mac held up both hands. "Sophie, I just don't—"

"I know you, Mac. You've been considering it, weighing the pros and cons. And the pros are winning. He's the perfect man for the job. Why not admit it?"

Picking up another carrot, Mac began to grate. "It's just that I'd planned on doing everything with a stranger."

Sophie moved closer and took the grater away, then shoved it out of reach. "I'm going to be brutally honest with you. That's what best friends are for, right? You're not going to hate me for saying this?"

Mac couldn't prevent her lips from curving. They'd always been able to be honest with each other. It was what had made their friendship last for so long. "I'm not going to hate you."

"Okay." Sophie reached for Mac's hand and gave it a squeeze. "I don't think you're going to be able to go through with your plan if you choose a stranger."

"You think I'm a coward."

"No!" Sophie's reply was quick and vehement. "You are one of the bravest people I know. But I've known you for a long time, and you're very…hesitant when it comes to relationships with the opposite sex."

"*Resistant* might be a more accurate word," Mac said.

Sophie grinned. "You know, one of the most endearing things about you is your ability to be brutally honest about yourself. Most of us sail through life telling ourselves whopping-big lies."

Mac frowned in puzzlement. "What's the point of doing that?"

"We think it helps. But to get back to you, this resistance you have to pursuing relationships with the opposite sex is the reason I think you might be much more successful with your plan if you choose someone you already know. I don't think you're going to be able to…let's say, *implement* these fantasies with a complete stranger. Plus, your ultimate goal is to use them on your husband. And he won't be a stranger. Isn't it best in a scientific experiment to try and reproduce all the circumstances to the best of your ability?"

"You really do listen when I rattle on about my work."

Sophie grinned at her. "Of course I do. And I'm right, aren't I—on both counts?"

Mac was very much afraid that she was. One of her own biggest fears was the idea of using her newfound knowledge on a stranger. Still… "Lucas wouldn't…I mean, he doesn't think of me that way."

Sophie's eyebrows shot up. "Well, there you go. Lucas represents the kind of challenge I think you should be looking for. Someone who would put your research to a true test. These men that your…*contacts* in the sex industry will put you in touch with are bound to be easy marks, don't you think? After all, they're eager enough to be paying for sex. Some of them might even be married and have started to wander, so to speak. And if your plan is all geared toward keeping a husband from straying in spite of his genetic mapping, then surely you ought to be able to seduce my brother."

Sophie had a point. Lucas Wainright would certainly offer her a challenge. And if she wasn't up to it, then she might as well forget her whole plan.

"Mac—" Sophie took her hands "—do this for me. I don't know if I can stand to think of you putting this research project into action with someone else. I know that Lucas, in spite of his many flaws, will be kind to you."

One glance at the concern in her friend's eyes, and Mac knew she was going to agree. She was about to, when Sophie continued, "And the truth is, you could do me a big favor at the same time."

"What?" Mac asked.

"On Wednesday, Lucas has made arrangements for me to join him at his hideaway cabin on one of the Keys. You know what they say about timing being everything! I want you to go in my place. I've never been there, but it seems to me that an isolated island in the Keys would be the perfect setting for you to put your plan into action. It will be just you and Lucas—hot, sunny days, palm trees, the ocean pounding on a sandy beach, warm, tropical nights. Just imagine it, Mac."

It sounded just a little bit too good to be true. She studied Sophie. "Why don't you want to go with him?"

"Because—" Sophie began to pace again "—every time I look at Lucas right now, I think of Bradley. My feelings are very raw, and having Lucas lecture me for a week on my abominable taste in men is the last thing I need. But he's adamant that I join him. I think he feels guilty and he wants to *bond* with me."

"What will you be doing while I'm down in the Keys seducing Lucas?" There. She'd actually said it aloud. Putting your fear into words was supposed to be half the battle.

Pacing back from the window, Sophie leaned against the counter. "I need to be by myself for a while. And I've found this great spa in North Carolina where I can hike in the mountains and ride and meditate. It's run entirely by women for women. When I read the brochure, it sounded like heaven to me. It's exactly what I need. Lucas is right about one thing. I do seem to attract men who are only interested in using me. An all-women retreat ought to at least protect me for a while."

"Lucas won't be happy about the switch," Mac pointed out.

Sophie patted Mac's hand. "If your research is as good as you say it is, he'll adjust. And I'll call him from the spa so that he'll know that I'm perfectly safe. Believe me, Lucas and I could both use a break from each other."

Mac drew in a deep breath. She'd never been able to refuse Sophie anything.

"Do this for me. Please."

"Okay."

"Great!" Sophie beamed a smile at her. "C'mon, the first thing I want to see is the wardrobe that Madame Gervais helped you select. Then we're going to shop for some additional pieces that will be appropriate for a holiday in the Keys. Have you ever worn a wig?"

"No. Why would I?"

"The better to create fantasies with, my dear. I'll explain everything while we shop."

CHAPTER THREE

"Is THERE ANYTHING I can get you before we take off, Ms. Wainright?"

Mac smiled at the young brunette, Captain Jill Roberts, who would fly her to Key West. "No thanks, I'm fine."

She hated that she had to lie to the woman, but Sophie's instructions were very explicit. Lucas's pilot had never met Sophie Wainright, and Mac was to keep up her impersonation until they had landed in the Keys. The blond wig was helping, and so were the clothes that Sophie had lent her.

No one could know that she was taking Sophie's place until she stepped off the plane in Key West. Sophie had been adamant about that because she was sure that Lucas was having her followed.

"The flight will take about two hours, and the galley is fully stocked."

"And Lucas is going to meet the plane?" Mac asked.

Captain Roberts smiled. "That's what he said. I spoke with him just as you were crossing the tarmac to come aboard, and I gave him the time I thought we would be touching down. That means I'd better get us airborne. If you want anything, the intercom button is right there on the armrest."

It was only as the captain disappeared into the cockpit that Mac allowed herself to relax a little. She felt as if she'd been caught up in a whirlwind ever since Sophie had breezed into her lab on Monday, but she had to admit that the plan was really working. It had been at Sophie's insistence that they'd switched identities.

The initial step had gone like clockwork thanks to a sudden summer storm that still held D.C. in its grip. Sophie had worn her red rain poncho, hood up, when she'd opened the antique shop at nine, and Mac had worn a bright yellow one, hood down, when she'd arrived fifteen minutes later. Once inside, they'd gone into the back room and changed clothes. As a final touch to their disguises, Sophie had donned a reddish-blond wig tied back into a bun, and Mac had put on a blond one.

They'd gotten the wigs and had them cut and styled on Monday when they'd gone shopping. The fact that they were almost identical in size and shape had helped. Friends in college had always remarked that they could have passed for sisters. Still, Mac had been amazed at just how much she resembled Sophie once she was wearing the blond wig. When they'd emerged from the shop, their hoods up and umbrellas open to hail separate cabs, she was sure that anyone watching "Sophie" would have been bound to follow "Mac," and vice versa.

Mac prayed that the rest of their plan would go as smoothly. Just the thought of facing Lucas Wainright and admitting that she'd purposely switched places with his sister had the butterflies dive-bombing around in her stomach. But it was much easier to concentrate on that first hurdle than the one that would come after, when she told him why she'd really taken Sophie's place.

"We've been cleared for takeoff, Ms. Wainright."

Mac jumped at the sound of Jill Roberts's voice pouring out of a nearby speaker.

"I'll let you know when you can move around the cabin,

but if you have any concerns or questions, don't hesitate to use the intercom button."

Mac found her gaze riveted to the button for several moments after the plane's engine roared to life. All she had to do was press it and she could call the whole thing off.

The plane vibrated, then moved forward.

Mac gripped her hands together. Whatever second thoughts she was having, she couldn't let Sophie down. Things had gone too far.

Leaning back in her seat, she took a deep breath and held it for the length of time that it took the plane to make its mad rush down the runway.

There was no need to panic. Years of experience in the lab had taught her that any project became simpler and much less inhibiting if she could just break it down into steps and take them one at a time. All she had to do was view her coming fieldwork in that light. Flying down to Key West to meet Lucas was just the first step. Telling Lucas about her plan would be the next—and a big one it would be.

The moment she felt the plane leave the ground, she let out the breath she was holding and took in another one. In her mind, she tried to picture herself taking the third step—making love to Lucas Wainright.

Every time she let herself think about that, a very vivid image of Lucas, totally naked, filled her mind. She could almost feel what it would be like to run her hands over the smooth tanned skin on his shoulders, down his chest to his waist and below. Of course, she'd fantasized about touching a man before. And that all-day seminar had certainly given her fantasies a lot of fuel. But never before had her hands tingled with anticipation. As she glanced down at them, grasped tightly in her lap, the realization streamed through her. She wanted to touch Lucas. Not just any man. She wanted to press her fingers against his hardness, to test his strength.

She could still recall how lean, how hard those muscles had felt through the thin cotton of his polo shirt. His whole body had been so hard. Even his hands. When she concentrated, she could still feel the pressure of each finger—on her back and, lower, on her hip. And there was that incredible stab of heat, the melting of muscle and bone.

She was still searching for a word to describe what she'd felt. *Hunger* was too mild a word for that needy, restless ache that had threatened to consume her. More than anything, she'd wanted him to—

"Ms. Wainright?"

Mac started as the voice flowed out of the speaker. Then, unclenching her hands, she pressed the button on the armrest. "Yes?"

"We've reached our cruising altitude. You can wander around the cabin or use your cell phone. Make yourself at home."

"Thanks."

Reaching into her bag, Mac took out her phone. She was about to press a button to speed-dial Sophie when she realized that it wasn't her phone. It was the color of white mother-of-pearl. Hers was black. A quick search of her bag confirmed her suspicion. When they'd switched outfits in the back of Sophie's shop, they'd switched the identical purses they'd bought too. After punching in her own number, she listened to it ring.

"Mac?" Sophie asked. "Where are you?"

"I'm in the air."

"Lucky you. I'm still on the ground, but we should be moving away from the gate soon. I take it everything went smoothly."

"Everything except that I have your purse."

"Yeah. I figured that out when I grabbed the phone. But it shouldn't be a problem. You have my permission to use my credit cards. I doubt that I'll need yours at the spa."

"Go ahead and use them if you have to."

"We're lucky that's the only thing that's gone wrong. I can't believe we've pulled this off."

"I hate to rain on your parade, but there's still the possibility that Lucas will send me packing and show up at your spa."

"They don't allow men on the premises. Besides, he's going to be much too busy engaging in those sexual fantasies you're going to create for him."

What if he doesn't? What if he refuses to—

"You're having second thoughts, aren't you?"

"No…well, maybe a few." Mac sighed.

"Stick to your first answer. And don't let my brother intimidate you. He's a man. And in spite of his numerous and infuriating faults, he's fair. The moment he realizes we've made a switch, he'll get me on my cell phone and lecture me. I'll make sure he knows this was all my idea— and then I'll suggest he have one of his hotshot security people check out the spa. Uh-oh. We're starting to pull away from the gate. Just remember that when Lucas finds out I'm perfectly safe, he'll calm right down. The rest is up to you."

For a few minutes after Sophie broke the connection, Mac stared straight in front of her. It *was* up to her. She was used to that kind of pressure in her lab. She could handle it there.

And she would handle it once she got to Key West. In the meantime, she was going to find something else to think about. An idea bloomed in her mind and she pushed the button on her armrest.

"What can I do for you, Ms. Wainright?"

"First, you can call me Sophie."

"Only if you agree to call me Jill."

"Do you ever fly with a copilot?"

Jill's laugh flowed into the cabin. "Frequently. In fact, when I fly with Mr. Wainright, I usually sit in the copilot's seat. He prefers to be in charge."

"A top gun?"

"You got it."

"Could I come up there with you? I'd love to learn about flying."

"Sure thing. I'd love the company."

"WHERE'S SOPHIE?" Lucas bit out the words as he glanced from MacKenzie Lloyd to the pilot of his private jet. Somehow he'd managed to keep his voice low and controlled—a sharp contrast to the feelings coursing through him. The first thing he'd felt when Mac had walked down the short flight of steps from the plane was pleasure. It had sprung to life so quickly that he'd barely had time to recognize it before he'd discovered that his sister was not with her. Then the fear had struck.

"Sophie's perfectly safe," Mac said. "She's at a spa in North Carolina. I...we switched places."

Lucas shifted his gaze to Jill Roberts who had descended the short flight of steps directly behind Mac. "Are you involved in this deception?"

Mac stepped in front of his pilot. "No. I told her the truth just as we landed. Before that, I was wearing a blond wig, and she believed I was Sophie. Please don't blame Captain Roberts. Sophie said you'd be fair."

Ruthlessly shoving his hands into the pockets of his shorts, Lucas narrowed his eyes. It was a look he'd honed to perfection when dealing with employees who'd displeased him. He kept Mac pinned with it while he considered what she'd said.

It would have been easy enough to fool his pilot. She hadn't worked for Wainright Enterprises that long, and he seldom used his private jet to transport family. He'd done it this time to ensure that Sophie arrived safely. And he was also blaming Mac for something he was almost certain his sister was behind. "I want to talk to Sophie."

"Of course." Instead of withering under his glance, Mac efficiently punched numbers into her cell phone, then handed it to him.

He listened to two rings.

"Lucas?"

His sister's voice had some of his fear fading. "Where in hell are you?"

"Didn't Mac tell you? I'm on my way to the Serenity Spa in Serenity, North Carolina."

"Hold on." Lucas cut her off, then directed his gaze at Mac and his pilot. "You two wait right here. We're not finished." Turning, he strode to the privacy and shade offered by a nearby hangar.

"Where exactly is this spa?"

"I told you, Serenity, North Carolina—about an hour's drive from Charlotte. I'll be quite safe. The place is run by women for women. No chance of any fortune hunters here—although you might argue the prices they charge puts them in that category. I'll give you their phone number and their Web site address. You can have one of your security men check it out."

"I intend to. They can do it in person when they pick you up and bring you here."

"Not a good idea, bro. I told you before, I won't have you running my life. You promised you'd back off for a while."

"And in return you agreed to spend some time with me down here in the Keys."

"You had me followed. That isn't backing off. And it's something I won't put up with."

Lucas sighed. "Soph, there's something I haven't told you. It's why I wanted you to come down here for a while. We need to talk."

"Talk is the last thing I need right now. I'm sorry. I know I agreed to come there, but I…just couldn't."

The quick change in her tone from anger to contrition pulled at him.

"I love you, Lucas. And I know that you did what you thought was best for the family. But being with you right now is only going to make me think of how lousy I am at choosing men. I really need to be alone."

It was the catch in her voice that had the pain shooting through him. He couldn't help recalling the scene in his office when he'd forced her to look at the evidence Tracker had gathered on Bradley Davis. It would be a long time before he could forget the words she'd hurled at him. They'd hurt much more than the right cross she'd managed to land on his chin. She'd accused him of having ice water in his veins, of being a ruthless dictator, of caring only about Wainright Enterprises.

What else could he expect her to say? He was prepared to go to almost any length to protect the company his grandfather had built and his father had almost destroyed. He stared past the low-slung buildings that formed the small private airport. The air was stifling, not even a hint of a breeze stirred the palms. If Sophie had a built-in homing device that seemed to attract fortune hunters, she'd inherited that gene directly from their father. His last and fifth divorce had come close to destroying Wainright Enterprises.

He'd tried to tell himself that Sophie would have been hurt even more if she'd gone ahead and married Bradley Davis. But that certainty hadn't helped a bit when she'd broken down and sobbed in his office.

"Please let me do this, Lucas. The spa has excellent security, and you can call the desk each day to check on me. You can even send one of your security people up here—as long as he's willing to camp in the woods. No males are allowed on the grounds."

For a moment Lucas said nothing as he ran the risks through his mind. A spa that was off-limits to men sounded secure, especially if he had Tracker assign one of his people to keep an eye on the place. While she was there, Sophie should be safe from any plot that Vincent Falcone might be hatching. Lucas drew in a deep breath. "As long as what you're telling me about this Serenity Spa is the truth."

"Check it out. I'm at the Charlotte airport now. Their van will be picking me up any minute. And whatever you do, don't blame Mac for this. I talked her into it. I can be very persuasive when I set my mind to it."

Lucas's lips curved in a smile. "Tell me about it. Don't worry, I'll have your friend back in D.C. by mid-afternoon."

"Oh, I don't think you should do that. She has a little problem she's depending on you to help her with, and I assured her that you were the perfect man for the job."

"What does she want me to do?" Lucas asked, glancing toward his plane. Mac had moved to the shade cast by one of the wings and was motioning his pilot to join her. Shaking her head, Captain Roberts stayed where she was. Evidently his order to stay put hadn't intimidated the doc. Courage had always appealed to him.

"I'm going to let Mac tell you that. But she may need a

little encouragement. And I don't suppose you were very welcoming when you saw she wasn't me."

No, he hadn't been welcoming, Lucas thought as he studied Dr. MacKenzie Lloyd. Part of that had been due to the fact that for the past four days he hadn't been able to get her out of his mind.

In the linen slacks and blouse, she looked prim, innocent and untouchable. It had never been those qualities that had drawn him to a woman before. Perhaps it was that detached way she had of summing up her opponent in a tennis match and then calmly going in for the kill. It was a skill she'd probably picked up in her lab work. But wherever she'd come by that single-minded determination, he couldn't help but admire it. Nor could he help but view it as a challenge.

"I'm depending on you to be fair, Lucas. Don't blame her for something that's not her fault."

Wasn't that exactly what he'd been doing—blaming her for that quick skip of delight he'd felt when she'd gotten off the plane?

"Mac doesn't have anyone else to turn to for advice. Her parents always lecture rather than listen."

"Ouch." Lucas winced. It was an accusation Sophie had hurled at him more than once.

"Please, Lucas. I'm asking a favor here. At least take her out to the island and hear her out."

Take her out to the island? Whatever second thoughts he might have had about the wisdom of doing that had to be dismissed. Sophie so rarely asked for favors. "All right. But at least give me a clue. What kind of problem?"

"It's personal. And she needs help from a man. That's all I can tell you."

Personal? Did it have to do with a boyfriend? An ex-lover? The possibility had him frowning. "I'll do what I can. In the meantime, I'm going to be checking in on you at that spa."

"I can't always promise to be available on my cell phone. They make you check them at the desk. But you can always have one of your security people pitch a tent on one of the hillsides and keep tabs on me that way."

Lucas sighed at the trace of bitterness he heard in her voice. "I love you, Soph."

"Ditto, bro. Enjoy."

As soon as Sophie ended the call, Lucas took out his own cell phone and pressed the number that would get him through to Tracker.

"What's up, boss?"

"Sophie tricked you."

"I followed her myself until she got on your private plane." There was a slight pause, and then he continued. "The raincoats. When she and Dr. Lloyd came out of her shop, they both had their hoods up and their umbrellas open…and I followed the blonde, just as she wanted me to. Damn! Let me check with the man I had tailing Dr. Lloyd."

"I can tell you where Sophie says she is—the Serenity Spa in Serenity, North Carolina. They don't allow men on the premises. She claimed she was calling me from the Charlotte airport. She says she wants some time alone, but I want you to make sure she's there."

"I'll check the flight manifests right after I check with Dr. Lloyd's tail. Am I right in assuming that the good doctor is with you?"

"Yeah. Sophie says she has a problem, so I may have another job for you."

"I'll be in touch."

SOPHIE ENDED her conversation with her brother, then crossed her fingers in the hope that Lucas had bought her story. Of course, he'd check out every detail. She knew from experience just how thorough he was.

However, she'd been thorough too. She glanced at her watch. The first thing Lucas would do would be to check out the flight manifests and see if an S. Wainright had indeed flown from National Airport to Charlotte that day. He would find that she had. Hopefully, he wouldn't find it too suspicious that an M. Lloyd had also made the same flight. She was banking on the fact that he would relax once he found that Sophie Wainright had checked into the Serenity Spa. Hannah Parker, the out-of-work actress she'd hired to do just that, should be arriving at the spa any minute, and once that final crucial step had been taken and Lucas had verified it, she should be free.

For the next week, she wasn't going to be Sophie Wainright. Instead, she would be MacKenzie Lloyd, a burned-out research biologist who was taking a little break from her lab.

She'd begun to formulate the plan when she and Mac had talked in the tree house on Sunday, but the details hadn't all fallen into place until Mac had finally agreed to trade places with her. Of course, she hadn't told Mac everything.

She knew her best friend too well to believe that she could lie to Lucas for an entire week. So she hadn't admitted to her that she'd switched purses on purpose. Nor had she confided to Mac that she never intended to go to the Serenity Spa.

Stifling the impulse to get up and pace, Sophie leaned back in her chair and scanned the occupants of the airport lounge. At nearly two in the afternoon, the lunch crowd had thinned to a few businessmen at the bar who were nursing beers as they talked nonstop into their cell phones. They'd been there when she'd entered, so she didn't think they were following her. And she doubted that the couple with four kids at a nearby table were being paid to keep tabs on her.

For a second, her gaze locked with one of the men at the bar. She was quick to glance away, then let out the breath she was holding when she saw him slide off his stool and leave in the direction of the departing flights.

Paranoia—that's what it was, pure and simple. If she wasn't careful, she'd turn into Lucas, forever afraid that everyone he met was trying to threaten Wainright Enterprises.

She couldn't, she wouldn't live her life that way.

Forcing herself to relax, Sophie took a sip of bottled water. Not that she hadn't borrowed a page from her brother's paranoia handbook. In making her plans for switching identities with Mac, she'd followed Lucas's number-one rule: Never underestimate the enemy.

Even after they'd each hailed their separate taxis in front of her shop, she'd made herself assume that she still had a tail. Though she couldn't think of a single reason why Lucas would be having Mac followed, she wasn't ever going to underestimate him again. That was why she'd waited to switch identities with Hannah Parker until they'd both entered the first available ladies' room at the airport in Charlotte.

It had been almost too simple to walk into adjoining stalls and then pass her poncho and a bag containing her identification, sunglasses and a duplicate of the red wig she was wearing to Hannah. Just in case Lucas *had* assigned someone to follow Mac, Hannah couldn't turn into the blond Sophie Wainright until she was safely in the van to the Serenity Spa.

For the space of about fifteen minutes, there had been two fake MacKenzie Lloyds in the Charlotte airport.

Sophie took another quick look around the lounge. No one was paying her the least bit of attention. She drummed her fingers on the table, then jumped when her cell phone rang. Grabbing it, she put it to her ear. "Yes?"

"It's Hannah. I just wanted to let you know. I'm all checked into the spa. You should see the room."

"Did everything go all right?"

"Like clockwork. The woman behind the desk told me that my brother had called. She was going to call him back and let him know I'd arrived safely."

"Have a great week," Sophie said as she ended the call. Then she lifted her bottled water in a toast to herself. "I'm free at last."

MAC GRIPPED the windshield of the boat tightly as Lucas let out the throttle and the *Adventurer* raced over the choppy water. She'd felt a certain kinship with the boat the moment she'd spotted the name. Together, they were racing off into the unknown.

With the wind whipping against her face, she concentrated on enjoying the feel of bright afternoon sun and the occasional salty spray against her cheeks. It wasn't hard. She would have enjoyed it even more though, if it hadn't been for the man standing only a few feet away at the helm of the boat.

Even when he wasn't looking at her or speaking to her, Lucas was a hard man to ignore. He projected...*something* that went beyond simple good looks. And it was mesmerizing. She'd barely taken her eyes off him as he'd gone about the task of casting off the boat, then steering it quickly and surely away from the marina toward the open sea.

She risked a sideways glance at him. Perhaps it was the mixture of competence and control that had her gawking like a teenager. No, she thought, it was more than that. There was also that hint of danger about Lucas that lurked just below the very civilized surface. She'd seen it in his eyes when he'd first realized that Sophie wasn't on board the plane—something hot, dangerous and lethal. It fascinated her.

And she was gawking again. Tearing her eyes away, she looked back at the marina that was fast becoming a speck on the shoreline behind them. A small plane lifted and soared out over the water as it climbed steadily into the sky. Jill Roberts was heading back to D.C. Only when it disappeared did she allow herself to look at Lucas again. He stood there, totally impassive, as if he were alone on the boat.

Clearly, he was still annoyed. He'd spoken only two words to her since he'd gotten off the phone with Sophie. Once Jill had disappeared into the plane, Lucas had turned to her, his expression neutral, and said, "This way."

His tone had been so cool she'd nearly shivered in spite of the hot southern Florida heat. They'd walked down to the small marina where he'd tied his boat. The moment she saw it, anxiety mixed with anticipation. It was her day for firsts, it seemed—her first time sitting in the cockpit of a plane and now her first time on a boat...to be topped off by her first time propositioning a man.

She glanced at him again. He stood completely at ease, his hands on the wheel, his feet planted apart, totally in control of the engine that roared beneath them. There was no sign now of the predator she'd glimpsed earlier. But it was still there, lurking. And it was touching off something in her. She pressed a hand against her stomach. The warm melting sensation that seemed to be centered there had nothing to do with the fact that the boat was beginning to bump more frequently into waves.

"Nervous?" Lucas had to shout the question.

"A little," she shouted back. "This is my first time on a boat."

"You're kidding."

She shook her head.

"How old are you?"

"Twenty-six."

"I can't imagine it. What did your family do on vacations?"

"They didn't take me with them."

"What about later?" Lucas asked. "You live in D.C. and you never went out on the water?"

"Too busy, I guess." She moved toward him then, carefully maintaining her grip on the side of the boat as she did. "Is it easy to steer?"

"For me it is. I've been doing it most of my life."

Suddenly, the boat struck a wave that lifted her feet right off the deck. The moment they smacked down, she felt them lift again, her stomach with them. The laugh escaped the moment she felt the boat solidly under her again.

The sound of Lucas's laughter mingling with hers had her turning toward him.

"You have the makings of a good sailor, Doc. Would you like to take a turn behind the wheel?"

At her nod, he stepped back and she slipped in front of him. Once her hands were on the wheel, he covered them with his. "Feet apart. Hands steady."

Lucas continued to talk, words of encouragement, but Mac's mind couldn't take it in. Just the sound of his voice in her ear was having the strangest effect on her breathing. And there were other sensations pouring through her. Instead of the salty air, it was Lucas's scent she inhaled. He smelled like sun and sweat and something else that she couldn't quite place. She could feel him too. His chest when it brushed against her back was like iron, and the hands trapping hers on the wheel were sure and firm, the palms surprisingly rough. For a moment, she closed her eyes and imagined what it might be like to have those hard hands pressed against other parts of her body.

Another wave had him shifting closer. His hands tightened on hers, pulling the wheel to the right. An arrow of heat shot through her, and her heart began to beat hard and fast, just as it had when she'd been lying on top of him.

"I'd better take over."

"Yes," she thought. Oh, yes.

"Doc, are you all right?"

Her eyes shot open as he turned her around to face him. "I'm…fine," she managed to say.

"You look a little weak in the knees. Why don't you sit down? You can see the island off there to your right."

Very carefully, Mac made it to the cushioned seat that ran along the side of the boat. Just as soon as Lucas wasn't actually touching her, some of her strength returned. It also helped that she wasn't looking at him.

Fascinating, she thought as she focused her attention on a tiny speck some distance away in the water. Her reaction the first time he'd held her hadn't been an aberration. Lucas Wainright could definitely turn her mind and body to mush.

And she liked it.

However, it would add complications to her research.

How was she supposed to keep her mind on creating male sexual fantasies if Lucas could scatter her thoughts and melt her into a puddle whenever he touched her?

Narrowing her eyes, she watched the speck become larger. It was a problem she'd have to solve.

CHAPTER FOUR

WHEN SHE STEPPED OUT onto the dock, Mac's eyes were first drawn to the white sand beach that stretched in both directions until it curved out of sight. Waves broke against it, then drew back to attack again in a steady rhythm. Fifty yards ahead, palm trees shaded a squat box of a cabin with a covered porch. Almost covered, she amended when she saw the ladder tipped against it, a pile of shingles stacked on its sloping roof.

Lucas grabbed her suitcase and climbed out of the boat. "I hope you're not expecting anything fancy. Every time I come down here I try to make a few improvements, but it's pretty rustic."

"It's lovely." Pausing as she stepped off the dock, she looked at the sweep of shore again. "I've never seen a beach that wasn't thronged with people. You must love it here."

He looked at her for a moment. "I do. None of the rest of my family does. They call this place Lucas's Folly."

It was impossible to imagine the confident man striding in front of her up the path to the cabin as being capable of folly. She found her gaze riveted on his broad shoulders. Beneath the thin polo shirt he was wearing, she could see the easy, sure movement of muscles as he swung her suitcase in rhythm with his stride. She'd learned in her research that from a psychological standpoint, a woman who was attracted to a man's muscular shoulders was probably looking for a strong emotional bond.

That was the last thing she wanted with Lucas Wainright, she reminded herself. If her plan was going to work at all, he was just someone she would practice on. A guinea pig.

She forced her gaze down the length of his back to his waist and below…. Suddenly, her mouth went dry as dust. He had what Madame Gervais would definitely call in her Parisian French a…

As she watched him climb the porch steps, the foreign words escaped her. "Great buns" was the only description she could think of in English. His cutoff jeans fit over his backside like a second skin, leaving very little to the imagination…just enough to make her wonder what his skin would feel like beneath that denim. Soft and smooth… firm and hard? Would it feel as hot as her own skin was beginning to feel?

The urge to find out was so sudden, so strong that Mac stopped dead in her tracks. If she hadn't, she was sure she would have reached out and actually placed the palm of her hand on Lucas's butt.

She made herself take a deep breath and let it out. In spite of the heat, the air felt cool compared to the fire that had started to burn in her body. What in the world was the matter with her? She'd never before found herself mesmerized by a man's *derriere*—that was the French word. According to Madame Gervais, women who were attracted to that particular body part were lusty adventurers who were looking for similar qualities in a man.

The thought of herself as a "lusty adventurer" nearly made her laugh. Still, it might be evidence that she did have a sensual side to her nature, after all.

It was only as Lucas opened the door of the cabin and

glanced back over his shoulder that she realized she was staring at that part of his anatomy.

"Are you all right?" Lucas asked.

"Fine." She moved quickly up the steps and into the cabin. The air was stuffy and even warmer than outside. Or perhaps it was her own inner temperature rising because she was standing close to Lucas again. Close enough to touch.

Pushing the thought out of her mind, she focused her full attention on the small, tidy interior of the room. Though the darkness contrasted sharply with the glaring brightness outside, she noted that the room was minimally furnished with a couch, a coffee table, a desk and a chair. At one end, a wooden counter with two stools tucked beneath its wide ledge framed a space for a tiny kitchen. There was no clutter, nothing to suggest that the place was occupied except for the laptop computer and thick, sturdy briefcase that sat on the desk.

It was then that she noticed the framed photographs that nearly covered the wall above. Curious, she moved closer to get a better look. Most of the pictures were snapshots of Sophie and her younger brothers, the step-twins. Nicholas and Nathaniel's high-school graduation, Sophie's graduation from college. She'd met Sophie five years ago when she'd been doing postdoctoral work and Sophie had been finishing her undergraduate degree. They'd been fast friends ever since.

Her gaze shifted to a shot of the opening of Sophie's antique shop in Georgetown. And there were others that captured less formal occasions—Sophie and the step-twins beneath a Christmas tree, a teenage Sophie standing by a red convertible dangling the keys from her fingers. There were twenty pictures in all, a sort of family album/mural, except that there were no parents in any of them. And no sign of Lucas.

Her attention was caught and held by the last photo in the bottom row. She was in it, standing next to Sophie. Lucas had snapped a victory picture after she and Sophie had beaten him at tennis.

Something moved through her then. Envy? Longing? Lifting her hand, she ran her fingers over the frame. The pictures were concrete evidence of something she already knew. Lucas Wainright valued his family.

"You played a great game. I'd be glad to make you a copy of the photo, if you'd like."

"Thanks." As she turned, she nearly bumped into him.

He handed her a bottle of water. "You'd better drink it all. In this kind of heat, it's easy to become dehydrated."

She took a long swallow, then watched as Lucas drained his bottle. She was close enough to see a drip of water run from the corner of his mouth to his chin, and then down the long column of his throat. In her mind, she imagined what it might be like to trace its path with her finger, to feel the coolness of the water, the heat of his skin underneath.

"Penny for your thoughts."

Mac reined them in. This was the second time in almost as many minutes that she'd fantasized about touching Lucas Wainright.

"Sophie says you have a problem you'd like my help with."

Her nerves slithered into a knot in her stomach, and she felt the bottle slip from her fingers.

Lucas caught it before it hit the floor and handed it back to her. "That bad, huh?"

Before she could reply, he took her arm and led her out

to the porch. "Why don't you sit down. You can finish that water while I fix some sandwiches. We'll talk about it over lunch."

In the doorway, he turned back to her. "You can stay here as long as you want. If it helps any, Sophie was pretty sure I could help. And I'm certainly willing to do anything I can."

WAS HE GOING CRAZY? Lucas spread slices of bread out on the counter. Standing on that boat with her body so close to his had turned his brain to mush and another part of his anatomy into something hard, erect and ready to go.

Except it wasn't going anywhere. Taking a calming breath, he slapped slices of ham, then cheese on the bread. MacKenzie Lloyd was his sister's best friend, and he could not, would not, get involved with her. He'd vowed a long time ago to keep his relationships with women entirely separate from his family. He never dated anyone in his family's social circle, and he never brought any of his women friends home. It was just one of the methods he used to ensure that the women in his life never nurtured the false expectation that he would marry them. His other method was to be totally honest with them up front.

What was he thinking when he'd invited MacKenzie Lloyd to stay as long as she wanted?

Dumb question. He reached into the small refrigerator for mustard and spread it liberally on the ham. He hadn't been thinking at all. His mind had been too busy remembering the way her scent had wrapped itself around him, the way her hair, whipped back by the wind, had felt against his chin. And once he'd led her into the cabin, his mind had taken the leap from memory to fantasy, and had totally immersed itself in imagining what it would be like to make love with Dr. MacKenzie Lloyd.

Even as she'd settled herself on the steps, the image had slipped into his mind of sitting right down beside her and slipping her out of that neat little blouse, then the slacks. He'd been wondering just what it was that she wore beneath that cool-looking linen. Thin, white, practical cotton—the kind that schoolgirls wore—was what he'd pictured. Once he'd discarded that, he could spend the entire afternoon pleasuring her until she was spent and limp beneath him. And then he could begin again.

Bending down, he grabbed two beers from the cooler. He couldn't recall another woman who'd aroused such erotic fantasies in him. And she'd yet to give him any indication that the attraction he felt was mutual.

Was that what fascinated him? That cool, seemingly unflappable image that she projected? Certainly, he was curious about what lay beneath the surface. He'd already discovered that she wasn't as serious as she seemed. It had been pure, innocent enjoyment he'd seen in her eyes when that wave had lifted her right up off the deck of the boat.

And her laugh. Just recalling the sound of it had him wanting to surprise another one out of her.

Maybe she wasn't as indifferent to him as she appeared to be. He could think of several interesting ways to test that theory.

And he'd be a fool to put any of them to the test. Slapping the sandwiches onto a plate, he snagged the beers with his free hand and walked back out onto the porch.

She wasn't there.

"Mac!"

He was off the steps and scanning the beach when she said, "I'm up here."

Fear shot through him when he saw her perched on the

sloping roof of the porch. "What the hell are you doing? You're afraid of heights."

"I'm also a coward. This is my way of summoning up some Dutch courage so that I can tell you why I'm here. But you may have to eat without me. I'm not sure I can get down."

Whatever else she was, MacKenzie Lloyd wasn't a coward. And what in the world had her so frightened that she'd climb onto a roof to screw up her courage? Tucking the bottles under his arm, he started up the ladder. "We'll eat up there then. I don't relish the thought of being flattened again if you decide to jump."

He had the pleasure of seeing her lips curve in a ghost of a smile as he settled himself beside her and distributed the sandwiches and beer. "Is it helping? To sit up here, I mean?"

"My stomach is still in a knot. But watching the water helps."

"Take a drink of the beer."

She glanced at it dubiously. "It'll make me want to take a nap."

"That's allowed. In fact, with the sun at its hottest, it's a very smart plan."

Damn tempting too. Lucas pushed away the image of lying down next to her on the narrow cot in his bedroom. He was trying not to think about the fact that he'd have to carry her down the ladder, but his body was already reacting to the possibility.

"Plan. Yes, that's what I wanted to talk to you about." She took a quick sip from the bottle, and when some beer dripped onto her wrist, she touched her tongue to it.

Lucas felt the hot lick of desire and took a long swallow of his own beer. "Sophie said you had a problem."

"That's because she didn't approve of my plan."

"She wants me to handle it."

"Exactly." Holding the bottle tightly in two hands, she kept her eyes on the sea. "I should begin by giving you some background. I want a family someday. For me that means kids and marriage. Not in that order, of course." She shot him a sideways glance. "I'm not one of those women who wants to raise children in a single-parent household. I know from experience that it can make for an unhappy childhood, so I want to avoid it at all costs. That's why I want to be prepared. A good plan is everything in the lab." She glanced at him briefly. "It must be the same way in a business deal."

"Yes," Lucas said. "But I'm not sure I'm following you."

Mac took another swallow of beer. "What are your feelings about divorce?"

Lucas's eyes narrowed. "I want to avoid it at all costs. That's why I'll never marry."

She nodded, then drank more beer. Lucas watched her lick the moisture from her lips as she lowered the bottle and turned to face him. "I want to avoid it too. We just differ in out approaches to the problem. I want to get married and my research is designed to make sure my marriage lasts forever."

Bells began to ring in Lucas's head—the ones that always warned him about women who were thinking about weddings. "I don't intend to get married. Ever."

"Of course you don't. You already have a family. I only had one until I was five. That's when my father's eye started to wander." She took another long swallow of beer, then glanced at the bottle. "You know, you were right about this. It is relaxing me."

"Maybe too much," Lucas muttered. "Have you had anything to eat today, Doc?"

"No. I never eat before I fly." She tipped the bottle up again and drank thirstily. "It's been ages since I've had beer. I didn't think I liked it, but I do."

"You were talking about wandering eyes." His own sure weren't wandering. They were glued to MacKenzie Lloyd's mouth as she licked the last trace of beer from her lips.

"First it's the eyes, and then it's the whole body. Did you know that infidelity is the number-one cause of divorce? And the number-one reason for one of the partners to stray is that monogamy usually leads to monotony? Hopefully, my plan will prevent that."

"How?"

"By making sure that my husband *never* gets bored in bed." Pausing, she rubbed the bottle against her cheek. "It's getting really warm up here."

"Tell me about it."

"I'm trying. I've done all this research on how to please a man in bed. Most of the data I've compiled is on male sexual fantasies. Did you know that the number-one fantasy of men is to make love with two women at once?"

"I think I read that somewhere."

When she turned to study him, he had the fleeting sensation of being put on a slide.

"Is that *your* favorite?" she finally asked.

"Not at the present moment."

"I haven't figured out exactly how to create that one, but I have a lot of other ones I'd like to try out. Are you going to finish your beer?"

Before he could reply, she plucked his bottle from his hand and replaced it with her empty one. Then she took a long swallow.

"Maybe you'd better spell out exactly how it is that I can help you."

As she turned to face him, she slid a little toward the end of the roof.

He gripped her arm. "Careful."

"There's a time in every research project when you have to put your theories to the test in the lab. I'm at that point right now. I feel like I'm bursting with research, and if I don't put some of it to use, I just might explode. Do you ever get that feeling?"

"Yeah."

"I feel that way in the lab too—and it's so exciting. That's why I need a man right now. I have to have someone to practice on. And Sophie suggested you."

Lucas's mouth went dry as dust. "You…" He cleared his throat. "You can't be serious."

"But I am. I tried to explain to Sophie. This is the exact procedure I follow in the lab. Theories always have to be tested. But you shouldn't feel pressured. I can certainly find someone else to test my research on. I have a friend in Paris who has several volunteers lined up. But Sophie insisted that I ask you first."

Lucas stared at her. It had to be the beer. He removed his bottle from her hand. "Let me make sure I have this straight. You're asking me to become your lover so that you can field-test your research on me?"

"Exactly. And it won't go any further than that. I promise that I'm not out to trap you into marriage. Sophie said you would be worried about that. This is strictly a no-strings arrangement. I've been on the Pill for three months, and I've always practiced safe sex, not that I've had to worry about it lately. What about you?"

Lucas stared at her, incredulous.

"Is there anything in your sexual history I should be concerned about," she asked.

"No, I'm a very careful man."

Mac nodded. "Of course, you could still use a condom as an extra precaution…"

"Of course. And if I agree to the arrangement…?"

"There are some particular male sexual fantasies that I want to try out. If you're willing." She took his bottle back and emptied it.

As her proposition swam around in his mind, Lucas watched a thin trickle of beer run down her throat. He imagined the bitter taste it would have, along with the sweeter, warmer flavor of her skin. But if he gave in to the temptation of leaning forward and following the path of the beer with his tongue, he wouldn't stop there. He would have to kiss her. And if he did, he wouldn't stop there either.

He felt as if he was fighting against a riptide that was carrying him farther and farther from shore, from his sanity. Even as the battle went on in his mind, he was leaning forward. Then the shingles moved beneath him.

"You're slipping." Mac grabbed his arm, and then she was sliding too.

In the instant it took him to realize that they were both going over the edge, he wrapped his arms around her and held her close. If he'd been alone, he would have simply tucked his arms in and rolled. As it was, the moment his feet hit the ground, he twisted and fell backward to take the brunt of the impact. It took his breath away.

As soon as he could, he loosened his grip on her. "Are you all right?"

She raised her head and looked down at him. "Fine. What about you?"

For a moment he didn't respond. All he could focus on was the way sunlight brought out the fiery glints in her hair and the way the amber flecks had brightened in her eyes. The way her body had softened until it fit perfectly against his.

He couldn't recall ever wanting a woman this much. "About your plan…"

"Oh," she said, her eyes suddenly narrowing. "Do you want to…? That would be great. If you'd like to get started…" She pushed against him. "I'll get the questionnaire."

"Questionnaire?"

"So I can tell which fantasies are your favorites."

He was thinking of carrying her down the beach to the small inlet where the palms touched overhead. There, he could make love to her until she couldn't think of anything, of anyone but him.

And the doc was thinking of paperwork!

"It won't take long. Once I know exactly what you like to fantasize about, I can run them through this program I created on my laptop."

"Wait a minute." When she tried to rise, he grabbed her wrist and sat up with her. The frantic skipping of her pulse against his thumb told him she wasn't anywhere near as cool as her voice had sounded.

Oh, she was excited all right. But was it about making love with him, or was it because she was thinking of her questionnaires and programs? "I stopped indulging in fantasies when I was twelve. I much prefer reality."

"Oh…are you saying you don't want to? I told Sophie that you don't think of me that way."

"I think of you that way." He couldn't stop himself from thinking of her that way.

"Then…" She moistened her lips. "You'll do it?"

The strength of his desire to agree had him releasing her wrist carefully. He had to think, to weigh the possible outcomes. And he couldn't think at all when she was sitting on his lap, her mouth only a breath away. "I never make snap decisions in business. I'm sure you never do in the lab."

"No, of course not."

"Then I suggest we take twenty-four hours to think it over before either of us jumps into anything. Agreed?"

"Agreed."

He saw something flicker in her eyes, but he wasn't sure whether it was relief or disappointment. Then to his complete astonishment, she settled her head on his shoulder and yawned.

"I feel so much better now that I've told you why I came here."

Better wasn't exactly the way he would choose to describe the mix of emotions moving through him. Desire, he could handle. But there was something unsettling about the warmth that was also spreading through him, solid and sure. And it shouldn't feel so damn right to have her sitting on his lap. He should be setting her away from him, but he hadn't been able to prevent his arms from moving around her.

And then he didn't move at all. For a few moments he allowed himself to simply sit and hold her. The silence was broken only by the sound of waves rushing onto the shore and the cry of a gull overhead.

Who in the hell was Dr. MacKenzie Lloyd? Was she the cool, unflappable scientist? Or was she the sensual woman who'd just offered to practice her sex research on him? And which one was having this effect on him?

Glancing down, he saw that her eyes were shut, her breathing even. She was asleep. Lucas frowned. Was she so indifferent to him that, one minute, she could tell him that she wanted to create sexual fantasies for him and then, the next, calmly doze off?

There was a part of him that wanted to wake her with a kiss. To catapult her from slumber to wakefulness by arousing in her at least some of the feelings that were tormenting him. He wondered if this was what that prince had felt when he'd fought his way into the castle and come upon Sleeping Beauty.

He'd always privately thought the poor guy had gotten more trouble than he'd bargained for when he'd kissed that beauty awake.

And Lucas Wainright hadn't gotten to where he was without looking before he leaped.

Twenty-four hours. He repeated the number to himself several times as he rose to his feet and carried Mac into the cabin. By the time he settled her on the bed and retreated from the cabin down to the beach, he wasn't sure whether it was a caution or a promise.

CHAPTER FIVE

WHEN SHE WOKE the next morning, the first thing Mac was aware of was the heat. Her entire body seemed to be on fire. Pushing herself into a sitting position, she felt a trickle of sweat run down her neck.

One quick glance around the room reminded her of where she was. Lucas's cabin. Then her eyes widened as the memory of just what she'd been dreaming about flooded into her mind. She'd been making love to Lucas, or more precisely, he'd been making love to her—touching her with those clever, callused hands. There hadn't been one part of her body that they'd left unexplored. She'd barely been able to breathe, let alone move. Even now, as she thought of the way those long, hard fingers had stroked her—down the length of her arms, her legs and then slowly, torturously up the inner side of her thigh—she could feel tiny little flames licking along her skin.

Mac sat up and scooted to the edge of the bed. She'd just had a fantasy! The one thing she'd discovered in her research was that she had a very dull fantasy life. Obviously, that was changing. Madame Gervais had insisted that she had a sensual side to her nature. Lucas Wainright seemed to be helping her discover it.

Pushing herself off the bed, Mac moved to the window, but even the breeze making its way into the room felt warm on her skin. No wonder. The sun was already quite high in the sky. A quick glance at her watch told her it was eleven o'clock. Another four hours to wait until Lucas would announce his decision.

What would it be?

Nothing in the way he'd acted the day before had given her the slightest clue. From the moment that she'd awakened from her nap, he'd been polite and attentive, encouraging her to walk along the beach while he fished in a lagoon for their dinner.

After they'd eaten, he'd taken her on a tour of the island. He'd even slept on the boat so that she could have the one narrow bed in the cabin.

In short, he'd been the perfect host. Other than that one terse statement—"I think about you that way"—he hadn't done one thing to indicate that he might be interested in becoming her...boy toy.

Moving toward the dresser, Mac gazed at her reflection. Better to face the facts. MacKenzie Lloyd was not a woman that most men had lustful thoughts about. Even with a new hair color and a head full of research, what did she really have to appeal to a man like Lucas Wainright?

The muffled ring of a cell phone had her moving quickly to the main room where she located her bag and fished it out. "Hello?"

"It's Sophie. If Lucas is there, pretend I'm someone from the university."

"He's not here." And she wasn't sure where he was. Mac went to the door of the cabin and spotted him on the deck of the boat polishing brass with a white cloth.

"Good. Whatever you do, don't tell him I called. As far as he knows, I had to check my cell phone in at the desk of the spa. The one thing that would spoil my week in paradise would be to have him calling me every day to check up on me."

"You're enjoying the spa?"

"It's heaven. For the first time in months I feel absolutely free. I wish you could see the view I have from my balcony. There are at least three air balloons suspended in the sky. They look like giant lollipops. I have to go up in one while I'm here. Wait…Mac, can you hold on a minute? I ordered something from room service. They're at the door."

In the background, Mac could hear voices, the sound of Sophie's laugh, then a deeper one. On the boat, Lucas continued to polish brass with sure, steady strokes. Odd that she'd never before pictured him as a man who would like to do any kind of work with his hands. It explained why they'd felt so hard when they'd settled over hers on the wheel of the boat. The memory had a sliver of heat shooting through her.

"You still there?" Sophie asked.

"Yes," Mac replied.

"Tell me how your plan's progressing."

"I asked him."

"Asked him what?" Sophie prompted. "Give me the details."

As she told Sophie what had happened, Mac once again replayed everything in her mind. Her stomach plummeted farther. "I don't think it was my most persuasive presentation."

"Surely he didn't turn you down?"

Mac smiled at the disbelief in her friend's voice. "Not exactly. He wants us both to think about it for twenty-four hours."

There was a great deal of exasperation in Sophie's sigh. "That is *so* typically Lucas. He's probably having one of his security people do a thorough background check on you to see if you're any threat to Wainright Enterprises. My advice is don't wait."

"What do you mean?"

"Seduce him into agreeing. That research of yours is worthless if you don't have the guts to use it."

"I don't know—"

"He who hesitates is lost. Picture yourself five years after you walk down the aisle with your future bridegroom. You're in your kitchen feeding two screaming kids and you're afraid your husband's eye is about to wander. Are you going to wait for *him* to make the first move?"

"No," Mac said softly.

"But? I hear a *but* in that sentence."

"I just imagined he might be a little more enthusiastic."

Sophie laughed. "Enthusiasm is contagious. Starting out by asking him to fill out a questionnaire was not your best move. As foreplay, it wouldn't rate very high on *my* list."

"Oh…I didn't think of that."

"I warned you that this plan of yours was not going to be like your usual experiments. You can't approach it like a job. Besides, it should be fun! And people are not like your docile little lab animals, Mac. Sometimes they need a little extra push."

The moment Lucas turned and glanced in her direction, Mac felt the impact of his gaze ripple through her. So what if his hormones weren't as stimulated as hers were. So what if he was just being kind to his kid sister's best friend. Didn't she have the kind of knowledge to change all that?

"Sometimes they need a big push," Sophie added.

Mac couldn't think of a man she'd rather push than Lucas. Slowly, she smiled as one of the fantasies from her research unfolded itself in her mind. "Thanks, Soph. I'm going to take your advice."

"You go, girl! And have some fun!"

SOPHIE HUNG UP her phone with a satisfied smile and glanced out at the view from her balcony. Covered in lush grapevines, the hillside rolled down to the valley below. There, the neat rows in the vineyards were crisscrossed by narrow roads until hills rose sharply again.

Napa Valley, California, was as far away from D.C., the Florida Keys and North Carolina as she could get without actually leaving the country. And since she'd never been here before, she doubted that Lucas would think of it. Her lips curved in a smile. Not that she expected him to be thinking about her at all for the next week. Mac should be able to handle that.

And she was going to handle the rest. For the next week, no one would know she was Sophie Wainright, least of all the man she'd agreed to meet today for lunch. When she'd first met him in that small café on Capitol Hill three weeks ago, she'd told him she was Susan Walker. The initials matched her own, but that was all that linked her to Sophie Wainright.

It was on the way home from that first meeting that she'd discovered she was being followed. Now she pushed herself away from the railing and began to pace back and forth along the length of her balcony. Just the thought of it made her furious.

Well, she'd made sure that no one had followed her here. Not once since she'd gotten off the plane in San Francisco had she had that prickling sensation at the back of her neck that had warned her before. Not even Mac knew where she was coming to spend time with the man who only knew her as Susan Walker. A man who wasn't just interested in her because she was Sophie Wainright.

Pausing, she leaned on the balcony railing to watch one of the air balloons make a soft landing on the valley floor. Then she smiled. Lucas would have a lot of trouble finding her even if he did discover that she wasn't in that dreadful spa. A bonus to switching identities with Mac was that she'd been able to make all her plane and hotel reservations in Mac's name.

Reaching for the coffee that room service had just delivered, she raised her cup in another toast. "To real freedom, at last."

THE MOMENT THAT Mac turned and strode back into the cabin, Lucas frowned and went back to polishing the brass trim that edged the deck of the *Adventurer*. Performing repetitive physical tasks always helped him to think and to put things in perspective. But he was no closer to sorting out what he was going to do about MacKenzie Lloyd's proposition than he'd been yesterday when he'd left her in his bedroom.

Could the doc possibly be as honest and disingenuous as she seemed? Gut instinct told him she was.

But experience told him that women usually had a hidden financial agenda.

That was the one lesson he'd learned from watching his father bounce through five marriages. He'd been ten when his mother had walked out for good. His father had reacted by marrying again on the rebound. It had been up to Lucas to help Sophie negotiate the emotional trauma. It wasn't until marriage three or four that he'd become aware of the financial toll that his father's behavior was taking on the company his grandfather had founded. By the time wife number five had departed, Wainright Enterprises had been deeply in debt. Not even Sophie knew how close they had come to losing everything.

When he'd taken over the company, he'd made a vow to himself never to make the same mistake his father had. He would never marry because he already had a family—Sophie and the stepbrothers his father had left behind.

MacKenzie Lloyd had seemed to understand and accept that. But maybe it had been the beer. Either way, she'd made him an offer he was finding it very difficult to refuse. The whole idea of researching men's fantasies and then offering to make them into a reality for some lucky guy was…almost irresistible.

When his cell phone rang, he put down his cloth and pulled it out of his pocket. "Yeah?"

"As far as I can tell, Sophie Wainright is somewhere in this damn spa," Tracker said.

"As far as you can tell?"

"I'm about fifty yards from the gates right now. The guard on duty says Sophie Wainright registered about three o'clock yesterday afternoon, but the people who run this place are a bunch of amazons who clearly have an aversion to men. If you have a Y chromosome, you can't set foot on their sacred ground. I'd feel more certain if I could get in there and see for myself."

"A little paranoid, are we?" Lucas asked.

"I'd prefer to think I'm being thorough," Tracker said. "I don't like that she pulled that switch on me, and I'd like to make sure she hasn't pulled another one."

"Your pride is wounded."

There was a slight pause at the other end. Tracker's drawl when it came was laced with humor. "Could be that. Could be the challenge too. I haven't figured a way in yet."

Lucas grinned. "I told you your policy on not hiring women would come back to bite you."

"No way, boss. I only hire people I can trust, and I don't trust the female of the species."

Lucas's grin faded. "Should I be worried about Sophie?"

"Not yet. If I thought she might be in danger, I'd go in there, grab her and get her out. And if you're worried about Falcone, he and his son have both flown to California. I've got a man on each of them. If there's any problem, I can be at the airport in an hour. Unless you want me out there right now."

Lucas considered it for a moment. "No. As long as you've got Falcone covered, you can indulge yourself with the challenge of getting into that all-female spa."

"Go ahead. Rub it in. What about the little doc? You find out what her problem is?"

"Yeah."

"You want me to do something about it?"

"No." The sharpness of his own tone surprised Lucas.

"You want me to butt out."

"Yes. No," Lucas said on a sigh. Tracker was a man he'd trust with his life and the only man he'd ever trusted with details of his business deals. "I think I'm going to have to tackle it myself."

"It's personal, I take it."

The delight in his friend's voice had him frowning. "It's complicated. And…it's confidential."

"Goes without saying."

Lucas kept his gaze on the cabin as he tried to think of the best way to summarize Mac's plan. Finally he began, "Long story short. She's done some research on how to keep a man pleased…" His frown deepened. "No, *pleasured* is a better word. In bed. So far all her data has come from books and interviews, and now she wants to put it… into practice."

"On you."

"Or on some other volunteer."

There was a beat of silence at the other end of the phone. Then Tracker said, "What's the problem?"

"Maybe it sounds too good to be true."

Tracker laughed. "You got a point there. Your little scenario has just moved to the number-one spot on my favorite-fantasy list. If you turn her down, please mention my name as a backup."

"No."

Tracker gave an exaggerated sigh. "Hands off. I get the picture."

"It's not that." But Lucas was all too afraid that it was just that. For some reason, he didn't like the idea of Mac taking her proposal elsewhere. It was bad enough to picture her with some anonymous man that one of her research contacts fixed her up with. But when he pictured her with Tracker, it was even worse. Tracker appreciated certain things about women, but he didn't trust them. And it occurred to Lucas that he wanted very much to protect Mac from getting hurt.

"If you're worried about her being after your money, I think you're safe there. I ran a financial check on her. She has a trust fund of two million from her parents, but she seems to live on what she makes as a full professor at the university. And she may get an influx of money in the near future. Several biotech firms are very interested in the research she's doing. It's some very promising stuff on slowing the aging process at the cellular level. One of them has been wining and dining her recently. That's all I've got so far, but she sure doesn't fit the profile of a fortune hunter."

"No, she doesn't."

"One other thing," Tracker said. "There was a break-in at her lab at the university. Must have happened when she was at your place on Sunday. According to campus security, there was no damage. Whoever it was got into the safe, but she told the police none of her research was stolen. She evidently keeps it elsewhere."

"Who would be after her research?"

"I figured you'd want to know, so I put a man on it. I assumed that might be the problem she wanted your help with. Look, boss, I'm going to give you some unsolicited and probably unwanted advice."

"Tracker..."

"No one works harder for your family than you do. Maybe it's time you relaxed and had a little fun. I say go for it."

Tracker's laughter was still ringing in his ear when he cut the connection. He'd come to pretty much the same decision on his own. If the doc was determined to create fantasies, he might as well be on the receiving end. Hell, he'd come up with several of his own he'd like to try out. And when the time came for the fantasies to end...he'd just have to let her down very easy. It was the one thing besides business that he'd worked to develop a skill for. He knew how to say goodbye.

MAC CAREFULLY CONSIDERED the two bathing suits she'd packed. The one still lying on top of her suitcase was a black tank top with a matching thong. The one she was wearing was a whisper-thin piece of silky latex in a shimmering emerald green. It covered her like a second skin from her breasts to her thighs, and it did everything that Madame Gervais said it would—revealing practically everything and suggesting more. More importantly, it fit the particular fantasy she wanted to create.

Picking up a flowered piece of silk, she wrapped it

around herself and tied it at the waist. Then she studied herself in the mirror and nodded.

Guilt-free sex with a beautiful, young island girl—that was the fantasy she'd chosen. She'd thought of it when she'd been talking to Sophie. It supposedly appealed to most men. Music from *South Pacific* hummed at the edges of her mind as she ran through the details in her mind. It would help if she could get Lucas to go into the water with her. Supposedly, men had very erotic fantasies about mermaids too. And since she didn't have the information that the questionnaire would have given her, a backup plan was a good idea.

Moving closer to the mirror, she ran her hands through her hair and studied herself more closely. Madame Gervais had told her that the right clothes could make all the difference. Mac was beginning to believe she was right. The outfit she was wearing did make her feel different, more confident.

When she stepped out that door, she was going to be a young girl who'd been born and raised in a village on this island. Lania was her name. And Lucas was a stranger who had been washed ashore by a storm. A dark handsome stranger she was strongly attracted to, a man whose touch she was beginning to crave. A man who would leave her soon, unless she convinced him to stay.

On impulse, she picked up the string of pearls she'd taken from her bag and fastened them around her neck. They fit well with the fantasy.

Turning, she headed toward the door of the cabin. She saw him even before she stepped out on the porch. He was hurrying up the path. In her mind, she pictured running to him across the sand. He would sweep her up into his arms and carry her down to a secluded section of the beach.

It was the water bottle she'd left on the top step that shattered the image forming in her mind. Her foot snagged on it, and she made a grab for the post. It kept her from falling, but it also swayed ominously, rattling more loose shingles on the roof. Three of them showered to the ground and one landed on Lucas's shoulder as he reached her.

"Are you all right?" he asked, brushing it off.

"Are you?" It was his quick grin that made her smile, and suddenly they were both laughing. When she reached for the post again to steady herself, he grabbed her hand.

"Please. I don't want to be hit by any more falling debris."

She felt a fresh wave of laughter bubbling up.

When it finally subsided, she found she was standing on the bottom step, his hands were at her waist, steadying her, and her eyes were level with his. Laughter had lightened the color, but the blue was already deepening, and his gaze had become intent. Her body reacted instantly, every nerve ending snapping to attention the way they always seemed to when he was close.

Her gaze dropped to his mouth. His lips were wide, not thin…not too full either. It was hard to tell if they would be hard or soft, and she had a sudden, compelling need to find out. In her dream, he'd touched her—everywhere. But he hadn't kissed her. She leaned closer.

"Doc…" Lucas cleared his throat as he tightened his grip on her waist, once more steadying her. "I came back to the cabin to tell you that I don't need twenty-four hours. I've reached a decision."

A quick skip of panic moved through her. He was going to say no. To forestall him, she pressed her fingers against his mouth. "I've reached a decision too."

"Go ahead."

The movement of his lips against her fingers sent a wave of heat through her. "I was coming down to the beach to…"

"Yes?"

Another wave of heat shot through her. "I wanted to… that is, I wondered if you…" It was hard to keep her mind on the fantasy, hard to think of anything but the pressure, the heat of his mouth on her fingers. What would his lips feel like on hers? What would they taste like? At the same time that she struggled to keep her focus, she couldn't seem to prevent herself from moving closer. "I have a fantasy in mind…"

"Yes."

In the fantasy that filled her mind, he gripped her wrist to pull her hand away. Then his mouth crushed hers, strong arms lifted her, carrying her into the cabin, and then the full weight of his body pressed her into the mattress of that narrow cot. Even as a sharp spear of pleasure streaked through her, she struggled to rid her mind of the image. She was supposed to be creating *his* fantasy, not hers.

Struggling to concentrate, she said, "My name is Lania. You're shipwrecked on my island. And every day I've come from the village to nurse you. To bring you food. There isn't a part of your body I haven't seen." She pictured it in her mind. "There isn't a part of you I haven't touched." She could feel the smooth skin stretched taut over long bones, solid muscles. "You've been growing stronger every day. You haven't noticed, but I've been watching you work on your boat. I know that you'll leave soon. But before you do…I want to—I need to—"

She wasn't sure what it was—the fantasy that her words were conjuring up in her mind or the heat that seemed to be steadily drawing her closer to him. But the need she felt to kiss him had twisted into something sharp and compelling inside her. She dragged her fingers away from his mouth, rubbing them over his bottom lip as she did.

"I just have to kiss you. I've been dreaming of doing this for so long." Framing his face with her hands, she touched her mouth to his. His lips were neither soft nor hard. "Just right," she murmured.

"What?"

She drew back slightly but she didn't meet his eyes. She couldn't seem to take her gaze from his lips. "Not too hard. Not too soft. Your mouth feels just right. I was wondering…"

This time when she pressed her mouth to his, she couldn't seem to prevent her tongue from slipping between his lips. If she'd thought he'd tasted good a moment before, this was heaven. Not sweet really, and not any flavor that she could remember tasting before. It reminded her just a little of her favorite childhood candy—the dark chocolate that her father would always send her on her birthdays and that her mother would take away from her and hide. It always tasted so delicious, so forbidden when she found it.

But Lucas's taste was much more potent. It seemed to be spreading through her, clouding her mind—and she had to focus. She'd forgotten for a moment the fantasy. In just a minute—or two—she'd have to get back to it.

And she would…definitely…just as soon as she tasted him one more time. Withdrawing a little, she nipped at his bottom lip, then let her tongue probe deeper. The tip of it brushed the edge of his teeth, then met his tongue. In the space of a heartbeat, the flavor changed again to something very dark and very male. As it streamed through her, she tightened her hands on him and felt her toes curl on the edge of the step. In the space of a heartbeat, each sensation intensified—the rough wood of the porch beneath her bare feet, the burning warmth of his thighs pressed against hers. Beneath her hands, she felt the sharp line of cheekbones, the hard strength of his jaw.

She wanted more. She wanted him to touch her, to kiss her back. And he was just standing there, letting her do whatever she wanted. Suddenly chilled, she drew away and met his eyes.

"What's wrong?" she asked.

"You stopped. Why?"

She blinked. "You're not kissing me back. I should have insisted that you fill out the questionnaire. Then I would have some idea—"

"Forget the questionnaire and kiss me again."

IT SEEMED LIKE an eternity to Lucas as he waited for her to bring her mouth to his again. He'd seen the confusion in her eyes and the hurt. He wanted to erase both. More than that, he wanted to ease her to the ground and run his hands over her, slowly, molding every inch of her until she felt as helpless as he did.

How could he possibly explain to her what he didn't understand himself? He hadn't touched her, he hadn't taken control of the kiss because he quite simply couldn't. Even now, he wasn't sure he could lift his arms.

Was it the fantasy that her words had conjured up? He'd imagined what it might be like to lie there, powerless, while she touched him—everywhere.

Or had it been the reality of her kiss—the softness of her lips and those tiny, tentative movements of her tongue as it glided over his? Perhaps it was the combination that had acted like a powerful drug on his system, pouring through him and trapping him in a world of sensations.

He wasn't sure of anything except that she'd weakened him. He'd never allowed a woman to do that to him before.

And it wouldn't happen again. This time he intended to be in control of himself, but the moment her mouth brushed against his, a short, explosive fuse ignited. Any intention he had of keeping the pressure light and teasing was blown away. Feelings she'd stirred up with that first kiss tore through him in a series of explosions, and wave after wave of sensations rocked him.

He'd never been so aware of a woman before—the helpless hitch of her breath when he nipped at her bottom lip, the husky, pleading sound of her moan as he swallowed it, and her skin…it was on fire. He could feel the flames licking at his fingers as they moved down her throat over her breasts, burning him even through the thin material of the bathing suit. And her taste, the deep ripe flavor poured through him.

He'd sensed this raw passion in her before, simmering beneath the surface, waiting to break free. He could feel it now in the way her hands gripped him, in the way her mouth met each of his demands with one of her own.

Though the ocean was over fifty yards away, he could have sworn he was standing in it, feeling the push and pull of the water as it sucked the sand out from beneath his feet. He pulled her closer for balance and felt her breasts crush against the hard line of his chest. It wasn't enough.

Desperation clawed at him as he ran his hands over her. He knew he was being rough. And in some distant part of his mind, he knew he should slow down, be patient. But his hands seemed to be operating of their own accord, following one directive—he simply had to get her closer to him. Impatient with the bathing suit, he stripped it down to her waist and cupped her breast in his hand. It was as soft as rainwater. Liquid silk. He wanted to savor it, taste it, but she arched against him, calling his name.

He had to have more.

"Mac." He cupped his free hand under her hip. "Scoot up. Wrap your legs around me."

With a murmur of acceptance, approval, she did. Then, arching against him again, she began to move, rubbing against his hardness. What he'd thought were flames before couldn't compare to the searing heat that sliced through him now. He'd felt need before, but not this kind—unreasonable, unmanageable. Something inside him snapped with the same quick finality of a switch being pulled. Then he wasn't thinking at all.

Sinking to his knees, he managed to pull down the zipper of his jeans, push aside the thin protection of her suit, and then he was sinking into her. But it still wasn't enough. With a quick, savage movement of his hips he went deeper, stretching her, feeling her slick, hot core take all of him. Gripped fiercely inside her, he felt his climax begin to build. His hips began to move, thrusting harder and faster. Swearing, he drove her, drove himself until the final release and the world went dark around him.

Shattered. That's what he felt like when sanity returned. He was lying on the rough boards of the porch beside Mac, but he had no idea how they'd gotten there. He couldn't move, could barely think.

And he was trembling. A small shiver of fear moved through him. Shame came next. He'd never before taken a woman with so little care. He wasn't even sure that she'd reached her climax. His own had been so quick, so consuming, and he'd been so totally lost in it.

Had he hurt her? He'd been close to violent, definitely out of control when he'd pushed into her. When he turned to look at her, he found wide amber eyes studying him intently. He had the uncomfortable feeling that he'd been smeared on a slide. He opened his mouth, but she spoke first. "That didn't go exactly as I'd planned."

The words were such a clear echo of the thoughts in his head that he blinked.

"I'm sorry."

She'd even stolen his apology. Suddenly, he frowned. "You don't have anything to be sorry about."

"I lost control. It wasn't supposed to end that quickly."

"No, it wasn't. But that was my fault."

"We were supposed to make it at least to the beach. I really wanted to get you in the water. Kissing underwater is supposed to be very erotic."

She was talking about the fantasy. Had she been kissing him or the sailor? And who had he just made love to?

She rubbed her fingers across her lips. "The way I react to your kiss is going to present a challenge that I didn't quite foresee." A fine line appeared on her forehead. "I'm going to have to make some adjustments to my plan."

It was the last thing he'd expected her to say. Whoever it was who'd been kissing him, it was definitely the doc who was talking to him now. And he wanted her even more than he had before.

"That is...." The frown line deepened. "I hope you're going to let me go ahead with my research."

Her lips were still swollen from his kisses. A pulse was still jackhammering at her throat, and yet he could hear the wheels turning in her head. "You're hard on a man's ego, Doc."

The corners of her mouth turned down slightly. "I don't mean to be. Next time I'll try to stay more focused on the fantasy."

"You do that, Doc." Next time he was going to make sure that she couldn't stay focused at all. With a quick grin, he said, "I may have to make some adjustments of my own."

For some perverse reason, derailing that one-track mind of hers was becoming his number-one desire. Perhaps it was the challenge she offered that was drawing him. He could swear that he was dealing with more than one woman—there was the doc and the island girl, Lania. And which one was the real MacKenzie Lloyd? One way or the other, he was going to figure her out.

"Before we go any further with this little experiment, I think we need a change of scene." He rose, then drew her to her feet. "Let's pack."

"Where are we going?" she asked as he ushered her into the cabin.

"Wainright Enterprises owns a resort hotel on Key West. It will provide us with a more romantic atmosphere."

"I don't need romance."

Lucas threw back his head and laughed. "I think I do. You'll just have to indulge me." Then, throwing an arm around her shoulders, he gave her a quick hug. "And you better start figuring out what to do when I kiss you again. I plan to do it again very soon."

CHAPTER SIX

TRACKER SWORE SOFTLY as he lowered his binoculars. The North Carolina mountains had too many damn trees, and he'd lost track of how many he'd climbed trying to get a good view of the guests at the Serenity Spa.

One problem was that the compound was spread out over a couple of square miles. A large building sat in the center on a hill. Fanning out from there were tennis courts, a glassed-in, Olympic-size swimming pool and acres of lawn set up for volleyball, badminton, croquet. One unpaved road connected the grounds to the highway a mile away. In the more than four hours since he'd had the place under surveillance, only two vehicles had used that road. One had been the spa van, the other a truck delivering fresh produce and bottled water to the main building.

Raising the binoculars, he focused them on the group of women who were gathering on one of the playing fields, watching to see if any of them walked with the confident, distinctive gait of the Princess. He'd dubbed Lucas's pampered and temperamental sister that the first time he'd seen her. His view was being hampered, not only by the branches of several trees, but also by the fact that the women were wearing what seemed to be the spa uniform—sweatpants and hooded jackets.

Huge gray clouds had settled like a lid over the mountains, and thunder growled overhead. As the hooded figures began to disperse, he shifted his gaze to the individual cabins, most of which were tucked away beneath the trees. The information he'd downloaded from the Serenity Spa website emphasized complete privacy. It promised clients a totally female environment, free from the "intrusion of any male vibrations."

Tracker couldn't prevent a grin. In the very near future, he was going to break their promise. He just hadn't figured out the best way to do it. If he forced his way in, the Princess would be furious. When the lady got all fired up, she reminded him of some warrior goddess about to wreak her vengeance on mere mortals.

She'd been mad as hell when she'd read the file he'd gathered on Bradley Davis. The heat of her anger had been aimed at her brother. And she'd taken him completely by surprise when she'd landed that right cross to her brother's chin. Just the memory had him grinning. Oh, she'd been quick as lightning. He couldn't help but admire her for it. And she was strong too. She might look as slender as a wand, but when he'd grabbed her, he'd had to put some effort into subduing her.

The Princess was smart too. No one he'd tailed had ever spotted him before. But she had. He could still recall the cold fury in her eyes when they'd met his in that Georgetown pub. He'd felt it like a blow in his gut.

He'd underestimated her. That had been his mistake—a moment of carelessness that he was paying for now, he thought as he shifted carefully on the branch to ease the sharp impressions the bark was leaving on his backside.

If she hadn't become aware that she was being tailed, she wouldn't have pulled that switch yesterday, and he'd know for sure if she was indeed escaping from "male vibrations" in one of those damn cabins.

A bird landed on a nearby branch, gave him a startled look and flew off.

"Good idea," he muttered as he started to lower himself to the ground. He'd hoped to study the women as they made their way to the main building for lunch, but the steady and insistent slap of rain meant that umbrellas would be out in full force.

After hitting the ground, he ran toward the main road. Time for plan B.

THE MOMENT LUCAS TURNED his attention to uncorking the champagne that had been waiting for them in the suite, Mac drew in a deep breath and slipped out onto the balcony. What she needed was a moment to plan and get back on track. He hadn't allowed her much time to do that on the boat trip to Key West. Instead, he'd seemed determined to distract her in any way he could.

Not that he'd kissed her again. He'd just taken every opportunity he could to touch her. A hand at her back as they'd walked down the dock, a firm grasp on her fingers as he'd helped her onto and off the boat, the brush of his body against hers as they'd stepped into the same slot of the revolving door that had spun them into the hotel lobby.

Each time he'd come in contact with her, her heart had made what felt like a somersault in her chest, and each and every nerve in her body had responded. So many images had filled her mind when the bellhop had given them a quick tour of the hotel suite. Every time he'd gestured to a different feature—from the oversize hot tub in the bathroom to the grand piano tucked into a corner of the sunken living room—she'd pictured Lucas making love to her in each spot.

Clearly, her ability to create sexual fantasies for herself was growing by leaps and bounds, and they all centered on Lucas Wainright. No other man had ever made love to her that way, with such intensity—as if he couldn't help himself. And she wanted him to do it again. And he would, just as soon as he followed her out onto the balcony. Just thinking about it was enough to make the muscles in her legs turn to water.

She had to get a grip. It would be so tempting to just give in to the spell that he seemed to weave around her. To enjoy it for however long it lasted.

As soon as he poured the champagne and followed her out here, she'd probably dissolve into a puddle at his feet.

No. If she allowed herself to give in to the temptation of what Lucas was offering, how could she fully field-test her research?

She had to focus on the fantasies. Resolutely, she walked to the railing of the balcony. A glance down at the man-made lagoon twisting like a turquoise snake around the hotel triggered a quick spurt of dizziness. The moment it passed, her gaze fixed on a waterfall tumbling over a small cave at the side of the lagoon. That definitely had possibilities. It would work for both the mermaid and the island-girl fantasies. The cave would also provide the perfect setting for making love in a semipublic place—another very popular male fantasy.

All she had to do was…

When the second wave of dizziness hit, Mac raised her eyes and concentrated on the view of the ocean stretching to the horizon. Taking a deep breath, she exhaled, then drew in another one. Her stomach settled, and her head cleared again.

The solution to keeping her plan on track was to get the jump on Lucas and draw him into a fantasy before he could totally mesmerize her as he had on his grandfather's island. Simple.

"What's wrong?"

She started, then turned. He was standing there studying her, and she felt the pull right down to where her toes curled in her sandals.

It was not going to be so simple.

"Tell me," he said, moving to the railing.

"Nothing. The room—everything—it's perfect."

"So perfect that you had to come out here to screw up your courage?" Taking her hand, he waited until she met his eyes.

"There's nothing wrong. No one has ever done anything like this for me. Sophie said you would be kind. But I didn't expect you to be sweet too."

"Sweet?"

The slightly disgruntled, slightly shocked look on his face made her smile. "It'll be our little secret. I won't tell a soul."

"Just tell *me*. What's wrong, Doc."

She shrugged. "I needed to come out here and think."

"Ah," he murmured, his forehead clearing. "Getting all your ducks lined up in a row?"

"Fear clears my mind. I know that might sound…" The rest of her sentence trailed off when he lifted her hand to his lips. He kissed the palm of her hand, then the veins at her wrist. For a moment, she couldn't say a thing. She was too busy absorbing the little waves of fire and ice that radiated up her arm. "You're trying to seduce me."

"You got me, Doc. I'm busted." He began to kiss her fingers one by one as if they were a delicacy he'd been waiting all day to sample. "I want to make up to you for what happened at the cabin."

She blinked and stared at him. "Why? I mean we both…I enjoyed it, really. It was my fault that I lost control."

"I lost control too, and I want to make it up to you."

"Wait." She pulled her hand away. "It's not necessary for you to make anything up. I don't think I've explained the essentials of my plan quite clearly enough. It's my job to seduce you."

He had her hand again, and she could feel a pull that went beyond the pressure of his fingers on hers.

"I'm not going to be able to create any fantasies if you keep distracting me," she continued weakly.

"What if I told you that I don't have any fantasies?" His eyes never left hers as he drew her fingers to his mouth. "I gave them up when I was a kid because I thought they were a waste of time. I much prefer reality. What I really want to do is to keep you in this suite and make love with you nonstop for the next three days."

The images that his statement conjured up nearly melted her knees again. And it didn't help one bit that he was touching her again, drawing one finger along her jawline, then down her neck to the hollow of her throat. She had to clear it to speak. "Sophie was right on the button when she bragged about your negotiating skills. You're trying to make me an offer I can't refuse."

His laugh erupted then, quick and infectious. The sound of it only added to the ribbons of heat spreading downward and upward from her center.

"I can never predict what you're going to say next. Maybe that's why you fascinate me, Doc."

She fascinated him? She'd never fascinated anyone in her life. It had to be the proposal she'd made him. Either that or he'd liked the island-girl fantasy. "I have some fantasies in mind that may fascinate you even more."

"I'd much rather spend some time with *you,* Doc. I've been wanting to touch you, really touch you, since you got off that plane yesterday morning. I don't know how much longer I can wait."

She felt her heart stutter.

"Why don't you come inside and let me show you?"

She was halfway to the door when she finally found the strength to dig in her heels. "Wait. Do you hear the way we're talking?"

"I know I'd like to stop talking."

"Just think about it. I said, 'I have some fantasies in mind for you.' You said, 'I want to touch you... Let me show you.' You see what that means, don't you?"

"We want each other?"

"More than that, we each want to be in charge. We're both control freaks, so to speak. Admit it. Don't you want to be in control when you're in a business deal?"

"You bet."

"And I am always in control in the lab. I have to be."

Lucas considered her for a minute. "What exactly are you saying, Doc?"

"We have a problem, and there's only one solution." She turned it over in her mind a few times, then said, "We'll have to take turns."

"Take turns?"

"Being in charge, calling the shots, whatever you want to call it. The first time we make love, I get to call the shots, create a fantasy, whatever I want. The next time, you're in charge. You can do whatever you want."

Lucas considered the idea for a moment. "How do you get to go first?"

She lifted her chin. "This whole thing was my idea. I flew all the way down here with the original proposition. And I just came up with a compromise so that two control freaks can work together. Clearly, I get to go first."

"How about we flip?" he asked, pulling a coin out of

his pocket. Before she could agree or protest, the coin was spinning upward into the sunshine.

"Heads," she called as he snatched it out of the air. Holding her breath, she watched his fingers slowly open.

"Heads it is," Lucas said.

Mac beamed a triumphant smile at him. "I'm going to freshen up. I'll meet you down in the lounge in thirty minutes."

"The lounge?" His face looked as incredulous as when she'd called him sweet. "Why do we have to go to the lounge when we have a perfectly good suite?"

"My call. And the fantasy I have in mind requires a different setting."

SHE WAS DRIVING him crazy. That much he knew. But now Lucas was beginning to suspect she was doing it on purpose. A glance at his watch told him that thirty minutes had lengthened into forty-five. No, forty-six.

Had he actually begun to count the minutes?

He glanced around the spacious but crowded lounge. Three TV sets hung from the ceiling over the bar, each one offering a muted version of a different sporting event. Other than that, the decor was rain forest, with moss dangling from the walls and ceiling, and exotic-looking plants bursting out of clay pots. Water dribbled steadily over rocks behind his booth and shot up in bright, colorful spouts from a pool twenty feet to the left of his table.

Directly ahead, beyond a wall of glass, the dimness gave way to light. Though the midday sun beat down mercilessly on the water, a few swimmers still sought relief from the heat in the coolness of the lagoon. Most guests were inside, enjoying the benefits of air-conditioning.

There was no sign of Mac anywhere. He lifted his beer, drained it, and thought of the perfectly good champagne he'd abandoned in the suite... And of what they could be doing right now. After what had happened at the cabin—he still couldn't figure it out. He'd never before desired a woman with that kind of intensity. And he'd never made love to a woman with less finesse.

He wanted to give Mac romance. There was a definite air of innocence about her that made him want to seduce her slowly—with champagne, soft music. When the bell-hop had given them that whirlwind tour of the suite, he'd pictured undressing her and making love with her on that large, smooth bed. Then he would have carried her to the Jacuzzi where they would have finished the rest of the champagne and then made love again. Very slowly.

But she'd decided he was a control freak. No one else he'd dated had ever complained.

But then Mac was unlike anyone else he'd ever wanted to make love to.

He tapped his fingers on the table. Maybe it had been a mistake to bring her here. If they'd stayed at the cabin, he wouldn't be sitting alone in a bar, nursing a beer. They could be lying right now on that narrow bed.

Leaning against the back of the booth, he allowed the image to slip into his mind—those smooth legs wrapping around him, drawing him closer, trapping him. Right now he could be pushing into her heat, withdrawing and push-ing in again. Deeper. He could almost feel her wet, silk heat closing around him.

"If you're not waiting for someone..."

Lucas's eyes shot open at the voice. It was Mac's. Per-haps a little huskier. But the blonde standing a few feet away from his table had to be a stranger. Still half caught up in the fantasy he'd fashioned in his mind, he blinked and tried to focus.

She wore a bright red skirt, barely the length of a dinner

napkin. It fit her like a second skin and seemed to stop where her legs began. His throat went dry as his gaze moved down the length of them, then back up to where the skirt rode high on her thighs. Was she wearing anything beneath it?

"That outfit…" he began.

When she whirled in front of him, the skirt inched even higher.

"You like it?"

"Mac?" He dragged his gaze from the miraculous legs up her body to her…. He could see her nipples through the stretchy fabric of the tank top—perfect little buds. With great effort he managed to focus on her face. Her blond hair looked mussed, as if some man had just run his hands through it several times. And her eyes—they were huge, heavy-lidded…and there was no mistaking that golden-brown color.

"Mac, what in hell are you doing?"

In a flash she had slid in beside him in the back of the booth. "Shh." She gave him a slow wink. "You're mistaken. I'm not Mac. I'm Sally. And you're…" She paused to slip a finger beneath the button of his polo shirt and flick it free of its hole. "You're John."

"John?"

"My first of the day." Leaning closer, she lowered her voice. "We're complete strangers. We've never met before. You saw me on the beach when you were docking your boat, and you've just invited me to join you in your very fancy hotel for a drink. I've never been in a place quite like this before."

Pausing, she glanced around, then dipped her finger into the water that ran over the rocks behind them. Slowly, she ran her damp finger along his jaw, then down his throat until she could unfasten the next button of his shirt.

"Mac—"

She leaned closer. "It's Sally. The fantasy will be more enjoyable if you let yourself get into it. Since you didn't want to fill out the questionnaire, I chose one of the most popular ones—sex with a perfect stranger."

She freed another button on his shirt.

"I'm hoping you'll like it. This too."

She set a package on the table. "I stopped in the gift shop and got you a surprise. Take a look and tell me what you think."

He was finding it difficult to think at all while he could feel the hard pebbles of her breasts brushing against his arm. But he found his gaze wandering to the bag. He couldn't remember the last time anyone had bought him a surprise. It had been sweet of Mac to think of it—except that it might not have been Mac but Sally who'd bought him the gift.

Her fingernail traced a line down the center of his chest, sending little ribbons of heat outward and downward. Then her fingers were on his belt, pulling it free. He clamped his fingers around her wrist. "Stop."

"You don't really want me to." Her free hand dropped to his thigh.

"We're in a public place." The ribbons of heat had burst into flames where her hand was resting. "Let's go."

"You're embarrassed. That's so cute."

"Cute?" He stared at her for a minute. All he could see was a mixture of amusement and excitement in her eyes. "You're enjoying this."

She leaned closer and dropped her voice to a whisper. "Because I'm *Sally*. Getting into these clothes really helped. I think you'd enjoy it too if you could get into the fantasy. In one survey, fifty-three percent of the men fantasized about having sex with a stranger they picked up in a bar. Thirty-five percent of those wanted the stranger to be a hooker. Have you ever had either of those fantasies?"

"No. I told you I don't have them."

"Never paid for sex?"

"No."

"A first-time John. My favorite," she said. He didn't think it was possible but she suddenly seemed closer. "Think about what I'd promised you we'd do when I persuaded you to invite me here." Her fingers traced a delicate pattern on his inner thigh as they moved higher.

"Doc, you can't." The words erupted on a moan.

"Want me to tell you what I promised to do?" The words were just a breath in his ear.

"Mr. Wainright, sir…"

Lucas turned to face a tall man wearing a conservatively cut suit with an insignia that marked him as a member of the hotel's staff.

"Is this lady bothering you?"

Immediately Lucas slipped an arm around Mac. "Not at all. This lady is my wife."

The man's glance slipped to Mac, then back to Lucas. "Your…I'm sorry, sir. I just thought…"

"You thought wrong."

"My apologies, Mr. Wainright. I…I'm sorry to have disturbed you. I hope you'll let me know what the staff can do to make your stay more pleasant." With a brief nod, the man turned and walked away.

The moment he was out of earshot, Mac spoke on a bubble of laughter. "'This lady is my wife!' How did you manage to say that with a straight face? I don't think he believed you."

"No, he didn't." Lucas kept his eyes on the man's retreating back until he was out of sight. "He was trying to do his job."

"He was going to throw me out, and you saved me. It was just like in *Pretty Woman* when Richard Gere brings Julia Roberts into that swanky Beverly Hills hotel. He doesn't let them throw her out either. Instead, he hires her for the whole week. Now *there's* a fantasy. How about it? Would you like to hire me for a week?"

Her hand was burning its way up his thigh again. Lucas covered it with his own, and when he turned to face her, he found that she was very close. It wasn't just her hair that was different. Her mouth was too—slicked with red the color of wild raspberries. It took all his willpower not to sample. "What I'd like to do can't be done here—" he tore his gaze from her lips "—unless you want to get us both thrown out. Let's take this to the room."

She smiled at him. "I'm not done yet."

Before he could prevent it, her hand slipped from beneath his to cover his erection.

"Ever fantasize about having sex in a public place?"

"Doc…" The word was barely audible. He couldn't breathe, didn't dare to move.

"I'm Sally, remember?"

Beneath the table, he grabbed her wrist and removed her hand very carefully. "This fantasy is over. We're getting out of here."

"Not until you kiss me. I've been dying for you to kiss me. I can't stop thinking about it."

Lucas gazed into her eyes. The teasing light was gone. In its place was something hot and needy. Was it Mac talking? Or Sally? And just who had brought him nearly to completion with her touch? At the moment that his mouth covered hers, he wasn't sure he cared.

CHAPTER SEVEN

KISS ME. The words had slipped out before she could prevent them. She hadn't meant to say them. But touching him, feeling the strength of his desire fill her hand had changed the fantasy into a desire so sharp she couldn't resist.

She hadn't even had time to blink before his mouth had crushed down on hers. The memory of their last kiss shattered as new sensations streamed through her. She welcomed the heat, the urgent demand, and wanted more.

The feelings racing through her were as exciting as the first time one of her theories had proven to be true in the lab. There was that breathless rush of pleasure, then the exhilaration that came with knowing that the results were just the beginning. That they could be taken to the next step and the next.

Touch me, she wanted to cry out. *Please touch me.*

And then he did. His hands were hard—and rough. One had clamped like a vise on the back of her neck. The other was running down her in a smooth, possessive stroke until it reached the top of her thigh. When he scraped his teeth over her bottom lip, a bolt of pleasure shot through her. She could feel everything—the soft give of the cushioned leather at her back, the hard line of his body pressing against her, and the beating of her own heart—so fast, so hard, she was sure it was going to pound its way right out of her chest.

And all the while, something inside her was beginning to boil like hot molten rock at the earth's center.

More. She arched toward him, and suddenly his hand was just where she wanted it to be. Right at the center of her heat.

"Excuse me."

The two words didn't register at first. All she was aware of was Lucas's abrupt withdrawal. First, he pulled his mouth from hers and then his hand. But he kept one arm around her as he turned.

"What is it?" Lucas's voice sounded like a snarl, and the perky little waitress took a quick step back from the table. At least he could talk. Mac's lips felt as if they were vibrating. She wondered if she could ever use them for forming words again.

"I'm sorry to interrupt," she said with a faltering attempt at a smile. "But my manager sent me over. There's a call for you at the main desk. He thought it might be important."

Mac could almost feel Lucas put a clamp on his anger. His voice was much milder when he said, "We'll take the bill."

"Thanks." She beamed a smile at him, then waited until he signed it and handed it back to her.

Mac didn't look at Lucas until the waitress left. He was studying her, and there was nothing on his face that gave away what he was thinking.

"You're trouble," he said.

She could have said the same about him and meant it. She didn't kid herself for one minute that she'd been successful at sustaining her fantasy for even a second after Lucas had begun to kiss her. One taste and Sally might just as well have been vaporized. She was the one who'd been kissing Lucas, wanting Lucas. And she hadn't wanted to stop.

He slid out of the booth and held out his hand. "We're getting out of here before we're arrested."

"I think I'm glad I'm with the owner of the hotel," Mac said as she grabbed the bag that contained his present, then tucked her free hand in his.

Lucas's lips twitched. "I'm glad I *am* the owner of the hotel."

They were both laughing as they walked out of the lounge.

THE LOBBY WAS CROWDED. Some people were clustered in groups, others wove their way toward the bank of elevators or up a curving sweep of stairs to the second level. The sun streamed down on them from a skylight as they circled a fountain in the open atrium.

At any other time, Lucas might have taken a moment to just mingle and observe how smoothly the staff was running the place, but two things were on his mind—the woman beside him and the phone call waiting for him at the desk. No one knew he was here at the hotel. Even if Tracker had guessed, he would have called him on his cell phone. After he solved that problem, he would have to figure out what he was going to do about the doc.

If he could just predict what she might do or suggest next, he might be able to get a handle on that. Clearly, his first priority was to get her back upstairs to their suite before she got them both arrested.

"Lucas Wainright," he said to the well-groomed young man at the reception desk. "I was told there was a call for me."

"Yes, sir. Just one minute, Mr. Wainright."

While he waited, he glanced over to where Mac was

leafing through one of the brochures stacked on a nearby table. She'd kicked off one of her high-heeled sandals, and he found himself wanting to slip her out of the other one.

Odd, but he'd never been particularly attracted to women who dressed in clothes that screamed casually available sex. He preferred his dates to wear elegant but conservative styles.

The outfit Mac was wearing was even more eye-catching than it had been in the dimness of the lounge. As he watched, the gaze of more than one passerby locked on her. One man stumbled, nearly falling into the man ahead of him. Another lurched into the woman at his side. Yet the doc seemed totally unaware that she was causing traffic mishaps.

Instead, she was totally engrossed in the brochure. Clearly, he was looking at Dr. Lloyd. His eyes narrowed. But there was a Sally lurking inside her. And he was beginning to think he was fascinated by them both.

He planned to have both of them in his bed tonight.

He let his gaze wander down the length of her legs. She'd taken off both sandals now, and she was rubbing the back of one foot against the calf of her leg. Evidently, the doc wasn't in the habit of wearing hooker shoes.

Very soon, he intended to have her out of the rest of her hooker outfit too. The tank top would go first. First one strap, then the other. And then he would slide the fabric down slowly until he could cup her breasts in his hands. Then he would—

"Sir, I have your call ready."

Turning, Lucas picked up the receiver. "Wainright here."

"Are you enjoying your vacation?"

Lucas recognized Vincent Falcone's voice immediately. "Very much. Are you enjoying the wine country?"

Falcone's laugh sounded relaxed in his ear. "You've been keeping tabs on me, I see."

And you've been doing the same with me. Lucas didn't like it one bit, but he didn't say the words aloud. He said nothing at all. A long time ago, he'd learned that silence was often more effective than a direct question in getting the information he wanted. While he waited, he let his gaze sweep the lobby. Did Falcone have a tail on him even now? He noted that Mac was chatting with the bellhop who had shown them to their rooms. In a moment, the young man was going to drool all over his uniform.

"You're much harder to locate than I am," Falcone said. "I heard a rumor that you were off to the Keys. I thought naturally of the Wainright Casa Marina, but I didn't really expect my call to strike pay dirt."

Right. And pigs fly. "It hasn't. Our business relationship is terminated."

"That's why I called. I have something in my possession that will change the picture."

"You'll have to be more specific."

There was a sigh of regret on the other end of the line. "I'm afraid I can't. Phone calls can be tapped. Let's just say that fortune has dealt me a few cards I didn't hold before. One of them might grab your attention."

Lucas wanted to hang up the phone. But he couldn't afford to. He knew the kind of ruthlessness that Falcone was capable of. That was why he'd wanted his sister with him and not in some damn spa. "A meeting then?"

"Ah. I thought you'd never ask. Saturday at my vineyard in Napa."

"Saturday in my offices in D.C."

Falcone's laugh lacked both humor and warmth. "My dear Lucas, this time it's my turn to call the shots. Three o'clock on Saturday at my vineyard. If you're curious, you'll come to me. If not, well, that could be very unfortunate."

Lucas listened to the phone go dead in his ear. *Hell would freeze over first.* There wasn't anything that the man could possibly offer him to renew their business relationship. Vincent Falcone was a crook. Hell, it had taken him four long years to find a way out of doing business with the man that wouldn't violate any of the contracts his father had signed.

He'd bided his time, making sure that any joint ventures Wainright had with Falcone's companies steadily lost money. Then when the man had come to him wanting the capital to invest in Lansing, a biotech company, Lucas had all the ammunition he needed. He'd given the older man Lansing as payment in full to buy him out of Wainright Enterprises.

Lucas reran Falcone's phone call over in his mind. He couldn't afford to underestimate him. A quick glance at his watch told him that it had been twenty-four hours since he'd talked to Tracker. Suddenly, he wanted to be very sure that Sophie was in that spa.

Pushing the numbers into his cell phone, he glanced over at Mac and stared. She'd perched herself on the table that held the brochures and crossed her legs. The skirt had inched about as high up her thighs as it could go. Three bellhops were now gathered around her, totally wrapped up in whatever she was saying, and the registration line had doubled.

Tracker wasn't picking up the call. Lucas disconnected it and punched the numbers in again. He hadn't taken his eyes off Mac.

"He wrote seventy percent of his works here—*A Fare-well to Arms, For Whom the Bell Tolls*," she was saying. "Can you tell me how to get to his house?"

She was talking about Ernest Hemingway. Lucas couldn't prevent a smile.

"Sure thing. I read *The Old Man and the Sea*," said the tallest of the three young men.

"I saw the movie once. I think," said another.

She was dressed like a tart, and she had three kids who were probably still in high school competing to admit they'd read Hemingway.

"My great-grandfather used to box with him on the front lawn."

"You're kidding," Mac said.

"No. There're pictures of him in the museum. You can see them if you go."

Clearly, being a descendant of someone who'd actually come into contact with Hemingway was much more impressive than merely reading his books. He might just have to tell her—Sally or the doc or both—that his own grandfather had fished with the novelist.

Lucas disconnected the second call and punched in the numbers again. The only time that Tracker didn't pick up a call was when he absolutely couldn't talk. Had he managed to get inside the spa? Each call he made would leave a message on Tracker's caller ID, and three calls in a row would let Tracker know that it was an emergency.

As the phone rang in his ear, Lucas saw one of his very able managers approaching. Obviously, the man didn't like that Mac had three of his bellhops enthralled—nor could he be too pleased that she was making a spectacle of herself, having captured the attention of most of the males waiting in the registration line. He'd taken two steps toward Mac, intending to remedy the situation, when Tracker picked up. "What's up?" he said.

"You're inside?" Lucas asked.

"Mr. Wainright?" The voice came at his elbow. "Sir, I hate to interrupt you."

"Hold on, Tracker," Lucas said as he turned to face the young manager. "What is it?"

"Do you think that Mrs. Wainright would be more comfortable in a chair? I'm having one brought down from the upper lobby."

A glance at the curving stairs told him that, indeed, a chair was making its way toward them. Lucas met the young man's eyes. "That's a very thoughtful idea, and I'm sure Mrs. Wainright will appreciate it. Her feet seem to be bothering her." Pausing, he glanced at the man's nametag. "Mr. Waldman, you're doing a nice job here."

Waldman nodded at him. "Thank you, sir."

"*Mrs.* Wainright?" Tracker asked in his ear.

"It's a long story."

"I've got time. My ride into the Serenity Spa won't be leaving for another hour. I'm being delivered with bottled water and organic produce, and I was in the middle of final negotiations with the driver when you called."

"Everything went well, I take it?"

Tracker laughed. "Piece of cake. I take it you're not at Lucas's Folly?"

That's debatable, Lucas thought. "No, I'm at the Wainright Casa Marina." He watched as the man scooped up Mac's high-heeled sandals, but she insisted on carrying the bag with his present in it herself. Waldman escorted her to the chair, and the bellhops were allowed to remain in attendance.

The only people who might be a tad disappointed were the men who were still waiting to register. Mac's skirt covered at least two inches more of her leg once she was seated in the chair, and they had to crane their necks to see her.

Waldman deserved a raise.

"You're at your Key West resort with a *Mrs.* Wainright. I'm assuming that's Mac. I'm also assuming that she's not really Mrs. Wainright because it does take time to get a license and so forth. But there are still a lot of gaps in your story, and I have at least another hour or so."

"I just got a call from Vincent Falcone."

Tracker was silent for a moment. "How did he get hold of your cell-phone number?"

"He didn't. He called me here at the hotel."

"I didn't even know you were there. How did he—"

"Exactly. No one could have known I was here unless—"

"He's having you followed." Tracker swore softly.

"He could have had Sophie followed too."

"I didn't see anyone, and I was looking." There was a pause. "But then I wasn't following Sophie. Maybe he believes she's with you."

Lucas sighed as he studied Mac. The waitress who'd served them in the lounge had just presented her with a drink. It looked like a Shirley Temple. She didn't look anything like the kind of woman who would be ordering a Shirley Temple. "He won't for very long. Right now Mac doesn't look anything like Sophie. She doesn't even look like Mac."

"I'm sensing some more interesting gaps in the story. C'mon, boss. It's raining here and I'm stuck in the back of a delivery truck. I could use a good story."

"Falcone wants to meet the day after tomorrow at his place in Napa at 3:00 p.m. His exact words were 'Fortune has dealt me a few cards I didn't hold before. One of them might grab your attention.'"

"Cards as in plural."

"Yeah." One of the things that Lucas admired most about his friend was the way Tracker's razor-sharp mind always cut right to the quick.

"If—*when* I find Sophie, you want me to get her out of here?"

Lucas thought for a moment. "No. And I don't want you to cause any disturbance. I just want you to make sure no one can get to her there."

"Right. I'll be able to verify she's here by morning even if I have to search each one of those damn cabins. I'll also have a look at their security system."

"Have fun."

Tracker laughed. "You too, boss."

The moment that Lucas disconnected the call, he strode purposefully toward Mac. It was time to salvage his reputation and the reputation of his hotel by escorting "Sally" to his suite. The moment he reached her chair, she jumped up, his present still clutched tightly in her hand.

"Shall we go, Sally?" he asked.

Rising up on tiptoe, she said in a low voice, "I'm not Sally anymore."

"I was beginning to like that fantasy," Lucas said, taking her arm and guiding her toward the bank of elevators. "I especially liked the way it was bound to end."

Mac dug in her heels near the fountain. "My turn isn't over yet."

"I think it is."

She shook her head. "We haven't made love yet, and

that was the deal. And I've got an even better fantasy in mind."

He studied her. Did he want to know? "What is it?"

She tapped one hand against the bag that contained his present. "It's right in here. You're going to love it."

CHAPTER EIGHT

"You're not really going to make me wait until Saturday afternoon to see you again."

Sophie turned in the front seat of the convertible to smile at the man behind the wheel. Sonny Falcone had been surprised and delighted when Susan Walker had called to invite him to lunch. "I'm booked solid with clients until Saturday morning."

Susan Walker had a business trip that would coincide with a party his family was throwing at their vineyard. That was the story she'd given Sonny in D.C. When he'd invited her to attend the party, she'd agreed. But at some point during the time they'd spent together that afternoon, she'd decided she didn't want her time in Napa dominated by Sonny.

He'd taken her to a lovely place in the hills where they'd sipped wine on a veranda that offered an even more enchanting view than the one she had from her hotel room. Then they'd had a late lunch at a small inn. He'd been charming, but less than totally attentive to all the lies she was telling him about herself and her business.

He was a very handsome man with the kind of body that had fascinated Italian sculptors for centuries. Perhaps that was why he was so totally self-absorbed.

"It was my good fortune that your plane got in early," Sonny murmured.

"Mine too." He'd mentioned that four times now. It wasn't really his fault that he was...dull.

Taking her hand, he raised it to his lips.

Sophie waited, hopeful.

Nothing happened. His practiced, romantic gesture only confirmed what she'd been gradually discovering all afternoon. However smooth the moves, when this man touched her, she didn't respond at all.

"I had a really lovely time," Sonny said. Very gently, he leaned forward and pressed his lips to hers. The kiss was very soft, very warm—an expert caress of tongue and lips.

And it left her unmoved.

When she drew back, she kept a smile on her face. His eyes told her that he at least had enjoyed the kiss.

"Are you going to invite me in for a drink?"

"I can't," she said, taking care to inject regret into her tone. "Just as soon as I freshen up, I have to race to meet a client. After that I have to prepare for my presentation tomorrow. But I am so looking forward to relaxing on Saturday. The bulk of my business will be over by then."

He reached out and ran a gentle hand down her hair. "We'll relax together. The vineyard will be crowded, but I have a special treat for you. I remember what you said about wanting to go up in a hot-air balloon, and I have one reserved for us."

"I'll be looking forward to it." Sophie let herself out of the car. At the archway that led into the courtyard of the hotel, she turned and waved. But it wasn't until the doors of the lobby swung shut behind her that she let out a sigh of relief.

Or was it regret? No, she wasn't going to let herself think that way. Dwelling on the fact that she'd switched identities with Mac just so that she could anonymously date a man she wasn't attracted to was not going to be productive.

Squaring her shoulders, she strode across the lobby. Sonny wasn't the only man in the Napa Valley. She would just have to find someone else to date anonymously while she was here. Turning on her heel, she walked back to the small desk where the concierge stood, talking into a phone. The moment he hung up, she beamed a smile at him. "My business dinner has just been canceled. Can you recommend a place nearby where a single girl could have some fun?"

"Sure thing." The concierge placed a list in front of her, then began to run down it, adding to the information that was on the paper. By the time he finished, she had two possibilities in mind.

"Dr. Lloyd…"

The man had to call the name again before Sophie remembered to turn around. He was tall, blond, casually dressed and wearing the kind of sunglasses that reflected back a mirror image. He held a basket of flowers in his hand. "I came in just as you were talking to the concierge. When I heard your name, I thought I might deliver these personally and save one of the bellhops a trip. You are Dr. Lloyd?"

"Yes," Sophie said, digging in her purse for a tip. She handed it to him in exchange for the basket. "Thanks."

"No problem. Enjoy the flowers."

Sophie couldn't help but enjoy the scent. She had to hand it to Sonny Falcone. He had all the moves down pat. Maybe her lack of reaction to him was due to jet lag, and she'd feel differently on Saturday. It wasn't until she got to the top of the stairs that it struck her.

Sonny didn't know her as MacKenzie Lloyd. He couldn't

have sent the flowers. Sitting down on the top step, she fished through the blossoms for a card.

There wasn't one.

WHAT IN THE WORLD was she going to come up with next? Lucas glanced down at the present in the hotel gift-shop bag Mac had been carrying around. To call the thin layer of latex he was wearing a bathing suit was a misnomer—unless you were an Olympic swimmer going for the minimum in aerodynamic resistance.

Turning his head and craning his neck, he attempted to get a view of the back. The suit revealed as much there as it did in the front.

"Are you ready?"

At the sound of Mac's voice, Lucas poked his head out of the cabana. "This suit doesn't cover much…" Neither did hers. In fact, it left enough bare to have his breath clogging his lungs. The tank top fit tighter than a second skin, and it stopped well above her navel. His gaze drifted over her soft, silky-looking skin to the bottom of the suit—a thin triangle of cloth that barely covered her—

"You're embarrassed again," she said, the amusement clear in her eyes.

"And you're definitely not." Stepping out of the cabana, Lucas took a quick look around the pool area to see how many other men were feasting their eyes on her. The heat had driven most of the hotel guests inside where they were either drinking in the lounge or resting up so they could sample some of the nightlife that Key West had to offer. He and Mac were alone except for the young man behind the towel booth about fifty yards away.

When they'd arrived, he'd introduced himself as Yancey and waved them toward the cabana, all the while assuring them that he'd guard Mac's duffel bag with his life should they care to swim off to a more private part of the lagoon.

"Very nice suit," Mac said.

When Lucas glanced toward the towel booth, he saw that Yancey was giving him a three-fingered wave.

"I think Yancey likes you," Mac said. "In a totally sex-object sort of way."

Lucas looked at her. "That seems to be the story of my life lately."

"Are you ready to get started?"

For one moment, he was tempted to grab her wrist and drag her into the cabana. The fantasy filled his mind of how quickly he could have her out of that suit. God, he wanted to touch her—to run his hands over that skin at her waist, pale as moonlight, soft as rainwater. He wanted to taste it. The need ripped at him like a rusty claw as he whispered, "Come here, Doc."

She took a step forward, then stopped. "You want to make love to me in the cabana."

"You think?"

"That's amazing. At least fifty-five percent of the men interviewed fantasize about making love in a place where they might get caught. I thought the number was a little high. Is that one of your favorite fantasies too?"

Lucas never before would have lumped himself in with that fifty-five percent. He couldn't ever recall wanting to take the kind of risk that she was talking about. That he was thinking about. But he'd come very close to doing something in that lounge that might have gotten him arrested. Truth told, he was skating on pretty thin ice again.

It was high time he took another tack. Walking toward her, he stopped when their bodies were almost brushing. Then he pitched his voice low so that only she could hear him. "I don't want to get caught. I want to make love to you where no one and nothing can interrupt us. I want to take my time and touch every single part of you. Then I want to taste you. The cabana is way too dark. I want to see your eyes when I'm inside you. And I want to stay inside you for a long, long time."

Mac released the breath she was holding on a shudder. "You're trying to distract me."

"I'm trying to seduce you." Unable to resist for a moment longer, he touched her, just the tips of her hair. She'd taken the blond wig off. He much preferred the richness of her own color—a mix of gold and fire.

Her breath shuddered out again.

He pressed his advantage, taking a step closer and bringing his body into contact with hers. Only the thinnest scraps of latex separated his flesh from hers. He felt the soft give of her breasts against his chest. She had to feel his hardness pressing against her.

For a moment, neither of them moved.

Then she said, "It's still my turn."

"Come back to the room with me, Doc."

"I'm not Doc. I'm Fiona—at least, that's the closest approximation in English."

When she responded, her voice was barely a whisper, the sound erotic on the still air.

She eyed him provocatively. "Aren't you even a little bit curious about the fantasy I have in mind?"

Twin desires warred within him. A part of him wanted to haul her over his shoulder and cart her off to the room. Another part of him wanted to indulge her. Hell, a part of him was becoming very curious about what she'd come up with next.

"It won't take long," she murmured.

Unable to resist a moment longer, he lowered his head

and nibbled along her jawline. Perhaps the room was too far away. But the cabana wasn't. "Come—"

"And we won't be in full view of the people in the lounge the way we would be in the cabana."

Lucas lifted his head and glanced over her shoulder. Hell, he'd forgotten that the lounge offered a panoramic view of this part of the lagoon. If he *had* dragged her into that cabana, they would have provided quite a sideshow for the hotel guests who were probably watching them even now.

"You're a damn good negotiator, Doc. If you ever get tired of working in that lab, I could use a mind like yours at Wainright Enterprises."

"You could?"

The quick leap of surprise and joy in her eyes sent a wave of feelings tumbling through him. It occurred to him that he would do a lot to see it there again. Often. "Absolutely."

"You really are—"

He put his fingers against her lips. "If you say *kind* or *sweet* again, you're going in the lagoon."

"Kind and sweet."

Before he could shove her, she twisted and dived into the water. He had one clear view of smooth, white cheeks before they disappeared below the surface of the water. It wasn't a bikini bottom she was wearing—but a thong.

While they'd been negotiating, everyone in the lounge had been treated to the view.

She was driving him crazy, and he was going to put a stop to it. He followed her into the water.

MAC BROKE the surface for air at the same time that Lucas did. The water was cold, and she'd needed the shock of it. She couldn't have held her own much longer—not with his body, his mouth touching hers. Especially when she could see that wild, reckless gleam in his eye. For just a moment—one glorious moment—she'd seen that he wanted to carry her off. And she would have gone.

The thought alone had the heat moving through her again. She hadn't known she had the power to make a man look at her that way. Treading water, she twisted to face Lucas.

The wild, reckless look had disappeared.

"That bathing suit is indecent," he said. "Do you realize that everyone sitting in that lounge must have had their eyes glued to your...your..."

"Do you think so? I never thought I'd ever have the courage to wear it. And I was right. I didn't."

"You did wear it. You've got the damn thing on."

Mac shook her head. "No, Sally was the one who put it on, under those outrageous clothes. Just as soon as I decided to be her, I suddenly had the courage to put it on. I didn't even have to go out on that balcony again."

His gaze narrowed and he stared at her for a long moment. "Who the hell are you?"

His question was a cue if she'd ever heard one—and her chance to bring that look back into his eyes. Moving closer, she said, "I told you. I'm Fiona now, a mermaid, and I've just lured you into the water."

"You're a...mermaid?"

He didn't sound at all convinced. Or even interested. Beneath the surface, her legs tangled briefly with his. "In the survey, over forty percent of the men said they had erotic dreams about mermaids. I find that very curious, don't you?"

Underwater, he trapped one of her legs with his. "Not particularly."

"Well, I've given it some thought—from a scientific viewpoint."

"Ah, and you'd like to share your conclusions."

In a swift movement, he trapped her other leg.

A strange wave of helplessness moved through her.

"Mermaids are exotic, different, and the stories of them date back to primeval times. Part of their allure could stem from that." The feeling of helplessness was growing, she discovered. They were touching nowhere else—just where his legs trapped hers in a vise. But she was very much aware that his legs were stronger. Her heartbeat was accelerating, and it was getting more difficult to breathe. "Then there's the fact that man came out of the water and will always be lured back to his origins."

"Sounds like a lot of scientific mumbo jumbo to me, Doc. I think my reality's a lot better than your fantasy." Quite suddenly, her legs were free, but he had her hand and was pulling her toward the edge of the lagoon.

"Wait." What had she been thinking? She'd been spouting off her research, and he was seeing her as Mac. That was the problem. "That's not the real reason I think that men have erotic dreams about mermaids."

"I told you, Doc. I've never thought of making love to a mermaid."

She moved closer so that their bodies were just brushing beneath the water. "Think about it now. Just how would you do it?"

His gaze narrowed. "What do you mean?"

"How would you make love to a mermaid? Maybe you couldn't—I mean, in the normal way. Certain important parts of her body are…another species." Lifting her hand, she drew it across his shoulder, over his throat, and slowly down his chest to his waist. She let her fingers rest just where skin gave way to the thin material of his bathing suit. "Right about here is where she changes. However, there are certain very specific ways in which she could pleasure you."

"Yes."

"Why don't you let me show you?"

For a moment, he said nothing, but she felt his grip tighten on her hand and saw the carefully guarded expression in his eyes change. This wasn't the recklessness she'd seen before, but something else—a raw hunger that she felt her whole body respond to. In that moment, she realized it could go either way. If he pulled her with him out of the water, she wouldn't resist. She would go back with him to the suite.

Finally, he let out the breath he'd been holding. "Not here."

She ran her fingers lightly along the waistband of his suit before she drew her hand away. "I have a more private place in mind. C'mon."

She pushed away from the edge, slicing the water with smooth, clean strokes. The waterfall she'd spotted from their balcony was on the other side of the hotel from where they were. The length of the swim would give her time to plan.

There wasn't a doubt in her mind that once they reached the cave, Lucas would make good on the promise she'd seen in his eyes and felt in his body's response to her. She'd been playing with fire for about as long as he was going to allow it. And if the truth be told, she wanted to be burned.

So what was causing the tight ball of fear to form in her stomach? Hadn't she proven to herself that if she could focus on the fantasy, she could do all the things she'd discovered in her research?

In the bar when she'd been pretending to be Sally, she

hadn't even had to plan anything out step by step. Everything she'd done to him had felt so natural because…she was Sally?

Or was it because he was Lucas?

She knew exactly when he drew beside her, even before she felt the brush of his hand along her shoulder and down her back. His touch was familiar, exciting, and with each lift of her right arm as she swam, she could see him. The lean muscled arms, the broad shoulders, the narrow waist and the…

She hadn't had a chance to appreciate before how he filled out that tiny bathing suit. Every time her face went into the water, her eyes homed in on the same target. Not that she hadn't vividly pictured him in her mind when she'd chosen the suit in the gift shop. But the reality of Lucas, nearly naked and well within reach, had the fear in her stomach turning into something else.

She really wanted him. As a biologist, she could dismiss what she felt as lust. But as a woman, she was very much afraid that it was personal.

As successful as she'd been in becoming Sally the hooker, Lucas had always been Lucas. There was that kindness, that sweetness that embarrassed him. More than that, there was the feeling she got when he looked at her— that he saw her as no one else ever had. He already knew her secrets, and they didn't frighten him away.

But it was dangerous to dwell on that, dangerous to want…

No, it was much safer to concentrate on the fantasy she was about to create and slip into the persona of Fiona.

Dragging her gaze away from Lucas, she checked her surroundings, then increased the speed of her stroke. The moment she rounded the curve, she spotted the churning in the water that told her the waterfall and the little rock cave were just ahead.

She summoned the image of a ladder into her mind. All she had to do was take it one step at a time. The first step was to create the mermaid fantasy. Concentrating, she focused on the water beyond Lucas. Though the lagoon was man-made, every effort had been made to create a facsimile of the real thing. Concrete in the shape of rocks lined the walls, and in the shade created by the palm trees on either side, the water was a deep, exotic blue-green. Shafts of sunlight lightened the color at intervals.

Slowly, inevitably, her gaze fastened on Lucas again. It was almost too easy to imagine that this was a man she'd rescued from the sea. She watched the steady ebb and flow of muscle beneath his copper-colored skin. He was so different from anyone she'd known before—so fascinating.

How often had she swum to the surface to watch him? Then the watching had turned to wanting. How she'd longed to touch him, to run her hands over that sleek, smooth skin. And now that she'd finally lured him to their destination she could reach out and…

Desire struck her then, so sharp and so piercing, she nearly doubled up from the ache. Oh, it was altogether too easy to fantasize that she was a mermaid, and Lucas was the human being she was prepared to give up everything for.

Touching him once on the shoulder, she angled to her left and swam ahead of him through the tumble of water and into the small cave.

FOR A FEW SECONDS after he'd made it through the waterfall, Lucas thought he'd entered another world. The inside of the cave was small, the light dimmed and filtered by the curtain of water falling from the rocks overhead.

Mac was sitting on one of the ledges that lined the walls, the lower half of her body submerged, her hair and face drenched with water. She looked like a creature of the sea—some primeval goddess that men would have followed anywhere.

And she was beautiful. Why hadn't he noticed that before? The ache that had built the whole time he'd been swimming beside her twisted low in his body and began to spread. For a moment he couldn't move, couldn't breathe. He could only want, and the torture was exquisite.

He watched, still mesmerized as she lifted one hand out of the water and beckoned.

"I want you."

He wasn't sure who'd spoken the words. But he knew they were real—the one real thing. She wasn't a mermaid. He wasn't some hapless sailor lured off course by her song. Fantasies were never real.

It was time he put an end to the game.

Even as he moved toward her, he glanced quickly over his shoulder. The thick curtain of water provided some privacy, and the cave faced the ocean, not the hotel. Still, all that separated them from anyone who happened by was water. When he turned back, they were facing each other eye to eye. Her lips were parted and wet. Real. It took all his control to touch only her hand. "Come with me," he said.

"Stay with me."

He brushed his lips over hers.

"We don't have to be who we really are as long as we're here. We have no past. No future," she said.

He traced her bottom lip with his tongue, then tasted each corner of her mouth in turn. And all the while her words burned through him, eating at his control like the hot, hungry flames of a bonfire.

"No regrets. No repercussions."

In some small part of his mind that hadn't completely shut down, he knew that her words were the worst kind of fantasy. Every action produced an effect as surely as a pebble made ripples when tossed in a pool. There would be a price to pay. There always was.

Unable to resist any longer, he crushed her lips with his. If he could just stop the words…but he couldn't seem to prevent her from making those small hungry sounds deep in her throat. They shot through him like electric shocks.

He grabbed her hands, bracketing them in one of his behind her back. Then with a quick groan of pleasure, he slipped his hand beneath the tank top, ran it up that smooth skin and cupped her breast. Helplessly, she arched toward him and moaned. It seemed he'd waited forever to touch her like this again.

He'd known hunger before, but it had never been this deep, this desperate. Suddenly impatient, he stripped her out of the tank top, and then arching her back over his arm, he lowered his mouth and feasted. The skin at her waist was taut, smooth and cool. He'd wanted to taste her there since he'd stepped out of the cabana. He lingered, using his teeth and his tongue until she was shuddering. Then he moved on, sampling her navel, then that slender, strong torso, until he reached her breasts. They were as soft as satin, as sweet as the most forbidden fruit. He wanted to go slowly, to torture her as she'd tortured him. But as he moved his lips and his tongue first over one silky curve and then the other, the soft, urgent sounds she made vibrated against his mouth and pounded into his brain.

Twin desires warred within him. He had to have her. Soon.

He had to draw out the pleasure for them both, for as long as he could.

Taking one cool, puckered nipple into his mouth, he moved his tongue over it, then closed his teeth around it. She arched back, her hair dipping into the water, and offered him more.

He slid the palm of his hand down the slick skin of her torso and dragged the bottom of her suit down her legs. Then he pressed his hand against her soft, hot center. When his finger penetrated her, she cried out, and he covered her mouth with his. Pushing in deeper, he felt tight, slick satin pulse and pull, begging, demanding.

Need slammed into him, not an ache this time but a chain saw with a rusted blade, shredding his restraint. Control streamed away as quickly and surely as the water crashing down overhead. He couldn't think. He had to be inside her, completely naked. He had to feel hot slickness pulling him in farther and farther.

"I...want...you." The hoarse sound of her voice had the need slicing deeper. "Now."

"You've got me." Slowly, he withdrew his finger. Then releasing her hands, he gripped her waist and settled her back on the submerged rock ledge. He ran his hands up the inner side of her thighs, pushing them apart.

Her fingers were already dragging his swimsuit down. The moment he was free, he grabbed her wrists. If she touched him now...

Drawing in a deep breath, he fought against the climax he knew was close.

Then, when he was sure he could, he took her hands and placed them on his shoulders. "Wrap your legs around me." He helped her, drawing her closer until his erection was pressed just inside her core. The searing heat of it—the promise of even more heat to come—nearly undid him. In spite of the coolness of the water swirling around them, he felt sweat pearl his forehead and slide down his spine. He'd never been this close to the edge before without letting go. His entire body was clenched tight, but the desire to take her warred with a greater need.

"Open your eyes." His words were only a whisper, but her lids opened.

"Say your name," he said.

She tightened her grip on his shoulders and met his eyes. "Fiona." Then she tightened her legs around him and began to draw him in.

It took all his control to resist. "No. Your real name."

"Mac."

"And mine."

"Lucas."

He thrust into her then, hot and deep and hard. For a moment he was sure his heart stopped. He thought he'd known what it would be like, but she was tighter, hotter, much better then he'd imagined. He knew he should wait, give her time to adjust, but he couldn't stop himself from withdrawing and thrusting again. And again. And again.

He watched her eyes grow darker even as the sheath she'd wrapped him in pulsed around him.

He wanted more than anything to stop—to draw out the moment—to prolong the feeling of oneness he'd never experienced before now. But he felt her convulsions start, felt them radiate through her, and he was lost. He had to thrust even more deeply into her until his own release began to rip through him. The pleasure built in wave after wave after wave—pulling him higher and higher—until it finally thrust him free. Holding her tight, he took her with him into a breathless, airless void.

CHAPTER NINE

WHEN SHE COULD BREATHE again, think again, Mac found herself sitting on Lucas's lap on the rock ledge that surrounded the little cave. His arms were around her and her head was cradled against his chest. Against her ear, she could hear the sure beat of his heart. Contentment spread through her, and she didn't want to move, to think.

That was not good. If she were in the lab, she would be feeling that sudden rush of elation that always came when an experiment went well. She would be running the whole thing through in her mind, evaluating what had worked, what needed to be improved.

But she didn't want to analyze. All she wanted to do was to hang on to the moment—to spin it out and to pretend just for now that Lucas had really wanted her, not Fiona.

That was not only wrong, it was dangerous. An impossible fantasy. Even as fear knotted in her stomach, she pushed it away. She couldn't afford to repeat the mistake she'd made all her life of wanting what she could never have. She had to settle for what was real—her research.

"Penny for your thoughts."

She jumped when the rumbling sound of his voice startled her.

"That bad, huh?"

She lifted her head and met his eyes. They were intent, guarded.

She struggled to reach the same level of control. "That went very well, I thought. But I'd like to try it again."

His eyes narrowed. "Something was wrong? Did I hurt you?"

"No, not at all. Except…" Slowly, she smiled—the way she imagined Fiona might. "I'd like to try it again, and this time you have to leave my hands free."

His hands tightened on her. And something flashed into his eyes—the wild recklessness she'd seen before. It ignited an answering response within her—a fierce, almost overwhelming need.

"That can be arranged. But not here. We've been lucky so far…"

The rest of his sentence trailed off when a head suddenly appeared beneath the curtain of the waterfall. In one quick, smooth movement, Lucas eased them both off the rock ledge so that the water came up to his chest and her neck. Mac was suddenly aware of two things. Lucas was easing himself back into his swimsuit. And she had no idea where hers was!

"Oh. Hi," said a plump woman in her mid-fifties. "We didn't mean to interrupt. Harold here just thought it would be fun to—"

While Harold surfaced and made a show of shaking out the water from the few strands of hair left on his head, Lucas moved in front of Mac, shielding her with his body. Running her hand along the rock ledge, Mac prayed that her suit was there.

"See, Nelly, these folks had the same idea I had, I bet."

"Nonsense." Winking at them, Nelly gave Harold a playful push. "Harold's a dirty old man."

"That's the best kind, isn't it?" Mac asked as her fingers closed around her tank top. As unobtrusively as she could, she drew it in front of her beneath the water.

Harold's guffaw filled the cave. "That's what I keep telling her, young lady. That's what I keep telling her."

"C'mon, Harold. We've interrupted this young couple."

Reaching behind him, Lucas gripped Mac's arm. "Not at all. We were just about to leave, weren't we, dear?"

Before she could reply, he was edging her toward the waterfall, shielding her as much as he could. As they moved past Harold, Lucas leaned toward him.

"My wife here thought that this might be just the kind of place a mermaid would lure some hapless sea captain, if you know what I mean."

"I think I catch your drift, son," Harold said and winked.

Without waiting to hear another word, Mac clutched the top of her bathing suit close and dived under the waterfall. When she surfaced she found Lucas at her side.

"What did you do that for?" she asked. "You practically told them what we were doing."

"I thought it might add to your research. Obviously, Harold fits into the forty to fifty percent of men who like the mermaid fantasy."

"Let's hope Nelly likes it too," Mac said.

Lucas threw back his head and laughed. The warm, rich sound of it was so infectious that she had to join him. Before they were finished, they were clinging to each other trying not to submerge.

"It's not funny," Mac said, trying to stave off another wave of laughter. "I only have half my bathing suit. I lost the thong."

"A real mermaid wouldn't need one," Lucas pointed out.

"A real mermaid wouldn't have to walk into the Wainright Casa Marina Hotel."

"Let this be a lesson to you, Doc. Fantasies can be dangerous."

And they could, Mac thought. But they were also fun. And she was enjoying this playful side of Lucas almost as much as she'd enjoyed the fiercely possessive lover that she'd encountered in the rock cave. Lifting her chin, she said, "I'm going to put the top half of my suit on, and while I'm doing that you can figure out how we're going to get to the room without getting thrown in jail."

But getting into the bathing suit wasn't as easy as it looked. The tank top wasn't in the mood to cooperate. The material didn't stretch as easily when it was wet. And to make matters worse, they kept laughing and sinking under the water. And it didn't help at all that Lucas's hands were on her more than they were on the suit. Each time they touched her, she couldn't seem to remember about the suit at all. By the time they got her arms through the holes and tugged the top down over her breasts, they'd both sunk to the bottom of the lagoon.

She would have pushed up to the surface, but his hands gripped her waist, anchoring her. In the wavering shafts of light piercing the turquoise water, he looked different, more like an undersea god than a mere mortal. Suddenly, she wanted him just as fiercely as she had in the rock cave. She only had time for that one thought before he pushed them both to the surface and shoved her against the side of the lagoon.

One of his hands gripped the back of her neck, his body pressed fully against hers. Then his mouth closed over hers.

Sensations streamed through her and around her, trapping her in a world of razor-edged contrasts. The chill of the water; the heat shooting through her in bright lightning bursts wherever his body touched hers. The hard pressure

of his hands at her waist and her neck; the incredible softness of his lips and the gentle insistence of his tongue as
it patiently explored her mouth—as if he had all the time
in the world to savor each flavor. Pleasure shot through
her in wave after wave. Seductive. Overpowering.

She was drowning. It was only as they once more broke
the surface of the water that she realized they'd sunk below
it again. Coughing and dragging in air, she stared at him.
His breathing was just as ragged as hers.

"I want you."

LUCAS WASN'T SURE who'd spoken the words aloud or if
they were merely a chant in his brain. All he knew was that
he'd never felt this way before. *Desire* seemed too tame
a word for it. What had gripped him at the bottom of the
lagoon had been so intense, so overpowering that he wasn't
sure how he'd managed to get them above the water.

He'd been laughing one minute, struggling with her suit,
then the need had snuck up on him and slammed into him
with a force that had driven everything else away.

She'd looked like a sea goddess, her hair a red-gold
crown. All he knew was that he had to have her. And
he'd very nearly taken her right there on the bottom of
the lagoon.

But it wasn't a mermaid who was facing him now, with
a mixture of desire and anticipation in her eyes. They were
no longer in danger of drowning. And the wanting had
only increased.

"I want you." This time he'd definitely said it aloud,
and the raspy sound of the words only seemed to inten-
sify the need pounding in his head and burning through
his blood. Using his body, he pushed her back against
the side of the lagoon, then slid a hand behind her and
gripped one of the rocks.

He tried to focus on looking around, checking to make sure they were alone. But any clear thoughts of decency and privacy were erased by the image of what he saw in her eyes, the perfect mirror of the desire that was coursing through his veins.

"Your hands are free this time," he said. "Use them."

As she grasped his shoulders, he wrapped her legs around him and, gripping the rock ledge behind her, he pushed into her slowly. The heat ate at his control.

"Tell me you want me." Slowly he withdrew nearly all the way. "Or do you want me to stop?"

"No," she whispered.

"No, you don't want me or no you don't want me to stop?"

"No...yes...please..."

He pushed into her again. Not fast enough, not far enough. "Hold on."

But she was already tightening her legs around him. Holding the rock ledge with both hands for all he was worth, he pushed as far as he could into her sleek, satiny heat.

She made a sound as she moved against him and drew him in even farther.

"Shh," he whispered against her lips. "You can't make any noise. Someone could come along at any moment. We can't let them know what we're doing."

He withdrew slowly, then entered her again, spinning the piercing pleasure into torture. "The water is working against us. It's going to take a long, long time."

"Lucas, please..."

"Shh," he managed to murmur. But the sound of his name had already shredded what was left of his control. Suddenly, he wasn't thinking. Couldn't think. All he knew was the dark, slippery grip of her as he withdrew as far as he could and pushed into her again. He wanted to go faster, had to go faster—but he'd spoken the truth. The depth of the water and their position against the side of the lagoon worked against him. Each time he withdrew, he felt as if he was leaving some vital part of himself behind. Then she stiffened, using all her strength to arch against him, and he felt himself shatter. Helpless, he pushed in as far as he could and poured himself into her.

For a long time, neither of them moved. Lucas wasn't sure he could. He knew he didn't want to. Palm leaves rustled overhead. The water around them gradually stilled. Then he heard the steady *slap, slap* of approaching sandals.

Tightening his grip on her waist, he drew back and eased himself out of her, then quickly adjusted his bathing suit and glanced around. Much to his relief, the area was deserted. Whoever was approaching was still hidden by the rock cave to his left.

Turning his attention back to Mac, he said, "Are you all right?"

Her eyes when they met his were focused and filled with delight. "Much better than all right." Then she leaned closer to plant a quick kiss on his lips. "It was even better than in the cave. And I like it when my hands are free. Next time I'll have to remember to use them."

He wasn't sure which surprised and delighted him more—her reply or the kiss. It had been so spontaneous, it had to have come from Mac, not her mermaid persona.

"Mr. Wainright! Mr. Wainright, sir..."

Glancing up, he saw Yancey, the young pool man, hurrying toward them and waving Mac's duffel bag. Lucas could cheerfully have murdered him. He released Mac, but used his arms to keep her caged against the side of the lagoon.

"Your cell phone has been ringing and ringing. I finally figured I should answer. Good thing too. A Mr. Tracker is trying to reach you. He ordered me to bring you the phone, so he can call back." Dropping the duffel at the edge of the lagoon, Yancey squatted to hand Lucas the phone. "Was your Mr. Tracker by any chance in the military? There's such a note of command in his voice," he asked, eyes bright with interest.

The cell phone rang.

"And he's so prompt too."

"Yes?" Lucas said into the phone.

"Are you okay?" Tracker asked.

"Of course."

"It's the first time someone else has ever answered your cell phone."

The amazement and concern in Tracker's voice had him frowning. For the first time since he'd followed Mac into the lagoon, reality was setting in. The truth was, he'd left the damn phone in the cabana along with his wallet and clothes. He hadn't given them a thought once he'd seen Mac in that swimsuit. And he hadn't been thinking of anything but her a moment ago when he'd taken her against the side of the lagoon.

He might have taken her there again if Yancey hadn't interrupted them. What was she doing to him?

"I'm inside," Tracker said.

"Inside?"

"The Serenity Spa. Look, am I interrupting something? If you and the doc—"

Lucas dragged his attention back to the phone call. "The doc and I are swimming. That's all. You can report."

"It's going to take me a while to verify that Sophie's here. I don't want to sneak into her cabin until she's asleep."

"You know which one it is?"

"Not yet. As soon as the coast is clear, I figure I'll be able to find her cabin number in the main office. Then I'll wait until everyone is asleep. I also have an updated report on the Falcones."

As he listened to Tracker give him a rundown on the two men's movements for the past twenty-four hours, Lucas found his attention refocusing on Mac as she retrieved her wallet from the duffel and gave Yancey a bill.

"I brought a couple of towels for you," Yancey was saying, "just in case you want to go into the hotel by the ocean-side entrance."

"You're a lifesaver. I'm going to tell the management to give you a raise," Mac said.

For someone who said she'd never gone on vacation with her family or stayed in a big resort before, she certainly had a knack for winding his staff right around her finger. First Waldman and the three bellhops in the main lobby and now the pool man. And, of course, the owner of the hotel. She had *him* forgetting his money, his cell phone and even the clothes off his back!

Pocketing the bill, Yancey gave them another three-fingered wave before he turned and strode away.

"You still there, boss?"

Dragging his attention back to Tracker, Lucas said, "Let me know the minute you verify..." He paused to watch Mac pull one of the towels into the water and fasten it around her waist. He thought of how easy it would be to pull it off of her once they got to the room. And there was that Jacuzzi. It would provide a much more private environment for a mermaid fantasy. They wouldn't be interrupted.

"The good doctor is very distracting, I take it," Tracker said.

"No. Yes." He had to get a grip. And the best way he knew how to do that was to put a stop to the fantasies she seemed bound and determined to ensnare him in. "Call me as soon as you can confirm anything."

CHAPTER TEN

THE SUN HAD MOVED nearly an hour closer to the horizon by the time Lucas let himself out onto the balcony of his suite. He'd urged Mac to use the larger of the two bathrooms, then taken his own shower in the smaller one. It had been a test—to see if he could stay away from her.

He wasn't sure he could pass it.

And that worried him.

The time he'd spent with Mac in the lagoon should have sated him. Making love to her in the cave had been risky enough, but what had happened afterward in the lagoon... He couldn't prevent his gaze from drifting down to the blue ribbon of water that snaked its way around the hotel. Even now he couldn't believe what they'd done, what might have happened if Yancey had come upon them a few minutes earlier. Never had he been that desperate, that reckless, not even when he was a teenager.

No other woman had ever driven him to do something that...crazy. For the life of him, he couldn't think of another word to describe it.

And there'd certainly been other women. He'd been quite young—only midway through his teens—when he'd discovered women were attracted to him. The realization that this had a lot to do with the Wainright name and wealth came later. By that time, his father had gone through three of his five marriages.

Lucas had no intention of ever following in his father's

footsteps. He'd always made sure that he was in control of any relationship he had with a woman.

Until MacKenzie Lloyd. And it wasn't just his control that she was sapping. Each time he made love with her, he was losing parts of himself. Maybe forever.

A ripple of fear moved through him. Then, dragging his gaze away from the lagoon, he paced down the length of the balcony. No woman had ever frightened him before either.

How could she have that kind of power over him? She might believe that he was buying into the fantasies, but he knew better. It was always MacKenzie Lloyd he was making love to, whoever she was.

A kaleidoscope of images poured into his mind. The shy, young girl he'd met at Sophie's party was only one facet of MacKenzie Lloyd. There'd been nothing of that woman in the way she'd looked on the tarmac when he'd demanded to know where Sophie was. That MacKenzie Lloyd had met his eyes with her chin lifted, determined to shield Jill Roberts from his anger. And she'd been yet another woman on his boat. He could still recall the excitement in her eyes and the recklessness of her laughter as the wind snatched it away.

And there was the doc, so intent and focused, aiming one of her killer serves across the net, or giving him that slow appraising look as if she were going to smear him on a slide and figure him out no matter how long it took.

Stopping suddenly, he stared back down at the lagoon. Then there were the fantasy women she'd created for him—the shy Lania, the exuberant and fun-loving Sally, and the brave and determined Fiona. They were all facets of MacKenzie Lloyd.

How many more women did she have inside her? He wanted to know—and he wanted to learn how to handle each one of them. To do that, he needed to get to know them better.

Turning, he looked back at the sliding glass doors he'd just stepped through. Not here. He knew exactly what would happen if they stayed in the suite. Incredibly, he felt fresh desire ripple through him. All he had to do was open the doors and go to her.

She was probably stepping out of the shower, pulling a towel around her and tucking the ends in at her breasts. He could slip his hands beneath the towel. There'd be no chance for her to think. He would make sure of that. Then he could lift her onto the vanity and gently separate her legs to make a place for himself between them. There would be no time for her to slip into one of those fantasies. No time for her to pretend that they were anyone else but who they really were—not with their images reflected on two walls.

And there wouldn't be the pressure to rush. No one would interrupt them. This time he would take her very slowly, drawing out the pleasure for them both. His hand had closed around the door handle before he stopped himself.

Turning, he paced down the length of the balcony again. He'd come out here to distance himself, and the desire he felt now was just as fierce as it had been in that damn rock cave. He was caught up in it as surely as if he were caught in one of the dangerous riptides that lurked beneath the surface of those seemingly gentle waves pushing onto the shore.

It was just as he focused his gaze on the sea that the idea came to him. Of course. He would take the doc out on a date. That would be very familiar territory for him. Thoughtfully, he considered his options. It would have to be someplace she'd like, someplace that would keep that very agile mind of hers occupied so that she wouldn't come up with a new fantasy.

Keeping his eyes on the water, Lucas began to sift through the possibilities.

USING A TOWEL to wipe steam off the bathroom mirror, Mac finally faced her reflection. As far as she could see, she looked exactly like the old MacKenzie Lloyd. But she certainly didn't feel like her. She felt wonderful, wild and frightened, all at the same time. Pressing a hand against her stomach, she drew in a deep breath.

Wonderful and wild, she understood. She'd done it! She'd brought three fantasies alive for Lucas. And his response had been more than she'd hoped for, more than she had ever imagined.

So why wasn't she feeling satisfied, the way she did in the lab when an experiment went even better than she'd hoped it could?

Why was there a bubble of fear in her stomach instead?

Foolish question. She knew exactly why it was there. It had to do with what had happened when they'd come out of the rock cave. She couldn't rid her mind of the way it had felt when he'd kissed her underwater—as if he was determined to know every secret she had. And she was sure she'd given them all away. Any kind of defenses she'd managed to build up had streamed away in the water. She'd felt parts of herself slipping away too.

Wrapping her arms around herself, she met her gaze steadily in the mirror. Years from now she'd remember what it had felt like to be wanted so much that he'd taken her right there at the side of the lagoon.

Correction, she reminded herself. He'd taken Fiona. It had been part of the fantasy. She'd had the whole time she'd spent in the shower to analyze it. When they'd been under the water, he'd looked like some kind of sea god to her. She must have looked the same to him. He'd been thinking about Fiona the whole time. She couldn't afford to let herself forget that.

She couldn't let herself want—

No. She blocked the rest of the thought from her mind, but she couldn't prevent the fear in her stomach from expanding. Why did she always have to want the one thing she couldn't have? Lucas had been right about one thing. Fantasies were dangerous.

At the sound of the phone ringing in the other room, she tucked the towel around herself and opened the bathroom door.

Another ring had her moving toward the phone on the desk.

Lucas wasn't in the bedroom. She told herself the sinking sensation in her stomach wasn't disappointment. Just as it hadn't been disappointment when he'd told her to go ahead and use the larger bathroom for her shower and he'd use a different one.

That one small suggestion had told her quite clearly that she wasn't Fiona to him any longer. She was just Mac. And that was fine—just as it should be.

As she picked up the extension of the hotel phone, she met her own gaze in the mirror. *Who was she kidding?*

Another insistent ring told her it wasn't the hotel phone that was making the racket. She raced to her purse and fished out Sophie's cell phone. "Hello?"

"I hope I'm interrupting a very erotic fantasy."

"Sophie." Smiling, Mac sank onto the foot of the bed.

There was a muffled groan. "I sincerely hope Lucas is not there. I would prefer not to have to talk to him."

"No, he's not here."

"What's wrong? And for that matter, why *isn't* he there? You did take my advice, didn't you? You've tested a few of those fantasies?"

"Yes."

"They didn't work?"

The astonishment in Sophie's voice nearly had Mac smiling again. She tried to force some enthusiasm into her voice. "Everything worked perfectly." *Too perfectly.* "I've turned a man who didn't like fantasies into a fantasy-aholic."

"You don't sound very enthused. Or triumphant. That *was* the purpose of your little experiment, wasn't it?"

"Of course." It was exactly what she'd wanted. Mac glanced down at her red-painted toenails. They were Sally's toes, and Lucas was totally fascinated by "Sally." She shifted her glance to her reflection in the mirror. Her hair, still mussed from the quick toweling she'd given it, was a tumble of locks around her head—the perfect mermaid do.

"You may be a brilliant scientist, but you're a lousy liar. Why don't you tell me what's really going on?"

"Things can't be that boring at the spa."

This time Sophie's reply was a sigh.

"That bad, huh? I thought you liked it. What happened to riding in a hot-air balloon?"

"This place…let's just say it isn't all it's cracked up to be. Maybe I ought to borrow one of your fantasies."

Mac blinked and thought. "I'm not sure I have anything appropriate for an all-women spa."

Sophie laughed. "You have such a wonderfully literal mind. But you can relax. If I were going to actually field-test one of your fantasies, I'd definitely go AWOL."

"Sophie—"

"Just kidding. After all this effort and subterfuge, I'm at

least going to stay the week out. But if you want to make sure I don't do something desperate, you're going to have to keep me entertained by telling me what's really going on."

Leaning back against the bed, Mac tried to find words for the thoughts that had been tumbling around in her head while she'd showered.

"Or maybe I should just take a wild guess. Lucas likes the research, but you'd rather he liked you."

Sophie's succinct summary of the situation had Mac bolting upright. "No."

"Denying the truth is never an effective way of dealing with reality."

The bubble of fear she'd felt before was sharpening, tightening in her stomach. "But I don't…he doesn't…I can't…"

Sophie laughed. "I love to hear the preciseness of a scientific mind at work."

Mac sank onto the bed again. "Lucas is not interested in me as me."

"What makes you so sure of that?"

"Island girls, mermaids and hookers are much more exciting. He's making love to them not me."

"Hookers I can figure out. Maybe even the island girls. But mermaids? When we have more time, you are definitely going to have to tell me about that one. In the meantime, there's one way to find out if Lucas wants you as you. Take a night off from the fantasies and be yourself. Seduce him all by yourself."

Mac glanced quickly at the closed door to the bedroom. "But I'm sure Lucas is expecting—"

"Don't give him what he expects. Surprise him. Surely your Madame Gervais included that piece of advice in her instructions."

"Well, yes, but—"

"The problem is you have no confidence in yourself. And the only way to build confidence is to practice. What have you got to lose, Mac?"

Everything.

"Just do it," Sophie said.

Once again, Mac stared at her reflection in the mirror. Did she have the courage to take that kind of risk?

"And for once in your life, don't plan it all out. Not that there would be much to plan on that island of my grandfather's."

"We're not on the island," Mac explained. "We're at the Wainright Casa Marina."

"You're what?"

"It was Lucas's idea to come here."

"Don't say anything else for a minute. I'm trying to picture in my mind hookers and mermaids in a public setting where Lucas could be seen and recognized." Sophie began to laugh. "This is just too delicious."

Mac found herself smiling in response. "I don't think Yancey, the pool man, recognized him at first, but Lucas told the manager in the lounge that we were married."

There were two beats of silence before Sophie said, "I don't think you need my advice, Mac. You seem to be doing fine on your own. Plus, I think I see the room service golf cart wending its way toward my door. Just tell Lucas I called and that I'm having the time of my life."

For a full minute after Sophie cut the connection, Mac stared at her cell phone. She could have sworn that Sophie was not having the time of her life. She was about to call her back when a knock at the door had her shooting to her feet. "Yes?"

"Are you decent?" Lucas asked.

Decent? This from the man she was becoming addicted to being indecent with?

"Yes."

Later she would wonder if Lania, Sally and Fiona had become permanent facets of her personality—or perhaps it was just one of those moments of perfect timing. But the moment that Lucas stepped into the room, the towel she'd wrapped herself in slipped silently to the floor.

TRACKER SWORE SILENTLY as he shifted in the tree he'd selected for his long vigil. It had taken him three hours and a lot of sweet-talking to get himself smuggled into the Serenity Spa. But he was beginning to believe he'd wasted five hours of his life dressed as a woman for nothing.

The Princess was going to pay for this.

He glanced down at the outfit he'd carefully selected at the general store in town—pale, stone-washed jeans, a pink shirt and a jean jacket. He didn't regret buying them. His pretty little informant, Millie Jean, had been right on the money. She'd sworn she couldn't smuggle him in on the floor of her van, and she'd been correct. The two amazons at the gate had searched it. But the wig and the makeup he'd worn had earned him only a cursory glance from the two guards before they'd waved them through. According to Millie Jean, they never bothered to check the van on the way out.

He shifted his attention to the main building that housed the kitchen, dining rooms and administration offices. Women were still drifting toward it in twos and threes, heading for dinner. So far, none of them walked with that confident, ground-covering stride that seemed to be so much a part of Princess Sophie.

But that didn't mean a thing. In the past hour, he'd seen the golf carts ferrying trays of food back and forth to various cabins. If Lucas's sister *was* here, he figured one of those golf carts had gone to her cabin.

Frowning, Tracker shifted again on his tree limb. What reason did he have to believe that she wasn't here—aside from instinct? The problem was, his gut instincts hadn't been working where Sophie was concerned since that day in Lucas's office when she'd begun to sob in his arms. He'd always thought himself immune to a woman's tears, but Sophie's had gotten to him. Perhaps because there hadn't been any weakness in the tears. She cried with as much energy as she fought.

And it hadn't been to get attention or to get her way. One minute she'd been fighting mad, and the next she was crying her heart out. All he could do was hold her until she stopped.

She'd really had feelings for that Davis jerk.

Well, he knew what it was like to be betrayed by someone you loved. That was why he'd taken it upon himself to look out for her. And she'd spotted him.

A good security professional didn't ever let his job get personal. He had, and now he was paying the price.

Muttering under his breath, Tracker shifted again. The damn tree limb was going to leave permanent markings on his backside. And to top it all off, he was beginning to suspect that he would find Sophie Wainright sound asleep and very safe in her bed.

A glance at his watch informed him that only three minutes had gone by since the last time he'd checked. The rain had stopped, but in the gray mist that clung to the mountains like a favorite cloak, it was impossible to guess exactly how long until sundown.

Tracker was literally counting the seconds. Sundown was nighty-night time at the Serenity Spa, and that meant that he could get into the offices and find Sophie's room number. He was allowing himself an hour to locate her, verify that she was here and then…

Well, then he figured he'd even have time for a nap before Millie Jean made her morning delivery.

And this time he was going to make sure the Princess never knew she'd been checked on.

As Lucas watched the towel drop to the floor, he was quite sure he'd never felt the blood drain so quickly from his head before.

In the soft glow of the bedside lamp, her skin had the pale, creamy hue of porcelain. He knew exactly what it would feel like beneath his hands—still cool and slightly damp from her shower. He could smell the soap even from a distance.

He hadn't moved. He didn't know if he could. In the back of his mind he knew that he'd had a purpose for coming into the room. But all he could do now was look at her. Knowing that she was here, naked in his bedroom, understanding that she could be his in the time it took him to take three quick strides across the room—all of that had the need to touch her boiling in his blood.

"Lucas…"

He wanted her beneath him on that bed. Now. That thought, along with a sharp stab of desire, freed him from the paralysis that had gripped him since her towel had dropped. He'd taken those three steps toward her before he stopped himself.

This wasn't what he'd planned. Ruthlessly, he tried to dredge up the details he'd carefully mapped out. He was going to take her out…on a date. For the life of him, he couldn't remember where.

"Lucas…"

If she continued to look at him that way, there wasn't going to be any date.

She moistened her lips with her tongue as she moved toward him and laid a hand on his chest. "What I have in mind is…"

Bells began to ring in his head. There was a shyness in her voice, a tentativeness in her approach that hadn't been there with Lania or Sally or even Fiona. If this was yet another fantasy, he had to nip it in the bud.

"You dropped something," he said. He saw the quick leap of surprise in her eyes and something else before she lowered her gaze. Embarrassment? Hurt? He stooped over to retrieve the towel, then handed it to her. As she wrapped it around herself and tucked it securely into place, he became certain of one thing. This was Mac standing in front of him. Lania, Sally and Fiona weren't shy at all. But Mac was. She was also very neat and thorough about the way she tied a towel around herself.

And he'd just hurt her. He knew he had to make it right. Wanted to with all he had. More than anything, he wanted to pull her into his arms and hold her. But he didn't trust himself to touch her. Still, he needed to erase the pain he'd seen in her eyes.

"Look at me, Mac."

When her eyes met his, he said, "For the record, I want to make love to you more than anything right now."

"Then why did you pick up my towel?"

"Because I was rough on you down in the lagoon, and I think we should both take a little break from… your research. And since it is finally my turn to call the shots—"

"It's not your turn."

Lucas frowned. "Time out. In the lobby earlier, you said

it was your turn until we made love. We did. That means it's my turn."

"We made love two times. The second time was your turn. Now it's mine."

She had a point. More importantly, the hurt look had vanished from her eyes. "Look, we can argue about this, or we can compromise. What I was going to suggest is that we go out—on a date."

Mac blinked. "A date?"

She sounded as if she'd never heard the word before, and quite suddenly Lucas began to enjoy himself. For the first time since Mac had stepped off his plane, he was beginning to feel as if he had a slight advantage. He intended to keep it. "That didn't pop up in your research? I'm thinking of the kind of thing where a guy asks a girl out to dinner, maybe dancing. It's an old-fashioned way of getting to know one another—"

"I've heard of a date before."

The dry tone had him grinning. "I think we're overdue for one, don't you?"

"But we know each other."

"Most definitely in the biblical sense. However, there are lots of things we don't know yet. What's your favorite flavor of ice cream?"

"Rum raisin."

"What do you have nightmares about?"

"Falling."

"Ah. That fits with the fear of heights. But the rum raisin is a surprise. I would have picked you for a strawberry girl."

She frowned, studying him as she turned over his proposal in her mind. Finally, she said, "This date wouldn't count as anyone's turn?"

"Scout's honor."

Still, she hesitated.

"Doc, it's just a date. I'm not asking for your hand in marriage. I want to go out with you for one evening in Key West. Just you and me. Mac and Lucas. We leave Lania, Sally and Fiona here in the room with John and the shipwrecked sailors."

She said nothing, and in the silence he could almost hear the wheels turning in her mind. He couldn't recall ever having a woman hesitate about accepting a date with him. Instead of being annoyed he had to clamp down on the urge to hug her.

"You're a tough sell, Doc. Let me sweeten the deal. If you'll come along quietly, I'll let you sneak in some of those questions on your questionnaire."

She studied him for one more minute before she held out her hand. "It's my turn when the date's over and we come back here to the room."

"You have my word on it."

While they were shaking on it, he said, "One other thing. I get final approval on what you're wearing this time."

"Don't push your luck."

CHAPTER ELEVEN

THE MOMENT THEY WALKED through the door, Mac felt her senses being bombarded from every direction at once. What she saw was a crowded, dimly lit room that might have been the set of a forties movie. If the lights had been brighter, she thought she might have even glimpsed Humphrey Bogart straddling one of the stools at the bar. She smelled perfume, liquor and cigarette smoke, mixing with the spicy scent of a pizza on the tray of a passing waiter. And through it all, she heard and felt the haunting, bluesy sound of a sax.

Nerves knotted in her stomach. How was she supposed to seduce a man in a crowded, noisy bar? Sally wouldn't have had a problem, but she'd promised to be Mac. And Mac didn't even have step one figured out in her mind.

"Lucas." A large man in tan slacks, a crisp white shirt and wide red suspenders slid from a bar stool and hurried toward them. Mac guessed his age to be in the seventies. "Welcome. It's been a long time." He grasped Lucas's hand and thumped him on the back. "I've got your grandfather's favorite table ready for you."

While Lucas introduced her to Joe Johnson, the current owner of the place, the large man ushered them past the band to a booth in a back corner. It was U-shaped with wooden partitions rising high on three sides and offering an illusion of privacy.

"You enjoy yourselves, hear?" Joe said as he left them.

"I've never been in a place like this," Mac said as she slid into the seat.

"Good."

But she wasn't so sure of that.

"I'd like to be able to tell you that Ernest Hemingway wrote *To Have and Have Not* while he was sitting at this very table."

She glanced down at the scarred wood of the table, then back at him. "But you're not telling me that."

"Not with absolute certainty. The place has been renovated since the days when he used to hang out here." He paused to glance around the room. "Some of the furniture goes back that far, I'm sure. What I can tell you is that this is the place where he wrote a lot of that novel—and others."

Mac stared at him. "But this isn't Sloppy Joe's. It says in the guidebooks that's where he wrote."

"This is the building that housed the original Sloppy Joe's. My grandfather used to bring me here, and then he'd tell me stories about the days when he and Papa Hemingway used to drink and fish. There's a back room they used to play pool in." He gestured toward a doorway next to the bar. "Each time he brought me here he'd swear that the table we were sitting at was the exact place where Hemingway had penned this or that story or scene."

Mac glanced quickly around the room. "Which one were you sitting at?"

Lucas grinned at her. "We were at a different table each time we came here."

She ran her hand reverently over the scarred wood in front of her. "But this was your grandfather's favorite. So it really could be the one?"

"Could be." He reached over and tucked a strand of hair behind her ear. "I heard you talking to the bellhops in the lobby of the hotel. I thought you might like this even better than the museum."

"I do." She met his eyes then. "Thank you. You're a very kind man."

"No." His grin faded as quickly as it had appeared. "Don't make the mistake of thinking that. Hasn't Sophie disabused you of that notion?"

Mac reached for his hand then. "Sophie appreciates that you care for her. Or she will as soon as she gets over that Bradley creep."

Lucas studied her for a moment. "When did you decide that Bradley was a creep?"

"The first time I met him."

"And Sophie knew your opinion?"

She shook her head. "Of course not, although sometimes I had to bite my tongue. She suspected that I didn't like him, but I would never have told her not to date him. Haven't you noticed that she immediately does the thing that she's been told not to do?"

Lucas laughed. "Yeah. I've noticed that pattern in her behavior."

"If you ever really want Sophie to do something, tell her the opposite," Mac said. "It's the forbidden-fruit syndrome. It works every time."

He could testify to that. His determination not to touch Mac was fueling his desire to do just that. And it had been growing steadily since he'd slid into the booth beside her—no, even before that, when she'd bent to get in the taxi and he'd caught a glimpse of that soft smooth skin at her navel, just below the spot where she'd knotted her shirt. He could reach out to brush his fingers along it right now.

It didn't help one bit that her hand was still in his. It would be so easy to raise her fingers to his lips, scrape his teeth over her knuckles and watch her eyes cloud. She was so responsive…so tempting. But he'd promised her a date, and he was going to give it to her.

When he caught himself staring at her mouth, he cleared his throat and said, "I'll have to remember that. About Sophie, I mean. The forbidden-fruit syndrome— the next time I want to handle her." Good grief, he was babbling. He had to focus. Ask a question. "Why are you so afraid of heights?"

Mac blinked and stared at him. "Why would you ask that?"

He settled himself against the back of the booth. "Because I want to know. You must have given it some thought—tried to analyze it."

She had, but it had been a long time since she'd dredged it up. She wasn't sure she wanted to now.

"C'mon. We're on our first date, remember. We get to ask questions so that we can learn more about each other. You can trust me, Mac."

The look in his eyes was so calm and patient, she found herself saying, "When I was five, my father built me a swing set in the backyard. There was a trapeze on it, and he'd been disappointed in me because I couldn't sit on it. I've never been very athletic."

"So?"

"My father had wanted a son. That's what my mother told me after he left us. Anyway, this one night I wanted to please him when he came home from work, and so I climbed up on the trapeze and tried to do this trick. I wanted to swing all the way around the trapeze bar like they do in the circus. I kept swinging higher and higher, but the trick wasn't as easy as it looked and I fell and broke my arm. My mother blamed my father for building the swing set, and my father was furious. The next day he packed up and left. Ever since then, I've been afraid of heights."

Lucas's fingers tightened on hers. "And you blamed yourself because your father left."

"At the time, I did. It was a long time before I understood that he'd found another woman he loved better than he loved my mother and me. She gave him the son he wanted. And eventually my mother found someone too. They're both very happy with their new families."

"And you're still afraid of heights."

She shrugged. "Fears aren't rational."

"No. It takes a brave person to battle them."

When he raised her hand to his lips and kissed it, Mac felt something inside her dissolve and stream away. No one had ever had this effect on her. She'd never allowed it. But when he looked at her the way he was now, she couldn't seem to prevent it. And she wanted, more than anything, she wanted to know that she truly was the person he'd made love to in the lagoon. Sophie's advice streamed into her mind—that she should seduce him as herself.

Wasn't it her plan to do just that?

"What can I get for you folks?" The waitress, a thin woman with a blond ponytail, beamed a smile at them.

"What kind of beer do you have on tap?" Lucas asked.

What if she wasn't the woman he'd made love to in the lagoon? What if she found out that Lucas was just being kind to his sister's friend? She'd forced herself to face other fears, but this—

She watched Lucas's eyes light with laughter at something the waitress said.

If she didn't at least try, she was the worst kind of coward. But she couldn't attack him the way Sally had. No, he would have to know it was Mac. She'd have to start with the questionnaire. When she pulled it out of her bag, her fingers were trembling.

The moment the woman hurried off, Mac smoothed it out on the table, "Before I drink any beer, I'm going to get you started on these questions."

"You know, I wish I had my camera with me. I'd like to capture that on film."

"What?" She glanced quickly around.

"The way you turn yourself from Mac, the woman who is enchanted because she might be sitting at a table where Hemingway wrote, into the focused, very serious-minded Dr. Lloyd."

"I didn't. I—"

"Oh yes, you did, the moment you pulled out that questionnaire. It wasn't quite as dramatic as Mr. Hyde turning into Dr. Jekyll. But I think I could definitely capture it on film. Your smile fades, then your eyes become darker, very intent, and I can almost hear the wheels start to turn in that pretty little head of yours."

As he talked, she studied him as closely as he was studying her. He was teasing her. She was almost sure of it. But there was something else in his eyes that she was equally sure was dead serious. "You're starting to make me feel like I have a split personality."

"Maybe you do, in a way. My theory is that you turn into the doc when you want to escape."

Mac stared at him. He was right. Why should it surprise her that he knew that about her?

"My question is, why? You're certainly not a coward."

"It's easier to be Dr. Lloyd." The words tumbled out before they'd been fully formed in her mind. "She can be clinically detached. She doesn't get hurt as easily."

For a moment she thought she saw a flash of understanding in his eyes.

Then the waitress appeared. "Two beers," she said as she slapped them on the table.

The moment the woman moved away again, Lucas said, "Okay, you can be the doc—for a few questions. Then I want Mac back."

Then I want Mac back. His words moved through her, weakening her and strengthening her at the same time. Blinking twice, she glanced down at the questionnaire and asked the first question she focused on. "Have you ever had anyone make love to you while you were blindfolded?"

"Blindfolded?"

"So that you can't see, and you can't tell what your lover is doing exactly. The sensual pleasure is incredibly heightened."

"Really."

She waited for a beat, then said, "You haven't answered the question. Have you ever let anyone make love to you while you were blindfolded?"

"No."

She nodded. "Because you want to stay in control."

"Perhaps. What's the next question?"

She glanced down. "What is your favorite position for sex?"

"My favorite position?"

She looked at him. "You know—on top, on the bottom, behind?"

"I know what you're asking. Let me see that." He pulled the papers closer and skimmed the page quickly. "Where did you get these questions?"

"I compiled them myself."

"And who else have you done this questionnaire with?"

"No one. I developed it especially for the man who would be my research partner."

"And that's me?"

She nodded and saw some of his tension ease. Was he jealous? Was that why he sounded so tense and annoyed? The possibility sent a little wave of pleasure through her. "You haven't answered the question yet." And she was suddenly curious. They certainly hadn't used any of the normal positions yet. "What *is* your favorite sexual position?"

Lifting his beer, he took a drink. "I pretty much like them all."

"That's not a very explicit answer."

He narrowed his eyes at her over the rim of his glass. "Give me another one. I'll try to do better."

She skimmed the page, then flipped to the next one. "Why don't I make it easier for you? There's a section here about sex toys. I'll just name them, and you can rate them on a scale of one to five—one meaning you've never used them and five meaning *wow*. All set?"

When she glanced up, she saw that his eyes had become very intent, and the dark, reckless gleam was back. Her throat went suddenly dry.

"I'll make it easy for you. Give them all a one. I've already told you I'm partial to reality."

Mac moistened her lips. Staring into Lucas's eyes for any length of time was paralyzing and, at the same time, exciting. She imagined a predator must look at his prey this way, just as he was about to spring. She forced her gaze back to the page and tried to focus. "No sex toys. Let me see…does it turn you on to watch your sex partner masturbate?"

When he didn't answer, she didn't meet his eyes. Already, she regretted the question. She didn't want to know, didn't want to picture him watching another woman pleasure herself.

When she finally did glance up, she found that he was close.

"I know that I would enjoy watching you touch yourself intimately." His hand moved to rest on her knee. "You could show me what you like, tell me what you'd like me to do. Explicitly."

His fingers began to trace a pattern on the inside of her knee. "Do you like this?"

Mac felt the heat rush through her. He was barely touching her, but her legs had already spread to give him more access.

"Ah, you do like this. Or do you want me to stop?" His hand stilled on the question.

"No." She didn't want him to stop. He hadn't touched her this way before. When he'd made love to her, his hands had been hard, demanding. Now she could barely feel the movement of his fingers. "But someone will see…"

Leaning closer, he feathered a kiss over her lips. "Tell me about your research. That way, no one passing by will know what we're doing."

"My research…?" His eyes and mouth were so close. His hand wasn't nearly close enough.

"Sophie says you had a breakthrough."

Mac tried to ignore the melting sensation in her lower body as his fingers moved a little higher. "I'm working on something—you…really shouldn't…"

"I can't seem to help myself. You started it with that question. Now I can't seem to stop picturing you touching yourself. Like this."

In his eyes, she could see the same mixture of emotions she'd seen when he'd backed her into the wall of the lagoon. Desire and something else too. Was it possible that he felt as vulnerable and as out of control as she did? Something softened within her.

"Have you made any progress?"

"Hmm?"

"On your research? Have you made any progress?"

He had made progress. The tiny circles that his fingers were making inched higher. What he was doing to her seemed even more erotic contrasted with what she was trying to think about, talk about. She drew in a shaky breath. "I've had some success with…" One of his fingers was stroking down the silk of her panty and was close to…

"Success with…?"

She dragged her thoughts back. "Animals," she managed to say. "They're not aging as quickly. Wilbur, one of my lab rats, has been with me from the beginning. He's lived to be…"

His finger slipped beneath her panties and entered her.

"Lucas…"

He leaned very close so that his lips were nearly brushing hers. "I can't do here what I could have done back at the hotel. If we were there, I would take you into the bathroom and sit you on the vanity. That's what I wanted to do when you dropped your towel. We could watch in the mirrors while I entered you. I want you to see both of us when I'm inside you. I want you to know it's just you and me. No fantasies."

But it was. It was the most seductive fantasy he could have conjured up. And she wanted it more than anything. She wanted Lucas to want her just the way she wanted him. Once more, Sophie's advice filled her mind.

"Come back to the suite with me, Mac."

No. Shaking her head to clear it, she met his eyes

steadily. If she went back there, it wouldn't matter whose turn it was, she would fall under his spell just the way she always did. Just the way she was right now. She had to know that she could seduce him. "One question first."

She watched his eyes narrow and darken. Here was the recklessness and the danger that had drawn her from the first. "Not from that damn questionnaire?"

"No, it's a simple date question. Would you play a game of pool with me?"

His hand finally stilled as he stared at her. "Are you always going to be able to surprise me?"

"I asked my question first."

"The answer is yes, just as long as I'm playing with Mac."

"You've got a deal." And, as Mac, she finally had a plan.

CHAPTER TWELVE

"MY GRANDFATHER TAUGHT ME to play pool in this room," Lucas said as he led the way through the door at the end of the bar. "I loved it." Past tense. Pool was the last thing on his mind right now. What he wanted to do more than anything was throw Mac over his shoulder and carry her back to the hotel. If they made it that far. The way he was acting, they might not make it farther than the first shadowy doorway along the street.

Ruthlessly, he pushed the image out of his mind. He'd asked her here on a date because he'd thought it would be safe.

Was there anyplace in the world where she would be safe from him? Or anyplace where he might be safe from wanting her?

He watched her walk over to the rack of cue sticks and run her hand down one. He couldn't blame his reaction on a fantasy this time. Mac was the one who'd set out to tease him with that questionnaire.

"Ready?" she asked as she turned back to him.

He glanced at the pool table. He was ready all right. And he could make sure that she was in seconds. All he would have to do...

A loud burst of laughter had him shifting his gaze to the open doorway. The crowd around the bar was growing, and the pool table was in plain sight.

Moving to the rack, he selected a stick. When he turned

to her, he found her looking at him in that quiet, intent way he was becoming familiar with.

"You really loved your grandfather, didn't you?" she asked.

"Yes. He was a remarkable man. He worked very hard to build Wainright Enterprises." He chuckled. "And he always took the time to play hard too."

"You were lucky to be able to spend time with him. I've heard that grandparents are a lot less judgmental than parents."

Lucas glanced up from racking the balls. "Your parents judged you a lot?"

"My mother. I think I'm a constant reminder to her that she failed in her first marriage."

He thought of his own parents—his mother who had left when he was barely five and his father who'd remarried within a year. "Mine pretty much left me to nannies, and whenever that didn't work out, my granddad took over."

Her eyebrows lifted. "The nannies didn't work out?"

"Bad things always seemed to happen to them—frogs in their beds, cockroaches in their tea cakes. It was almost as if the house were haunted."

"Shades of *Turn of the Screw?*"

Grinning, he propped a hip against the pool table. "Not quite that bad. Just enough to get my grandfather's attention. What about you? What's the worst thing you ever did to your nannies?"

A smile hovered at the corners of her mouth. "The worst I ever did was to give them the slip and disappear for the day."

"I can't picture Dr. Lloyd playing hooky, so it must have been Mac." He tucked the new insight away. "What did you do when you gave them the slip?"

Her chin lifted. "Maybe I learned to shoot pool."

"Did you?"

"You're about to find out." Turning, she walked toward the table.

"It's a good idea to chalk the sticks first."

After he demonstrated, he watched her imitate his actions perfectly. "You're a very quick study, Doc."

She shot him a very level look. "I'm Mac. Or did you forget?"

His grin widened. "Touché. When Grandfather and I played, we always used to have a friendly wager, just to keep the game more interesting."

"Sure. Have you ever played strip pool?"

Lucas stared at her.

"It's basically like strip poker. When you win the first game, you tell me to take something off, and—"

"I know what the wager in strip poker is." She'd tossed it out as if she'd been playing pool for years, and that was her usual bet. And she was suddenly close enough to run a finger down the buttons of his shirt.

"Of course, we probably couldn't really strip—not here. Not if I have to be Mac and you have to be Lucas. But we *could* pretend. I could tell you exactly what I'm taking off, and you could imagine." She leaned closer until her body just brushed against his. "You do have a pretty good imagination, don't you?"

"Yeah." His imagination was both excellent *and* fertile. The picture of what she'd looked like standing in his bedroom earlier had beamed itself right into his mind. Now he was projecting what she would look like lying on that pool table, wearing absolutely nothing.

"I'll go first."

His gaze tracked her as she moved to where he'd racked

the balls, and he managed to follow her just in time to see the skirt she was wearing hike up a full two inches when she leaned over the table.

Glancing over her shoulder, she said, "Any suggestions on what I should do next?"

Later he would wonder if it was the heat in her look, the sultry invitation of her tone or the images she'd managed to conjure up in his mind. Perhaps it was the whole package. The only thing he was really aware of was that he couldn't resist her. And if he moved toward her now, touched her now, he was afraid...

He'd taken one step when she straightened and grinned at him. "I can't believe it."

"What?" He was amazed that he'd managed to get the word out.

"I was just being myself. Mac. I swear I was. I didn't know I could do that. And it was *working!* I could see it in your face, in your eyes."

Lucas narrowed his eyes. She was baiting him. She'd known exactly what her suggestion had done to him and precisely how her skirt would hike up when she'd leaned over that table.

"You amaze me," he said. And he realized that nothing he said could have been truer. He wondered if he would ever figure her out. But he did know that two could play at the little game she'd begun. He tapped his cue stick against hers. "Why don't you turn around and I'll show you how to break the balls?"

She grinned at him. "I don't think so." She shot a quick look at the open door they'd walked through.

When he followed her gaze, he saw the crowd in the bar had grown even more, so that there were groups standing, drinks in hand, just outside the room.

"Even as Lucas, I don't think you'd want to get arrested

for…" She glanced back at him, the laughter clear in her eyes. "What exactly was it you had in mind a few seconds ago?"

"You're playing with fire, Mac."

When she laughed, he couldn't help but smile.

"You stand over there like a good boy," she said.

Lucas very nearly laughed, himself, when he did exactly what he was told. Meekness had never been one of his strongest virtues, probably because he didn't believe that the meek would one day inherit the earth. But then, thanks to the doc, he'd done a lot of things out of character in the past day and a half. Of course, it wasn't the doc ordering him around now. It was Mac.

Leaning against the wall, he watched her take the rack off the balls and bend over the table. As she ran the stick through her fingers in short little strokes, he watched her hands. Her fingers were long, delicate-looking. But he recalled how strong they'd felt on his skin, pressing, demanding. Taking.

Straightening, Mac lifted, then relaxed her shoulders in a circular motion. This time, she planted her feet farther apart before she bent back over the table.

If they were alone, he could walk right up to her and… Out of the corner of his eye, he saw someone glance into the room, then walk away. He could easily shut the door and prop a chair against it. Then he could go to her, lean over the table with her… She would gasp in surprise as he pressed against her, pinning her against the table. Then he would whisper in her ear, "You don't know me. I'm not even going to tell you my name." He would tell her exactly what he was going to do, describe every action, even as he did it. He'd make quick work of pushing the skirt up to her waist. Then he'd release his zipper and free himself so that she could feel him pressing against her with nothing but her panties separating them. All he would have to do then was push her down against the table and tear away that last, thin, silky barrier. Then he could bury himself in her. Lose himself—

The sharp crack of the cue ball smacking against the others sent Lucas's fantasy splintering off in as many directions as the balls. Drawing in a deep breath, he let it out slowly and dragged his attention back to the pool table. He thought he saw three balls sink into pockets.

"Aren't you going to congratulate me?" Mac beamed a smile at him as she moved to the other side of the table.

"Congratulations." He struggled to free his mind of the remnants of the fantasy he'd woven.

"That doesn't sound very sincere. I don't think you were paying attention."

Could she see into his mind?

"Watch," she said as if she were talking to a recalcitrant child. "I'll show you again."

To Lucas's astonishment, she did.

"Well?"

"Do it again," he challenged. This time he watched more carefully as she set up a complicated bank shot. It wasn't the one he would have chosen, but the moment she set it into motion, the cue ball careened off the side of the table into three others and sent them spinning into three different pockets.

"You hustled me," he said.

"I did no such thing," she said, moving toward him. "You assumed I didn't know how to play, and you're the one who wanted to make a little wager, just to keep the game more interesting."

"Were you telling the truth? Did you really learn to shoot pool when you were playing hooky from your nannies?"

"I learned in college. I was too young to date, but there were a lot of guys who didn't mind a kid sister-type tagging along. Especially if she could tutor them in physics or biology or calculus."

"That's all they wanted you to do? Tutor them?"

"I started college at fourteen. The deans and the resident directors had read all the guys the riot act. Not that they were tempted. I was a total geek, a one-hundred-percent nerd."

Mac at fourteen. Lucas tried to form a picture of it in his mind. It reminded him of the person he'd glimpsed at Sophie's party—a timid little bird, eager to help but determined to remain on the sidelines. Probably because she was so sure she wouldn't fit in.

"Did you beat them all at pool?"

She shrugged. "It wasn't hard. Getting them to see the utter simplicity of calculus was hard."

"I'll bet." He could barely keep a straight face at the seriousness of her expression. He wanted to grab her and hug her, twirl her around the room. But he didn't trust himself to touch her at all. And if he was patient now, he might learn more about the woman who hid behind the facade of Dr. Lloyd. Look how much he'd learned already. It was a good enough excuse to wait—almost.

He watched her lean across the table for a very long shot. She could have taken it more comfortably from the other side of the table. Was she doing it because she didn't see that, or was she doing it so that he could see the lacy edge of her panties when her skirt moved up? He took another drink of his beer to ease the dryness in his throat and watched the ball sink.

By the time she'd cleared the table, he'd had several more views of the edge of her panties. He was just about through waiting.

She collected and racked the balls before she approached him. Then she put a hand on his arm and said in a voice only he could hear, "Time to pay up. Picture this— I'm taking your pants off right now. Of course, I can't really take them off." She glanced toward the doorway. "Someone might come in, so we'll just have to imagine that you have to take your shots wearing only your boxer shorts."

He leaned down and whispered into her ear. "I'm not wearing boxers *or* briefs. Picture that."

The quick hitch of her breath had him grinning as he moved to the door, shut it and jammed a chair beneath the knob.

When he turned back to her, she was taking off the string of pearls she'd worn around her neck. "Now you can really take off your pants."

He walked toward her. "Now I can do a lot of things I've been planning."

She let the pearls swing from two fingers. "I've been thinking of something too."

He lifted her onto the pool table and began to ease off her panties.

"You were supposed to take off yours first."

There was laughter mixed with the excitement in her eyes. He couldn't have wanted her more. "No problem." Pulling the belt loose, he let his pants slip to the floor.

"I suppose you're going to insist on going ahead with your plan first."

"Absolutely," he said as he gripped her hips and pulled her to the edge of the table. "But I promise to let you have your turn next."

VERY SLOWLY, Sophie twisted around on the bar stool and let her gaze move over the crowd. The room was dim, the music live and pulsing with bass. Laced through it was the din of conversation and laughter.

She was in her element. She should be having a good time.

And the prickling sensation at the back of her neck was just due to the fact that she was in a place where people came to meet other people. Of course, they would be looking at her—perhaps even staring. She glanced down at the dress. Hadn't she chosen it just to get some attention?

She'd bought it Monday on that shopping trip with Mac. The green color went particularly well with the red wig she was wearing tonight. When she'd walked through the lobby of the hotel and caught a glimpse of herself in the mirror, she'd been amazed at her resemblance to Mac.

Lifting her glass, she took a sip. Tonight she was Mac-Kenzie Lloyd and not Sophie Wainright, and she *was* going to have a good time.

The concierge at her hotel had been right on the money with his recommendation. The Side Street Grill was crowded with people, mostly singles, or at least pretending to be. The last man she'd danced with had forgotten to take off his wedding ring. Tables circled a dance floor, and on the second level, pressed against a balcony railing. On one wall, tall glass windows looked out on a patio lit with Chinese lanterns.

She caught herself rubbing the back of her neck again and immediately dropped her hand to her lap. She was being ridiculous, paranoid. Gripping her wineglass between her fingers, she began to turn it in slow circles on the bar.

Why not admit the truth? She was bored. Lifting her wineglass, she licked a drop off the rim, then set it back down.

Perhaps she should go back to D.C. If only Mac were

here to talk to, or even— She set the glass down so fast she nearly overturned it. She couldn't be wishing that the *Shadow* were here, could she?

Definitely not! She wanted to torture the man, slowly, not…what? She certainly wasn't thinking of using some of Mac's research on him! She didn't know anything about him, other than that he was big, bigger than Lucas even. And strong. Smart too. When she'd cooled down enough to read the file he'd compiled on Bradley, she'd found his report thorough, well written and concise.

And he'd held her when she'd cried. A lot of men couldn't stand a woman's tears, but the Shadow hadn't been fazed.

She ran her finger around the rim of her wineglass. Well, she certainly wasn't going to soften toward him because of that.

And if she was wishing him here, it was just because it would give her great satisfaction to give him the slip again. Although if she were to consider using Mac's research on him… She ran her finger around the top of her wineglass again. There was more than one way to torture a man. She dipped her finger into the wine, then licked the drops off.

"I've never seen anyone do quite so many things to a wineglass without actually drinking the wine."

Sophie froze in her chair. Damn! She knew that voice— Sonny Falcone. Had he recognized her in spite of the wig? How would she explain that she'd told him she'd had to work on her presentation?

"Why don't you let me buy you a fresh glass? I can recommend one from a local vineyard."

He hadn't recognized her. But he still might.

Pushing down the nerves in her stomach, Sophie turned.

"No thank you. One is my limit, and I made the mistake of ordering a second one."

"You know, I have the funniest feeling we've met before. And that's not a pickup line. You remind me of someone…"

"I do that to a lot of people. But we haven't met. I just arrived in California today."

"It's probably the lighting in this place. But I can see I was mistaken. If I'd seen you before, I wouldn't have forgotten your face."

Oh, please! What had she ever seen in this man? Had her breakup from Bradley made her this blind? This desperate?

"If I can't buy you a glass a wine, perhaps I could persuade you to dance?"

"I'd love to dance." She risked a quick meeting of eyes and felt the nerves settle. He still didn't recognize her. And she would make sure that he didn't. "But first I need to freshen up."

"I'll be waiting right here."

For longer than you'd probably like. Sliding from the stool, Sophie threaded her way through the crowd in the direction of the ladies' room. But she didn't go inside when she reached it. Instead, she pulled open the door next to it marked Exit. The cool night air was refreshing after the smoky closeness of the bar. Drawing it in, she hurried down the path to the parking lot.

A glance at her watch told her she could still catch the red-eye. Her decision made, she suddenly felt free. Happy. There was only one thing she regretted. She was going to head back to D.C. without ever going up in that hot-air balloon.

But there had to be places to take a balloon ride in Maryland or Virginia. It would be a nice wild-goose chase to take the Shadow on. She was still thinking of that, laughing almost, when she reached her car.

It all happened very quickly. Arms grabbing her, holding her tight. A prick in her arm, and darkness swallowing her up.

CHAPTER THIRTEEN

MOONLIGHT POOLED on the bed, spilling over Mac as she slept.

Mac. Propping himself up on an elbow, Lucas shifted slightly so that he could see her better. She'd fallen sound asleep in the taxi on the way home from the bar. The last thing she'd said to him before she snuggled her head against his shoulder was that since he'd enjoyed the pearls, she knew he would love being wrapped in plastic wrap.

"Plastic wrap?" he'd asked.

"Mummification," she mumbled against his shirt. "It turns some men on. You can't move. I can. I can do anything I want. I bet you'll like it."

"I don't think I'll enjoy smothering to death."

"You won't." She'd giggled then and yawned. "I'll leave your mouth and nose free and, I think, one other part of you. Maybe I'll use the pearls again." He felt her mouth curve against his chest as she moved her hand from where it rested against his chest to the waistband of his slacks. He gripped it there.

"The picture is becoming clearer."

"The moment you told me you weren't wearing any boxers or briefs, I knew I had to try the pearls. And they worked."

They worked all right. Just thinking of the way she'd looped them around his erection and drawn them slowly upward...

She'd moved then, wiggling against him, exactly where he'd grown very hard. "I bet you'll enjoy the plastic wrap too. I packed a whole roll. We can do it right after we get back to the hotel."

But they hadn't gotten to it. They hadn't gotten to anything. Yet.

MacKenzie Lloyd slept like a rock. He'd had to carry her into the hotel, and he hadn't had the heart to wake her when they reached the suite. As he'd undressed her and tucked her in, he'd noticed the dark smudges under her eyes. She was exhausted.

And no wonder. When he thought of what they'd done on that pool table. They'd taken turns, and when she'd suggested a position he'd never heard of before, they'd even compromised. He was going to have to get a hold of her research. He certainly was never going to be able to concentrate on his pool game again.

Because he couldn't help himself, he brushed one finger lightly over the fullness of her bottom lip.

At last he'd met the real MacKenzie Lloyd. And if the glimpses that he'd caught of her before had intrigued him and surprised him, the real deal fascinated him. She played pool as if she'd been raised in a pool hall. Yet he'd seen traces of the scientist too, in the way she set up her shots and measured the angles, almost as if she was solving some kind of problem.

He reached out to brush a curl back from her forehead. But it wasn't just the logical side of her brain that he admired. It was the imaginative side that quite literally had knocked his socks off.

And when she set out to seduce him, she drove him… crazy.

Tracing a finger down the soft curve of her cheek, he

smiled. Who would have thought that the prim and proper Dr. Lloyd had an alter ego who was wicked and wild?

But then he'd never thought of himself as a man who could get caught up in wild fantasies or risky sexual games. What they'd done tonight had been plenty risky— but fun.

Anything might be fun with Mac.

Except for the plastic-wrap thing. He was going to have to draw the line at being rolled up in that. Then suddenly he grinned. Perhaps he'd have to turn the tables on her and see just how much she liked "mummification." He traced a finger lightly down her throat and over the rise of one breast until he let it rest on the peak. Of course, he'd have to leave some parts free.

As the images began to fill his mind, he shook his head to clear it. If he allowed himself to pursue that fantasy, he wouldn't let her sleep. He wouldn't get any sleep himself. And they would have plenty of time.

Time. Just that one word sent the first little ripple of unease through him.

He wanted to go on seeing Mac. And he could. There was nothing to prevent their spending more time together when they returned to D.C. He could picture her there even now. In his apartment, in his office…in his life?

The direction his thoughts were taking had the ripple of unease growing into a full-blown wave.

As quietly as he could, Lucas slipped from beneath the sheet and eased himself up from the bed. After glancing back once to make sure that she hadn't stirred, Lucas pulled on his slacks and let himself out of the bedroom.

Moonlight streamed into the large sitting area, bright enough to have him squinting a little as he crossed to the bar and poured himself a snifter of brandy. He had to think, to plan. Somehow, lying there beside Mac, he'd stopped doing that. He'd felt so—he struggled to find the right word—content.

Lifting the glass to his lips, he took a long swallow and welcomed the burn as it slid down his throat. He didn't want to feel that way. It didn't last. There was no one that you could allow yourself to depend on that much. Those were the rules he'd lived by. Survived by.

Moving to the balcony door, he opened it and slipped through. The moon was full and bright. Beneath it, the ocean was black, laced with flashes of silver. His granddad had told him once that the sea was a lot like life—always dangerous, often surprising and, every so often, magical. For a while he stood there, just concentrating on the flashes of silver.

What would Mac think if he told her he wanted her in his life once they got back to D.C.? Somehow, he didn't think she'd be any more pleased with the idea than he was. He took another taste of his brandy, just a sip this time. She might run.

He would catch her.

Or she might come on this very balcony to get her courage revved up. He'd recognized, though, that she had no understanding at all of how really brave she was.

Surely brave enough to take the same risk he was taking. And if she wasn't, he'd just have to convince her. He smiled slowly. With plastic wrap, if nothing else worked.

Tossing off the rest of his brandy, Lucas glanced at his watch—3:00 a.m. He could wake her and begin his campaign right now.

Or he could catch what little sleep he could and wake her when the sun came up. The wide yawn that suddenly overtook him had him choosing the latter. His resolution strong in his mind, he turned and walked back toward the bedroom.

AT 3:00 A.M. TRACKER glanced at his watch, then aimed a murderous glance through the crack in the closet door. His back was killing him and he wasn't sure if his legs would ever unbend again. If looks could have maimed or killed, the woman sitting at the desk would have died a very painful death several hours ago.

He'd waited until after eleven to break in. By that time, all the lights had been turned out except the ones illuminating the walkways between the cabins. He'd no sooner let himself into the office than he'd heard the key turn in the outer door.

The closet had been his home ever since.

The sudden whir of the computer told him that the blond amazon might have finally finished her nocturnal bookkeeping. He would have put her out of commission earlier, but Lucas's orders had been very clear. He didn't want any kind of disturbance at the spa that might alert Sophie to the fact that her big brother was keeping tabs on her.

The moment the computer stopped whirring, the blond amazon closed the ledger and put it in the top drawer. Tracker pinched himself just to make sure that he wasn't dreaming when she rose and moved toward the door of the office.

He waited two minutes before he crawled out of the closet. When it only took him another five to find what he was looking for, he swore softly beneath his breath. If he'd climbed out of that tree ten minutes earlier, he would have had the number of Sophie's cabin before that blond amazon had ever settled in for her nighttime rendezvous with the books, and wouldn't have wasted so much time.

Quickly he checked the number against the map on the wall and discovered that the cabin Sophie had been assigned to, number 58, was nearby. Perhaps his luck was about to change.

Once he let himself out of the building, he slid into the shadows offered by the trees and made his way to number 58. The kinks had just about worked themselves out of his legs when he reached it.

A light poured through one of the windows and pooled on the flower beds below.

Did anyone sleep normal hours around here?

Ducking low, Tracker moved quietly to the cabin. Then pressing his back against the logs, he rose slowly, inched his face closer to the window and risked a quick peek.

It was the bedroom window all right. A woman had propped herself up against a pillow to read. The good news was she hadn't seen him.

The bad news was that the woman wasn't Sophie.

Tracker ran through the evidence in his mind as he moved quietly to the front door of the cabin. It always paid to be thorough. The porch light confirmed that this was indeed Sophie's cabin. So he hadn't made a mistake. And the blond wig he'd spotted sitting on the dresser had been styled to resemble Sophie's hairdo.

There were times he hated it when his instincts were right. He let himself quietly into the cabin. The time for careful subterfuge was over. He intended to get some answers.

WHEN SHE DRIFTED UP through the layers of sleep in the early hours of the morning, Mac discovered she and Lucas were nestled in bed together like spoons. She felt his breath warm on her ear, his body even warmer along her backside. One of her feet was trapped between his legs, and he had one arm wrapped around her waist, the other hand planted firmly on her thigh. Just as if he wasn't planning on letting her go.

She didn't want to go anywhere.

She opened her eyes only a crack, only long enough to see that thin gray light was creeping into the room.

Closing them tightly again, she tried to recapture the dream she'd had—of Lucas slipping in beside her during the night and pulling her to him. He'd touched her so gently, loved her so softly, she'd known she was dreaming. His lovemaking had been nothing like the other times. There had been none of the desperation, none of the demand. She had never felt so cared for, so cherished. Each time she'd drifted close to the surface, he'd whispered to her to go back to sleep, to dream, to just feel how much he wanted her.

In the dream, Lucas had wanted *her,* not just the fantasies she'd conjured up for him. He'd wanted Mac. When he'd whispered that in her ear, the pleasure had streamed through her so sweetly, so deeply, that she'd shattered into a million pieces.

It had been the most wonderful dream she'd ever had. And as impossible as it was, she wanted it to go on and on. She wanted it to be true.

In the half light of dawn, still wrapped in his arms, she could admit that she'd fallen in love with Lucas Wainright. She'd known it with the same certainty she felt at times in the lab, just when an experiment was about to go right. If she wanted to be Dr. Lloyd and analyze it, all she had to do was remember her research. When admiration was mixed with physical attraction, the chances for combustion were greatly enhanced. Mix in liking and trust, and you might have the perfect formula for love.

Mac didn't need the analysis. She just knew it was

true. She never could have attempted what she had in that poolroom if she hadn't been doing it to Lucas.

She loved him.

Keeping her eyes tightly closed, she hugged the dream and the knowledge closer. As long as she did, she wouldn't have to allow the part of her that was Dr. Lloyd to spoil this moment by coming up with a tidy list of reasons why a future with Lucas Wainright was impossible. That would come soon enough. For now she'd let the Mac she was discovering inside of herself rule. Because Mac knew how to dream.

The first ring of the cell phone had her frowning and opening one eye. Sophie surely couldn't be calling her at this hour, not if she was bound and determined to avoid speaking to Lucas. In fact, Sophie didn't even get out of bed at this hour.

The second insistent ring had Lucas stirring behind her and another thought springing into her mind. What if Sophie was in trouble?

Mac struggled to free herself, but Lucas only tightened his grip.

"The phone," she said. "I have to answer it."

"Why?"

His voice was sleepy, but his body wasn't.

"It could be So—I mean, there could be a problem... at the lab." There. If it was Sophie, she could still pretend it was someone else.

The second Lucas relaxed his arms, she slid from the bed and raced to the dresser for her purse. Dumping the contents, she grabbed the cell phone.

"Just how often do you have trouble at your lab?" he asked, sounding more awake.

"There was only that once." She flipped open her phone. "Last weekend someone broke in. Hello."

The third ring sounded.

"It's mine," Lucas said.

It wasn't until she turned back to him that she realized she wasn't wearing any clothes. They were lying neatly folded next to the pants Lucas was lifting off a nearby chair. Mac couldn't remember taking hers off. In fact, the last thing she recalled was falling asleep in the taxi on their way back to the hotel.

She never slept in the nude. But she'd definitely been nude when she'd dreamed that Lucas had made love to her. Or had it been a dream?

"Yeah?" Lucas rubbed a hand over his face as he spoke into the phone. "No…okay." Dropping the phone to his side, he turned to her. "My security man has a rather lengthy report to make. I thought I saw the makings for coffee out at the bar. Do you think you could…?"

"Sure." She moved quickly to the chair, but before she could pick up her clothes, he handed her his shirt.

"I want to have coffee with Mac, not Dr. Lloyd."

He wanted to have coffee with Mac. Forgetting to slip into the shirt, she hugged the thought to her all the way to the door.

A SMILE CURVED his mouth as Lucas watched her walk out of the bedroom. He had to clamp down on the urge to follow her. Making love to her during the night had only whetted his appetite. He wanted more, and this time he wanted her wide awake and alert to every sensation when he was inside her. He wanted her to know exactly who it was who was touching her, tasting her, making her come.

He started toward the door. Hell, the coffee could wait. And so could Tracker's report. Lifting the phone to his ear, he said, "I'm going to have to get back to you."

"Sophie's not at the Serenity Spa."

Lucas stopped dead in his tracks. "You're sure."

"I've spent the past two hours confirming it. Once I found an impostor in her cabin, I decided the time for disguise was over. I even persuaded the amazon in charge of this place to let me check every single client at their morning yoga exercises."

As Tracker filled him in, Lucas paced the length of the bedroom and back. Fear flooded through him along with questions. He clamped down on both of them, concentrating on the facts that Tracker was feeding him.

"They switched at the airport in Charlotte?"

"According to the actress Sophie hired to impersonate her, they both went into stalls in the ladies' room where they donned wigs and changed clothes. Then they exited at different times."

"And it was shortly after that Sophie called me to let me know where she was, and I told you Mac was with me."

"Right. The actress in Sophie's cabin swears she knows nothing about where Sophie was going. I believe her mostly because I don't think Sophie would have told her. She planned this thing out pretty carefully. She wouldn't want us to be able to trace her easily. I've got men checking the flight manifests out of Charlotte right now. So far, they haven't come up with anything."

"Falcone's got her."

"We don't know that."

"I know it. That's what the phone call was about. He told me he had something that would make me reconsider. He was talking about Sophie."

There was a pause before Tracker replied, "He won't hurt her. He wouldn't dare."

The fact that Tracker wasn't arguing with him sharpened the fear in his stomach. He had to believe Falcone wouldn't hurt Sophie. Turning, Lucas paced the length of the room again. He had to keep telling himself that. More than that, he had to think, to plan.

As he strode by the dresser, his gaze fell on the stuff Mac had dumped out of her purse. In addition to the cell phone, which matched the same pearl color of his sister's, a wallet, a small plastic makeup case and loose change littered the top of the dresser.

"My office is checking the flight manifests out of Charlotte. So far they haven't found any record of a Sophie Wainright flying out."

"Maybe she used another name," Lucas said.

"Easier said than done. With the new security, she'd need a pretty accurate picture ID. And I already checked. She flew into Charlotte on a round-trip ticket under her own name."

"Maybe the actress used that ticket." Turning suddenly, Lucas walked back to the dresser and stared down at the cell phone. The evidence was right there.

Dr. Lloyd wouldn't have loose change lying in the bottom of her purse. Nor could he imagine her having a pearl-colored phone. Hers would be black, practical. He pictured Mac as she'd stepped off the plane. She'd taken off the blond wig, but if she'd been wearing it, she would have looked a lot like Sophie.

The sharp, jagged fear that had been slicing through him suddenly turned cold and hard. He knew even before he opened the wallet what he would find.

Sophie's picture on the driver's license stared up at him.

"Sophie used Dr. Lloyd's ID," Lucas said. He could feel the fury beginning to bubble up, but he clamped down on it tightly.

"Dammit," Tracker said. "I should have thought of that.

The two of them must have switched everything before they left Sophie's shop."

"Yeah," he murmured. "I should have figured it too."

With one part of his mind, he listened to Tracker outline what he was going to do. But another part of his mind was sifting through everything that the doc had done in the past twenty hours. Images and sensations swirled through him.

Nothing could have been calculated to keep him more distracted. Hell, he hadn't been thinking straight since he'd seen her step off that plane.

Had it been all her idea—or was she merely following a scenario that his sister had mapped out? Pain sliced through him, deep and sharp. Suddenly he recalled Mac's initial reaction when the ringing of the cell phone had wakened him.

It could be So—

She'd expected it to be Sophie.

"Does the doc know where your sister is?" Tracker asked.

"I'm going to find that out right now."

CHAPTER FOURTEEN

LUCAS FOUND HER on the balcony standing in the same spot where he'd realized that he wanted her in his life.

He shoved the thought out of his mind. But it wasn't so easy to shove the woman out, or the feelings coursing through him. It hurt to look at her. Pain shimmered inside him, fueled by the fact that he still wanted her. He took a step toward her, and when she turned, for one second he allowed himself to absorb the look on her face.

Then he reminded himself that it was a lie. She was a lie.

"Where's Sophie?" he asked.

"At the spa. In North Carolina."

"No, she's not. She never went there."

He watched each and every emotion flicker over her face—surprise, confusion and a trace of concern. She was good.

"I don't understand. She told me she was there."

He held out the wallet then in the palm of his hand. "You've got her wallet, her driver's license. Does she have yours?"

"Yes. We switched by accident in her shop."

"By accident? And was it an accident that she hired an actress to impersonate her at the spa?"

She stared a him. "An actress? What are you—"

"Let me spell it out for you, Dr. Lloyd. My sister was very angry with me, so she decided to teach me a little lesson. I'm sure she shared all this with you. She hired someone to take her place at a spa. Then she got you to fly down here in her place and distract me so that she could disappear. You tell me she's at the spa. She calls me and pretends she's there. If I call there, they tell me she's all checked in, and as far as they're concerned, she is. Still, I might have checked further, but she told me you have a problem you wanted to discuss and asked me to help you out. I've got to hand it to the two of you—it was a brilliant plan to distract me."

Mac lifted a hand, then dropped it. "I know what it looks like, but I—I didn't know—I—"

He studied her as she spoke, but he couldn't trust himself to read her. She'd made him lose his objectivity, his control. She'd made him lose everything. "How many times has she gotten in touch with you since you got off my plane?"

"Two…no, three times."

"And she never once told you where she'd really gone?"

"She told me she was at the spa. She was happy there at first. Last night I thought she sounded a little restless and bored, but she denied it."

"And you expect me to believe that? You're not that good a liar, Dr. Lloyd."

He watched the hurt spring to her eyes and the color drain from her face. There was some satisfaction to be gained from that. It wasn't enough. "You played me, Doc." He took a step toward her then and watched her step back into the railing. The need boiled up within him to grab her and shake her hard, make her tell him the truth.

But there was fear too—that if he touched her even now, he wouldn't be able to let her go. Fisting his hands, he shoved them deep into his pockets.

"The two of you must have had a few good laughs at my expense. How long was the charade supposed to go on? And who dreamed up the little research project on sexual fantasies?"

She flinched at each of his questions as if he'd slapped her, and he felt disgust roll through him. Struggling for control, he turned away from her. He had to focus on the fact that all signs pointed against her. Drawing in a deep breath, he said, "Look, I'm begging you to just tell me where she is. I wanted her down here in the Keys with me for a reason. I've made an enemy in the last week. She could be in danger."

"I'd tell you if I knew. She told me she was at the spa."

He whirled on her then. "Then why did you agree to the switch in identities?"

"I didn't. We took each other's purses by accident when we put the wigs on in her shop."

"And the wigs were for…?"

She raised her hands and dropped them. "The fantasies."

"Of course. Well, I have to hand it to you. They were very good. Just one question, Doc. Is there anything about you that's real?"

She didn't answer. But he heard the sharp catch in her breath, saw the tears, just a flash of them, before she lowered her eyes. They only seemed to increase the hurt that threatened to consume him. Digging deep within himself, he struggled to rebuild the shield that for so many years had protected him. "One last time. If you know where my sister is, tell me."

She didn't look up but merely shook her head.

He moved to the glass doors, turning back only when

he'd stepped through them. "Congratulations, Doc. You led me right down the garden path."

Never again. He didn't say the words aloud, but they drummed in his mind as he walked away.

GRABBING HER CLOTHES out of the closet, Mac stuffed them into her suitcase, hangers and all. She had to get out of the suite, out of the hotel. Once she did, she could stop thinking about Lucas. Then she'd be fine.

In the bathroom, she swept everything on the vanity into her cosmetics bag. A plastic bottle of shampoo hit the floor and bounced. Bending over, she scooped it up, but it slipped out of her hand and bounced off the floor again, this time onto her foot. A kick sent it sailing into the wall, and this time it boomeranged back into her leg.

Taking a deep breath, she made herself stand perfectly still. This wasn't like her at all. She usually packed meticulously. And she'd never before had a fight with a shampoo bottle.

Turning, she held tightly to the edge of the vanity. She had to get a grip. She made herself look in the mirror. The dark circles under her eyes didn't surprise her, but the tears stunned her. She couldn't remember the last time she'd cried. Dr. MacKenzie Lloyd never cried. Evidently, Mac did.

Who was she?

Before she'd met Lucas, she thought she'd known the answer. She was a research scientist who had a job she liked and whose work was going well. The only thing that had been lacking in her life had been a family of her own.

She'd taken the first step toward solving that problem just the way she would have approached a problem in the lab. It had seemed so logical, so simple. Maybe Dr. Lloyd's plan would have worked, if it hadn't been for Mac.

Sinking onto the toilet seat, she buried her face in her hands. She just needed to get back to D.C. She still had her work. She could go to her lab and bury herself in it. With time she would forget Lucas Wainright. And the way he'd looked at her before he'd left the suite.

He had every right to be furious with her. She'd deceived him. And she could never forgive herself if she'd put Sophie in any kind of danger. It might have been Sophie's suggestion that she fly down to the Keys in a disguise, but she'd gone along with it easily enough. She could see now that it was Mac who'd gone along with it because she'd wanted to try out her research on Lucas. Had she loved him even then?

No, she wouldn't let herself think about it. Turning, she walked into the bedroom. She was going to pack and get out of this room that smelled like him.

The chimes rang just as she was jamming her cosmetics bag into the suitcase. One thought filled her mind as she raced to the door. Lucas.

But it was the manager who'd gotten the chair for her in the lobby, and he was shaking his head at her. "Mrs. Wainright, you really shouldn't open your door without ascertaining who's there."

"I thought it might be Mr. Wainright."

He smiled at her. "That's why I'm here. Mr. Wainright spoke with me before he left. He told me to tell you that the staff has instructions to make your stay, for however long you wish to remain, as pleasant as possible."

Mac blinked back the sting of new tears. Lucas was furious with her, and yet he'd taken the time to make sure the hotel would take care of her.

"Is there anything I can do for you right now?"

"Yes," Mac said. "I'd like you to make a plane reservation for me back to D.C."

"Oh. Well, of course. Although we'd much prefer that you stay, I'd be happy to take care of that. If you'll just give me your first initial, Mrs. Wainright? They'll want to know for the reservation."

For just a moment, Mac hesitated. Then she said, "S. For Sophie." If she had to fly in a commercial plane, she would have to present a picture ID to get on the flight. She'd just have to use Sophie's, and she'd have to wear the blond wig so she'd look like Sophie's picture.

"I'll see to it right away."

She was closing the door to the suite when it struck her. Had Sophie used her ID in the same way?

Leaning back against the door, she forced herself to think. It had been fun buying the wigs and then putting them on in the back room of Sophie's shop. But what if it had been more than just a lark for Sophie? Was it possible that she *had* switched the purses on purpose?

Thinking back, Mac tried to recall Sophie's exact words in the tree house. *The next time I find a man I like, I'm going to make sure he doesn't know I'm Sophie Wainright.*

It had been Sophie's idea to buy the wigs and the matching purses and raincoats. She'd blamed it on the fact that Lucas was having her followed, and that she desperately needed a break. What if her plan all along had been to go somewhere and actually pretend to be someone else? *Like MacKenzie Lloyd.*

Mac strode down the hall to get her bag. The sooner she got to D.C., the sooner she would be able to figure out where Sophie had gone.

"REPORT." Vincent Falcone gestured his son into a chair on the other side of his desk. In his hand, he held a glass of Falcone Vineyards 1998 Cabernet Franc. Currently it was his favorite vintage, and it would only improve with age. Beyond the glass that walled his office on two sides, grapevines marched in neat little rows until they began to climb the hills in the distance.

"A crew will be here shortly after three on Saturday to inflate the hot-air balloons. They can take any of our guests up until sunset."

Vincent lifted his glass of wine and watched the play of light in its depths. Sonny had purchased four hot-air balloons just last week. Offering free rides would draw crowds to the vineyards and sell more wine, Sonny had said in defense of his expenditure.

"And about the other business?" Vincent asked.

"Everything's going as planned."

"You have a signed contract?"

Sonny shifted in his chair. "I will by Saturday."

"You said you'd have it last week."

"I know, but there's been a little delay."

"In business, delays can be fatal."

"I have a man on the inside who assures me that I will have the contract by Saturday."

Vincent said nothing.

Sonny shifted again in his chair. "I am perfectly capable of running Lansing Biotech. I know you don't trust me. But I've got everything under control."

His son was lying. Worse than that, he was a fool. Vincent took a sip of his wine and let the flavors linger on his tongue. There were fools in every family, almost as if the stronger genes that ran in a bloodline had to take a break before they could appear again.

In the Wainright family, the weak genes had made their appearance in Lucas's father. It was too bad that Lucas hadn't inherited more of those weaknesses and fewer of his grandfather's strengths.

But in the end, it wouldn't make any difference. Vincent was not going to allow his business connection with Wainright Enterprises to be severed. That was why he'd arranged for Lucas's sister and Sonny to meet in Georgetown.

And that was why he'd held his tongue about the balloons when he'd learned that they were part of Sonny's campaign to impress Sophie Wainright. Vincent could picture her now, riding in one of them with Sonny just as Lucas arrived at the party. A picture was often worth a thousand words.

"Why don't you bring Sophie here for dinner tonight?" he said as he lifted his glass to his lips and took another sip.

"She's busy. She has to make a presentation tomorrow."

"A presentation? I thought she flew out here specifically to see you."

Sonny frowned. "She did. But...she hasn't yet admitted to me that she's really Sophie Wainright. She's still pretending to be this Susan Walker person. I thought of telling her today that I'm aware of the masquerade."

Vincent shook his head. "Best to wait until she tells you." And the fact that she hadn't told him wasn't a good sign. Sonny had always had a way with women, so bringing the two of them together had been worth a shot.

Setting his glass down on his desk, he said, "You'd better go work on that contract."

He waited for his son to leave the office before he sighed.

It was a damn good thing he had a backup plan to handle Lucas Wainright.

HOME. It was the foremost thought in Mac's mind as she paid the taxi driver and climbed the porch steps of her duplex. She knew where Sophie was, and she was safe. Just as soon as she got inside, she would face the task of calling Lucas's office to let him know. He wouldn't take the call though. She'd convinced herself of that. He wouldn't want to speak with her ever again, so she wouldn't have to hear his voice. All she'd have to do was leave the information with his secretary.

Setting her bag down, she fished in her purse for her keys. All she'd had to do was call the 800 number on her credit card and ask for the latest posted charges. It was all there—an airline ticket to San Francisco and another charge to the Châfateau Mirabeau in the Napa Valley. Sophie hadn't answered the phone when she'd called, but the desk clerk had promised to give her the message.

She swept her hand one last time across the bottom of her purse. Where were her keys? Then it hit her. She didn't have them because Sophie had her purse. Moving quickly to her neighbor's door, she knocked but without much hope. The stockbroker who shared the Georgetown duplex with her wasn't likely to be home from the office yet.

After a few moments, she dropped her bag on the porch and hurried around the side of the house. She was going to have to break in, and one of the basement windows was her best bet. Dropping to her knees, she picked up a good-size rock. Then, just to make sure, she leaned close and peered through the glass. The latch was secure.

"Ma'am?"

Startled, Mac whirled to face the man standing directly behind her. "Who are you?"

"Detective Ramsey, District of Columbia Police Department." He showed her the badge he'd removed from his pocket. "Now, why don't you tell me who you are?"

"I'm MacKenzie Lloyd. I live here."

"And the rock in your hand is for…?"

Mac quickly put the rock down on the ground. "I don't have my key, and my neighbor isn't home to give me the spare."

The detective studied her for a moment. "You have some ID?"

"Yes." She was reaching into her purse when she realized that she didn't. "No. My friend and I switched purses. Her name is Sophie Wainright and I have her ID." She handed the detective her wallet.

After glancing through it briefly, he said, "According to the security people at the university, MacKenzie Lloyd has red hair. Yours is blond."

Mac lifted off the wig. "I had to wear it so that I could get on the plane. All I had was Sophie's ID." Running her hands through her hair, she glanced up at him. "Isn't this where you advise me that I have the right to remain silent?"

Fishing a photo out of his pocket, he glanced at it, then at her. "I don't think that will be necessary. You look a lot like the picture I have of Dr. Lloyd. We've been trying very hard to get ahold of you, Doctor. Don't you ever answer your cell phone?"

"Yes, of course." She pulled it out of her bag and then stared at it. It just hadn't been her cell phone she'd been answering. "My friend has mine."

Detective Ramsey nodded. "Well, she's not answering it either. Where have you been, Dr. Lloyd?"

"I took a few days off and went down to the Florida Keys."

He nodded. "That fits with what the university told us. But they were worried when they couldn't get hold of you. I have some bad news for you. Sometime on Wednesday, your apartment was broken into. One of your neighbors called it in, and then tried to reach you at the university. Somebody high up at the college is very concerned about you and your research and they called us. They think the break-in here and the one at the university are related. They also said you'd planned to take a few days off, but no one at the lab, not even your colleague Dr. Stafford, knew where you were. The timing of this break-in made them worry that perhaps...you hadn't gone away voluntarily."

Mac's eyes widened. "They thought I was kidnapped?"

"They wanted to file a missing persons report. Officially, we can't let anyone do that for forty-eight hours. In the meantime, the commissioner assigned me to keep an eye on your place. A lot of people are going to be relieved that you're back."

Mac stared at him. "I just went to the Florida Keys for a little...vacation. I'm fine."

"Well, the bad news is your apartment isn't. Whoever broke in was looking for something and they were pretty thorough. If you feel up to it, I'd like you to take a look and tell me what's missing, or what they might have been after."

"Of course." She could hardly refuse. But she wanted to. During the short time it took the detective to lead her back to the front porch and open the door, she tried to prepare, to steel herself for the sight. She still remembered what it had felt like when she'd first learned about the break-in at the lab. Her head pounded, her stomach clutched at the memory. This would be easier, she told herself as Ramsey led her inside.

It wasn't. The place was in a shambles—sofas and chairs overturned, lamps shattered, pictures torn out of their frames. In the kitchen, the cupboards and even the refrigerator had been emptied. Shards of glass and china lay over everything.

Drawing in a deep breath, she tried to reach for control. Lucas had weakened it, but it still had to be there. If she could just reach deep enough.

"Is there any way to tell if they found your research?"

Mac shook her head. "It's not here. Why would they do this?"

"They were angry," Detective Ramsey said. "Probably because they couldn't find what they were after."

"All they did at the lab was break into the safe and search through my file drawers."

"There are some very influential people at the university who think they might have been after more than the formulas here," Ramsey said as he led her back out to the porch.

"What then?"

"According to the university security people, you usually work in your lab on Sundays. The Sunday of the break-in, you didn't. Then you should have been home on Wednesday. Your voice mail on campus was letting all callers know that's where you were."

Mac drew in another breath. "What exactly are you saying, Detective?"

"It's possible that whoever did this to your lab and your apartment might have been looking for you. When you weren't here, they got upset and trashed the place."

She didn't want to believe it, not for a moment.

Then she thought of Sophie who'd been using

MacKenzie Lloyd's name and traveling with her ID. And it was Sophie who'd disappeared. If there was any chance that what Ramsey was saying was true, she'd just learned how easy it was to find out where MacKenzie Lloyd was staying.

"Detective, if you're right, there's someone I have to get in touch with right away."

CHAPTER FIFTEEN

SOPHIE DRIFTED in that gray world, halfway between wakefulness and sleep. Once or twice, she'd nearly reached consciousness only to slip back under. But gradually, moment by moment, awareness was creeping in. The throbbing in her head grew more intense. As did the light, growing steadily brighter beyond her eyelids. And she was lying on a rock—a hard and lumpy one.

It was only when she tried to shift to a more comfortable position that she realized she couldn't move her arms or legs. A quick spurt of alarm shot through her.

It had to be a dream. That had to be why she felt paralyzed. Clinging hard to consciousness, she struggled to wake up.

The memories came then—in bits and pieces. California, that's where she was. And Sonny... As his face appeared in her mind, she tried to focus. She'd come to California to see him...to teach Lucas and his security chief a lesson. The flash of satisfaction was short-lived, erased by a wave of fear.

She couldn't move her hands and feet because they were bound. She couldn't see or move her lips. They were covered by something. What? How? Why?

Even as the questions poured into her mind, she turned over to one side and ran into a solid wall. A quick, panicked roll in the other direction led her smack into another wall.

Where was she?

This time she took her time, but she reached the opposite wall in three rolls. A small room. A cell? She fought against the fear even as it clawed its way to her throat. Breathe, she told herself. The air was fresh, warm. There had to be an open window nearby. Drawing in another breath, she felt the sharpness of her fear fading. And her mind was clearing.

Think, she told herself. She was in California—where?

And then she remembered—running into Sonny, slipping out of the restaurant, the sharp sting in her arm.

Someone had drugged her. Who?

"You gave her too much of that stuff, I tell you."

The voice came from close by. Acting purely on instinct, Sophie curled into her original position.

"You wanted it quick and clean. You got exactly what you asked for."

"The boss wants to talk to her."

There was a sound nearby, and Sophie could have sworn that the floor she was lying on shook as if someone had jumped on it.

"Relax. She's probably coming around right now."

The voice came from over her head, then the same noise she'd heard before, and the floor shook again. She braced herself. If they wanted her to come around, it was the last thing she was going to do.

"She's still out. She hasn't moved since the last time we checked her."

"Let's just see."

She had just enough time to steel herself before she felt the sharp slap on her cheek.

"I told you. You gave her too much."

Fingers gripped her pulse. "If you don't shut up I'll give you a dose."

"It's not me you have to worry about. He's not going to tolerate any more mistakes."

"Will you relax?" The voice sharpened even as her wrist was freed. "Her pulse is steady. She's fine. Besides, he won't be out here to see her until tomorrow."

"I don't like it."

Sophie barely let herself breathe until she was sure the two men had gone. Wherever she was, it was a place the men had entered from above. There had been no sound of a door.

Was she on some sort of truck bed?

And who wanted to see her? Sonny? Had he recognized her in the bar after all?

But that didn't make any sense. Why would Sonny Falcone kidnap her? The motive for that was money. And he didn't even know who she really was.

When the headache behind her eyes began to throb, Sophie pushed the questions aside. The answers wouldn't get her out of her present predicament. Rolling over, she drew her legs up until she could touch her ankles.

Tape. That's what was binding her legs and hands. Moving to the wall, she wiggled and pushed herself into a sitting position. The first thing she was going to do was see if she could find anything to cut herself loose.

LUCAS PACED back and forth in his office listening to Tracker's report over his cell phone. They'd been in constant contact all day.

"So you're telling me that you know where Sophie is staying but she's disappeared?"

"What I'm saying is that she's not here right now. Last Wednesday, she registered as MacKenzie Lloyd at the Châfateau Mirabeau in the Napa Valley. I've questioned nearly everyone who works here. The clerk says that she went out last night. No one has seen her this morning and the maid claims her bed hasn't been slept in."

"Have you notified the police?"

"No. I don't think we should do that just yet. We may be overreacting."

Lucas began to pace again. "My sister has been missing all night and you think we're overreacting if we notify the police?"

"Just hear me out. The tail that I had on Sonny Falcone says that a blond woman matching Sophie's description had lunch with him on Thursday."

"Are you suggesting that she may have flown out there on purpose just to be with Sonny, and she may be with him now?"

"I'm not liking it, but that's what I'm saying. You told me yourself that she doesn't know anything about what goes on at Wainright. She wouldn't even know the name Falcone, let alone about Vincent's other less legitimate business dealings. And Sonny has a reputation for being a real ladies' man."

Lucas stopped pacing in front of his window. The heat of the day still clung in a misty shroud around the Washington Monument. For the first time in his life he questioned his decision to keep his family isolated from all the problems at Wainright Enterprises.

Maybe Tracker was right and he was overreacting. He'd been letting fear and anger cloud his mind ever since he'd realized Sophie was missing. He had to start thinking clearly if he was going to help his sister. More than that, he had to stop thinking about Mac. He was hundreds of miles away, and he still couldn't get her out of his mind.

"Boss, you still there?"

"Yeah. I don't like what you're saying, but you may be right."

"I don't like it myself, but I want to check it out. I have someone finding out whether or not she stayed at Falcone's villa last night. It will take a little time, but I should know something soon. In the meantime, I'm going to personally check out the list of places that the concierge recommended to Sophie last night. Have you heard anything from Vincent Falcone yet?"

"No."

"For what it's worth, I don't think he had anything to do with your sister's disappearance. I know you don't trust him, but think about it. If he wants to reestablish a business connection with you, kidnapping your sister is not his best move."

Lucas sat on the edge of his desk. "He might be planning to use her as a pawn to blackmail me into investing with him again."

"Thought of that. But you always said he's a shrewd businessman. After threatening your sister, he'd have to figure it wouldn't be long before you got your revenge."

Everything Tracker was saying made sense. As much as he didn't like it, he'd much rather imagine his sister dating Sonny Falcone than being at the mercy of Sonny's father.

"If Falcone is aware that Sonny and Sophie are an item, that could be the reason he told you that his connection with Wainright Enterprises isn't finished yet. That could also be the reason he's invited you out to his vineyard. Dr. Lloyd's pretty smart, and she knows Sophie. Why don't you run my theory by her and see what she thinks?"

"She's not here. I didn't bring her back to D.C."

Tracker didn't reply.

Restless, Lucas began to pace again, until he caught himself. He never paced. Since MacKenzie Lloyd had come into his life, he'd done a lot of things he'd never done before.

"Aren't you going to ask me why I left her there?"

"None of my business."

"She lied to me." Lucas listened to the words as they hung on the air. He'd needed to say them out loud. But they didn't ease the hurt. They only made it grow.

"Women are known for that. Pretending they want one thing when they're really after something else. The best way to handle that problem is to nip the relationship in the bud."

"Exactly."

"No offense, but I think your sister wins the prize when it comes to lies. If I'm right about what's going on, that is."

"Yeah." Lucas rubbed his free hand over his face. How long was it going to be before he could get rid of the image of Mac standing there on the balcony as he left their suite? The whole time he'd packed his things, she'd just remained at the railing, staring out to sea. "Do you have a contact in Key West, someone who could check on her and see that she's all right?"

"Dr. Lloyd? Sure thing, boss. I'll get right on it."

Tracker had no sooner cut the connection when the intercom on his desk buzzed.

Lucas pressed a button. "Yes?"

"There's someone— Miss, you can't go in there."

The door to the office opened, and Lucas started forward the moment he saw his sister framed there.

"Sophie—" He stopped short the moment she pulled off the wig.

It was Mac. No, he corrected himself again. It wasn't Mac either. It was the doc. She was wearing her hair pulled back and she was dressed in jeans and a T-shirt. And she looked vulnerable. He took a step toward her before he stopped, reminding himself that he couldn't trust anything he thought or felt about her.

"Mr. Wainright?"

It was only then that he noticed the man standing behind her.

"Who are you?" he asked.

"I'm Detective Ramsey."

Lucas glanced at the badge the man produced.

"I just want to make sure that Dr. Lloyd is in good hands. She can't stay at her apartment tonight, and she shouldn't be alone."

Just seeing Mac had so many feelings tumbling through him. Guilt, desire, bitterness. He tried to hold on to the last one.

"I'm sorry about the wig," she said. "I had to wear it on the plane, and I just forgot to take it off."

"Why are you here?" he asked as he took another step forward. For a moment he thought she would turn and run, but she held her ground.

He knew in that moment that he might not have let her run.

"I may know where Sophie is staying. Or was staying. And she may be in danger."

CHAPTER SIXTEEN

TAKING A LONG SWALLOW of the water that Lucas had poured for her, Mac tried to focus her attention on Detective Ramsey as he summarized what they'd discussed at her apartment. It hadn't been until she'd said the words out loud to Lucas that the fear had struck her full force. Sophie might be in real danger because of her. Setting her water on a low table, she saw her hand was shaking and curled her fingers into a fist.

"So, you believe that there's someone so desperate to get control of Dr. Lloyd's research that they would kidnap her?" Lucas said.

"More importantly, there are some higher-ups at the university who believe it," Detective Ramsey said. "According to them, there are a lot of pharmaceutical and biotech companies who've been showing some interest and offering money. Greed is a big motivator when it comes to crime. And someone has enough power to get my bosses to pay attention. Otherwise, I wouldn't be here. My usual job is to investigate robberies, murders and rapes—crimes that have already happened. In D.C., we don't have much time or manpower for prevention. I came over here at Dr. Lloyd's insistence. She seems much more concerned about Miss Wainright's safety than about her own. She says that your sister has been traveling as MacKenzie Lloyd, using that ID instead of her own, and now she's missing. She's afraid that Ms. Wainright's disappearance might be related to the incidents at her lab and her home. How long has your sister been missing?"

The detective's words had a new wave of fear settling in Mac's throat. If she'd been thinking more clearly, she could have warned Lucas before he'd left Key West. She should have figured out what Sophie was doing earlier. Maybe she could have prevented this, if she hadn't been so distracted by Lucas.

Lucas showed no emotion on his face as he glanced at his watch. "Sophie's been missing a little less than twenty-four hours. My security people traced her the same way that Dr. Lloyd did. Sophie went out last night and didn't come back to her hotel room, but I have a man in California checking the restaurant that the concierge recommended to her. We think she may have met a man there, someone she flew out there to be with. There's a possibility that she may be with him."

"No," Mac said.

Both men turned to look at her.

"She's not with him. She'd decided she didn't like him after all. She was going to cut her trip short."

Ramsey turned to Lucas. "Could be she's on her way back then. Do you have a way to check that out?"

Lucas nodded. "I'll have my security people check the flights out of San Francisco."

"Keep me posted. Here's my card. If you need me to contact the local law enforcement, just give me a call. I have to get back to the station." He met Lucas's eyes. "Now that I've warned Dr. Lloyd, there's not much else I can do."

Lucas nodded. "I'll take care of it."

As the two men moved toward the door of the office, Mac clasped her hands together in her lap. In a moment she'd be alone with Lucas. That had been the one thing she'd wanted to avoid. She could still leave. Even as the impulse moved through her to stand and run after Detective Ramsey, she heard the door click shut and her throat went dry. She was reaching for her glass when she saw the blond wig lying on the table where she'd tossed it. Quickly she dropped her hand to her side. If only she had refused to go along with Sophie's plan....

Rising, she steeled herself to meet Lucas's eyes, something she'd avoided since she'd first walked into the room. In that instant when she'd taken off the wig and he'd recognized her, she thought she'd seen...what? Relief? Pleasure? Or had it only been a fantasy, a projection of the feelings that had been running through her?

Pushing the hope down, she lifted her gaze to his...and saw nothing. His eyes were perfectly blank. She might have been a stranger he was meeting for the first time on the street. Drawing in a deep breath, she managed not to shiver. She told herself that she preferred blankness to the cold detachment she'd seen in the hotel room. "This is all my fault. All of it."

He took a step forward, then stopped. "Blame is beside the point right now, don't you think?" His tone was as neutral as his expression.

"Of course. Tell me what I can do."

"Do?" He took two more steps toward her and stopped again.

This close she could see that he wasn't as carefully controlled as she'd thought. For a moment the silence stretched between them, and her heart began to drum.

The ringing of the phone made them both start. Then Lucas moved to grab it.

"Yes, Ms. Burns?"

"Mr. Falcone on line two."

"Put him through."

"I HOPE YOUR FLIGHT from the Keys was uneventful, Lucas."

"To the point of being boring." Lucas was pleased to note that his voice was cool. Because he wasn't. He hadn't been since Mac had walked into the room. And it wasn't merely the news that his sister might have been kidnapped. Even now as he looked at Mac, she unlocked feelings in him that he couldn't seem to control. And what he'd feared most seemed to be true. In spite of everything, he still wanted her.

"You shouldn't have left your little playmate behind at the hotel. She could have amused you on the flight."

Fear was a copper taste in his mouth as several possibilities flooded his mind. He'd known that Falcone was monitoring his movements. How else would he have known to call him at the Wainright Casa Marina? And yet he'd left Mac there alone without any thought that Falcone might make a move on her. But she was here. She was safe even if it was no thanks to him.

Tearing his gaze away from Mac, he said, "I came to the same conclusion. That's why she's with me right now." Lucas sat on the edge of the desk and concentrated on relaxing every muscle in his body. He had to get some grip on his control or Falcone would believe he had the upper hand.

"Ah."

He hadn't known that, Lucas thought with some satisfaction.

"She seemed to be much different than your usual choice of companion. But I'm told she is very entertaining."

When his free hand tightened into a fist, Lucas relaxed it. "Surely you haven't called merely to comment on how I'm keeping myself entertained?"

Soft laughter rippled into his ear. "Of course not. I called to remind you of my party tomorrow at the vineyard. Bring your new little friend if you wish. For old times' sake, I'd like you to be there."

"The old times are over."

"Perhaps I can persuade you to create some new ones. Your sister has accepted my invitation."

"Sophie?" The surprise he heard in his voice was genuine. He hadn't expected Falcone to mention her. Had he already discovered that she was impersonating Mac? He felt the flutter of panic in his throat and swallowed it.

"She and Sonny have become very close over the past few weeks. He's persuaded her to come."

Falcone was choosing his words carefully. He was purposely creating the idea that his son and Sophie were intimate. Could Mac's theory be wrong? Was Tracker right and Sophie had merely spent the night with Sonny at the estate? Pushing the questions aside, Lucas concentrated on the one thing he could depend on. The old man wanted him frightened and angry. Therefore, he couldn't afford to be. "I'm sure you'll treat her as an honored guest. For old times' sake. Give Sophie my best."

There was a beat of silence, just long enough for Lucas to know he'd scored a point.

"There's another reason you should come. We have business to discuss."

Lucas waited a beat this time. "I don't think so."

"The pharmaceutical company you paid me off with, Lansing Biotech. We're about to get exclusive rights to some very promising research. You might be interested in buying back in. If not, I'll go directly to your board before the news hits the street."

Lucas said nothing, but his mind was racing. Lansing

Biotech. Why hadn't he put it together sooner? Lansing Biotech gave Vincent Falcone the perfect motive to kidnap MacKenzie Lloyd.

Falcone's laugh was softer than before. "I'll see you tomorrow at...three, shall we say? I have a special bottle of wine I want to share with you."

For a moment after he hung up the phone, Lucas turned this new information over in his mind.

"Is Sophie safe?"

He glanced up at Mac's question. She had to have guessed that he'd been talking about her to Falcone, but all he could see was concern for Sophie in her eyes. "I don't know. I think I know who's got her. As far as I can tell, he thinks he's got both of you. He's an enemy of mine, and he says Sophie's going to be at his party tomorrow, and he's about to get exclusive rights to some exciting new research. How many pharmaceutical companies have been wooing you to come with them?"

"Three. It all started after I published that article last month. My results are preliminary, as I told you. But the enzymes I'm using are having very promising effects on rats."

"What did you tell the companies?"

"That I wasn't interested. I was afraid that once I signed papers, they'd own me. That's why I prefer the university setting. There's much more freedom."

Lucas's eyebrows shot up. "Less money too."

She shrugged. "Money isn't everything."

"Did anyone give you a hard time when you refused to sign?"

"One of them was hard to discourage. My fault, really. I dated the representative a few times. I thought he might be interested in me until he made his pitch. He wanted me to sign a contract that would give his company exclusive rights to manufacture the results of my research. He told me that I wouldn't have to come to work for them, that I could stay at the university. He was very upset when I didn't sign."

"What was the name of the company?" he asked.

"Lansing Biotech."

"Bingo," Lucas said even as fear flooded through him, leaving a bitter taste in his mouth. "How long ago was it when you gave the rep his walking papers?"

"Just a few days before Sophie's birthday."

"That could explain why they went to plan B," he said. "They broke into your lab that Sunday, which means they're desperate to get your signature on that contract."

"But they must realize that if they kidnapped me and forced me to sign I could go to the police afterward, explain about the kidnapping and swear I signed the contract under duress."

Lucas nodded. "Sure, you could do that. But I'm betting that Falcone has covered his tracks well. And that company rep you dated may have a different story. You wouldn't have any proof about when you signed the papers, and your signature would be authentic. It would take the courts a while to settle it. And if I'm right about what Falcone is planning to do, he'll only need to produce your signature to convince my board to invest in his company before the stock goes up. He'll make sure Wainright Enterprises makes a killing before the legal battles start. And if he could get his hands on your research notes, he wouldn't really need you anymore."

"He won't get my research notes. They're safe. It's Sophie who's in trouble. What will happen when they find out she's not me?"

It was the question he hadn't wanted to ask himself.

Mac reached for his hands then. "We're going to find her before that happens."

The words, just the fact that she said them out loud, stilled the fear that had been ripping through him. Before he could prevent himself, he linked his fingers with hers. There was comfort there, he thought, a kind he'd never hoped to have. He couldn't afford to trust it any more than he could prevent himself from clinging to it—for just a moment. "Mac..."

The phone on his desk rang again. Releasing her hands, Lucas reached for it and heard Tracker's voice in his ear.

"I'm at the Side Street Grill, the restaurant the concierge recommended to Sophie. Sonny Falcone was here for a short time last night. The bartender doesn't recall anyone who fits Sophie's description, but he remembers a redhead—someone he'd never seen before—talking to Sonny. Next thing he knows, she's gone. Sonny hung around until the place closed down."

"Mac's here, and she says that Sophie told her she was bored with Sonny and planned on heading home." Quickly he summarized the rest of what he'd learned from Ramsey, Mac and his phone conversation with Vincent Falcone.

"Damn," Tracker said. "I'd like it a hell of a lot better if I knew who was who. You got any orders?"

"Any chance you could scout out Falcone's vineyard?"

"Can a duck swim? I was going to head out there anyway."

Lucas's lips curved slightly as he glanced at his watch. "I should be able to get there in five hours."

"What about Dr. Lloyd?"

Lucas glanced at Mac. "No. I'll make arrangements for her here. Just tell me who to call."

Lucas jotted down the instructions Tracker gave him, but he'd no sooner hung up when Mac said, "I'm going with you."

"It's not safe."

"You know who's got Sophie, don't you? Who is it?"

"I'm pretty sure it's an old enemy of mine by the name of Vincent Falcone. That's why I wanted Sophie with me down at my grandfather's cabin. I didn't foresee that he would go after you. I wasn't prepared for that at all." Lifting the phone, he punched in the numbers that Tracker had given him. "I'm going to leave you with someone who'll keep you safe."

"If I go with you, they'll know that they don't have the right person. They'll have to let her go."

Lucas frowned at her. "It's not that simple. Vincent Falcone is really after me. And I don't trust him." He filled her in on what Tracker had told him. "If he finds out that he's got the wrong woman, I don't think he'd hesitate to use Sophie to get what he wants."

"You still need me," Mac said. "He'll release her if I sign the papers he wants. I'll give him my research."

Lucas stared at her. "You can't do that. I couldn't allow it."

She moved to him then, until they were standing toe to toe. "You might be able to tell Sophie what to do, but not me. I can always do more research. I could never replace Sophie. If you don't take me with you, I'll go on my own."

Lucas studied her. She looked as fearless as he'd always imagined Joan of Arc would look as she was being led to the stake. And just as naive.

He didn't doubt for a minute that she would do what she said.

"If I agree to take you, there are some ground rules we'll have to set."

She leaned down to pick up her bag. "I can do rules. They're a scientist's way of life. Why don't we discuss them on the way?"

MAC LAY CURLED on the seat opposite him. As soon as his private plane had lifted into the air, she'd been out like a light.

Little wonder. Exhaustion bruised her eyes even in sleep. Sipping his wine, Lucas willed himself to relax. How much had either one of them slept in the past—what was it? Three days?

Was that all it had been? He felt as if he'd known her forever. Yet, as he watched her sleep, he wondered if he knew her at all.

Leaning back in his seat, he shifted his gaze out the small window at his elbow. Ever since they'd taken off from D.C., they'd been chasing the sunset. The light outside was soft and glowing. Focusing on it, he tried to think of other things. Tracker had called with information on the party, and the layout of Falcone's vineyard. They'd even mapped out a tentative plan for searching both the villa and the other buildings. But he didn't kid himself that Vincent Falcone wouldn't take excellent precautions. He might not even be keeping Sophie on the premises. They might not find her. He might not see her again.

Closing his eyes, he pressed two fingers against the bridge of his nose and dismissed the *might nots* from his mind. When he opened them, he found his gaze resting on Mac again, and he thought instead of another time he'd watched her sleep, little more than twelve hours ago. She'd been snuggled against him in bed, and he'd been making love to her, slowly, thoroughly. Even as he thought about it, an achy, edgy desire crawled through him anew.

That much hadn't changed. She'd looked fragile and defenseless then too. Someone a man should protect. And everything had been a lie.

Or had it?

Rising, he moved into the small galley and poured more wine into his glass. Ever since he'd learned about Sophie's deception, he'd convinced himself Mac had been playacting with him from start to finish. He'd told himself that nothing about her could be trusted. Nothing was real.

He'd been wrong. Her loyalty, her love for his sister was very real.

What else was? Turning, he moved back to settle himself in the seat opposite her.

Her dedication to her work. Her courage. She might think of herself as a coward, but she would risk her own safety, without a second thought, to save Sophie.

That was why he wasn't going to let her out of his sight until he'd settled things with Falcone. He couldn't forget the cold fear that had sliced through him when Falcone had revealed that he'd known Lucas had left Mac behind in Florida. What if Falcone had known she was MacKenzie Lloyd and gone after her then? He'd been careless about her safety. He couldn't forgive himself for that. And he wouldn't be careless again.

He lifted his glass of wine, then frowned and set it down. His determination to protect her wasn't the only reason he'd agreed to bring her along. He didn't like lies, and self-deception was the worst kind. He wanted Mac-Kenzie Lloyd. It was just that simple. Just that vital.

Sitting here watching her sleep was enough to have his blood nearly boiling. He wanted to know everything about her, to discover what made her tick. He wanted to touch her, to discover what pleased her, to watch her come alive when he was inside her again.

He wanted all of her.

If he could make love to her—just once again without any kind of pretense between them—maybe then he could get her out of his system.

And if he couldn't? He'd just have to face that when he got to it.

He moved to her then, lifting her into his arms and carrying her into the small bedroom at the back of the plane.

SHE SHOT FROM deep sleep to half sleep with a swiftness that had her mind and senses reeling. Blood heating, pulse racing, she was trapped in a place where all she could feel was Lucas—his body pressed tightly against hers at every possible contact point, his hands holding her wrists. And his mouth, insatiable and possessive, moved over hers, drawing everything from her.

Freeing one of her hands, she ran it over his shoulder, testing the hard muscles, craving the warm smooth skin beneath the shirt. Hers. The word brought pleasure and a hint of panic. He was only hers for as long as she could hold on to the dream.

"Wake up. All the way now."

The voice was soft, seductive. She struggled against it.

His teeth nipped at her bottom lip. "C'mon, Mac. Wake up for me."

It was the sound of her name that had her eyes snapping open. All she could see was him, his mouth only inches from hers, his eyes dark and so hot.

"What?" She struggled to think. "Where?"

"Shh." He brushed his lips against hers. "We're on my private plane. Remember?"

Memories flooded back. They were flying to California to find Sophie. She was in danger. Mac tried to move and found she couldn't. His body truly was pressed against hers at every possible contact point. It hadn't been a dream.

"I figure we must be about forty thousand feet over Kansas right now."

"Lucas." The word sounded breathless.

"Shh." He continued to nibble at her lips. "We have to be very quiet. I don't think you want my pilot to know what we're doing."

She felt the rush of heat flood her face, felt the warmth of his chuckle at her ear.

"You're blushing, Mac. Did I ever tell you how much it excites me when you blush?" He spoke the words against her skin as he traced kisses along her jaw, down her neck. "And I don't think that Sally the hooker or Fiona the mermaid are genetically capable of being embarrassed. What's your expert opinion on that?"

"Stop," she managed to say. "If this is your way of punishing me…"

"Uh-oh. Now the doc is back. I don't think she blushes either. She's always so busy analyzing or planning." When he scraped his teeth along her throat, she moaned.

"Still want me to stop?"

Even as she struggled to form the word, he shifted his weight. For one moment she felt cold, bereft. Then his hands freed the snap of her jeans, pulling and tugging them down her legs.

"Yes," she breathed as his clever fingers began to move up her inner thighs. "Oh, yes." She no longer knew what question she was answering.

Pushing aside her panties, he slipped one finger inside her. "I'll stop anytime you say."

"Yes. Don't…stop." Pleasure streaked through her as she arched into his hand.

"I'm getting mixed signals here. Why don't you open your eyes and tell me exactly what you want me to do next?"

She saw his face above hers, his eyes so hot that she was sure they alone were causing the flames within her. Drawing in a deep breath, she tried to bank the fire, tried to find some shred of control. "We were going to lay down some rules."

She saw his lips curve just before he lowered them to hers. "I'm following the ones you laid down before. It's my turn, my fantasy."

He *was* punishing her, Mac thought as he withdrew his fingers and then slipped them inside again. But the pleasure was exquisite, irresistible. She moaned again when he did something with his thumb, and his fingers moved deeper.

"I never did admit to you what my fantasy was," he murmured as he trailed kisses from her temple to her jaw. "My fantasy is just you and me, Mac. Just the two of us alone with nothing to do but pleasure each other."

She should be able to resist. But she couldn't prevent her arms from going around him. She knew he didn't mean it. He couldn't mean it, not when he'd been so angry with her. He was just trying to get even. Still, she threaded her fingers through his hair. She couldn't, she wouldn't, push him away when she might never have this chance again.

"Just enjoy." The rhythm of his fingers increased, and suddenly her body grew taut. She lifted her hips from the bed, reaching. Very slowly, he withdrew his fingers.

"Not yet," he whispered as he kissed her forehead, her eyelids, her chin.

"Please," she whispered, gripping his shoulders.

His thumb teased her again. "Look at me."

When she did, she saw the heat in his and the reflection of herself.

"Tell me that you want me."

He was giving her a choice. She could say no. In some part of her mind she knew that. Her eyes never wavered from his when she said, "I want you."

He made a place for himself between her legs. "Look at me, Mac. Say my name."

"Lucas."

Even then he didn't enter her, not all the way. Instead, he leaned down and pressed his mouth to hers. The tenderness of the kiss shuddered through her, melting her. She was trembling, but her eyes were open and on his when he finally pushed into her.

This was the way he'd imagined her. This was exactly how he wanted her—pliant and warm beneath him, her muscles limber. But he hadn't anticipated the sweetness of her surrender. He hadn't realized how the piercing pleasure of it would pull at his control. Would it always be this way?

The moment that he began to move, she moved with him, absorbing and matching each stroke. She was his. He tried to keep the pace slow and easy because he wanted to spin out the moment. He wanted to remember the way she looked, her cheeks flushed, her eyes dark with desire.

But each time he sank into her, he was losing a part of himself. He should have been able to slow down or pull back. All he could do was move faster. And still she moved with him. When she ran one possessive hand down his back, he knew he was lost.

"Come with me." His voice was raspy, raw as he increased his rhythm and they began to race together to the finish. He felt the climax move through her, then heard his name mingle with hers as he held her tight and surged within her.

FOR A WHILE, Mac let herself drift, absorbing the sensations. His head was still buried in her hair, her hand was still tangled in his. She could feel the rapid beat of his heart. Or was it her own?

She'd never been taken so completely by anyone. She'd never even imagined anything like it. In a minute she was sure she would start to form a list in her mind of all the reasons why she shouldn't have let Lucas Wainright seduce her.

Right now she didn't care. She didn't want to think, to analyze, to plan. Outside the window, the light had softened to a glow. Day was teetering on the brink of tumbling into night. And it would. No one could hold off tomorrow. All one could do was cling to the present.

A sudden, enormous thump shook the cabin.

Lucas raised his head. "What the...?"

The plane lurched suddenly and they tumbled off the narrow bed to the floor. Another lurch sent them rolling, and her head rapped smartly against the wall.

"Are you all right?" Lucas asked, holding tight as the plane banked sharply. This time he managed to keep them from rolling, but they still slid into the bed.

Mac made a strangled sound.

"You're hurt," he said.

"No."

When she lifted her head, he saw that her eyes were filled with laughter. She clamped a quick hand over her mouth and turned a giggle into a gurgle.

Relief nearly made him giddy.

"Sorry about that." Jill Roberts's voice poured out of the speaker. "The turbulence was a little rougher than predicted or I would have warned you. I hope you had your seat belts fastened."

"We're fine."

Mac buried her head against his chest to muffle a fresh wave of giggles.

"I'm climbing out of it now, but there may be a few more bumps. Keep your belts fastened."

"Thanks, Jill," Lucas said. The moment he heard the intercom click off, he gave Mac a shake. "You want to tell me what's so funny."

When she lifted her head, her hand was still clamped over her mouth. Lowering it, she took a deep breath, then paused to swallow a giggle. "I just remembered when we fell off the bed. Doing it on a plane—it's one of the top ten fantasies of men. They even have a club you can join. You must have heard of it."

"The mile-high club? I still don't see what's tickling your funny bone."

The plane banked again and they rolled into the wall so that he held her pinned against it as laughter moved through her.

"Some men even charter a plane so that they can join the club. My question is why? So they can roll around and nearly kill themselves?"

She had a point. He was willing to bet that they'd both have bruises. "On a commercial jet, there'd be the challenge, the added excitement of not getting caught. That seems to be a big factor in your research."

"Yeah, but it seems to me that the chances of coitus interruptus are greatly increased."

He laughed then and held her tight. "I don't think I'm

ever going to figure out how your mind works. But I'm going to try. How's this?" He shifted so that she was beneath him.

She read his intent immediately. "Stop."

"Just a little experiment, Doc. This is step number one," he murmured as he slipped into her.

"Ohhh."

The hitch in her breath sent the heat shooting through him. "Ready for step number two?"

"We shouldn't," she managed to say.

"I thought scientists always wanted to find out answers. Why is having sex at forty thousand feet one of the top ten fantasies? Wasn't that your question? Ahhh," he sighed as her sleek softness pulsed around him, pulling him deeper. "There you go, Doc. You're already ahead of me on step number two."

Her fingers pressed into his hips.

"And three," he murmured as he began to move.

CHAPTER SEVENTEEN

TRACKER MET THEM at a little all-night diner where the Golden Gate Bridge could just be seen glimmering in the distance.

"Dr. Lloyd, I presume," he said, shaking her hand with a perfectly straight face. But his eyes were filled with humor.

Mac decided she liked him on the spot. "And you, I'll bet, are the Shadow."

His eyebrows snapped together. "The what?"

"That's what Sophie calls you, because you're always slipping into them," she explained. "You frustrate her."

"Yeah, well I guess you could say that the feeling is mutual."

"But I think she admires you."

"That's mutual too."

Mac wasn't even aware that Tracker hadn't released her hand until Lucas took her arm and nudged her into a nearby booth.

"Were you followed?" Tracker asked as Lucas slid in beside her.

"No. We checked into the St. Francis, then slipped out by way of the delivery dock. We came the rest of the way on foot."

And her feet were still complaining, Mac thought, wincing. Not to mention her shins. They'd run up a very steep hill before they'd angled their way down again toward the water.

"What? You're not having fun yet?" Tracker winked at her.

Fun. It only took the mention of the word to have her thoughts flying back to the plane trip and what they'd done in the small bedroom at the back of the aircraft. Heat flooded her cheeks. She'd never thought that lovemaking could be fun. But it had been. Lucas had shown her that. When this was over, when they found Sophie and she went back to her work, she would still have that.

She risked giving Lucas a sideways glance and found that he was looking at her. He ran a finger down the side of her cheek before he shifted his gaze back to Tracker.

"You're awfully cheerful," Lucas said dryly.

"I could say the same about you. I guess we both got lucky after I talked to you last."

"You found out where Sophie is?"

"I hung around the Side Street Grill after I talked to the bartender. Couple of valets came on duty around six-thirty. One of them saw a woman pass out in the parking lot last night, just about the time the bartender says that the redhead disappeared. The kid says it was dark, and he didn't get a good look at the woman. He wouldn't have thought much about it. Figured she was drunk. But he had his eye on the car these two guys helped her into, thinking you never know when something could be not quite right. It was a silver RV and he gave me a detailed description of it, including its performance capabilities *and* a license-plate number. After a little research, guess who I found out it belongs to?"

"Falcone?" Lucas asked.

"Sonny."

"He stayed at the bar after she left."

Tracker nodded. "That gives him an alibi. Might have been a perfect plan if he hadn't used one of his family's cars to drive her off in."

"No one said he was Einstein."

"Can we go after her?" Mac asked.

"We will," Tracker assured her. And this time there wasn't a trace of laughter in his eyes. Then he shifted his gaze back to Lucas. "My question is who Sonny thought he was kidnapping? She was wearing a wig and using Mac's credit card last night. But she wasn't wearing any kind of disguise when she went out with Sonny in D.C. And my man definitely saw him eat lunch with a blonde on Thursday."

"Sophie might not have given him her real name," Mac said, and the two men turned to stare at her. "Last weekend, when we were talking in the tree house, she told me that she wasn't going to tell the next man she dated that she was Sophie Wainright. Her experience with Bradley Davis had really gotten her down. Then she got a call on her cell phone, and I had the feeling it was from someone she was already seeing. Could it have been Sonny?"

Lucas and Tracker exchanged glances.

"Could she have told this man that she was you?" Lucas asked.

Mac thought for a minute. "No, I don't think that Sophie would have done that. I mean, she might have pretended to be someone else. But I don't think…" She let the sentence trail off as she met Lucas's eyes. "But then I figured she was really at that spa. And I can't explain why she was wearing the wig and pretending to be me last night. I wish we'd never bought those foolish wigs. If we hadn't, none of this would have happened."

For a moment Lucas said nothing. He merely looked at her with an unreadable expression on his face.

"Look," Tracker said. "None of this makes sense right now. All we know for sure is that someone snatched Sophie out of that parking lot last night."

"Can't we go to the police with that much?" Mac asked.

"Right now it would be tricky," Tracker said. "Sonny stayed at the Side Street Grill until well after midnight. He can always claim that his RV was stolen."

"And while he's shielding himself behind his father's legal team, something could happen to Sophie," Lucas said. "You think she's on the estate?"

Tracker waited until the waitress, a woman named Leona, had slapped down mugs of coffee and taken their orders. The moment she waddled back to the kitchen, he pulled out a hand-drawn map and spread it on the table.

"I took a little tour of the Falcone Vineyards this afternoon, along with thirty or so other tourists. Of course, I kind of got lost. Falcone's security is pretty good, and they weren't happy when they caught up with me. Before they did, I found the silver RV safe and sound in the garage along with six other cars."

Pausing, he pointed to one of the boxes he'd drawn on the map. "This is the garage. The main house right next to it has three stories with decks on each level. There seem to be several guests staying there already and all have access to the cars."

"Do you think Sophie is being kept at the house?" Mac asked.

Tracker shrugged. "I'm not ruling it out, but it'd be tricky with all the people around. What if she cries for help?"

Mac found Lucas's hand and gripped it.

"The outbuildings where the actual wine is made are

nestled together over here." Tracker tapped a finger on the map closer to the highway.

"That's even riskier," Lucas said.

"Yeah." Tracker took a quick swallow of coffee. "Too many people in and out on the tours. But there are places they don't let the tourists into. The tents for the party this weekend are being built here." He moved his finger in a straight line to a point halfway between the winery and the main house. "There's going to be a lot of traffic to and from this point tomorrow and Sunday. But the house won't be open to the public, only to a few invited guests."

"And we'll be among them," Lucas said.

Both men stopped talking as the waitress placed heaping platters onto the table. Mac glanced down at the mountain of eggs, bacon and home fries and wondered where to begin. Lucas and Tracker reached simultaneously for the saltshaker. When their hands collided, Lucas settled for the pepper, and then they switched. Their movements were so smooth that Mac was sure they'd done this before. How similar they were, it occurred to her as she watched them sample their eggs, then reach for the ketchup.

"You've worked together before, haven't you?" she asked.

Both men shot her a look of surprise.

"How do you know that?" Tracker asked.

Mac shrugged. "You've shared meals before, and you can practically finish each other's sentences."

Lucas looked at Tracker. "The doc has a sharp, analytical mind."

"Welcome aboard, Dr. Lloyd," Tracker said as he poured more salt on his home fries. "We're going to need all the help we can get."

They even looked alike, she thought as she watched them attack the mountain of food. Each had the dark good looks of a Brontâue hero. Tracker's edges were rugged, Lucas's more polished. But both had a capacity for stillness, and both of them exuded that hint of danger. In Lucas, that threat of danger might be hidden under a more civilized veneer, but it was there, and it had never been more apparent than now when she saw him with Tracker.

Lucas Wainright certainly didn't fit the profile of the man she'd thought she would fall in love with. She should be afraid of him, but she wasn't. Perhaps because he had that other side too—that streak of boyish mischief that lay hidden beneath the surface. It was something that he didn't share very often. She was sure he shared it with his friend Tracker. And he'd shared it with her. In spite of his harsh words, he must still trust her a little. She hugged the knowledge to her.

Tracker shoveled in a final mouthful of scrambled eggs, chewed and swallowed. "I'm betting that Sophie's somewhere on the estate. There are apartments over the garage that I didn't get a chance to check. Falcone's security is top of the line. Electronic surveillance as well as human. The two who helped Sophie into the RV were probably part of his crew."

"It might help if we knew who they thought they snatched in the parking lot last night," Lucas said.

"Tell me about it," Tracker said.

"The D.C. police think that there have been two attempts to snatch Mac here because of her research. So it's probable that whoever took Sophie last night thinks they have Mac. When she wasn't in her apartment on Thursday morning, they could have traced her eventually the same way we did."

"Yeah. And they have every right to think they have Dr. Lloyd," Tracker pointed out. "Sophie was registered as the doc and she was dressed up impersonating the doc. Plus she was using the doc's credit card at the bar."

"But if Sonny dated Sophie in D.C., he might have seen through her disguise last night," Mac said. "In those wigs, we do look a lot alike. But if I was wearing the blond wig right now, you'd still know it was me."

Lucas turned to her. "What are you saying?"

"Only that if Sonny thought he was dating me and had an inside track to my research, and he suddenly found out that Sophie wasn't me…"

"He could have snatched her in the heat of the moment, so to speak, and he could be using her as a pawn," Tracker said. "She's got a point."

"Looking at it objectively as possible, there's only one fact we can be sure of. Sophie was taken last night in that silver van," Mac said. "The rest is just theory. We won't know if it's true until we test it. Therefore, it's only logical that you take me along to the party because that will give you so much more flexibility in solving the problem. If I have to, I can sign papers on the spot, give them what they want, and we can walk out of there with Sophie."

Lucas stared at her. "But you don't want to sign those papers."

She met his gaze steadily. "Sophie wouldn't be in this situation if it weren't for me. Everything you said to me in Florida was true. I did lie to you. I didn't tell you the whole truth. If I had, she wouldn't be where she is right now."

"Mac—" Lucas began.

"She's my best friend and I love her."

There was a beat of silence. Mac thought she saw something in his eyes, but then it was gone.

"You can't fault her logic," Tracker said.

"Thank you." Mac sent him a crooked smile.

"Anytime," Tracker said. "You gonna finish your home fries?"

Mac pushed her plate toward him.

"You hardly ate anything," Lucas said with a frown.

"I ate a lot," Mac said. "I knocked at least two inches off the top of this mountain."

"No bickering, kids," Tracker managed to say around a mouthful. "Whoever they think they've got, the way I see it, our job is to get in there and get her out."

"The question is how to do that," Lucas said.

Tracker sighed. "You always ask the tough questions."

"There ought to be a lot of confusion when I show up as the real Dr. MacKenzie Lloyd."

"No." Tracker and Lucas spoke in unison.

"You can make your move then, while I'm distracting them," Mac insisted.

"You can't show up as yourself. It's too risky. And it could put Sophie in even more danger," Lucas said.

"Then I'll come as Sally."

"Sally?"

"Sally made quite an impression on the staff at the Wainright Casa Marina. Lucas even introduced me as his wife," Mac said. "I bet Mr. Falcone won't be surprised if you bring me. And I can help."

"She could be right," Tracker said.

Lucas hesitated for a moment, then said, "We'll have to lay down some ground rules."

CHAPTER EIGHTEEN

IT WAS NEARLY DAWN when Lucas rose and slipped from the bed. Moving quietly, he went into the living room of the suite at the St. Francis. Through the wide expanse of window, he could see the lights winking on the Golden Gate Bridge.

A quick glance at his watch told him that it would be at least four hours before Tracker would arrive, and the time could best be utilized by sleeping.

But sleep did not seem to be a possibility as long as he was in the same bed with Mac. He couldn't seem to be anywhere near her and not make love to her. It hadn't even mattered that she'd been asleep when he'd finally lost the battle he'd been waging with himself and crawled in next to her. Immediately she'd snuggled her backside into him so that they were lying side by side, nestled like spoons in a drawer. And immediately, his body had responded, growing hard.

It had been the same trusting way she'd slept with him in Florida, except, this time, he hadn't been gentleman enough to just watch her. Just thinking of how he'd slipped his arms around her and eased his hand beneath the elastic of her panties was enough to have his body hardening all over again.

She'd been so soft and warm, as if she'd been waiting just for him. She hadn't awakened right away, moving only slightly as he'd eased her panties off. She'd stirred again as he'd probed her from behind and then entered her. But she'd only fully surfaced when he'd begun to thrust into her with long, slow strokes. Even now he could hear her soft cries, urging him, pleading with him to go faster.

He hadn't.

Instead, he'd touched her, brushing his fingers under her breasts and lightly over her nipples, then down her torso and lower. Then he would begin the whole process again. He'd purposely kept the pace slow, building the pleasure and then retreating until it had become so intense that neither one of them could bear it. Only then had he allowed her to climax. When she'd cried out his name, he'd finally sought his own release.

Afterward, she hadn't been able to stop trembling. He'd held her close until she'd drifted off to sleep again. It had occurred to him that he could have gone on holding her just that way for a very long time.

The problem was that while his mind had found some kind of contentment, his body hadn't. She'd barely dozed off when he'd wanted to wake her again.

Lucas made his way to the couch. He couldn't stay in the same bed with her and not want to take her again. And again. At least if he stayed on the couch, one of them could get some sleep. He frowned down at the cramped space thoughtfully. Maybe if he hung his feet over one edge, and his head over the other...

Settling himself on the sofa, he twisted one way, turned the other, then tucked one arm beneath his head.

In his mind, he tried to focus on the plan that Tracker had outlined before they'd left the diner—where Mac had barely touched her food, he recalled with a frown. Of course, the food there hadn't been the best introduction to San Francisco cuisine, he thought ruefully. He could think of several restaurants he wanted to take her to the next time they visited.

The next time?

The two words had him rising again and pacing to the window. Oh, there was going to be a next time, all right. He was going to make it happen.

Because he was almost sure he was falling in love with her.

Slowly, he lowered himself to the arm of a chair. If it hadn't been directly behind him, he might have sat down right on the floor. He hadn't planned on falling in love. In fact, he'd spent most of his life making sure that it would never happen.

Hadn't his father always said that it was more fun when it sort of sneaked up on you and blindsided you? He'd always thought his father a fool for letting it just happen— for not building up a sort of protective armor against it.

His own armor hadn't been able to stand up against Mac.

And just how did she feel about him? Oh, she was enjoying the sex part. There wasn't enough dishonesty in her to be faking that. And, after all, that had been what her whole little experiment had been about—acquiring the skill that it would take to keep a man's eye from wandering.

But he hadn't been thinking about contributing to her research on the plane or just now in the bedroom.

All he'd been thinking about was Mac. There were so many women inside her. Not only was she Dr. Lloyd, the focused, serious-minded scientist, but she was also Mac, who wouldn't be left behind when her best friend was in danger. She had the loyal, nurturing nature of Lania, yet there was a very passionately playful and reckless side to her that was very much like Sally.

His gaze shifted to the bedroom door. And there

was also a part of her who was Fiona—a part that desperately needed to be loved, without restraint, without inhibitions.

And heaven help him, he was in love with all of them.

Rising, he moved back to the sofa and stretched out on it again. He would do something about that once he made sure that both Sophie and Mac were safe. Twisting, he settled himself into the cushions. He had an idea that rescuing his sister was going to be an easier task than getting a restful night's sleep on a piece of furniture that seemed to be designed for children.

VOICES PIERCED the dream Sophie was having.

"She's got to be awake. It's been over twenty-four hours."

Instantly, she tried to clear her mind. How long had she slept? It was hotter now than the last time she'd awakened. In her earlier investigation, she'd figured out that she was lying on burlap bags filled with sand. And the place where she was being held was isolated. All she'd heard besides the voices of her captors were the sound of birds and the buzz of insects.

The floor beneath her shook.

"The drug we gave her was more powerful than we thought."

The man who'd spoken was so close she could smell his breath. Strong hands gripped her shoulders and drew her into a sitting position.

"She's faking."

Sophie couldn't prevent the wince when the blow struck her cheek.

"C'mon, lady. Wake up." The hands on her shoulders shook her roughly.

"I need her signature on the papers."

She hadn't heard that voice before; it didn't belong to either of her captors. Suddenly, Sophie frowned. Or had she? There was something familiar...

Hands shook her again until her head snapped. She felt the wig being pulled off.

"You fools."

She knew that voice. Where had she heard it before?

"You've got the wrong woman."

"HOW LOVELY," Mac said as the limo Lucas had hired wound its way along a drive banked on either side by multicolored flowers. Even as she said the words, she knew they were inadequate. Lavish was closer to the mark. And the place was certainly well guarded. They'd been stopped at a set of heavy iron gates, and a uniformed security guard had verified their invitation by calling the main house.

The buildings where the wine was made were just as Tracker had described them, sleek and modern in structure, their tall gray windows glinting in the afternoon sun. But it was the villa itself that had sparked her comment. The modern, three-story structure of gray wood and glass was large enough to be a small hotel.

"Falcone has some very lucrative business interests," Lucas said.

Mac blinked. It was the first sentence Lucas had addressed directly to her since they'd been in the diner the night before. He hadn't even spoken when he'd come to her bed and made love to her.

Made love to her. That's what it had felt like. Everything he'd done to her on the plane and in the hotel last night had *felt* as if he was making love. Last night he'd been so tender, so gentle that she'd thought it was a dream at first.

And it had been so erotic. No one had ever done anything like that to her. Just thinking about it had her blood heating and her body melting again.

Then he'd left—without a word.

When she'd awakened, the bed had been empty. But his scent was still on her skin and on the pillow next to hers. She'd found him in the suite devouring another huge breakfast with Tracker.

It was then that she'd made herself face facts—a scientist wasn't worth her weight in salt unless she did that. Whatever they'd shared in the past few days had been just sex to him. He'd agreed to help her with her research, and he desired her. That did not equal love. She'd learned from her research that emotions didn't have to play much of a role when it came to men and sex.

Of course, she'd made it equally clear at the outset that she neither wanted nor expected anything more than to experiment on him like a guinea pig.

She hadn't wanted and she hadn't expected to fall in love with him.

"You know what to do?" Tracker asked from where he sat in the limo.

"Hmm?" Dragging her eyes away from Lucas, she turned to him.

"You know what to do?" he repeated.

"Yes," she said. A moron could have played the part they'd created for her. She was to be "Sally Maxwell," a woman Lucas was currently too infatuated with to leave behind at his hotel. Her dress was more conservative than what the Key West "Sally" might have worn. And she wasn't supposed to do anything to draw attention to herself. But since Falcone had invited her, it wouldn't cause much speculation if "Sally" was to appear as Lucas's guest.

And Tracker's role was to play her brother, Jerry. Turning, Mac checked out Tracker's disguise again. In her opinion, it was perfect. She barely recognized the man who'd sat across from her in the diner last night. "Jerry" was slighter in build. She would have sworn to it in court. His hair was long enough to be pulled back in a ponytail and he wore a diamond stud in his left ear. She would have guessed he was gay. Not Tracker, but this man who was supposed to be her brother was definitely effeminate in the way he talked and walked.

"At some point, Falcone will want to see me alone," Lucas said.

"And that's my cue to mix with the crowd. I'll introduce myself to men. That's the kind of friendly girl Sally is," Mac said.

"While you keep yourself highly visible among the guests, I sneak off to the upper floors and investigate," Tracker finished as the limo pulled to a stop in front of the house. "The moment I find Sophie, I'll take her out. Once we're clear of the estate, I'll call Lucas."

Lucas turned to Mac. "I don't like leaving you alone. As soon as Falcone and I finish our business, I'll come for you. Until then, stay with the other guests. There's always the chance that he'll guess who you really are. The man's smart. I'm banking on the fact that he's not likely to try anything where there are witnesses."

"I don't see why I can't slip away to look for Sophie too. We'd have a better chance of finding her."

"We've been over that," Lucas said. "Falcone will have someone watching all of us. It will be difficult enough for Tracker to—"

Whatever else Lucas would have said was cut off when the driver of the limo opened the door. Tracker slid out first. Mac had one foot on the ground when she caught a glimpse of a tall man with a mane of white hair walking down a shallow set of steps to greet them. She could feel Lucas stiffen behind her just before his arms gripped her shoulders and turned her back toward him.

"Follow orders," he warned in a low voice. Then without warning, his mouth covered hers. The kiss was hard and thorough. And her response was immediate. Her thoughts seemed to explode, then fade into nothing, drowned out by the beat of her heart. She had to get closer. Her hands moved to his shoulders and into his hair. There was no one, nothing but him.

He released her so suddenly that she blinked. Then he was urging her out of the car. As the man she'd spotted earlier reached them and Lucas made the introductions, she concentrated on breathing and keeping her balance.

"Lucas. Welcome, my dear boy." Vincent Falcone enveloped Lucas in a hug. "And I completely understand why you brought Ms. Maxwell. I wouldn't have left her behind at a hotel either."

"I knew you'd understand, and since you mentioned her..." Lucas ran his hand down her arm in a lingering, possessive stroke.

He'd only kissed her for show. Everything he was doing was an act to impress Falcone. Pushing the hurt and the anger down, Mac concentrated on Sophie.

"Anyone you wish to bring is welcome. I want you to think of my home as yours." Turning to Mac, he extended his arm, then waited for her to place her hand on it. "First, Ms. Maxwell, I want you to meet some of my guests. Then while Lucas and I discuss a little business, perhaps you and your brother can enjoy the party?"

She gave him her best "Sally" smile. The sooner he pried Lucas loose from her, the sooner she could look for Sophie. "We'd be delighted."

"Lucas is a very lucky man," Falcone said as he led them into the house.

LUCAS HELD HIS GLASS up to the light pouring through the glass windows of Vincent Falcone's office. From here, he could see the multicolored tents on the lawn, the rows upon rows of vines fanning out beyond and the winery buildings to his far right.

He took a sip of the pale, gold-green liquid.

"What do you think?" Vincent asked.

"It's quite nice, but I think you didn't ask me in here to solicit my opinion on your prize-winning chardonnay."

Vincent sighed. "Do you ever take a break from business?"

Lucas raised his eyebrows. "Isn't that what you invited me in here to discuss? I'd like to conclude it as quickly as possible."

"Ah, yes. You wish to return to your Sally. A charming girl. Perhaps this will ease your concerns." Moving to a wall, he pushed a button and the panel of a Renoir print slipped silently out of sight. The clear glass that remained offered a view of the main room of the house.

Tracker was talking to a tall blond woman, Falcone's hostess for the party. It took him a second longer to find Mac who was laughing at something an older gentleman was saying, her hand on his arm. He could almost hear the sound of her laughter in his ear. When the man leaned down to whisper in hers, he felt a sharp stab in his gut.

"She's not your usual type," Vincent said.

Lucas set his glass down with a snap. "That is not the topic of our business either."

"Your grandfather would have liked her," Vincent said.

"What would you know—" Lucas caught himself. What was the matter with him? Mac was flirting with that old man because that was what she was supposed to do. This was the second time that he'd let her distract him. He never should have grabbed and kissed her like that in the limo. It was out of character for him, and it was just the thing that would put Falcone on the alert. He'd better keep his mind on what he had to do. Shifting his gaze to Falcone, he said, "I didn't come in here with you to discuss my grandfather either."

"That's where you're wrong. Our business begins and ends with him." Moving to another painting on the wall, he pushed it aside and began to turn the knob on a small safe. When it was open, he extracted an envelope and held it out to Lucas. "Read this first and then we'll talk."

"Tiny Morelli's the name, and you are?"

Mac felt her hand gripped in a vise. When she glanced up, her first thought was that the name was a misnomer. Tiny Morelli was huge. He towered at least a foot above her and his hand was easily the length of her forearm.

"Sally Maxwell."

"Ever been to the Napa Valley before?"

"No." Tiny was the third man who'd gravitated to her since Lucas had disappeared with Vincent Falcone. This one was younger than the other two. But it didn't seem to matter. "Sally" was a definite man magnet. There didn't seem to be a male in the room who was immune to a woman in a short skirt, a top that showed cleavage and very high heels.

Added to that, she was a stranger. If she'd doubted the validity of her male-fantasy research before, she certainly didn't now. A week ago, this verification would have thrilled her.

"How about a dance, sugar?"

"I can't leave. My fiancé made me promise to stay here."

"Then we'll dance right here."

Mac blinked and stared. The only music in the room came from a string quartet. "It's a little hard to dance to Mozart."

"We'll improvise," Tiny said, placing his wineglass on the tray of a passing waiter. "I got some moves we'll both enjoy."

She just bet he did. Out of the corner of her eye, she noticed that Tracker had worked his way to the archway that led to the hall. He was nearly home free. Trying to ignore the quick stab of envy, she turned up the wattage on her smile and flicked her gaze back to the man whose fingers were now sliding up the inside of her arm. The one thing she wasn't supposed to do was call attention to herself.

"I shouldn't really," she pointed out. "My fiancé wouldn't like it."

"Who cares?" he murmured as he leaned a little closer. Then to her astonishment, she felt the backs of his fingers brush very deliberately along the side of her breast. She took a quick step back into a waiter. Wineglasses clinked and jiggled on his tray, and one dropped to the floor. In the midst of the confusion, Mac upended the contents of hers down the front of Tiny's shirt.

"I'm so sorry," she said.

"Why, you little…" Tiny paused to glare at her as he searched for a word. "You did that on purpose."

Mac lifted her chin. "That's not a very nice thing to accuse a lady of."

"Sally, my dear, is there a problem?"

Mac turned to find Tracker pushing through a circle of people. "I spilled my wine."

"She poured it over me on purpose," Tiny maintained.

Whipping out a hankie, Tracker began to brush it down the front of Tiny's shirt. "You're so lucky it was white wine. Red wine stains are so difficult to take out." Pausing, he ran his finger down the cloth. "Oh my. This is silk. And chardonnays have been known to leave a mark."

The man slapped Tracker's hand away. "Leave it, will you?"

Tracker made a tsking sound. "Just to be sure, you should rinse it immediately with cold water." He gave the shirt one last brush with his hankie. "I can show you where the men's room is."

"Never mind," Tiny said, backing away. "I can find it on my own."

"You weren't supposed to create a scene," Tracker said under his breath as he took her arm and parted a way for them through the little crowd that had gathered.

"I don't like to be fondled in public," she said. Then it occurred to her that she'd just told an outright lie. Hadn't Lucas touched her almost as intimately in front of Vincent Falcone? "At least not by strangers."

"C'mon, let's get you a breath of fresh air." Taking her arm, Tracker guided her through a glass door to a redwood deck.

"I'm sorry."

"The boss has you rattled, doesn't he?"

She sighed as she turned to him. "Yes. But I shouldn't be letting it interfere. I should be able to put it out of my mind until we find—" Cutting herself off, she glanced quickly around. They were alone on one of the wide decks she'd spotted from the limo. Beyond Tracker's shoulder, she could see the flight of steps that led to the upper levels. Shifting her eyes back to Tracker, she said, "In the lab, I never lose my focus."

"He's rattled too, if that helps. As far as making my escape goes, I think we've just found a better way to get to the upper levels of this little hotel. C'mon."

"I'm supposed to keep myself visible," Mac said. The stairs looked steeper and steeper as they drew closer to them.

"Been there. Done that," Tracker said as he began to climb. "And since you've called a little too much attention to yourself, it's time for plan B. Besides, I think you're safer with me right now than you are with Tiny."

"But we can be seen by anyone who glances this way." Drawing in a deep breath, she took the first step, then the second. This was what she wanted, wasn't it? She wanted to help find Sophie.

"It's the best kind of cover," he explained in a low tone as he turned to draw her up the last steps. "If someone asks, we're just trying to get a better view of the whole estate." He guided her toward the railing and raised his voice. "Mr. Falcone wanted us to make ourselves at home. And the view is so much better from here. Look, there's even a telescope we can use."

Mac was sure that the view was incredible, but it was hard to enjoy it with the way her stomach had started to pitch and roll. She gripped the edge of the railing.

Tracker leaned close and whispered, "One of the glass doors behind us is ajar. I'm going to wander in, then check out the room and the floor. You stay here and keep watch. Any trouble, you head down to the party. Okay?"

"Sure." Mac managed a nod. She wasn't sure she could

get back down the stairs, but she wasn't going to keep Tracker from doing his job.

In a louder voice, he said, "Nature is calling, sweetie. Be right back."

Mac kept her eyes directly in front of her as Tracker slipped away. The view was spectacular. If she kept her attention focused on that, the dizziness would fade. From this level, she could see the neat patterns that the rows of vines made as they crisscrossed in the distance. She let her gaze follow one pattern into the next as she drew in deep breaths and let them out. Any minute now, the queasiness would pass. Out of the corner of her eye, she caught a flash of color.

Turning, she saw just the edge of a colored cloth spread across the grass. She inched her way along the railing as it curved around the side of the house until she spotted the baskets and the splashes of colored silk. Deflated hot-air balloons.

Sophie had mentioned taking a ride in one—how long ago? Two days? Mac recalled the excitement in her friend's voice, and now she wondered if Sophie would ever…

No, she wasn't going to let herself think that way. They were going to find Sophie. She was going to be all right. Tracker could be finding her right now.

Suddenly, she narrowed her eyes. She'd just seen it again, that flash of color. Something had caused one of the swatches of red and green silk spread along the ground to ripple a little. That was what must have caught her eye a few moments ago.

What was causing it? There wasn't any wind, but she was sure she'd seen the cloth move. She waited and watched.

"What in hell am I supposed to do now?"

The sudden break in the silence made Mac jump. It was

coming from the section of the deck below her where she and Tracker had been standing only moments before. And the voice was familiar.

"I promised my father that I would have exclusive rights to MacKenzie Lloyd's research by today. You promised me that I would."

"Look. I was sure that you would have it too. But you know how difficult she is to deal with."

Mac's hands tightened on the railing. The second voice was more than familiar; she recognized it instantly. Leaning over the railing, she confirmed what she already knew. The second man was Professor Gil Stafford, her department chair at the university. And the first was Vincent Smith, the representative from Lansing Biotech who'd dated her in the hopes that she'd sign with his company.

"You assured me it was a done deal," Vincent said.

"It's just a minor glitch. She left town unexpectedly. Once I can get her out here, she'll sign the papers. I guarantee it." Gil Stafford's voice was as smooth as an oil slick, and just as dangerous.

"You've been wrong about her before. You told me that all I would have to do was get her to fall in love with me and she would sign everything over to Lansing Biotech. That didn't work. And I've guaranteed my father that he can make this announcement today."

"Calm down, Sonny."

Another wave of dizziness hit at the same instant that everything clicked in Mac's mind. She pulled her head up slowly and focused on the colorful balloon silk in the distance. The man who had introduced himself to her and romanced her as Vincent Smith of Lansing Biotech had to be none other than Sonny Falcone. She took a deep breath and let it out.

What name had he used when he'd been dating Sophie?

she wondered. Then she clamped down ruthlessly on the hysterical bubble of laughter that threatened to erupt. There would be time to laugh with Sophie later. Right now she had to listen and think.

"I admit I misjudged Dr. Lloyd at first. When she turned down the money you were offering, I thought she might be persuaded by romance. She's such a little mouse. But everyone has a price." Gil's tone was soothing, his laugh soft. "I now have something that she wants—something that she will do anything to get back. I guarantee it."

"Then why isn't she here, signing the papers right now?"

"I told you. I have to get her out here first."

For the first time, Mac heard a hint of anger and frustration in Gil Stafford's voice.

"The important thing is not to let your father know that there's a problem, right?" Gil said. "No need in getting him all upset when everything will work out in the end."

"As long as you're sure…"

"When he calls you into his office, just tell him that the paperwork will be here shortly. Dr. Lloyd is sending it by special messenger."

Mac heard footsteps then. They were taking the outside stairs to the lower level. As the voices faded, she focused her eyes on the bright silk cloth. This time it wasn't the thoughts spinning around in her head or even the height of the deck that was making her dizzy. It was the fear blooming inside her. If Gil Stafford had something she wanted, it must mean that he had Sophie—and he knew it was her.

Just then the silk rippled. And this time she saw what was causing it. One of the baskets had swayed, tipping one way and then righting itself.

Moving quickly to the telescope, she focused it on the balloon. Someone had to be in it, making it move. Then she caught a glimpse of a head with blond hair. Sophie?

Whirling, she made her way to the stairs. Two flights. The moment she glanced down, the panic slammed into her and stopped her short. Closing her eyes, she gripped the railing and took a steadying breath. But it didn't seem to help.

There was a sliding glass door behind her. She could go back into the house and find Tracker. But that would take time. And Sophie—if it had been Sophie that she'd seen—needed her help now.

I've been promised a balloon ride. The words slipped into her mind as clearly as if Sophie had spoken them aloud. She'd said them the first time she'd called from the spa. Except she'd been here in California.

Keeping her eyes closed, Mac took another deep breath and let it out. This time she wasn't going to let the fear stop her. All she had to do was take the stairs one step at a time. Gripping the railing, she placed her foot on the first one.

CHAPTER NINETEEN

LUCAS COULD HEAR the ticking of the clock on Vincent Falcone's desk as he read the letter for the second time.

> My dear Ham,
>   If you are reading this, it means that my friend Vince is calling in an old debt. Since I owe him my life, I hope you will find it possible to grant him his request.
>
>   All my love,
>   Green Eggs

The words hadn't changed since the first time he'd read them. As always his grandfather had been brief. Lucas Wainright believed that brevity was one of the cardinal virtues. But the conciseness of the letter wasn't the only detail convincing him that it was authentic. The signature, too, was his grandfather's. Of course, Falcone was resourceful enough to hire an excellent forger. But as far as Lucas knew, no one else had ever known the secret code name his grandfather and he had used whenever they had gone on one of their private vacations to the cabin.

So this had been the source of the slow, sinking certainty in his gut he'd been experiencing ever since Falcone had walked out of his office that day—the one that always told him when his opponent had something up his sleeve.

At least it was good to know that his instincts weren't failing him.

Raising his eyes from the letter, Lucas looked at the older man. He was standing at the drawn curtain, gazing at the group of people he'd gathered together to celebrate the fifth anniversary of the vineyard. The ruler surveying his happy subjects. That was what he should have looked like in his moment of triumph. But to Lucas, Vincent Falcone suddenly seemed older and more frail. He was reminded of the way his grandfather had looked shortly before he'd died.

Shaking the impression off, he said, "My grandfather owed you his life."

Falcone threw back his head and laughed, and a sound of genuine amusement filled the room as he turned to face Lucas. "You are so very much like him. You accept the facts and cut right to the heart of the matter. No quibbling. Your father would have argued forever, questioning the authenticity of the letter, arguing that he wasn't bound by it."

Lucas shrugged. "I'm pretty certain my grandfather wrote it."

Falcone moved toward him and took the seat behind his desk. The negotiations were about to begin, Lucas thought.

"I could give you some time. If you check, you'll find his prints on both the note and the envelope, along with your own. I've always used gloves when I've touched it. And the handwriting will also check out."

When Lucas said nothing, the older man said, "And, yes, I did save your grandfather's life. We fought in the same unit in France. We were very young, barely eighteen. I have no proof of that, by the way. Only the two of us knew about it."

Lucas's eyes narrowed. "What happened?"

"We were the last two left in a bunker. Everyone else in our unit had been shot or had made a run for it. The shelling was heavy and the hits were getting closer." Vincent Falcone leaned back in his chair, a half smile of remembrance on his face. "I knew we were just sitting ducks and I wanted to get out. Your grandfather felt it was safer to stay. We had a fight. Luckily, I knocked him out, then carried him with me to safety. The bunker was leveled about ten minutes after we cleared out."

Lucas nodded. His grandfather had told him the story more than once—about the man who hadn't been afraid to take a risk. He'd credited the man, not only with saving his life, but with showing him how to live it.

And that man was Vincent Falcone, a man he'd viewed as an enemy for the past five years. "Did my father receive one of the letters too? Is that how he came to get mixed up with you?"

Falcone shook his head. "Your grandfather wrote only one letter. He sent it to me shortly before he died. It wasn't long after that your father came to me and asked for money."

"Which you were only too happy to lend him."

"It served my interests well. I won't mince words. Your father was a weak man." He turned a hand over, palm upward. "The strong will always take advantage of the weak."

Lucas folded his grandfather's letter and put it back into the envelope. "What do you want?"

Falcone's lips curved. "You might as well be your grandfather's clone."

"Then you know that I will not let you back into Wainright Enterprises." He placed the envelope between them on the desk. "My grandfather would not have asked me to do that."

"No, he wouldn't."

"So?" Lucas asked. "Play your hole card."

For a moment, Falcone studied him, eyes narrowing. Then once again, Lucas thought he caught a glimpse of frailty. Finally, the older man said, "I have a favor I want to ask you. No, it's a favor I want to collect from you. My doctors tell me that I am going to die within the year."

Lucas managed to keep his astonishment masked. Whatever he'd expected to hear when he'd followed Falcone into the office, it hadn't been this. What kind of game was the old man playing?

"I've been making certain preparations. One step is that I've sold off all my business interests that are not what you might refer to as legitimate."

Lucas said nothing.

"Your grandfather and I never associated publicly after we came home from the war, but we kept in touch over the years. I took a few vacations with him on that island of his. He used to talk about how he was disappointed in his son, your father. He said that the future of Wainright Enterprises would depend on you. I have come to accept that the future of the Falcone fortunes will depend on my grandchild."

Lucas's eyes narrowed. "Sonny is...?"

The older man rose from his desk and moved toward the one-way glass. "No, my grandchild hasn't been conceived yet. I won't live to see him. Or her. I had hopes that perhaps Sonny and your sister would hit it off. He's a nice enough looking young man."

Lucas followed the direction of Falcone's gaze and saw that Sonny had joined the gathering in the other room.

"He didn't have any more luck with her than he seems

to be having at Lansing Biotech. I thought for a while he was on the right track there. He hired a research scientist as a consultant. It's what I would have done. That's him, the tall blond man right there next to my son. According to Sonny, they're very close to getting exclusive rights to some very important research."

"What kind of research?" Lucas asked. But it was beginning to take some effort to remain patient and play the dupe.

Falcone waved a hand. "Something on slowing down the aging process. I had it checked into, and the research was indeed legitimate and very promising. It's also on the up-and-up to have these scientists sign these contracts. Lansing Biotech finances some of the cost of the research in return for exclusive rights to manufacture any results in the future. Sonny was supposed to have all the papers signed so that I could make the announcement today."

"But he doesn't."

"We wouldn't be having this conversation if he did."

"What exactly is it that you want me to do?" Lucas asked.

Vincent Falcone met his eyes, and there was no trace of the frailty he'd glimpsed earlier. "I want you to take Sonny under your wing and make sure that my two remaining businesses prosper until one of my grandchildren can take over. Sonny swore he'd prove to me that he was capable of running both businesses, but he's made a mess of it. I advanced him some money—told him to show me what he could do with it to increase profits here at the vineyard. He bought hot-air balloons."

"Balloons?" Lucas asked.

"My reaction exactly. He could have used the money for research, he could have imported some old vines from France or Italy. Instead, he bought hot-air balloons so that he could offer the tourists who stop by an aerial tour of the valley." Falcone sighed. "But that's not the worst of it. To be perfectly honest, he's gotten himself into a bit of a scrape."

Finally, Lucas thought. We're getting to the hole card.

"The simplest way to put it is that I believe he's kidnapped that young scientist who was at your house party last weekend, and I need your help."

Lucas studied the older man for a moment, trying to come to a decision. Vincent Falcone was a consummate actor, but the request seemed to be costing him. In the end he decided to trust the man who had saved his grandfather's life. "Do you know where she is now?"

Falcone shook his head. "I had some men keeping an eye on her, but they lost her last night. She met my son at a restaurant, the Side Street Grill. One minute she was talking to him, then she went to the ladies' room and never came back. She hasn't been back to her hotel either."

"And you think your son is involved?" Lucas asked.

"He told me he was going to have her signature on a contract by today. He also told me that he would be bringing your sister to this party. Neither event has come to pass yet. In his effort to prove himself to me, he may have panicked. Look at him. Does he look like he has good news to tell me?"

Lucas did just that. Sonny didn't look happy. Neither did the man standing next to him as he stopped a passing waiter to exchange an empty glass for a full one.

Lucas scanned the room. There was no sign of Tracker or Mac. "Tell me everything else you know."

As she neared the end of the row of vines she'd been following, Mac paused to catch her breath. The clearing with the balloons had been a lot farther away than it had appeared to be from the deck, and Sally's shoes were not made for running.

During the time it had taken her to get there, all four balloons had become bright balls of color in the air.

Keeping her head down, Mac inched her way to the edge of the row. Her stomach sank. The four balloon baskets floated about fifteen feet in the air. A rope ladder hung from each one, and other ropes anchored each to the ground.

Her gaze lingered on the red-and-green one. There was no way to tell if the person she'd spotted from the deck was still in there.

"What the hell were you thinking?"

The deep voice had Mac ducking low and flattening herself against the nearest grapevine.

"They said they had orders from Sonny Falcone to get the balloons in the air. There were two of them and only one of me. What was I supposed to do?"

"You didn't have to help them."

"At least I kept them from discovering the girl. And I convinced them to take a break and get some beers in the kitchen."

There were a few beats of silence. Mac waited, hardly daring to breathe.

"They'll discover her soon enough once they start offering the party guests rides."

"I'm getting out of here."

"You can't. All we have to do is get her out of there. Stash her someplace else."

"You want to hang around and have somebody catch you? Fine. But I've got a feeling that this whole job is going south. First, he tells us we've kidnapped the wrong girl. Then he wants us to keep her here in this damn basket until the right one comes calling. I'm hitting the road."

Mac held her breath while she counted the receding footsteps of the man who'd just spoken.

"Hell, wait up… Wait up, I said."

Mac waited, counting to ten as the sound of the footsteps faded. In the distance, she could hear the music of the band. Closer, she could hear the drone of insects. Just to make sure, she counted to ten again. Then she straightened and raced across the clearing to the red-and-green balloon.

It appeared to be even higher off the ground than she'd first thought.

"Sophie," she called.

There was no answer.

She tried again. "Sophie."

There was still no answer.

CHAPTER TWENTY

"SHE WASN'T SUPPOSED to leave the room," Lucas said, more to himself than to Tracker. "All she had to do was mingle. She wasn't supposed to call attention to herself. She sure as hell wasn't supposed to dump a glass of wine over one of Falcone's guests."

"It was my fault she left the room," Tracker said as he pulled on the steering wheel and took the jeep Vincent Falcone had lent them into a two-wheeled turn. Once the vehicle had stabilized, he continued, "But I told her to stay put on that deck until I got back."

"She never does anything you tell her. She can't even do what you expect her to do. She's..." It occurred to Lucas that he didn't have a word that would describe Mac. He might never have one.

"She'll be fine," Tracker said.

Lucas wished he could believe that. It was Tracker who'd spotted her through the telescope from the upper deck of the villa. The quick surge of relief had given way to a sharp stab of fear as he'd watched her start up one of the rope ladders attached to a balloon.

"She's found Sophie," Tracker had said.

It made sense, Lucas thought. She'd no doubt spotted something through the telescope and taken off. Thank God Tracker was thinking clearly, because he wasn't. He couldn't rid his mind of the image of Mac climbing up that rope ladder.

"How much farther?"

Tracker merely grunted as he dragged the Jeep into another two-wheeled turn that shot them off in another direction. Vincent Falcone had given them directions to the clearing, but the dirt road zigged and zagged, slowing their progress.

They didn't seem to be getting any closer. Fear ate like acid in the back of Lucas's throat.

"She was alone," Tracker said. "There was no one else in the clearing."

Lucas tightened his grip on the side of the Jeep. "We saw her. Someone else could have seen her too."

"Falcone's got Sonny in his study."

What Tracker didn't say, what neither of them had spoken aloud, was that Sonny had denied everything hotly. Oh, he'd admitted to wining and dining both women— the doctor because he wanted her name on a contract and Sophie to please his father. That much Tracker had intimidated out of him. He'd even confessed that he'd talked to a redhead at the Side Street Grill. But it hadn't been MacKenzie Lloyd. On that point he'd been adamant.

"You think Sonny's behind this?" Lucas asked as Tracker eased up on the gas.

"That boy's as dumb as a rock," Tracker said.

Under other circumstances Lucas might have grinned. "We're on the same page there."

"Beats me that he had the business savvy to want to sign Mac in the first place."

"My thought exactly," Lucas said.

The Jeep careened around another curve. Dust spewed up, tires spun, then gripped the dirt again.

"You're thinking little Sonny might have a silent partner that he doesn't want to talk about in front of Daddy."

"Bingo. Pull over here. We'll go the rest of the way on foot."

CLOSING HER EYES Mac wiped one damp hand on her skirt, then gripped the next rung of the rope ladder. Her heart was beating so loudly that she could hear it above the sound of the band in the distance. She had no idea how high she'd climbed, and she wasn't sure she could go any farther.

Running back to the villa for help just hadn't been an option. There was no time. Sophie might be hurt.

Reaching up, Mac wrapped her hands around the rope. Every instinct she had told her that Sophie was here, and she had to get her out. *One step at a time. Just one.* This was the easy part. She wasn't even going to think about climbing down. Drawing in a deep breath, she moved her hands and her feet to the next rung. The moment the swaying stopped and the rope steadied, she made herself repeat the process.

"You can stop right where you are."

Mac recognized Gil Stafford's voice immediately. And this time she felt what she hadn't allowed herself to feel before—anger.

"Turn around."

She clamped down on her anger just as she had on her fear. Then she made herself face Gil. The gun in his hand was pointed at her. When the nausea hit, she pushed it away and concentrated on his face. If her disguise worked, she might have a chance.

"MacKenzie, I've been waiting for you."

His voice was soft, the tone falsely welcoming. It was the look of hatred in Gil Stafford's eyes more than the gun in his hand that sent an icy shiver sliding up her spine.

"Gil. What are you doing here?"

"I think you know. I saw you climb down from the upper level of the deck." His lips curved in a smile that never made it to his eyes. "Oh, the disguise is quite good. It might have fooled even me, but I saw the way you hesitated on the stairs, the way you gripped the railing. I remembered your telling me about how frightened you were of heights. You should have worked that through with a therapist long ago. It's a dead giveaway."

Mac's chin lifted, but she clamped her lips tight on the words that wanted to tumble out. It wouldn't do her any good to provoke a man with a gun in his hand.

"As it is, you're going to have a very scary ride ahead of you."

Mac's heart leaped to her throat as she watched him move to one of the ropes that anchored the balloon to the ground and pull it free. "What are you—"

The basket above her lurched, and she clung tightly to the ladder as it swayed crazily, swinging her back and forth.

"We're going away—you, me and your friend Sophie Wainright."

"No," Mac managed to say. Then she forced herself to open her eyes. "Gil, you have to let Sophie go. She has nothing to do with this."

Gil grabbed the bottom rung of the rope ladder and gave it a shake. "She was pretending to be you. And she ruined everything."

Sweat, cold and clammy, broke out on her skin. Mac couldn't move. For a moment, she couldn't even think. Clinging to the rope, she lifted her gaze from the ground, tried to focus on something else. Her vision grayed, the edges blurring with fear, but a movement at the edge of the vineyard registered. She made herself blink hard and saw Lucas at the edge of one of the rows of vines. If she could just stall Gil... Slowly, she lowered her eyes to his. "Why are you doing this?"

"Because your research is going to make you rich one day, and part of that money belongs to me. The school promised me time and money for my research. Then they hired you and decided to pour their money into your project. They even installed you in the lab they'd promised me."

Mac let out the breath she was holding and drew another in. She couldn't let herself look to see where Lucas was. She had to keep Gil's attention focused on her. "If you'd let me know, I would have done something."

"What?" Gil's laugh was bitter. "What would you have done? Would you have told me you were sorry? Or given up your work, moved somewhere else?"

She stared at him. The hatred she saw in his eyes was hot and lethal. Then he moved to the second anchor rope and began to twist it free. Mac fought against a fresh wave of dizziness as the ladder swung out and in.

"Lansing Biotech was going to pay me a half-million dollars for getting your signature on a contract. But you couldn't even do that."

"If you let Sophie go, I'll sign anything you want."

Gil twisted the freed anchor rope around his wrist, then grabbed the bottom rung of the ladder. Closing her eyes, Mac held on for dear life.

"No, I have a much better plan. I think that Lucas Wainright might pay handsomely for the safety of his sister, don't you?"

"No, I won't. Drop the gun."

Gil whirled around, one hand on the rope ladder, a gun in the other. He aimed it at Lucas. "Drop yours or I'll free the balloon, and your sister and Dr. Lloyd will go for a little ride all by themselves."

Lucas stopped dead in his tracks. "All right. I'm putting it down." Bending over, he placed his weapon on the ground. "We should talk about this. You're not going to accomplish anything by letting that balloon go."

Mac felt the balloon already struggling to rise, saw the anchor rope slipping free of Gil's wrist. Frozen with fear, she watched Gil place one foot on the bottom rung of the ladder. He was going to climb up. The moment his other foot left the ground, they would be airborne.

"No," Lucas said as he moved forward.

A shot rang out.

The sound had the fear streaming through her, but Lucas didn't fall. Instead, he took another step forward.

"This time, I won't miss," Gil said as he steadied his aim.

Mac let go of the rope and jumped. She felt her body slam into Gil's, heard another shot ring out as they both tumbled to the ground. Then the blackness enveloped her.

SOPHIE SAT on a crowded counter in Mac's kitchen, swinging her feet back and forth. "It's nice to see that everything's back to normal."

Mac looked up from the carrot she was shredding for Wilbur, then glanced around the room. It was perfectly back in order. When she'd thanked her landlord, he'd told her that someone from Wainright Enterprises had arranged to have it cleaned. Lucas.

Quickly, she pushed the name and all the images that

came with it away and focused her gaze on Sophie. "Yes, everything's fine."

It was such a lie Mac wondered that her nose didn't grow three inches. Or that Sophie didn't hoot right out loud.

But all Sophie did was nod as she grabbed one of the carrots Mac was shredding. "Absolutely. Wilbur's happy you're back, you have that extra space in your lab you've always wanted, your hair's back in that unattractive bun, and you're wearing your old drab clothes. And, as a bonus, you're going to be in the *Guinness Book of World Records* for shredding five pounds of carrots in ten minutes flat."

Mac's gaze sharpened. She had a good idea where the conversation was leading, and she was going to head it off. "We agreed that we're not going to discuss your brother."

Sophie raised both hands, palms out. "I never mentioned him. Did I say his name or refer to him in any way?"

"You said I was back in my drab clothes. The before—" She caught herself before she said his name. It hurt too much to say it out loud. *The before Lucas clothes.*

It was bad enough to think his name. She hadn't seen him since she'd taken that flying leap onto Gil Stafford. When she'd woken up in one of the guest rooms at the Falcone villa, she'd been sure that Lucas had been shot. Sophie had assured her that he was fine and dandy. And later, when Sophie had left, Tracker had stopped by to fill her in on everything that had happened. Gil Stafford had been arrested along with the two men who'd kidnapped Sophie. Even Sonny Falcone and his father had dropped in to apologize and to tell her that Lansing Biotech wouldn't pressure her anymore.

But Lucas hadn't stopped by even once. He had some

loose ends to tie up, Tracker had said. That had been a week ago—seven whole days. Sophie had spent the first five badgering her to call Lucas.

But she hadn't. She couldn't. They'd agreed that when her research was over, they'd go back to their own lives. No strings.

Her whole body ached from missing him. She couldn't fall asleep without dreaming about him, without reliving every moment that they'd spent together.

"So now I can't even mention your clothes." Whipping a notebook from her purse, Sophie plucked a pen out of a nearby cup and began to scribble. "Don't mention her dreary, drab clothes even if they make you wretch. There." She glanced up at Mac. "Anything else that's off-limits?"

Mac frowned. "Don't be ridiculous. I'm sorry. I…you can talk to me about my clothes. You always have. This…" She raised her hands and dropped them. "I wish I'd never gone to that island. It's ruined everything."

"The person whose name we're not mentioning has a way of doing that. I'm annoyed with him myself." Sophie bit into a carrot and chewed. When Mac continued to shred in silence, she said, "I still don't know what was really going on down there in California. Why wasn't Sonny Falcone arrested?"

"He didn't have anything to do with the kidnapping. As I understand it, Sonny was trying desperately to prove to his father that he has the wherewithal to run both Lansing Biotech and the vineyard."

"Sonny? He didn't impress me as having a lot going for him upstairs. Well, maybe at first he did," Sophie said. "But I was in a rebellious mood. I don't know what I was thinking when I agreed to go out there to California—except that it would be a good way to defy Lucas. Whoops!"

She slapped a hand over her mouth, then mumbled, "Sorry. It just slipped out." Dropping her hand, she shot an apologetic glance at Mac. "Anyway, to get back to Sonny. I can see him being duped by someone else. But I still don't understand what Gil Stafford hoped to gain by kidnapping me. I mean you. Your signature on a Lansing Biotech contract wouldn't have been worth anything once you explained how you were forced to sign the contract."

"The way I understand it—and I was sworn to secrecy on this—Gil knew that the Falcone family has...I guess you'd have to say *connections* to organized crime, and he was assuming that once Sonny had my name on the contract, I would be strongly *encouraged* to cooperate."

Sophie stared at her. "*Encouraged* as in broken kneecaps?"

Mac shrugged. "Something like that."

Sophie let out a low whistle. "I never would have figured that a man with his education and intelligence would get himself involved in something like that."

"At first, I think his plan was just to cash in on my research. He approached Sonny and convinced him to offer me a contract on behalf of Lansing Biotech. Gil was the one who introduced me to Vincent Smith, a.k.a. Sonny, and he did everything he could to get me to sign. When his plan didn't work, Gil got desperate."

"So he hired those two goons who kidnapped me to break into the safe at the lab?"

Mac nodded. "He thought the formulas were in the safe. Of course, he had the combination, but he had to make it look as if someone else had done it. But the formula wasn't in the safe."

"Why not?" Sophie asked.

"It's the first place a thief would look, so I've always

kept it at the bottom of Wilbur's cage. I can't think of anybody who'd want to look there."

"And they searched your house too."

"Yes. And when they came up empty there, they got desperate. That's when Gil decided to hire someone to kidnap me. He figured that was the way that the Falcones would handle things. Only he figured wrong. Whatever shady connections the Falcones have had in the past, Lansing Biotech and the vineyard are one-hundred-percent legitimate businesses and Sonny's going to testify against Gil."

Sophie narrowed her eyes as she studied Mac for a moment. "You are a lot more well informed about this whole thing than I am. It sounds to me like you *have* been talking to my brother."

"No." Mac set down a nub of carrot and chose another from the plate. "Tracker told me."

Sophie's eyes widened. "Tracker McGuire? You mean you've actually been in contact with the Shadow?"

"Several times. I think he's been told to keep an eye on me. He's stopped by here and the lab almost every day." Mac felt a little band of pain tighten around her heart even as she said the words.

"Well!" The word came out on an annoyed huff of breath. "Do you think he'll be stopping by tonight?"

Mac concentrated hard on rubbing the carrot back and forth on the grater. If she just concentrated on small details, just one step, then the next, she was going to survive. Tracker's continuous visits over the past week was just one of the signs that told her she would never see Lucas again. Of course, he would want to tie up any loose ends. That was what Tracker had said he was doing in California. But she knew Lucas was distancing himself, using Tracker as his go-between. "I told him it's not necessary. I'm not in any danger. But it's very kind of…your brother to want to make sure. But everything's fine."

"Mac!"

She looked down and realized she'd grated right down to her knuckle and was now bleeding all over the grater.

"Here, let me." Sophie took Mac's hand and drew it under running water. When she was satisfied that the wounds were clean, she reached into a nearby cupboard.

"Did I ever tell you how much I hate people who are stupid?" Sophie asked as she applied disinfectant and bandages to Mac's fingers.

"Several times." Mac felt her lips curve slightly.

Sophie turned to face her. "I'm going to say this just once. You and my brother are being very stupid." At Mac's frown, she hurried on. "That's it. I don't intend to elaborate or lecture. My experience with stupid people is that you can't ever get them to change their minds. So, I've merely stated a fact."

Mac was saved from replying by the ringing of a cell phone. Both women moved toward their purses. Sophie dragged hers out on the third ring. "Yes? Okay." A frown appeared on her forehead as she listened. "Tell him I'll be there."

When she turned back to Mac, she had a smile on her face, but her shoulders were tense. "The person whose name I can't mention is arriving in D.C. this evening and wants to see me in his office tomorrow. He was too busy to lecture me in California. But that was his secretary. It turns out he had me penciled in for tomorrow, and she's just calling to confirm his calendar."

"Sophie, he loves you."

"But he's going to play big brother. That's why he isn't calling himself." She sighed. "Not that I don't deserve the lecture. My little rebellion got me kidnapped. And I don't want to think about what might have happened if Gil Stafford had let go of that rope. It seems that whatever I do, I just can't measure up to what Lucas wants."

Moving forward, Mac took Sophie's hands. "That's the way I've felt about my family my whole life—that I could never measure up. But they never really loved me. Not the way Lucas loves you."

Sophie managed a smile as she hugged Mac. "I know that. And on that note, I'm leaving."

In the doorway to the kitchen, she turned back. "But before I go, I do have a suggestion."

Mac frowned.

"Don't give me that look. It doesn't have anything to do with the person whose name I promised not to mention. I'm just going to say that since you did give your research a little field test down in the Keys, you should be ready to put it into action for real, right?"

Mac blinked. She hadn't given any thought to her fantasy research for the past week—other than reliving every single thing she'd tried out on Lucas. Without saying a word, she studied her friend. Oh, Sophie's face wore an innocent enough expression, but Mac didn't trust her. She trusted her even less as she saw puzzlement fill Sophie's eyes.

"The whole plan was geared to keep hold of a husband once you found him, wasn't it?"

"Yes." It seemed like a lifetime ago, Mac thought.

"Step one, as I recall, was to test the research."

"Yes," Mac repeated, wondering why she felt as if she was being led down the garden path.

"Then it's time for step two—finding the husband."

"Sophie, I—"

"I'll be happy to come along with you. Come on, Mac. Wilbur's got enough carrots there to keep him going for a month. It's high time you got dressed up in some of your fantasy clothes from Madame Gervais and we did a little manhunting in Georgetown."

"Soph—"

Sophie cut her off with a raised hand. "I'm not taking no for an answer. The best way to get over a man is to move on to the next one. We've both been through a rough time, and we need to do this for ourselves."

Mac might have said no, but she could see that Sophie needed it too. "Okay."

"Good. I'll be back in an hour."

CHAPTER TWENTY-ONE

"THIS ISN'T THE OFFICE," Lucas said.

"No," Tracker said.

He'd been so lost in thought that he hadn't even noticed where they were until Tracker had parked at the curb. The sun had set, but in the thin light of dusk he could see the tree-lined street, the small but carefully tended lawns. Georgetown.

"Mind telling me why we're here?" Lucas asked.

"*She's* here. You asked about the doc twice when you called from the plane and two more times since I picked you up at the airport. Obviously, you have some doubts about my ability to keep an eye on her, so I figured you wanted to take over."

"No. I'm not...I—" It was one of the only times in his thirty-two years that Lucas found himself at a loss for words. He had a plan for handling MacKenzie Lloyd. He'd come up with it during the seven nights he'd spent at Vincent Falcone's villa. Seven sleepless nights. Without Mac. He'd shared a bed with her...what? Only twice. And now he couldn't seem to sleep without her. Even on the plane ride home, he hadn't been able to concentrate. All he could think about was her.

"You're not what?" Tracker asked. "Worried about her? Head over heels in love with her?"

"She doesn't... I don't... We...."

"See. You can't even finish a sentence. She's not in much better shape herself."

Lucas whirled on him then and grabbed the front of his shirt. "You said she was all right."

"She's fine, except for the fact that she asks about you just about as often as you ask about her. The two of you are gaga over each other."

"I'm just tired." Lucas relaxed his grip, knowing that he hadn't told the truth. For the first time in his life, he was truly afraid. It was the same cold deadly fear that had bit into him when he'd seen her hanging from the balloon while Gil Stafford pointed a gun at her heart.

He couldn't lose her. The words had screamed through his mind. After that, he wasn't sure of the exact sequence of events. Mac had jumped and landed on Stafford, a gun had gone off, he'd felt the heat of a bullet pass by his cheek. Later, they'd told him that while he was breaking Stafford's jaw, Tracker had climbed the rope ladder and landed the balloon and Sophie safely. But his only clear memory was of what Mac had looked like, lying on the ground, so pale, so still. For one moment, until he'd felt the pulse at her throat, he was sure she was gone.

Lucas rubbed the heels of his hands over his eyes. That heart-stopping moment had been what had prevented him from contacting Mac over the past seven days. The mind-numbing, body-aching, out-of-control fear that had ripped through him had scared him. He'd never been someone to lose control and Mac had a way of making him do just that on a continual basis.

"You can think of this as an intervention, if you want. But I can't see you getting anything accomplished at the office until you settle things with the doc. That deal you made with Falcone—promising to mentor Sonny until his heir can take over—that was not something a sane man does. You're not making any money for Wainright Enterprises on that one."

"It's an old debt," Lucas said. "A personal one."

Tracker paused for a moment as he digested that. "Okay. But I still say the office isn't the place for you right now. You can either go in there and settle things with the doc or you and I are going to get rip-roaring drunk."

Lucas nearly smiled. "Do you remember the last time?"

"Small town near Trinidad."

"Istanbul. I'll never forget carrying you back to the hotel."

"It was Trinidad and I carried you. You never could hold your booze."

"You passed out first."

For a few moments, silence settled over the car.

"You're right," Lucas finally said. "I love her."

"You got a plan?"

"I don't have a clue." Lucas opened the door and stepped out.

STEPPING OUT of her shower, Mac grabbed a towel and wrapped herself in it. She had barely ten minutes until Sophie would be back, and she hadn't yet decided what to wear. Every time she looked at one of the outfits she'd shopped for with Madame Gervais, she began to imagine wearing it with Lucas.

Lucas. As sadness bloomed within her, she reached to rub the steam off the mirror so that she could see her image clearly.

She was a mess. And she was going to stay that way until she got a grip.

As a scientist, she knew that it was essential to face the facts. Number one, she had fallen in love with Lucas

Wainright. Number two, he did not love her back. So what was she going to do about that?

Tightening the towel around her, she began to pace back and forth in the small bathroom. There had to be a solution. She could always find one in the lab. Frowning, she began to pace faster. What she had on her hands was a man who didn't want her.

Stopping short, she stared at herself in the mirror. *A man who didn't want her!* Her father hadn't wanted her either. He'd walked away, and she hadn't been able to stop him.

But she wasn't a child anymore. And wasn't the whole point of her research to make sure that her future husband never walked away from her?

Striding into the bedroom, she studied her clothes. She was going to go manhunting all right. And she wasn't going to give up until she had tried every single bit of her research on Lucas Wainright III.

She was reaching for a short red leather skirt when the doorbell rang. Sophie. Tightening the knot on her towel, she raced down the hall and opened the door.

For one moment she couldn't speak. The joy was sharp and bright, the panic racing behind it fast and fierce.

"What the hell do you think you're doing?" Lucas asked as he stepped into the room and slammed the door behind him. "You couldn't know who was knocking. You just threw open the door, dressed in practically nothing."

He was angry, she noted as he began to pace. Furious. She watched his legs eat up the length of her living-room floor in four paces. She sensed the same leashed violence in him that she'd felt that morning at the Wainright Casa Marina when he'd discovered she'd lied to him about Sophie. Her stomach sank as he whirled to face her.

It was only then that she noticed how tired he looked.

Nerves jumping, she said, "Would you like something to drink? Wine? Coffee? I have a very nice brandy that Sophie gave me for my birthday."

She was babbling. She had to stop and think.

"Brandy."

She had to move past him—close enough to catch his scent, feel his heat. It was enough to make her knees weak, so weak that she wasn't sure how she made it to the kitchen. It didn't help one bit that he dogged her steps.

"I came to clear up some matters between us."

Her stomach sank to her feet. He was tying up loose ends. She didn't feel it at all when the brandy snifter slipped out of her hand and splintered on the floor.

"Don't move. Where do you keep your broom?"

She didn't say a word as he opened a closet and found what he was looking for. Instead, she drew in a deep breath, unfastened the towel she was wearing, and let it slip to the floor.

The moment Lucas turned around, he felt as if he'd been poleaxed. Her skin had the milky, translucent look of fine porcelain, and the glass shards at her feet glinted like diamonds. But it was her eyes that drew him. In them he saw the same mixture of hope and fear that he was feeling. In them he saw his future.

"Don't move," he said again as he dropped the broom and moved toward her. Gripping her hips, he lifted her onto the counter.

But she didn't obey. Even as his hands moved over her, she was busy, pulling at his belt, loosening his slacks. Then her mouth moved on his, teeth nipping, tongue probing, as her fingers closed around him.

"Now," she murmured, inching closer and wrapping her legs around him. "Right now."

It took him only seconds, an eternity, to free himself

and push into her, to feel her flesh part then pulse and tighten around him. For a moment he was sure his heart stopped. It was like coming home.

Then she arched against him.

"No, don't," he managed to say as he gripped her hips and held her still. His voice sounded hoarse, strange. His whole body was straining to move, to drive himself into her. "Do you know how long I've been waiting to do this?"

"Seven days, three hours, and... If you'd let me move, I could check my watch and tell you the minutes. Not that I've been keeping track."

Lucas grinned. And though he didn't know how in the world it was possible in his present position, he felt some of his tension ease. It was the first time he'd smiled in seven days too. She never said what he expected. She never did what he expected. Was he ever going to get used to that? He used one hand to tip back her head so that he could see her eyes. "I wasn't talking about the sex. I've waited all my life for you."

He watched her eyes widen.

"I just didn't know what I was waiting for. I didn't even fully realize how empty my life was until..." No, he wasn't going to spoil this by thinking of what might have been. "I love you, Mac."

Her eyes went even wider. "Lucas—"

"No, let me finish. I know that it's too soon. I know what we agreed on. No strings. I had a strategy all mapped out. I was going to call you tomorrow and ask you out on a traditional date—flowers, champagne, dancing under the stars. I figured after a month, I'd propose."

"Propose?"

The stunned look on her face sent a bolt of panic shooting through him.

"Lucas, you don't even know me. I'm just beginning to know myself."

"We'll work on it together, over a lifetime. I'm not going to take no for an answer. I'll hound you until—"

"Yes."

Feelings tumbled through him. Joy. Relief. He barely had time to absorb them before she was tightening her grip on him with her arms and legs and the hot, moist inner part of her.

"There's just one condition."

His eyes narrowed. "And that would be?"

Her lips curved. "That I get to start moving now."

He felt the laughter bubble up. It might have broken free, but she wasn't waiting for his permission. Her mouth was on his again, her body arching. He thought his brain might just evaporate into steam.

"Now," she murmured over and over until it became a chant in his blood. Not that he needed any encouragement. Still, he struggled to keep his rhythm under control so that the pleasure could stretch out and build. Each time he sank into her and felt that slick, wet grip pull him deeper, he knew that he was losing part of himself, gaining part of her.

"Quick. Now." Her voice was breathless, her body agile.

He started to move then, hard and fast. He felt the moment that her climax tore through her; it was more than enough to draw him with her into a dark vortex of pleasure.

Afterward, they clung, trying to catch their breaths. He could feel hers, tickling his neck. "I love you, MacKenzie Lloyd."

"I love you too."

He didn't know until she said it how much he'd wanted to hear the words from her.

"I have a secret to tell you."

She drew back then to look at him. "I hope you're not going to tell me that you have a crazy wife hidden away in the attic."

With a quick chuckle, he rested his head against her forehead. "No. Not that. This is something that you can add to your research. I've just discovered what my favorite sexual fantasy is."

Her eyebrows arched. "And that would be?"

"Coming home from work to find a naked woman in my kitchen."

"No problem," she said as he lifted her and started down the hall in search of the bedroom. "But I'm going to change that."

"You think?"

"I *know*," she assured him. "You're going to love being wrapped in plastic wrap."

They were both laughing when they tumbled together onto the bed.

EPILOGUE

Lucas let himself into his house, smiling at the spicy scent of cinnamon and…apples? It had to mean Mac was cooking. In his bachelor days, he'd rarely used the kitchen, preferring instead to eat out or order food brought in. Since their wedding three months ago, Mac had insisted on fixing dinner at least three times a week.

Wives should know how to cook, she'd insisted. After all, how hard could it be? Surely not more difficult than one of her experiments in the lab.

His smile widening, Lucas set down his briefcase and began to loosen his tie as he strode down the hall. "Mac the chef" was just one more delightful personality that was part of MacKenzie Lloyd. She cooked with the same total focus and precision that she did everything else. The food was…getting better. Coming home to find his wife elbow deep in pots and bowls and finding a way to lure her off task, well, that was quite simply the best.

His wife. Just thinking the word sent a wave of joy through him. And this was the first night she'd cooked all week because she hadn't been feeling up to par. Each night they'd ordered in from a different restaurant, but nothing had tempted her. She must be feeling better.

Perhaps well enough to create his favorite fantasy? He quickened his stride, but when he entered the kitchen, there was no naked woman waiting for him.

There was no sign of Mac either. The room was pristine

clean except for the items lined up on one counter. The moment his gaze swept over them, he began to smile again. A bowl of thick whipped cream, a tall squeeze bottle of chocolate syrup, a large economy-size roll of plastic wrap and a string of pearls.

A very long string of pearls. Lifting it, he drew it out to its full length—nearly three feet. Lucas felt himself grow hard just imagining...

The bell on the microwave dinged. Opening it, he discovered a glass mug with a cinnamon stick in it. Hot spiced apple cider?

He knew the moment she entered the kitchen, and he slowly turned to face her. Three months of marriage and he still wasn't used to the shock of pleasure that moved through him when he saw her in his house and realized that she was his to keep, to cherish. "You're not naked."

And she wasn't. She was wearing one of his shirts, opened just enough to let him know that she was wearing nothing underneath it, and she'd knotted a black tie loosely around her neck. Her hair was mussed and her feet were bare, the toenails painted a pale shade of pink. Desire speared through him.

"I thought I would dress for dinner tonight."

He glanced at the counter, surprised at the effort it took not to go to her and take her where she stood. But three months of marriage had taught him that sometimes it was better to give over control and go along for the ride.

"New pearls?" he asked.

"Do you like them?"

"I don't think I want to eat them."

She smiled then, and he realized that it was the first time she had. And she hadn't moved toward him yet.

"What would you like to start off with?" she asked.

"My choice?"

"The first one is. Then it will be my turn."

He wanted to laugh then. But there was something in her eyes beneath the excitement…apprehension?

He glanced again at the selection lined up on the counter. "It's quite a feast. Why don't you come here and help me select?"

He noticed the slight hesitation before she moved toward him. Once he had her hand tucked safely in his, he said, "I'm kind of leaning toward the whipped cream and chocolate syrup myself."

"Good choice. If we top that off with the hot apple cider, I figure we've hit at least two-thirds of the food pyramid—fruit, dairy and protein."

"I'm lucky to have a scientist keeping my diet on track."

"Want to know what I have in mind for the cider?" Mac asked.

"I always want to know what you have in mind," he said as he tucked a strand of flyaway hair behind her ear. The apprehension hadn't vanished yet from her eyes.

"I melted those little red-hot cinnamon pieces in it, so it's doubly hot. I'm going to drink it and then taste you." Her hand unerringly found the part of him that she was thinking of tasting.

With a sigh that ended on a moan, he rested his head against her forehead. "You're going to be the death of me." Then he carefully removed her hand from his erection. "Before we get to that, why don't you tell me the reason for the feast. Are we celebrating a special occasion?"

"Yes."

Now it was his turn to be apprehensive. Had he forgotten an anniversary of some sort?

Licking her lips, she continued, "I did a little experiment today. And then I reran it five times. I wanted to make sure."

He smiled at her. "You had a breakthrough at the lab. Don't tell me—let me guess. Wilbur is going to live to be a hundred."

"Not exactly. I mean, I didn't do it at the lab. I did it here."

"Here?"

"It came out positive. All five times. And the pharmacist told me the test has a very high accuracy rating. I'm… we're…pregnant."

"Pregnant?" Even as he said the word aloud, he struggled to take it in.

"Yes. That's why I have to get started, using my research, I mean. I'm going to get fat. I can't afford to let you get bored."

"Pregnant." He was beginning to absorb it. He could tell by the joy that was zinging through him. "You're pregnant." Lifting her off her feet, he swung her around and around, then abruptly stopped and set her on the counter. "I shouldn't be doing that. Are you all right?"

"I'm fine." Eye to eye, she studied him for a moment. "You're happy?"

He grinned at her. "Very."

Her expression remained serious. "I don't want to bore you. I don't want to lose you…ever."

He kissed her softly, coaxing her into it, pouring everything he felt into it until they were both nearly drowning. Finally, he drew away. "You're not going to lose me. Ever. And I don't know how I'm supposed to get bored. There are so many parts of you that I love. So many parts that I'm still discovering. I can't wait to meet Mac the mother."

She hugged him then, and he felt her lips curve against his chest. Her sigh moved through him. "Let's get started on dinner. You grab the chocolate and whipped cream. I'll bring the cider and the other stuff."

"Appetizers first," he said as he quickly wrapped her legs around him and pulled down his zipper.

"Appetizers?" Her breath hitched as she took him in.

"I'm very hungry."

"You are?"

"Oh, yes. And the appetizer is always the first step to enjoying a great meal. You do like to take everything one step at a time, right?"

"Absolutely," Mac managed.

The laughter, the overwhelming joy welled up between them as they began to move together in a steady and familiar rhythm.

"We'll take it slowly," Lucas promised as he struggled to do just that. But already he could feel her climax begin to move through her. As always, his own control began to slip away. Drawing her closer, he spoke softly. "And when you reach the heights, I'll be right there…with you. Always."

And he was.

* * * * *

A GLIMPSE OF FIRE

Debbi Rawlins

This is for Steve and E.
I'm so glad you found each other.
You're everything I write about.

CHAPTER ONE

DALLAS SHEA CHECKED HER WATCH and then shoved her keys and two twenties into her jeans pocket. She'd planned on walking the eighteen blocks up midtown but now she had to catch a cab or she'd be late.

"Oh, good, you're still here." Her roommate burst out of the tiny bathroom they shared while she pulled her long red hair up into a ponytail. Behind her a heap of towels lay near the foot of the ancient claw-foot tub.

Dallas sighed. The woman was the consummate slob. Funny, spontaneous, ambitious and a loyal friend but a total slob. "Not for long. I'm on my way out."

"Can you walk Bruiser first?"

"No."

The furry black mutt heard his name and came from behind the green floral couch, which was the extent of their tiny living room, wagging his tail, looking up at Dallas with soulful black eyes. He had to be up to seven pounds by now—big difference from three months ago, when Wendy found him scrounging for food in an alley near Nineteenth Street.

"Please, Dallas. I'll make dinner."

Giving Wendy a dry look, Dallas headed for the door, trying to avoid looking at Bruiser. If she did, she'd give in. "That's what you said the last time."

"I came through, didn't I?"

"Hot dogs from Howie's cart is not my idea of dinner."

"Come on, please. I have an audition." Wendy hopped on one leg as she pulled on a tennis shoe over her purple tights. "It's really important. A new musical and they need twelve dancers. This time I'm going to get it. I know it. Right here." She pressed a palm to her tummy. "This is gonna be my big break."

Dallas undid the dead bolt. Then hesitated, reminding herself this wasn't her business. But Wendy was crazy for chasing after these jobs. Sadly, at twenty-nine, she was already too old for Broadway. A new crop of eager, energetic young twenty-somethings were getting all the gigs.

She looked at her friend and then down at Bruiser, whose expectant eyes met hers, his tail still wagging. Even he'd already figured out what a pushover Dallas was.

Sighing, she opened the door for Wendy. "Go."

Grinning, Wendy hopped toward her as she slid on her other sneaker. "You're the best."

"Be careful of those feet. I need your share of the rent." Dallas scooped up Bruiser before he made a break for the open door, then grabbed his leash off the hook on the wall. "Don't worry about dinner. I'm meeting Trudie."

"Tell her I said hey."

"Break a leg," Dallas said as Wendy slipped out into the hall and closed the door.

She put Bruiser down and crouched to secure his leash. "What are you looking at me like that for? Huh?" She stroked his curly black fur, laughed when he licked her chin, rearing back just in the nick of time to avoid a sloppy kiss.

"Okay, boy, I know it's been a while since I've had a date but I like my guys a little taller." She stood, grabbing the plastic bag she needed to clean up after Bruiser.

In a way she envied Wendy. She never gave up. Her

optimism and enthusiasm seemed boundless. Even after she'd lost the contract with Revalyn last year. A week after her twenty-eighth birthday, the company decided they needed someone with younger-looking hands for their print ads. Thank God feet didn't age as quickly.

Dallas sighed. Boy, was she glad she'd gotten out of that world quickly. She'd modeled for a year during her senior year in college. After the blowup with her parents when they'd cut her off, she'd needed the money. But that had been enough. There had always been someone taller, slimmer, prettier. She'd hated every minute of it.

She led Bruiser out of the apartment, careful to double lock the door, then checked her watch as she waited for the elevator, hoping the damn thing wasn't on a milk run. Of course, that it was working at all was cause for celebration. If she had the money, she'd move out, but finding and affording another apartment without having to move to Brooklyn would mean working a whole lot of overtime. Or worse, taking another job. The kind her parents would approve. The thought made her shudder.

"THANK GOD YOU'RE HERE." Trudie looked up from a pink phone slip on her desk, her heavily outlined brown eyes filled with worry. "Close the door, would you?"

"Sure." Dallas did as asked and then dropped into the worn burgundy leather guest chair. "What's up?"

"I'm totally screwed."

Dallas tried not to smile. Her friend had a penchant for drama. Their circle of college friends had been certain Trudie would end up on Broadway and not dressing department store windows. "What's wrong?"

"I'm in charge of doing the Fifth Avenue window display for the Fourth of July sale. It's also the store's tenth anniversary."

"Sounds like a big deal."

"Yes," Trudie said miserably. "And I'm about to blow it big-time."

"How?"

Trudie shoved the pink slip she'd been studying across her crowded desk, between a stack of fashion magazines and a pile of fabric swatches.

Dallas picked up the phone message. It was from someone named Starla Jenkins. It simply said she had a stomach virus and had to cancel tomorrow evening.

"Okay," Dallas said slowly, sliding the pink slip back toward Trudie. Her friend was obviously upset, so she forwent the wisecrack that came to mind. "And?"

"I am so screwed."

"Who's Starla Jenkins?"

"A model I'd hired." Trudie exhaled sharply. "Stomach virus, my ass. I haven't heard of anything going around."

"So? I'm sure there are fifteen others who'd love to take her place. Call the agency."

"It's not that simple," Trudie said and then remained silent as she stared at Dallas with an odd expression on her face. Her gaze dropped to Dallas's hands and she wrinkled her nose. "Your nails are horrible."

Dallas reflexively balled them into fists. "I just got off work."

"That's okay." Trudie flashed her a quick smile. "We can fix them."

"I don't want them fixed." She studied her friend for a moment, a bad feeling growing in the pit of her stomach. "Look, if you need to cancel dinner so you can find a replacement, I totally understand."

Trudie's gaze stayed steady. "I already have."

Dallas stared back, feeling uneasy. Trudie couldn't

possibly be thinking— No, of course not. Ridiculous. She knew better. But just in case… "No."

"Come on, Dallas. I'm not asking you to do it for free."

"Why ask me period? You could find a replacement in half an hour."

"No way, toots." Trudie shook her head. "I promised my manager something special. A live mannequin."

Dallas's mouth opened but didn't cooperate any further.

"*You* gave me the idea," Trudie said in an accusatory tone. "Remember how in college you used to fake everyone out. Jill and I'd take bets you could stay perfectly still for a half hour at a time. Hell, we used to clean up. Pay for all our gas and entertainment."

"That was eight years ago."

"You did it again at the Christmas party last year and took fifty bucks off that snobby Chandler Whitestone."

"That was different. He ticked me off."

"Please, Dallas. You have to bail me out."

Dallas sighed. Did she have *Sucker* written across her forehead or something? "I have faith you'll find someone else. Or come up with another window display."

"By tomorrow?"

"I'm not standing in a damn department store window. I'm too out of shape."

"Bull. You should have never left the business." Trudie glanced at Dallas's hands again. "Your nails suck, but other than that you're every bit as pretty and—"

"I'm twenty-nine."

Trudie's mouth twisted wryly. "There's that."

Dallas stood. "Moot point. Are we doing dinner or not?"

"Look, my career's on the line here." Trudie hesitated. "I wouldn't ask if I wasn't desperate."

"Have you *even tried* to find someone else?"

"Yes. I swear."

Dallas sank back into the chair. She believed her. Trudie wasn't one to ask for favors. Even after her jerk of a boyfriend had moved out along with half of Trudie's furniture and the next month's rent, she hadn't asked Dallas or Wendy for a thing. Hadn't accepted anything that was offered either.

"Come on, Dallas. As soon as Starla gets over her virus or whatever, she'll call and you'll be off the hook."

"I'm not on the hook."

"Oh, God, are you going to make me beg? Do I have to get down on my knees?"

Dallas sighed, knowing she was going to regret this. "Okay," she said slowly. "How long do I have to pose and what do I have to wear?"

Trudie's smile faltered. "Come on, let's go have a drink or two first."

"Trudie…"

Her friend got up from her desk, grabbed her purse and headed out the door. "I'm buying."

Dallas followed. She was not going to like this. Not one bit.

ERIC HARMON PAID THE CABDRIVER and got out near Sixth and Lexington. No sign of Tom. He checked his watch. Traffic had been surprisingly cooperative, and he'd apparently beaten his friend to the rendezvous point a block from their office where they both worked for Webber and Thornton Advertising.

He squinted up at the twentieth floor and counted four

windows from the corner, which was Tom's office. The light was still on. But of course, so was the light in Eric's office, two over from Tom's, and Eric had no intention of returning to work. Not today. He was too beat.

They really should've met at Pete's Grille, he realized. After the meeting he had just left, he could really use a double scotch about now. He checked his watch again, moved out of the way as a horde of pedestrians left the crosswalk and headed for him, then withdrew his cell phone from his suit jacket pocket.

"Put that away. I'm right behind you."

He turned toward Tom's voice and slid the phone back into his pocket. "I need a drink."

"Me, too."

Eric looked down at the briefcase his friend was holding. "Since when do you take work home?"

Tom shook his head, his expression grim. "I don't care how bad your meeting went, be damn glad you weren't in the office this afternoon."

"Great. Tell me it doesn't have to do with the Mercer account." The advertising business could be a bitch. When you bonded with the client, you were on top of the world. But then there were those times when you thought about ordering a one-way ticket to Siberia.

"I'm not talking work until after I have a scotch." Tom stepped back, accidentally bumping into a short blonde in a khaki suit. "Excuse me."

At his dimpled smile, her irritation promptly vanished. "No problem." She returned the smile, laced with a brief but obvious invitation.

Eric sighed. "Come on, Romeo. Let's get to Pete's before your wife calls and tells you to get your ass home."

Tom gave the blonde's swaying rear end a final appreciative look before turning toward Fourth Avenue. "Speaking of wives, since *you* don't have one—" Tom said as if it were a crime "—who are you taking to Webber's annual thanks-for-the-job-well-done-but-you're-not-getting-a-bonus party?"

"Who says I have to take anyone?"

"Unspoken rule, my friend. You always show up and you don't show up alone. The guy's old school. He thinks everyone should be married and settled by the time they're thirty. A mark you've already bypassed. Besides, didn't you get the picture after the Christmas party? He didn't like it that you were the only one flying solo."

Eric scoffed. "That attitude's not only ridiculously antiquated, it's illegal."

"Tell him that." Tom's head swung around after a redheaded jogger in a skintight green tank and running shorts who'd passed them.

"And then there are some guys who just shouldn't be married."

"What?" Tom glanced at him and laughed. "Only looking, pal. Only looking. Something you should be doing more of."

Frankly he didn't know how Tom did it. Juggle a wife, a successful but demanding career and an active and strategic social life. Of course, Tom's first putt in life came with a handicap. Prominent Westchester family. Ivy League education. No student loans to repay. A wife with an impressive social pedigree.

Must be nice. Eric wouldn't know. His background was Pittsburgh blue-collar all the way. Of his entire extended family, he'd been the first to graduate from college and escape a life sweating in the steel mills.

"Seriously, Eric," he continued, "when was the last time you brought someone to a company function?"

"Why are we discussing this?"

"Tell me when and I'll drop it."

"Why would I subject a date to one of Webber's boring parties?" He was about to cross the street when the light turned red. Normally that wouldn't stop him, except a stretch limo came barreling around the corner from Lexington.

"See? Good reason to get married. Then the girl's gotta go and be bored."

"Right."

Tom elbowed him. "Check out the blonde at three o'clock. The one in the red stiletto heels."

Eric casually glanced in that direction. "Not bad."

"Not bad? Are you nuts? That one could put you in intensive care for a month."

Eric started to cross the street as soon as the light changed. Two cabs ran the red light and honked at the pedestrians who'd entered the crosswalk. Across the street several other cabs blasted their horns for no apparent reason. You'd never know the city imposed a three-hundred-fifty-dollar fine for unnecessary honking.

They'd barely made it across Fifth Avenue when Tom started in again. "Okay, I want you to point out your idea of the perfect woman." He gestured toward the mass of people, mostly women in suits and running shoes, coming toward them. "You have a wide variety right here."

"What is with you today?"

"Humor me."

Eric shook his head in disgust, at the same time catching sight of a department store window display, taken aback by the realistic beach scene. Sand, sun, a threatening wave that looked as if it were about to crash over two incredibly lifelike mannequins and then right through the window onto the sidewalk. Computer generated, obviously, but realistic enough to earn some gasps from the crowd of onlookers and send an older couple back several steps.

Remarkable as the special effects were, what caught his attention was the blond mannequin in the red bikini. She looked so damn real. And perfect. Long honey-blond hair, sexy blue eyes, full lips that formed a tempting bow. And man did she have legs....

"Are you listening?" Tom got in his face.

"What?" Eric hadn't realized he'd stopped. Right in the middle of the sidewalk, blocking everyone's way. People muttered curses and stepped around him. "No."

He looked back at the window. At the mannequin. She was amazing. Incredible. Too bad that kind of perfection could only be synthetic.

Tom followed his gaze just as another wave swelled threateningly, and he ducked. Clearly realizing his foolish reaction, he straightened and glanced around. Several other onlookers had done the same.

"Damn, that's amazing."

Eric nodded. "Genius. Pure genius. Look at how many people the window's attracting."

"No shit. This should earn someone a nice little bonus."

Eric shook his head. Lately with Tom it was always about money or women. As if he needed to worry about either. "Let's go."

"Wait. No more changing the subject. You have an assortment of lovelies right here. Blondes, brunettes, redheads." Ignoring a sharp look he received from a well-dressed older woman who'd obviously overheard, he gestured toward a group staring at the window. "I'm not moving until you choose one."

Eric shrugged and turned to leave. "I'll say hey to everyone at Pete's for you."

Tom snagged his coat sleeve. "Come on."

Eric sighed. His gaze went back to the mannequin, to the tiny beauty mark at the corner of her lush mouth. "Her," he said with a jut of his chin.

"Who?" Tom scanned the group of women close to the window. "Which one?"

"There." Eric barely contained a smile as he fixed his gaze on the mannequin. "She's perfect."

It took Tom a moment for it to register and then he laughed. "Why, because she can't talk?"

"A big bonus, you have to admit."

"I'll give you that." Tom studied the mannequin. "Great legs, too. I wonder if she's busy this weekend."

Eric shook his head and headed across the street. "I'm gonna go have a drink. You do what you want."

Tom started after him when he heard the crowd gasp. He turned just in time to see the two mannequins throwing their hands up as if frightened by the wave, and then they repositioned themselves, again going perfectly still.

The crowd began murmuring and talking excitedly, loud enough that Eric turned around to see what was happening. Tom took off after him.

"What's going on?" Eric asked.

"Nothing. Another wave." Tom shouldered him, urging him to keep walking. "Let's go before my keeper calls."

Tom could barely contain himself. This was rich. Totally awesome. He wasn't sure what he was going to do yet, but the opportunity for something really big was there.

Like Saturday night—the company dinner. God, this was too perfect.

In his excitement, he nearly tripped over his own feet.

All he had to do was keep Eric away from that window for the next two days.

CHAPTER TWO

TEN MORE MINUTES. FIFTEEN TOPS, AND the store would be closing, judging by the steady stream of shoppers exiting the Fifth Avenue doors. She could do this. Wait fifteen minutes before she sprinted to the bathroom. Dallas simply had to stop thinking about how her bladder was ready to explode.

Even though she'd purposely laid off the coffee and Cokes made available in the dressing room, the knowledge that she was stuck in the window and couldn't leave was enough to make her desperate for a pit stop. One five-minute break in four hours just didn't cut it. She and Trudie were going to have a serious discussion tomorrow.

Dallas heard her partner's stomach growl and used every ounce of self-control to keep a straight face. Steve did an admirable job of remaining impassive himself, and she kept her gaze fixed on the fire hydrant across the street. It was easier that way, to focus on one particular object until the soft beep told them it was time to change positions. Besides, making eye contact with anyone in the crowd outside wasn't a good idea. Made it much harder to keep a straight face and not blink.

She'd almost blown it earlier. Two yuppies had stopped and stared, obviously more interested in her bikini than the window display. The taller one had caught her eye with his dark wavy hair and light eyes and a tanned face with a deep cleft in his strong chin that had a way of sending her thoughts in a dangerous direction.

The announcement came that the store would be closing in five minutes.

Freedom. Hallelujah!

She and Steve exchanged a brief glance.

That's when she noticed him. Approaching the window. One of the guys she'd seen earlier. Not the good-looking one with the dimpled chin but the shorter one.

He stopped dead center and stared at her intensely, thoroughly, as if she were a museum exhibit. She tried not to move, not to give any sign of acknowledgement. Then he mouthed something to her, but still she refused to focus on his lips or try to understand what he was saying.

Panic knotted her tummy, and she tried to disguise the deep unsteady breath she took. Just what she needed— some pervert following her home later. She'd have to duck out the employee door, maybe even get Steve to share a cab with her.

The guy walked up to the security guard, who stood at the door making sure no one slipped inside, and the two men shook hands. They apparently knew each other, which brought Dallas some relief.

Behind her, Trudie's assistant opened the door to the window, at the same time dimming the display lights, a signal it was over. They were free. At least until tomorrow night. She and Steve looked at each other. He smiled. She groaned. Of course, he looked as if he were barely out of his teens. His back and legs probably didn't ache as hers did.

"You okay?" he asked, his incredibly pretty blue eyes clouding with genuine concern. Nice guy. Idaho born and bred, he'd only moved to the city six months ago. He'd change. They all did.

"Terrific."

"You look awful."

"Thank you."

"I didn't mean it like that." He actually blushed as he stepped aside to let her out first.

She grinned. Too bad he wasn't older. "Aren't you a little stiff?"

His brows rose in surprise. "Why?"

"Never mind."

She climbed out, smiling ruefully to herself. It wasn't that she was in bad shape. Just the opposite. Working in construction for the past year and a half had probably gotten her into the best condition she'd ever been. This was different. Holding the same position for an hour at a time wasn't easy. Nothing like it had been eight years ago in college.

A couple of stragglers leaving the store stopped to stare at her. She accepted a robe from Trudie's assistant and pulled it on over the tiny red bikini before heading for the dressing room. The lights flickered—the store's final warning for everyone to leave.

"Hey, you wanna go for a drink?" Steve threw his robe over his shoulder.

Drink? Bathroom? Oh, God. "How about a rain check?" she said without breaking her stride.

"Sure." He shrugged, smiled. "See you tomorrow evening."

Dallas sighed as he walked ahead of her. He sure was pretty. Young but pretty.

"Excuse me."

Dallas heard the voice behind her and glanced over her shoulder. It was him. The guy who'd been standing outside a moment ago. Her chest tightened. "The store is closed. You'll have to leave."

He gave her a boyish grin. "I know the security guard. Besides, I only need a minute of your time."

"I don't have a minute."

"Look, I want to hire you." He produced a business card from his jacket pocket. "For Saturday night. Your usual modeling fee, of course."

She barely glanced at the card. "I'm not a model. I'm doing this as a favor for a friend." She tried to hand him back the card but he wouldn't take it.

"Call my office," he said. "Check me out. Or ask Jimmy." He inclined his head toward the security guard.

She shook her head. "Look, I—"

"I'm not a kook or a pervert." His boyish grin took a chink out of her resolve. "Well, my friends may argue that point. But seriously, I only want to play a practical joke on my friend. He was here earlier with me and saw you and…well, we have a company dinner at the boss's house this Saturday and I thought it would be pretty funny if you showed up."

Of course she remembered the guy. His face was surprisingly clear in her mind. That strong, dimpled jaw stood out in particular.

"He thinks you're a mannequin."

That startled a laugh out of her. Oops! Bad move. She squeezed her thighs together. "I'll think about it and call you, okay?" she said as she started toward the bathroom.

"Tom!" The security guard motioned the man to the door. "I gotta lock up."

"I'll be waiting to hear from you." Tom backed toward the door. "Either way, call me, will you?"

"Sure," she said, amazed that she was even considering it.

"I THINK YOU'RE NUTS IF YOU *don't* go." Wendy plopped down on the love seat with a bowl of buttered popcorn that she placed between her thighs. "How totally cool. You'd be like the mystery woman."

If Dallas denied being intrigued by the prospect, she'd be a liar, but the situation was just so way out there. "Pass me some popcorn, would you?"

"You won't like it. I used a whole block of butter," she said, licking her fingers.

"I don't suppose you set any popcorn aside for me."

"Sorry."

"Thanks." Dallas sighed as she pushed off the purple beanbag chair. Some things never changed.

They'd been roommates for three years, but Wendy still hadn't grasped the concept of sharing. She had other good qualities, Dallas reminded herself as she grabbed an apple from the basket of fruit they kept on top of the refrigerator—the only spare spot in the minuscule kitchen.

"So, you saw this guy, right?" Wendy asked between handfuls of popcorn.

"Briefly. Anyway, it's not like it's a blind date. Just a prank."

"What does he look like?"

"Tall, kind of wiry, athletic-type body, dark hair, hazel eyes, strong square jaw."

Wendy snorted. "Just a brief look, huh?"

"Keep stuffing your face and shut up." Dallas sank back into the chair and stretched her legs out. "I called that guy Tom's office. I didn't talk to him. Just made sure he really worked there."

"And what about Saturday night? How do you know it's legit?"

"I pretended I was a florist and wanted to confirm the delivery date for the dinner."

"Very sneaky. I'm impressed."

Dallas groaned. "But I still don't know if I should do this."

"Did Trudie have an opinion?"

"Please, you need to ask? She thinks I'd be crazy to do it."

"Screw it. She's gotten too conservative since she caved in and got a nine-to-fiver. Go. Be daring. Have fun. What else do you have to do Saturday, anyway?"

Dallas watched a popcorn kernel slip from Wendy's hand and fall to the floor to join several of its friends. Dallas sighed. Wendy was right. What else did she have to do Saturday night besides clean up Wendy's mess?

ERIC FINISHED HIS COGNAC and debated having another one before he slipped out. As usual he'd come late, forgoing the cocktail hour and arriving just minutes before dinner had been served, along with a different wine with each course. Easy to get stupid with all that booze. And he made it a policy never to get stupid in front of the brass.

Webber, of course, was here. It was his house. He always threw the parties. New money. He still had a lot of showing off to do. The firm's other partner, Joseph Thornton IV, came from old money. Nice guy, old-school polite, but with the exception of Webber, no one from the office had ever seen the inside of his house. At least no one Eric knew of. Not that he was the type to be invited to the Thornton estate. But some day…hell, some day he'd have a nice three-story brownstone like this with a view of Central Park.

Near the white marble fireplace, Tom and Serena were talking to Harold Carter, the company's controller and possibly the most boring human being in Manhattan. Eric wasn't in the mood to make small talk, so he circled around the room, heading for the bar.

"Another cognac?" The bartender reached for the bottle.

"Yep, one for the road." Eric put down his empty snifter. Most bartenders had amazing memories. "Go ahead and refill this one."

He'd picked up a clean glass but set it aside. "No argument from me. One less to wash."

Eric glanced at the guy's name tag. He remembered him from the Webber's Christmas party. "Tell me something, Chuck. You ever get tired of these private parties?"

Chuck shrugged. "They aren't so bad. Pays the rent."

Eric sighed. "Yep, that's what it's all about." He surveyed the plush living room, impeccably decorated in gold and burgundy, a van Gogh over the fireplace and, if he wasn't mistaken, a couple of Gauguins on the dining room wall. He hated these affairs. Ridiculously formal and mandatory—unspoken, of course. "Money."

Chuck grinned. "Nothing wrong with that."

"Not a thing." Eric had to agree. Not to would make him a hypocrite. Wasn't that why he was here when he'd rather be just about anyplace else? Not just because he was the only guest without a date—something which Webber had again commented on. But that was Eric's choice. He could have brought a date if he'd wanted.

Most of the time he could be political and schmooze the bosses with the best of them. He certainly did his share when necessary. Frankly he had to. It was all part of the game. But social situations weren't his favorite milieu. He always felt at such a disadvantage.

"The class of people at these private affairs are better than working the bars." Chuck motioned with his chin toward the foyer. "Like her. What a knockout! Can't believe I didn't notice her earlier."

Eric looked in that direction and saw the blonde entering the foyer. The Webber's maid had just let her in the double glass front doors. No escort. Just her and that slinky black dress.

She turned in his direction and his jaw dropped. That face. Those lips. That tiny beauty mark near her mouth. Those legs. He knew her....

Impossible.

He blinked. Took a deep shuddering breath. Exhaled slowly.

Chuck muttered an oath. "Sorry, man, I hope that isn't your wife or anything."

"What?" Eric barely glanced at the bartender before his gaze drew helplessly back to the woman. "No, I, um, I don't know her."

"In that case, I'd go introduce myself if I were you, dude." Chuck grabbed a crystal flute and poured some champagne. "Here. Take this to her."

Eric didn't move. He just stared. Blinked hard. Stared again. In total shock. The woman's resemblance to the mannequin he'd seen three days ago was remarkable. The hair on the back of his neck went straight up as he watched her enter the living room and take Mrs. Webber's extended hand.

"I need a scotch," he said to Chuck, his eyes never leaving the woman.

"Hey, dude, you okay?"

No, he wasn't okay. He was friggin' hallucinating. He finished his cognac and set it aside as he waited for Chuck to pour the scotch, and then he downed it in one gulp.

Tom.

Eric peered toward the marble fireplace where he'd last

seen his friend. Where the hell was he? Tom had seen her in the window the other night, too. He could prove Eric wasn't going crazy.

Eric left the empty glass on the bar and moved toward the fireplace area while trying to keep the blonde in his sights. Wasn't hard. Everyone else seemed to be eyeing her, too. Of course, all the other guests knew each other. But it wasn't just that she was an outsider. She was stunning.

He spotted Tom, but before he could get to him, the blonde and Mrs. Webber approached him and his wife. Tom and Serena shook hands with the blonde. Not a trace of recognition on Tom's face.

Eric took a step back. Obviously he'd been working too hard lately. He was losing it. He needed to sit down. Have another drink. Better yet, go home.

"Hey, Eric. Come here." Tom motioned him toward them. "I'd like you to meet someone."

The blonde smiled. Her teeth were dazzlingly white and perfect. So was her skin. Flawless. Golden and creamy. And her honey-colored hair...the way the light from the chandelier touched it, lighting it with shimmering highlights, was a work of art.

A tiny half-moon-shaped scar near her jawline surprised him. Nothing bad or ugly but certainly unnecessary. A cosmetic surgeon could probably eliminate the imperfection with a thirty-minute office visit.

Too late to retreat gracefully, Eric moved forward and forced a smile.

Mrs. Webber leaned over and straightened his tie. "Don't leave too soon, okay? I have a very special dessert planned," she said with a twinkle in her eyes before drifting across the room.

"This is Eric Harmon," Tom said to the woman. "And Eric, this is Dallas."

She smiled and extended her hand. Eric's palm was so clammy, he was embarrassed to touch her. He took her fingers and brought her hand to his lips, pressing a light kiss to the back, which earned a choked snicker out of Tom.

"A pleasure meeting you," Eric said and released her hand as quickly as he could without seeming rude.

She blinked, surprise flickering across her face. "The pleasure is mine," she whispered, her voice soft and breathy and matching her perfectly.

The heady scent of roses and mystery swarmed his senses and he actually felt weak in the knees. His lips tingled from the silky warmth of her skin.

Too much scotch. That's all.

He caught the tail end of the amused look Tom and Serena had exchanged and he cleared his throat. "Tom, could I speak with you for a moment in private?"

Tom hesitated. Long enough for their boss, Morgan Webber, to call for Tom and motion for him across the room.

"Sorry, pal," Tom said, looking anything but as he hurried across the room toward Webber, Serena in tow.

Eric took a deep breath and turned back to Dallas. Her long, delicate fingers absently stroked the gold chain she wore around her neck. It held a small ruby heart that followed the deep V of her dress and rested in the tantalizing valley between her breasts.

He tried his damnedest not to stare. Forced his gaze up to the slender column of her neck, to her lush peach-tinted lips, the cute upward tilt of her nose and then to dive headfirst into eyes so sexy and blue, he thought he might have to loosen his collar to breathe.

He cleared his throat. "It's nice to see a new face at one of these parties. They get pretty stale after a while." He stopped, swore under his breath. "Tell me you aren't the Webbers' niece."

She smiled and shook her head.

"Or in any way related."

This time she laughed, the simple innocent sound seductive as hell. "No, you're safe."

Eric exaggerated a sigh of relief and then smiled. Up close he realized the scar on her jaw wasn't that old. Maybe a year or so. At least he knew she was a real live person.

God, he was losing it. He had to talk to Tom. Or then again, maybe he shouldn't. His friend was likely to have him committed. "How do you know the Webbers?"

Dallas looked blankly at him for a moment. And then her gaze shifted past him. "Would you get that waiter's attention, please? I'd really like a glass of wine."

"Of course." Damn, he should've brought the champagne Chuck had poured.

Eric snagged the waiter's attention. On his tray he had both white and red wine and flutes of champagne. Eric turned back to her to ask which she preferred and was surprised to find her nibbling nervously at her lower lip.

Their eyes met, and her lips immediately stretched into a smile, her expression one of utter composure.

"Red, white or champagne?" he asked.

"Red, thank you."

He lifted the glass off the tray and handed it to her. He thought about having another drink himself but decided he needed a clear head to survive the twilight zone.

"At the risk of sounding tedious, have we met before?" he asked and then waited for her to finish her sip.

She lowered the glass, and a tiny droplet of wine shimmered from her upper lip. Battling the urge to lick it was bad enough, but when she pursed her mouth, her lips forming a tempting pout, he totally lost his train of thought. What the hell had they been talking about?

"I'm sure I would remember," she said finally.

"Oh, yeah, right. Me, too." He should have had another drink. Never had he been so tongue-tied or at such a loss for words with a woman. "I mean, Dallas is an unusual name."

"Not in my family. My sister's name is Dakota. My brother's name is Cody."

"I'm sensing a pattern."

Her lips curved in a wry smile. "Very astute."

He smiled back. "Cody isn't so unusual."

"Not now. Thirty-three years ago it was, and he hated it with a passion."

"Ah, he must be your much older brother."

Laughter sparkled in her eyes. "*Much* older."

He guessed she was in her midtwenties, not that it mattered. "Where do you fall in the pecking order? Middle?"

Her eyebrows rose, and she seemed a little annoyed. "Does it show?"

Eric shrugged. "I haven't been around you long enough to know."

She didn't say anything but sipped her wine, still looking a little put off.

He understood her touchiness, which he wisely didn't point out. As far as he was concerned, whoever had come up with the "middle child syndrome" theory was on to something. He knew firsthand. "I'm right smack in the middle myself. A brother three years older and one three years younger. Both pains in the ass."

Her smile returned. "But you love them anyway."

"Yep, though I admit I don't always like them."

"Amen."

"We have something in common then."

Her voice lowering to a husky pitch, she said, "I wonder what else we have in common."

This had to be a joke. She was too perfect. And she'd just handed him the perfect opening. "How about we find out over dinner sometime?"

She blinked, uncertainty flitting across her face.

Eric silently cleared his throat. Had he misread the signal? Had he screwed up? It wasn't as if he'd been pushy. "Look, I—"

The lights flickered once, twice.

The room quieted for a few seconds, until the tinkling sound of metal meeting crystal broke the silence.

"May I have your attention?" Mrs. Webber stood with a crystal goblet in one hand and a silver spoon in the other. "I'd like you all to return to the table. We have a special dessert we're about to serve."

Great. Just how he wanted to spend the next hour. Eric turned back to Dallas.

She was gone.

CHAPTER THREE

AFTER EVERYONE WAS SEATED, THE LIGHTS went out and two waiters carried trays of flaming Baked Alaska high above their heads into the dining room. Several people clapped, and during a chorus of oohs and aahs, the lights came back on.

Across the long table, where Tom had made sure Dallas was seated with him and his wife, Eric's eyes bored into hers as if the lights had never gone out. As if even in the dark he'd been drawn unerringly to her. And like a deer caught in the headlights, Dallas held his gaze, totally powerless to look away.

"This is rich. This is just too friggin' rich," Tom murmured, drawing her attention. "I should have brought a damn camera."

Thankfully the waiters began serving the Baked Alaska, and Dallas used the distraction to pull herself together. If she were smart, she'd excuse herself from the table and leave the party. Between his staring and the other guests' curiosity, she was bound to trip up. Make a fool of herself.

She'd purposely come after dinner so that she could flit about the room just out of his reach, engage in some harmless flirting, make him a little crazy and then disappear. The last thing she'd wanted was to be stuck at the table. Damn, she didn't even like Baked Alaska.

Her gaze drew back to him. Sitting beside him, a slim

fortyish woman wearing too many diamonds on her fingers and an unhealthy tan had managed to monopolize his attention. Dallas used the opportunity to give him a once-over. Watch the way his mouth quirked up on one side in a sort of lopsided smile.

He really was good-looking in a conservative way. She'd like to see his hair a little longer, but that was cosmetic. The basics—the structural stuff, like the strong square chin—were there. Great lips, too. Nice and full on the bottom.

Then again, the clean-cut look wasn't bad for a change. Many of the guys she worked with had hair long enough to tie into a ponytail. Except for her best bud Tony, and even his dark, shaggy mop rested on his collar.

Tom made an odd gurgling noise behind his napkin, trying to stifle a laugh. "Look at him. He's in a daze talking to Miriam Lancaster. Doesn't even know what hit him. Did you see when he was trying to get my attention earlier? Do I have a poker face, or what?"

"Tom, stop it." Serena's warning voice was low, but both Dallas and the woman next to her heard. Serena's voice dropped a few pitches. "Besides making an ass out of yourself, you're going to blow it."

"Okay, okay." He stared at his plate until he was able to compose himself. It lasted three seconds before he started to chuckle again. "Did you see his face when—?"

"Tom, I mean it. I'll leave." Serena glanced at Dallas. "This is so incredibly juvenile. I'm sorry he involved you."

"Juvenile, hell. This is priceless." Tom's eyes gleamed until Serena picked the linen napkin off her lap and started to fold it, preparing to get up. "All right, I'll shut up."

She hesitated and then laid the napkin back down on

her lap. Tom cast another glance at Eric and then at Dallas, pressed his lips together and picked up his fork.

Through the rest of dessert, Dallas sat quietly even though her heart raced like a thoroughbred rushing for the finish line. She'd figured she'd be nervous. And she was a little. Had almost backed out at the last minute. She'd certainly never expected the exhilaration she felt or the giddy headiness of power and control that continued to build.

While Eric knew nothing about her, she knew a lot about him. Knew he was a Columbia graduate who'd been steadily climbing the ladder of success from the day after he'd graduated. His hard work had paid off, and he was a rising star with Webber and Thornton, a company that believed in family and socializing outside of the office. Eric was the only holdout, unmarried and never even bringing a date to the company functions.

She liked that about him. A rebel, kind of like herself. But the similarity ended there. His friends and acquaintances belonged to an elite circle. The kind she shunned. No, not shunned, really. That wasn't accurate. But her world was definitely more eclectic. By choice.

But that's what made tonight's cameo appearance fun. No one knew anything about her. Not even Tom. He assumed she was a freelance model. She hadn't bothered to correct him. Wouldn't he be surprised if he discovered the truth?

She surveyed the other guests, all dressed to the nines, every hair in place, perfect manicures and polite smiles. They'd all be surprised to learn what she really did for a living. Disgusted maybe. As her parents were. To some extent, at least her brother and sister understood her need for autonomy. Not that they approved of her choices.

Dessert seemed to go on forever. Lots of cognac and

fancy liqueurs were served. Fortunately enough subdued chatter muffled private conversations that she was able to easily fend off the polite curiosity of the other guests before Eric could get wind of their exchange.

According to Tom, only he, Serena and Mrs. Webber knew about the joke. Everyone else thought she was a visiting friend of the Webbers' absent daughter. Dallas stuck to the story, and curiosity generally died quickly.

Not Eric's, though. His gaze often strayed in her direction, although to his credit, the woman beside him would never know he was distracted. He smiled and inclined his head toward her when she spoke, did all the courteous things expected of him.

Only Dallas knew his thoughts were about her, that more than curiosity burned in his eyes when they met hers. Every nerve ending in her body reacted. As if two live wires connected and sparked with each look.

She tried to avoid the contact. Pretended interest in a boring conversation with Serena about the upcoming Heart Ball and the local celebrities who'd be attending. But she was just as hopeless, her gaze drawing back to him, admiring the breadth of his shoulders, the generosity of his smile, as the woman kept him busy.

He looked at her suddenly as if he'd felt the weight of her stare. To her amazement, she didn't look guiltily away. She held his gaze for a long, torturous moment, gave him a slow smile that invited all sorts of possibilities.

He wasn't shy about returning the volley. His gaze wandered down the front of her dress, lingering just long enough on her breasts to remain respectful yet make her tingle all the way down to her toes.

She finally had to look away. Or end up in an embarrassing puddle on the floor. He had the most incredibly intense eyes. The eyes of a man who knew what he wanted and went after it with everything he had in his arsenal. The thought frightened her, fascinated her, and then she remembered that she had the power here. Anything that happened would be by her design. She was no Cinderella hoping to be swept off her feet, rescued from life's drudgery.

Dallas's life was just fine, with or without a man. Less reliance on the old vibrator might be nice for a change, but that didn't mean she was willing to settle for just anyone. But Eric...well, he was looking like a pretty damn good substitute. Smart, attractive, successful, ambitious. Not that his view of success was important to her. In fact, her lack of interest in such matters was what put her at odds with her family.

But all that along with his standing in the business community made him a safe bet. At least for a couple of nights. What would it hurt? He didn't even know who she was. Even if he tried to contact her through the store, Trudie was the only one who knew her and Trudie wouldn't tell him anything. Trudie thought she was insane for doing this as it was.

Maybe she was crazy. This certainly wasn't her style. Her gaze drew to Eric again. He'd been watching her. Her pulse skidded. She nearly dropped her fork. This was going to be one hell of a night.

HE HAD TO TALK TO HER AGAIN. Alone. Away from the party. The Baked Alaska dishes had been cleared from the table. Cognac had been served. People had begun milling around. In about a half an hour they would start leaving. He had to make his move.

If he could find her. She'd left the table five minutes ago. He'd tried to follow but gotten waylaid by Brian Sutter's wife. Brian motioned for her a moment later, but Eric couldn't get away before Eve Dinton ambushed him.

Tonight of all nights it seemed as if everyone had to talk to him. Normally he didn't mind making polite conversation with his coworkers' wives, but if he heard about another unfair Little League game or about the rising cost of produce, he'd jump off the...

"Hello again."

Her feminine scent tickled his senses even before he turned to find her directly behind him. His attention immediately went to her glistening peach-tinted lips. They parted slightly and she drew back a step.

"I'm sorry. I didn't mean to intrude," she said almost in a whisper, and he realized he was just standing there. Staring. Speechless. Like an idiot.

"You didn't." He touched her arm when it looked as if she might take off. "Not at all."

She smiled tentatively. "You seemed so deep in thought."

"The truth is—" he lowered his voice "—I was thinking about the Webbers' rooftop garden."

"Oh." Her eyebrows drew together, and she hesitated, looking confused. "You like to garden?"

He laughed. "I was thinking about jumping off."

Her eyes widened.

"This isn't exactly my first choice for spending an evening."

"Ah, I see."

"Nice people." He shrugged. "But I see most of them every day at the office."

"Coworkers are kind of like family. You don't choose them," she said thoughtfully. "But you do have to make nice whether you like them or not."

He snorted. "That's debatable."

She smiled. "You get a point for honesty."

"Does that mean you'll go someplace for a drink with me?"

"Leave here?"

"I know this bar right around the corner. It's a nice place with piano music and—"

She'd started shaking her head. "I can't."

"Okay," he said slowly, "no problem."

"I'd like to, really…"

"But?"

She glanced over at Tom and Serena still sitting at the table. "I just don't think I should leave."

"Tell you what, how about we take a couple of cognacs up to the garden?"

"On the roof?"

"Sure. It's quiet. Great view of Central Park and Columbus Circle."

She seemed reluctant though definitely interested. "Won't the Webbers mind?"

"Not a bit."

"Sounds like you've done this before."

He smiled. "Actually I've only been up there once, when Mrs. Webber gave the grand tour a couple of years ago."

She glanced at her watch. "I suppose it would be all right for a few minutes."

"Then you turn into a pumpkin?"

Her lips curved in a mysterious smile. "Something like that."

THE GARDEN AREA WASN'T LARGE. Dimly lit, about the size of a guest room, flowers grew everywhere. Red geraniums, white daisies and sprays of pink blossoms spilled from several barrel-size stone urns. A trellis leaning against the reddish brick was covered with tiny climbing white roses that perfumed the air with their seductive scent.

Beyond the decorative black wrought iron that surrounded the rooftop garden were the lights of Manhattan and the shadows of Central Park.

"What a fantastic view." Hands gripping the rail, she leaned out, a gentle breeze blowing back her honey-blond hair, giving him an unobstructed view of her profile. The small, slightly upturned nose and skin that was remarkably flawless except for the scar.

Eric's curiosity got the better of him and he asked, "How did you get that?"

She turned to look at him and he pointed to his own chin. Her hand shot up to touch the marked area, her mouth twisting wryly.

She rolled her eyes. "Totally my fault. I got it at work when I wasn't paying attention."

"At work? How?"

She looked away. "This is a beautiful view. I wonder how much one of these co-ops cost." She smiled. "Not that I'd ever be able to afford one."

"I will someday."

Her eyebrows rose. "Ambitious or optimistic?"

He laughed. "Both."

"I wish you luck." She gave him a peculiar smile and then turned away to look out over Central Park.

"You must make good money modeling."

A smile played at the corners of her mouth. "What makes you think I'm a model?"

He stared, waiting for a telltale flicker to cross her face. She didn't even blink. "Aren't you?"

"No. But I'm flattered." She seemed so damned sincere. Maybe he was going crazy.

"Then what do you do?"

A GLIMPSE OF FIRE

"Why?"

He shrugged. "Just making conversation."

"Then you won't mind talking about something else." Her lips curved in a smile that made him her slave.

A totally new experience for him. He liked women, of course, but he hadn't found one yet that had him thinking with the wrong head. Not since high school, anyway. "You like being the mystery woman, huh?"

The smile lingering on her lips, she lifted her chin and shook back her hair, lifting her face to the balmy breeze.

"So, if I can't get more than your name, how am I going to ask you out to dinner?"

After a moment's hesitation she looked directly at him and asked, "When?"

"Tomorrow night." God, he hoped he could get a reservation this late. "Amuse Bouche. It's that new restaurant at the—"

"I know it." Amusement lit her eyes. "Trying to impress me?"

"Damn right."

She laughed. "Another point for honesty. But unless you had another date cancel on you, we will not be getting into Amuse Bouche tomorrow night."

"I confess. No reservations, but I know the maître d'."

"Ever been to Hakata on West Forty-eighth?"

He frowned. "Sushi place, isn't it?"

"Among other things."

Just his luck, the woman was one of those adventurous-eater types. That was the trouble with New Yorkers. They weren't happy with a simple steak. "You wanna go there?"

She grinned. "Ever tried sushi?"

He sighed. All the guys in the office kidded him. When they went for sushi, he went to McDonald's. "I have a feeling I'm about to."

"Your enthusiasm is overwhelming."

"The stuff is raw. Can't be good for you."

She laughed. "Common misconception. Sushi can include raw fish but not necessarily. Don't worry. I'm a pro at ordering for neophytes. I'll be gentle with you."

He cleared his throat and tried not to make anything of the way she moistened her lips. Tried not to stare at her glistening lower lip. "Not too gentle. That would take out all the excitement."

Her eyebrows rose.

Eric smiled. "Bring it on."

She laughed, deep and throaty, and the sound skated down his spine. "You're giving me carte blanche?"

"I'm all yours." He hoped they weren't talking about sushi. Or he was screwed.

"Hmm…"

He moved closer. She didn't retreat. Excellent sign. "So, what would you like to do with me?"

"Oh, I never tip my hand too soon."

"Oh, right. A woman of mystery and surprise."

"You have no idea."

"I'm willing to stick around until I get an idea."

She smiled. "You get another point for being adventurous."

"Yeah? And what exactly are these points worth?"

She tilted her head to the side and pursed those sexy lips of hers. "I'll have to think about it."

"I don't." He took her hand, and when she didn't resist, he pulled her against him and slid his arms around her narrow waist.

She tilted her head back, her eyes glittering with unmistakable challenge. He lowered his head and she lifted her chin to meet his lips. They touched, gently at first, tentative, searching, exploring, and then she opened her mouth to him.

He slid his tongue between her lips and tasted her eagerness. That's all the permission he needed to plunge deeper. When she put her hands on his chest and slid her palms up to his shoulders, the tips of her fingers doing this little stroking thing that drove him crazy, he stifled a moan, willed his sudden hard-on to calm down before he scared the hell out of her.

But he couldn't calm down and she didn't scare. Instead she moved her hips, taunting him, driving him beyond insane. He cupped her backside, not sure if he wanted to stop her or make her grind harder.

Taking the decision out of his hands, abruptly she moved back, stared at him for a moment and then let her hands slide down his chest. "I have to go."

"Now?"

She smiled. "Tomorrow?"

"Yeah, sure— Wait!"

She'd already headed for the door that led to the stairs but stopped hesitantly and then turned to him.

"Dallas?"

"I'll be there at seven," she said and then took off.

CHAPTER FOUR

DALLAS HAD BARELY FINISHED HER FIRST cup of coffee when Wendy plodded into the kitchen, still wearing red boxers and a white tank top—her preferred pajamas.

"What are you doing up so early?" Dallas asked, wondering the same thing about herself. She'd only had four hours' sleep, tops. After she'd gotten home, she'd been so wired, she'd stayed up and watched *Pretty Woman* for the twentieth time.

Well, she hadn't actually watched it. Stared, really. While she'd replayed the kiss over and over again in her head. While she'd imagined his hands curving over her butt, drawing her against his erection.

"I'm dying to hear about last night." Wendy got her usual morning cola out of the fridge. "Did he totally freak when he saw you?"

Dallas smiled, thinking about the stunned look on his face as he'd approached her. "He pretty much kept his act together when we were introduced. Although I'm not sure when he first spotted me."

"Who did he think you were?" She popped the tab of the can, sat cross-legged on the love seat and then yawned before taking her first sip.

"A friend of his boss's daughter. But we kept it vague."

"How late were you out?"

"I got in around midnight. You need a haircut."

Wendy's hand went to her spiky hair, and she hopelessly tried to pat it down. "I know. As soon as I get a few bucks together, I will. Maybe next Friday."

Dallas forced herself to keep her mouth shut. She was always ready to bail someone out. It wasn't that she was a pushover. She preferred to think of herself as a nurturer. Anyway, even if she offered Wendy a loan, she wouldn't take it. To her credit, Wendy watched her finances. "Any news on the audition?"

"I didn't make the final cut."

"I'm sorry."

"*C'est la vie.*" Wendy shrugged. "Maybe I should start sleeping with directors."

"Right." Dallas rolled her eyes. "That would be a good move."

"Hey, I didn't get up early to talk about how I screwed up yet another audition. Tell me about last night."

Dallas briefly turned away to pour another cup of strong black coffee. "Speaking of getting up early, I had to walk Bruiser again."

"Oh, no. Sorry. You should have knocked on my door."

"He yelped and howled for five minutes. If he couldn't get you up, I doubt I could have."

Wendy sighed, and then her lips started to curve as the curly black mutt, having heard his name, lumbered out of his cushioned basket and then stretched before leaping up onto the love seat with Wendy. "He's so cute, isn't he?"

"Adorable. Especially at six in the morning."

Wendy gave her a sheepish look but then narrowed her eyes. "You're trying to avoid talking about last night."

Dallas rubbed the back of her neck. "Not really," she said, even as she privately acknowledged there was some truth there. "Last night was great. More fun than I'd expected."

"Yeah?"

"Yeah." Dallas leaned with her elbows on the kitchen counter that served as their table and a room divider. She cradled her mug in her hands and stared at the black liquid. "Eric is really a nice guy."

"And?"

"And I'm seeing him again tonight."

Wendy's hand froze in Bruiser's curly black fur. "You're kidding."

"Why not?"

"Alone?"

"At a restaurant. I'm not totally insane."

"This is so totally not you."

"That's the fun part." Dallas grinned. "It's not me."

Wendy put down her cola, linked her fingers together as she often did when she angsted over something, which wasn't often enough. She generally acted first, thought later. "Okay, what's really going on here?"

"Nothing." Dallas straightened, her defenses rising. "What's with you?"

"You're worrying me."

"This coming from someone who'd sleep with a director for a role?" Dallas snorted. "Besides, you're the one who encouraged me to go last night."

"Hey, I was kidding about the director." Wendy rubbed her eyes and sighed heavily. "How much did you tell this guy about yourself?"

"I haven't told him anything."

"Nothing?"

"Nothing."

Wendy studied her with an annoying mixture of curiosity and concern. "You don't trust him enough to tell him anything about yourself but you're willing to date him."

"It's not about trust. And I'm not dating him. It's one time. Jeez." Dallas sipped her coffee and took a mental time-out.

"I don't like the idea of you seeing him alone."

"We won't be alone, *Mom*. That's why I chose a restaurant."

"Which one?"

"Like I'm going to tell you."

"Why not?"

"I don't want you spying on me."

"Would I do something like that?"

In a New York minute. Dallas didn't bother to answer. Only gave her a look.

"Okay, what if I promise not to?"

"What does it matter which restaurant?"

"If he turns out to be a serial killer and no one ever sees you again, I need something to tell the police."

Dallas groaned. "He's not a serial killer. He works for Webber and Thornton Advertising, for goodness' sakes. If anything, he's too conservative for me."

"Really?" Wendy smiled. "So, why are you going tonight?"

Dallas stared blankly at her friend. The truth was she had no idea.

SHE'D LIED. TO WENDY AND to herself. As soon as she saw him, Dallas knew why she'd agreed to come. She wanted him. Even for just one night. The situation presented the perfect opportunity. Anonymous sex. Behavior she normally wasn't into. But something about him really drew her. Sparked a need she'd suppressed for a long time.

He stood near the register, stoically watching the guys

making sushi behind the bar. He'd beaten her to the restaurant. And she was five minutes early.

After spending more time deciding what to wear than she'd care to admit, she'd chosen her newest pair of low-riding jeans and a light blue stretchy top that exposed about an inch and a half of her midriff and showed off her new tan, courtesy of Trudie. Casual but not sloppy.

Eric had dressed up a little more, in khakis and a hunter-green designer polo shirt, his tasseled loafers perfectly polished. She glanced down at her sequined flip-flops. At least her toes were polished; an electric pink, again courtesy of Trudie.

His fascinated interest in the sushi-making process came to an abrupt halt and he took a step back. The chef presented a plate of intimidating *hamachi*-and-eel sushi he'd been working on to a couple at the bar. Dallas smiled, and taking pity on Eric, she moved toward him.

"Hi."

He turned to her with relief in his eyes. "You showed up."

"Of course. I suggested the place, remember?"

He half smiled, and she realized he wasn't talking about the sushi.

The petite Japanese hostess returned from seating another couple and grabbed two menus off the counter. "How many?" she asked without a trace of an accent.

"Two," Dallas said, "and we'd prefer a table in the back if you have one."

"Let's see…"

While the woman searched the crowded restaurant, Eric whispered, "We can still make a break. There's a steak house right around the corner."

Dallas laughed. "Behave yourself and I won't make you eat anything raw."

"Follow me, please." The woman led them toward the back, her waist-long black hair swaying and shimmering like expensive silk as she wove in between tables. "Is this all right?" she asked, waving a perfectly manicured hand with long red fingernails at a table for two in the far corner.

"Perfect." Eric flashed her a grin that put a sparkle in her dark eyes.

"Enjoy your meal." She left the menus on the table and moved back toward the front as if she were gliding on air.

Dallas sighed as she took her seat. She really didn't mind being so tall, liked it usually, but sometimes she envied the seemingly effortless femininity of petite women.

Eric sat, too, his back toward the other diners. He didn't pick up his menu, only stared at her. Not in a rude way but enough to make her uneasy.

She cleared her throat. "Do you trust me to order for you?"

"Is this where the 'I'll be gentle' part comes in?"

"I thought you didn't like gentle."

"Depends."

"On what?"

His lips curved as he thoughtfully studied her for a moment. "So, that's how you wanna play."

She smiled back. "I'm not playing."

Challenge flickered in his eyes, but before he could deliver a comeback, the waitress appeared for their drink orders. He asked for a scotch, and Dallas ordered white wine. But that would be it for her. Work started at seven tomorrow.

"You come here often?" he asked, glancing around at

the other diners, mostly tourists, mostly couples but a few families.

"This is only the third time, but the food is good and reasonable considering they advertise in one of those tourist magazines." She stopped herself from volunteering that it was also close to her apartment.

"Yeah, I was surprised you chose a tourists' hangout. I figured you must live nearby."

She smiled and picked up the menu even though she knew exactly what she'd order. "You'd better have a look at the menu."

"I already know what I want."

The huskiness in his tone made her look up. She met his eyes and there was little doubt as to what he meant. She held his gaze but only for a moment before she had to look away. He didn't scare her. She frightened herself. Never before had the reckless urge to shun common sense been so strong. To jump in headfirst and consider the consequences later.

What the hell was it about him that made her want to be foolish? She pretended to study the menu, hoping her ridiculous desire to skip dinner and go straight to a hotel room would pass.

"What are you going to have?" she asked, keeping her eyes lowered to the menu.

"The teriyaki rib eye steak."

"You big chicken," she said, shaking her head at him.

"Hey, it's not like I'd ask them to leave off the teriyaki sauce."

They both laughed.

She laid down the menu. "How adventurous of you."

"You have no idea."

"Where are you from?"

"The Pittsburgh area. And you?"

She'd expected the return question and saw no harm in answering. "Right here. I was born at New York General, although I grew up mostly in Tarrytown. It's about forty minutes away."

"I know the area. Nice."

She nodded. "So green and pretty. I miss it but I like living in the city."

"Which part is that?"

She smiled. "How long have you lived here?"

"In Manhattan, about five years." His gaze roamed her face, lingered on her mouth. "I think our drinks are coming. Ready to order dinner?"

"Are you in a hurry?"

He gave her that sexy look again. "As a matter of fact, I am."

THEY LEFT THE RESTAURANT AN hour later. The sun had set, but there was still another half hour of light left. No way would Eric let this evening end. He still didn't know her last name or anything else about her. Other than she was from Tarrytown but now lived in the city.

Of course, knowing she'd grown up in Tarrytown provided more insight. He could safely bet his Rolex that her family had some money. The upper-middle-class community was a far cry from the steel-mill neighborhood where he'd grown up. Hell, even the Rockefellers had an estate there.

Although he didn't need particulars to know she came from a genteel background. Breeding showed in every step she took. The softness in her voice. The graceful way she moved. Modeling, of course, gave her polish, but she had her own natural panache that couldn't be learned or faked.

"How about a walk?" he asked before she could flag a cab and disappear.

"Sure. It's nice out. Not as sticky as last week."

"I say we head for Central Park."

Her eyebrows rose. "It'll start getting dark by the time we get there."

"Afraid of the big bad wolf?"

"Should I be?"

He smiled. "I think Tom probably assured you that I'm an okay guy."

"Tom?"

He shoved his hands in his pockets as they turned down Sixth Avenue. He badly wanted to touch her, but he'd wait for a signal. Let her call the shots. That's what she wanted. That's why she insisted on the secrecy.

"Was Tom at the party?" She seemed genuinely confused, which gave him pause.

"I figured it out, Dallas. We both saw you in the display window. Tom had to have put you up to this."

"What are you talking about?" She slid him a sidelong glance, her eyebrows drawn together in a skeptical frown.

"There's no other explanation."

She shook her head with a wry smile. "Maybe we ought to skip the walk. You need some serious rest."

"Yeah, I hardly slept last night." He kept watching her, noticed her near misstep, the way her cheeks colored a little. "What about you?"

"Fine. I slept just fine."

"Good. Then you shouldn't be in any hurry to get home."

She laughed. "Very sly."

"Look out." He grabbed her arm and pulled her close

when she nearly collided with a shabbily dressed man staggering wildly, obviously drunk.

"Thanks." She leaned against Eric as she glanced over her shoulder at the man, who'd already passed by—but not so his rank odor. "Sad, isn't it?"

The compassion in her eyes touched him, as misplaced as it was. He took another look at the guy, evidently homeless and drunk. "He needs a good meal instead of spending his money on booze."

"You don't know his circumstances." She pulled away. "He may have just lost his job or received some horrible news."

"You're right." He drew her back against him and slipped an arm around her shoulders. "I shouldn't have said that. But there were a lot of steel mills where I grew up. I saw what happened to men who lost their jobs."

Looking away, she murmured, "Yeah, I've seen it, too."

That surprised him. What did she understand about that world? About the blue-collar laborer who was so readily sacrificed to improve the bottom line of a corporation's financial statement? He understood. Too well. His brothers were fools for languishing in the mills, and settling for the same scraps their father had.

He caught a glimpse of Central Park a couple of blocks away, along with the lineup of carriages and horses with their colorful hats. "I have an idea. How about a carriage ride?"

"Are you serious?" She laughed softly. "Only tourists do that."

"Correct me if I'm wrong, but didn't we just eat in a touristy restaurant?"

"Touché."

"Come on. Let's pick out a horse."

She made a face. "We don't have much time before it gets dark."

He smiled, his body thrumming with anticipation. "Sometimes interesting things happen in the dark."

CHAPTER FIVE

BY THE TIME THEY GOT TO THE FOURTH horse—wearing a straw hat with an orange band and large drooping yellow daisies—Dallas knew Penelope was the one for them. The chestnut-colored mare had sweet, soulful eyes and a soft neigh, and Dallas immediately bonded with her.

She stroked her velvety head. "Penelope's definitely the one."

"You're sure now?"

"Positive." Glancing at Eric, she realized he was teasing her and she lightly punched him in the arm.

"Okay." He laughed. "Penelope it is."

He spoke to the driver a moment—an older man with drooping eyes and a face lined and brown as shoe leather—and then helped Dallas into the carriage. In seconds they were trotting into the park, the sound of Penelope's clopping hooves on the asphalt stirring a wistfulness in Dallas.

She sighed. "I haven't ridden in ages. I used to ride every weekend when I was in high school."

"Where?"

"At my grandparents'. They had a couple of Arabians and a palomino."

"Am I allowed to ask where?"

She smiled. "In Connecticut."

He slid his arm around the back of the seat and she snuggled closer. "They have ranches in Connecticut?"

"I didn't say they owned a ranch."

"Just recreational stables."

"You ask too many questions."

"I believe that was a statement."

She just shook her head. He chuckled, and then they rode in silence for a while, enjoying the slight breeze produced by the movement of the carriage.

Ironically, more and more questions about him paraded through her head. Based on what Tom had told her, she'd figured she knew exactly who Eric was. The Rolex around his wrist, the Gucci shoes, the designer clothes—all accessories of an image-conscious social climber—confirmed her belief.

Eric was exactly the kind of man her parents wished she'd bring home. He was precisely the type she never would.

But his comments about the steel mill usurped her logic. Made her wonder about his link to the other side of the coin. Not just because he had lived in an industrial city like Pittsburgh. A variety of jobs existed there just as in any other city. But there had been something personal in his voice, a tinge of bitterness that came from firsthand experience.

"See? Playing tourist isn't so bad, is it?" he whispered, his mouth so close to her ear that his warm breath sent a shiver down her spine.

"I'll admit this is nice." She turned her head toward him, knowing exactly what would happen.

His lips brushed hers lightly, a teasing swipe that left her wanting more. She angled toward him, resting her palm on his thigh. She heard his sharp intake of breath and realized just how high up she'd placed her hand. Resisting the urge to jerk back, she pressed her lips harder against his.

He ran the tip of his tongue across the seam of her lips until she opened to him. She heard voices along the path, someone giggling, but she didn't care. Her pulse raced with every swipe he took with his tongue, exploring the fleshy inside of her mouth, leisurely tracing her teeth.

Heat spread through her chest and up her neck. And then the warmth flooded her belly, spiraled lower, until she had to squeeze her thighs together.

Eric moved his hand to her waist, his fingers probing her bare skin where her shirt ended. She sucked in a breath as he explored her belly and then moved his hand higher so that he cupped the underside of her breast.

The driver started to whistle an unfamiliar tune. He hadn't turned around and seen them, she was relatively certain, but the reminder that they were out in public put a damper on her excitement.

Eric obviously sensed her retreat and stilled his hand. He broke the kiss and pulled back to look at her. She couldn't see his face very well. It seemed to have gotten dark so quickly.

"Something wrong?" he asked, his fingers idly stroking her skin.

"Other than the fact that we're in the middle of Central Park acting like two hormonal teenagers, no." She snarled. "Nothing's wrong."

"It's too dusky. No one saw anything other than us kissing."

She shifted so that his hand fell away from her belly.

"Tell you what, let's use the blanket." He reached behind him and brought out the small stadium-style blanket that had been left on the seat.

"It's too warm for a blanket."

"Exactly." He shook it out. "So why else do you think the driver left it."

She laughed. "He did not."

"Ask him."

"Right."

He laid the blanket across their laps. "Trust me. We aren't the first couple to neck in Central Park."

"I've always had a problem with the term 'trust me.'"

The carriage ran over a small bump and she fell against him.

"Sorry, folks," the driver muttered half over his shoulder without turning around.

Eric slid both his arms around her and brought her back against his chest. "Isn't that more comfortable?"

"It would be if I could—" She gasped as his hands moved up to cup her breasts. She leaned her head back and he kissed the side of her neck.

He inhaled deeply and whispered, "You smell good." He kissed her neck again, trailing his tongue to the area just below her ear. "You taste good."

She turned her head so that their lips met and slipped a hand between his thighs. Something he clearly hadn't expected. But wasted no time in using to his advantage.

He shifted his hips, and her palm slid against his bulging fly. His hardness startled her. Excited her. Empowered her. She twisted toward him, deepening the kiss, letting him slide his hand underneath her shirt. He reached her bra and worked his fingers inside, gently stroking the sensitive flesh around her nipple.

With her free hand she clutched the blanket to her chest. Not just for privacy but because he was making her crazy. What was she doing? She'd only met him last night. This wasn't her style.

She breathed in deeply. This was her fantasy, she reminded herself. She wasn't hurting anyone. In fact, it had been a long time since she'd felt this good. Felt the uncontrollable burning in her belly. Felt like saying *screw everything* and dragging him down to the grass.

He took her nipple between his fingers and she whimpered softly. He smothered the sound with his mouth, delving in deep with his tongue until she couldn't breathe. Couldn't think. Couldn't feel anything but his heat searing her skin, the feverish desire in his touch.

Like a sound echoing in a distant cave, she heard voices murmuring, laughing. Momentarily disoriented, she shifted, let her head fall back against his shoulder.

Approaching them on the path was another couple, on foot, not so far away. Dallas moved away from him and tugged down her bra and shirt. The blanket still hid them from view, but the spell had been broken.

Eric didn't move. He continued to hold her, his warm breath dancing over the side of her neck and ear. Once the couple had passed, he whispered, "My apartment isn't far from here."

She bit her lip. God, it was tempting. Incredibly tempting. She liked him. The chemistry was certainly there. This is what she wanted. So, what held her back?

She did have to get up early tomorrow.

What a load of crap. Her reluctance was about the whole fantasy thing. It would end. No more mystery woman. He'd find out she was an ordinary woman, working in construction, trying to pay off her student loan.

The polished nails and perfect hair, the sensational tan, the nice clothes—none of it was really her. If he passed her on the street while she was working in her normal torn jeans or coveralls, her hair tied back in its usual messy ponytail, he wouldn't give her a second look.

But then again, he'd only find out if she told him.

Which she'd probably blurt out once they'd made love. Except it would only be sex. Very different. So maybe...

"Dallas?"

Lost in thought, she jerked at the sound of his voice.

"Look, I didn't mean to push you. It's okay."

"It's not that. Really."

He kissed her briefly on the lips. "On Wednesday night one of my clients is having a reception. I'd like you to go with me." He paused, watching her closely. "Unless you have to work Wednesday night."

She did everything in her power not to laugh. His fishing was so obvious. Fortunately the original model had recovered and was back to work. "I don't work nights. Where's the reception?"

"At an art gallery on the Upper East Side. They'll be serving champagne and hors d'oeuvres. We can go out to dinner afterward." He kissed the side of her jaw. "Anywhere you want. Say you'll come with me."

The carriage began to slow just as the driver said, "End of the line, folks. Hope you enjoyed the ride." He slowly turned and grinned at them. "For thirty bucks, I'll take you around again."

"No, thanks." Dallas straightened and made sure she was put together before dropping the blanket. "I really do have to get up early tomorrow," she said to Eric and started to climb down.

"Wait. Let me go first." He hopped down before she could protest and then grasped her around the waist and lowered her to the ground.

"Thank you," she murmured, stopping herself from informing him that she was perfectly capable of climbing down by herself. She wasn't normally treated so chivalrously. In fact, she made it a point to be one of the guys. As it was, they needed little ammunition to harass her and the only other woman on the crew.

Eric handed the driver a couple of bills. She resisted

arguing over who should pay. They'd already gone that round in the restaurant.

It didn't matter that it was a Sunday night. Around Fifth Avenue and Fifty-ninth there were always people on the streets, mostly tourists, returning from Broadway or dinner or watching the street entertainers.

Not far from the corner a magician transfixed his audience with disappearing balls and trinkets, earning him delighted gasps and fistfuls of change dropped into his proffered top hat.

"I know a place that makes the best cappuccino." Eric raised his hand to hail a cab.

Dallas smiled. "I'll have to pass."

"It's only five minutes away."

"Sorry."

He muttered a mild curse. "I've screwed up."

"No, you haven't," she said, touching his hand. "Not at all."

He turned his hand over until their palms met and squeezed gently. "Am I going to see you again?"

She nodded just as a cab pulled alongside the curb.

"Will you go with me on Wednesday night?"

"Yes."

"I don't have your phone number." He opened the cab door and stood aside for her.

"I'll call you."

"What if I can't wait until Wednesday?"

She smiled. "You can take this cab. There's another one behind it."

One side of his mouth hiked up. "I don't suppose you'd let me ride with you to your place."

"I don't suppose I would." She leaned toward him for a kiss. A brief, friendly good-night kiss.

He wanted more and took it.

He tugged her forward and she came up against him, her still-sensitive breasts pressed to his chest. He cupped her nape, and as she opened her mouth to his demanding kiss, he held her steady while he got his fill.

The impatient cabbie muttered something about turning on the meter. The interruption saved her from ending up on the sidewalk in a boneless mess. She pulled away from Eric, her knees close to giving out, and crawled into the backseat, yanking the door closed behind her.

On the other side of the closed window, Eric smiled and then mouthed *Good night.*

The cab pulled away. She tried to wave. She didn't have the strength.

"YO, SHEA," TONY ST. ANGELO called from hands cupped around his mouth. "You ready for lunch?"

"Five more minutes," Dallas hollered back and then used her sleeve to wipe the sweat off her brow.

Today was way too hot to be working outdoors. But that was the breaks. Just part of the job. That's why she got paid the big bucks.

Right.

She adjusted her sunglasses and then dug for her bottle of water without letting go of the heavy Stop sign she'd been holding most of the damn morning. She hated traffic duty. With a passion. Even shoveling rocks and brick from a razed building was preferable. But this was a punishment she often received. For no other reason than being a woman working in a man's world.

Tony was one of the good guys. One of the pathetically few who didn't blame her for "taking a man's job away from him." He always waited to have lunch with her, though he was allowed to break at any time. The two traffic workers had the only formally scheduled breaks. She even had to get permission to go to the bathroom.

She waited for the radio message and then dutifully carried her sign to the middle of the road, bringing traffic to a halt and enduring angry honking until the back loader cleared the intersection. Then she radioed to her partner on the other end to resume traffic and waited for someone to come and relieve her for lunch. She pushed back the top of her glove and checked her watch. As usual her relief wasn't in any hurry.

In the beginning, with the exception of Tony and Sam— and Billy, when the other guys weren't around—the rest of them had treated her like a pariah, pulling seniority and giving her jobs that no one else wanted. They had made snide remarks, sometimes crude ones, under their breaths when no one but she could hear. Even so, after they'd clocked out for the day, half of the stupid bastards had hit on her at least once.

That had mostly changed after she'd made it clear she wouldn't put up with that ridiculous behavior. Of course there were two exceptions who insisted on acting like macho idiots, but they were easy to ignore.

What really got to her was that Nancy—the other woman on the crew—put up with their harassment. She accepted after-work drink offers even though she couldn't stand the guys. But she was a single mother with limited skills who desperately needed the job and felt she had to play nice no matter what.

Dallas, on the other hand, stuck around partly out of stubbornness but mostly because she didn't know what else to do with her life. Nothing really called to her; she had no passion. Not like her brother or sister who both lived and breathed the intricacies of the law, or her father, a well-respected judge, whose views on education and child abuse had achieved national notoriety. Even her mother had made a name for herself in the science community. Dallas envied them their passion and focus. While in graduate school, after she'd become disgusted with modeling, she'd gone to a temporary agency for work. She'd quickly found she hated sitting in front of a computer all day. Adding columns of numbers hadn't turned out to be her thing either.

Then a new temp agency had mistakenly placed her on a construction site. To her amazement, she'd found she liked working outdoors. She no longer had to worry about every morsel she ate or what to wear, or how many mistakes she made typing. After she punched her time card, she didn't have to worry about anything related to work.

"Okay, Shea. Lunch." Rocky roughly grabbed the sign out of her hand. He was one of the two Neanderthals left and hated relieving her. "That's thirty minutes only. Got it?"

"Really?" She raised her eyebrows and looked at him over her sunglasses. "It hasn't changed?"

"Don't be a smart-ass," he mumbled and snatched the radio.

"I wouldn't want to take away your job." She smiled sweetly and walked away from his barrage of curses.

Tony was waiting for her at the curb with both of their lunch pails. "He giving you a bad time again?"

"What's new?"

"Damn low-life bottom-feeder. I still think you should report him."

"Like that would help." She took her *Aladdin* lunch pail—a gag gift from Wendy— from him and they both turned toward the small park they'd found last week. "He's in so tight with old man Capshaw, it's pathetic."

"Yeah, he's either kissing ass or sleeping with the old guy."

Dallas laughed. "You would think of that."

"Tell you what, how about I just punch him out in the meantime?"

"Hey, if that's what I wanted, I'd do it myself."

This time Tony laughed. "Yeah, you probably would. Seriously, though, I don't care how tight Rocky is with Capshaw, this is a legal issue. Capshaw's Construction is too big. He can't afford to ignore a complaint and get ripped apart by the EEO, ERA or whoever the hell is involved."

"You're right. But I don't think that's enough. One complaint would only get a wrist slapping."

"Both you and Nancy need to—"

"You're preaching to the choir."

"Yeah, I know. It just pisses me off that you have to put up with so much crap when you do a better job than half those losers." They'd sat under a tree and he opened his lunch pail. "Shit, peanut butter and jelly again."

Dallas shook her head as she removed her gloves, and then brought out her cheese and crackers and fruit. "Tony, you aren't married. You made your own lunch."

"Yeah, I know." He gave her that wide grin that had surely broken many hearts. "I haven't grocery shopped in a while."

She took off her baseball cap, tightened her ponytail, replaced the cap and then got out the hand sanitizer. "Why haven't you gotten married?"

"I've been saving myself for you. Wanna cola? I have an extra one."

"Come on. I'm serious."

"And nosy."

"Yeah, so," she said, laughing as she took the cola he offered.

He shrugged a shoulder. "Hell, I'm only thirty-one. I've got time."

"Here." She gave him a hunk of her Gouda.

"What about you?" he asked, his dark eyes suddenly full of curiosity. "Every time we go for a drink after work, you turn every guy's head in the bar. But you don't even talk about dating anyone."

"I keep waiting for you to ask."

He stared, speechless.

"I'm kidding." She winked. "You're my only friend here. I don't want to ruin a good thing."

"Yeah, that's what I'm thinking." He checked his watch and then bit into his sandwich.

She watched him chew, studying the clean lines of his jaw, the straight, almost patrician nose. His dark wavy hair was pulled back in a short ponytail. He was a really good-looking guy. The way his muscled biceps strained against his T-shirt sleeves caught the attention of nearly every woman who walked by.

But Dallas had never felt anything other than camaraderie with him. She had no idea why. Just no chemistry. No sparks like she had with Eric.

Just thinking about him made her all tingly inside.

How was she going to stand not seeing him until Wednesday night? That was almost forty-eight hours from now. Tomorrow night she had her meeting. Since she was the organizer, she damn well had better show up. Anyway, she had to get a dress for the reception on Wednesday night.

Thoughtfully she took a sip of cola. Tonight she wasn't doing anything. Her heart started to race as she summoned her courage. What the hell? She didn't have anything to lose. She was the mystery woman.

She checked her watch. Eight minutes left.

"Hey, Tony, I've got to make a phone call," she said as she started to gather her stuff. "You want the rest of this cheese and crackers?"

"You talkin' to me?" He grinned at his lousy imitation. "Leave everything. I'll pick it up. Go."

She smiled her thanks. Her cell phone already out of her pocket.

CHAPTER SIX

ERIC GOT HIMSELF A SOFT DRINK OUT of the refrigerator in the coffee room. The pastrami sandwich he'd ordered from the corner deli would be here any minute. On the few occasions he'd ordered lunch in, they'd delivered promptly.

Never in his life had he waited for a woman to call. Not even in high school when he'd had the hots for Tammy McIntosh, who'd had the best breasts east of the Mississippi and had given him his first and thankfully only hickey. Every guy in school had wanted to take her out, and he'd had the pleasure three or four times. When things had started to cool between them, he'd moved on. No waiting around by the phone for him.

But today he waited. Even skipped going out to lunch with Tom just in case Dallas called. Tom hadn't volunteered squat about Saturday night. Which was really ticking Eric off. His so-called friend's innocent act had gotten real old. That's why Eric hadn't told him about dinner last night. Screw him.

On his way down the hall back to his office, he heard the delivery kid at the reception desk. He'd already left money with the receptionist so he needed only to grab the bag on his way back to his office.

"You had a call," his secretary said as he approached his office.

"What? Who?" Damn it. He'd been gone less than two minutes.

Looking confused and curious, Lucy handed him the pink message slip. "A woman. She said you'd understand."

"I told you to page me if I had any calls."

Lucy shrugged. "She wouldn't wait."

He frowned at the message. And then he smiled. It read: *Tonight. By the magician. Six-thirty. Dallas.*

"What's this?"

At the sound of Tom's voice behind him, Eric pocketed the message. "None of your business."

Lucy's eyes widened.

Tom laughed. "Testy today, aren't we?"

Eric sighed and went into his office.

Tom followed. "Is that your secret meeting place? By the magician?"

Eric sat at his desk and glared at him. "You read my message?"

"Yeah, but just over your shoulder. I'm assuming this is the same woman from Saturday night."

Ignoring him, Eric set aside the ad campaign he'd been working on for his newest client. Ironically an upscale take-out sushi place. He opened the white paper sack and brought out his sandwich. Normally he'd give Tom the dill pickle. Screw him.

"Come on." Tom sat in the burgundy leather chair opposite Eric's desk. "What's going on?"

"You tell me."

"What are you talking about?" The corner of Tom's mouth twitched. He could barely contain a grin.

"I'm not stupid. I know you set up Saturday night."

Tom frowned, pretending confusion. "Saturday night? I don't get it."

Eric unwrapped his sandwich. Forget it. He didn't need Tom to admit his involvement. In fact, he probably should be thanking the pain in the ass. "Don't you have work to do?"

"Come on. Tell your buddy Tom what's going on."

Lucy briefly ducked her head in. "Tom, Mr. Webber is looking for you."

"Thanks." He got to his feet and, with an annoying grin, said, "Later," before he disappeared.

Eric leaned back in his chair and stared at his diploma and awards on the opposite wall. His office wasn't much to write home about. Fairly small, sparse, just like all the other offices except for Webber's and Thornton's corner suites. The money and attention had gone into the conference room, where the ad execs met with clients.

He forgot about his sandwich. Forgot about the new ad campaign. Forgot about Tom and his stupid antics. All he could think about was seeing Dallas tonight.

By the magician.

Interesting choice. She could have named a restaurant. Or any number of places. Why Central Park, near the magician? Of course, having had to leave a message probably had something to do with not getting specific. Or maybe...

His heart started to pound. Blood rushed straight to his groin. He'd told her he didn't live far from there. Maybe she wanted to go to his place.

The thought took hold and wouldn't dissolve. He barely remembered eating his sandwich. But suddenly it was gone and he was crumpling up the wrapper.

The rest of the afternoon was a total loss. Flashes from last night haunted him. Consumed his concentration. He swore he could smell her honeyed scent, could feel the weight of her breasts in his palms. His body responded fiercely to the memory of her slipping her hand between his thighs. After that, he couldn't even get comfortable.

An hour earlier than usual he packed it up. He hadn't gotten a damn bit of work done for three hours. All he could think about was Dallas.

SHE LEFT THE PLAZA HOTEL, where she'd stopped for a drink with Trudie, five minutes before the appointed hour. Trudie thought Dallas was insane for carrying on this charade. But, of course, Trudie's idea of adventure was trying out a new grocery store.

This was perfectly harmless, Dallas assured herself. She knew she wasn't the type of woman he wanted. He wasn't her type either. Not that she had a type. She'd had a couple long-term relationships, including going steady with Steve O'Neil for three chaste years in high school. Every one of the guys had been different. With the exception of Steve, she'd been the one to break off the relationship. The truth was, she didn't know what she wanted.

But she hadn't lied to Eric about herself. She simply hadn't told him anything. He knew all he needed to. Simple sex required no history, no promises.

Eric was already there. He was listening to a couple playing the sax and singing on the corner. Her pulse already starting to race, she slowed to watch him a moment, enjoying the way his jeans hugged his long, lean legs. He had on a black T-shirt this time, but she'd bet anything it had some kind of designer logo on it. That was okay. She was glad he'd dressed more casually than last night. In fact, what she had in mind didn't require clothes at all.

The song ended, and Eric threw some bills in the basket at the couple's feet, then stepped away from the crowd and turned in her direction. He spotted her and smiled.

The way her heart seemed to flip-flop was totally ridiculous. Amazingly foolish. But only because he had such a good body. Not muscular but kind of lean and wiry, like a long-distance runner.

"Hi." He took her hand and bent to kiss her briefly on the lips.

The familiarity surprised her, and she stiffened.

He released her hand. "Guess I shouldn't have done that."

"No. I mean, it's fine. Really." She shrugged a shoulder, feeling awkward suddenly. "You just took me by surprise."

"So did you. Thanks for calling."

"I wasn't sure you'd show up."

He reared his head back. "You gotta be kidding."

She smiled, her confidence returning. "You could have had a meeting or something."

"I would have canceled it."

"Just like that?"

"Uh-huh." He smiled, his gaze slowly taking in the clingy peach-colored V-neck top she'd borrowed from Wendy. Probably a tad too small for Dallas, but she loved the color. "You look great. I mean, really terrific."

"Thanks," she murmured, a little embarrassed by his obvious appreciation but also glad she'd splurged on a trendy new pair of white capris after work. Might as well show off her tan while it lasted.

He took her arm and they started walking. "You have anything in mind?"

She nearly missed a step and had to take a deep breath before she answered. "A drink maybe."

"How about some dinner?"

"Okay." She wasn't the least bit hungry. But she supposed dinner could be a start. "Have any place in mind?"

"Hmm…" He thought for a moment. "You like Chinese?"

"Love it. But this time it's my treat. Nonnegotiable."

He smiled. "There's a hole-in-the-wall five blocks from here. Great food. They even cook everything."

She laughed. "You were a good sport last night."

"I still think that California roll had something raw in it."

"See? You're still alive."

He stopped and stared at her. "You swore there was nothing raw in—"

She burst out laughing. "Teasing. Only teasing." She held up her hands. "I swear."

With phony gruffness he grabbed one of her hands and pulled her toward him. An older lady wearing a huge straw hat and walking a Chihuahua had to sidestep them and she muttered a surprising oath about them blocking the sidewalk.

Eric apologized, though unable to lose the smile, then steered them off to the side. "I thought she was going to sic Bruno on us."

"Don't underestimate those little suckers. One of my college roommates had a Chihuahua. He had me cornered a couple of times."

They'd started down Fifty-ninth again, and he looked over at her. "Where did you go to school?"

She hesitated. "Cornell."

"Whoa. Nice. Scholarship?"

"Partial."

He nodded. "What was your major?"

Dallas stalled a moment. She really didn't want to get into this personal a conversation, but nor did she want to ruin the evening. "Let's just say that much to my parents' delight, I'm not working in the same field in which I studied."

"Which would be?"

She smiled. "Are we there yet?"

He gave her a speculative look and then decided to drop it. "Almost. Hungry?"

She nodded, which was a lie but she'd effectively changed the subject. "Hope they aren't too crowded."

He took a long time looking at his watch. "They probably will be." He looked at her as they stopped for a red light. "I usually take out."

She held his gaze. "Fine."

"My place okay?" he asked slowly.

"Sure."

His eyes seemed to bore into hers. "It's only a block from Chun's."

"Let's go." The light turned green and they hurried across the street with the few other pedestrians who hadn't ignored the stop signal.

Eric didn't say much for the next block, which made Dallas nervous. Although she hadn't volunteered much conversation either. Her thoughts kept straying to later. When they got to his place. Of course, nothing had to happen. They could just have dinner. Talk. Kiss a little.

Yeah, right.

She was getting damp just thinking about being alone with him. About the way he'd kissed her last night and how she'd felt the warm, gooey sensation down to her toes. About how he'd gently cradled her breasts.

Her breathing came so quickly that he even glanced over at her. "Are you okay?"

Heat climbed her neck. "Yeah, I'm fine. Really." Fortunately she spotted a sign for Chun's on the corner. "We're almost there."

"Yeah, that's it," he said with a final concerned look before taking her arm and ushering her to the door.

He hadn't been kidding. The place truly was a hole-in-the-wall. Really tiny, with only four tables, all taken, and a counter crowded with paper bags, presumably containing take-out orders. Several people waited in line as a young Asian woman efficiently yanked slips from the bags, called names and rang up bills at the cash register.

The aroma of onions and garlic and exotic spices permeated the air. This place was obviously the real deal and not a watered-down version to appease Western tastes.

Behind the counter an older man and woman worked side by side, stirring pots and tending a large grill against the far wall, speaking loudly to each other in Chinese. One of the customers got up from the table and went to the corner, where there were pitchers of water and iced tea and a bucket of ice. Sitting on a hot plate was a glass carafe of hot tea. He poured himself some and then returned to the table and his two companions.

Dallas smiled. She liked the place already. Kind of homey and friendly.

"I know it smells pretty bad, but I promise the food is terrific," Eric said as he took her hand and pushed his way inside.

"Are you kidding? I think it smells great."

The cashier looked up and smiled broadly.

"Eric." She glanced over her shoulder. "Mom, Dad, look who's here."

The short, graying man at the grill turned around. He spotted Eric and put down the long wooden chopsticks he was using, his big grin displaying a gold-capped tooth. "My friend, where have you been? I haven't seen you for three weeks, I think."

"Been busy working."

The man wiped his hands on his apron and gave Dallas a curious glance. "I see."

Unlike his daughter, who had no trace of an accent, the

man's English was heavily coated with his native dialect. The sly look he gave Eric, however, was universal.

"This is my friend, Dallas. And this is Jimmy Chun, owner and chef of this wonderful establishment."

Jimmy chuckled. "He likes to use funny words," he said and gave his palm another swipe across his stained apron before extending his hand to Dallas.

"Uh, Jimmy, I think you can skip the formality," Eric said, one eyebrow lifted at his friend's slightly soiled hand.

"Pleased to meet you." Dallas readily accepted the man's hand. If Eric only knew what her hands went through on a daily basis. Even wearing gloves all the time at work didn't totally protect them.

Jimmy grinned, a flicker of approval in his eyes. "You are most welcome here."

Eric waved to the woman still cooking. "Jimmy's wife, Ruth."

She smiled and then said something to her husband in Chinese, her tone slightly brusque. Dallas could sure guess what was said, with all the people lined up for their orders. Two more guys came in after they did, and the phone had rung twice. The place was really hopping. The food had to be good.

"Maybe we should come back," she whispered to Eric.

Jimmy heard. "No, no, you come with me."

He pushed aside the low swinging gate that separated the galleylike kitchen from the eating area and motioned for them to follow. Jimmy led them into a small kitchen where a young man wearing headphones and singing was dumping a huge pot of cooked rice into a wok heating on a stove.

Jimmy touched him on the shoulder and the man

stopped singing, turned toward them, a sheepish smile twisting his lips.

The kitchen was crowded with a stainless-steel commercial refrigerator, a double sink and a small stove. Too small for a business, but that's all that would fit. There was barely enough room for all four of them to be in there. Nevertheless she was impressed with how spotless the kitchen was kept.

"You tell me what you want. Anything." Jimmy jabbed a thumb into his chest. "You tell Jimmy and I cook for you. You like some orange chicken? Garlic shrimp?"

Eric put a hand on the shorter man's shoulder. "I'll give you an order, but no rush. I'll pick it up later. You need to go help Ruth. You have a lot of customers out there."

Jimmy waved a dismissive hand. "I have so many customers because of you. They can wait." With his hands motioning wildly, he barked instructions in Chinese to the young man.

"Jimmy, honestly we're not ready to eat. We have someplace to go." Eric briefly met her eyes and purposefully looked at his watch. "We'd like to pick up dinner in about an hour and a half, if that's okay."

"Anything for you, my friend." Jimmy looked at Dallas. "Something special for the lady? Our shrimp is very, very fresh today. Or how about some—"

"I love all kinds of food. Surprise us." She winked at Eric. "I hate to be rude, but we're going to be late."

"Right. I'll be back to pick up dinner in an hour and a half."

"You want us deliver?" Jimmy asked. "We deliver to you. One hour and a half."

"I'll call and let you know."

Grinning, Jimmy nodded. "Anything for my friend. You call."

"Thanks." Eric shook his hand. "Okay if we go out the back way?"

"Yes, yes. Please." He gestured toward the door.

Ruth called out something in Chinese, to which Jimmy responded in kind.

"See you later, Jimmy." Eric opened the door and motioned for Dallas to precede him.

"See you, my friend." Jimmy grinned with a raised hand and watched them go, seeming in no hurry to go back out and help his wife.

They ended up in a short alley with a foul odor thanks to the Dumpster stationed not more than four feet from the door and hurried to the street.

Eric made a face and muttered, "Sorry, who knew the place would be so jammed on a Monday."

"No problem." She shrugged. "We can eat anywhere. At the park if you like."

He gave her an odd look. "You're really something."

The appreciation warming in his eyes made her blush. "What?"

He kept staring at her, paying no attention to where they were walking, and then he said half under his breath, "You're going to be trouble, Dallas. Big trouble."

CHAPTER SEVEN

SHE WAS TRULY REMARKABLE. ERIC thought about how Tom's wife, Serena, would have reacted to the whole Chun's experience. Or Ryan's wife or Grant's wife. All nice, attractive ladies, but they would have been totally freaked out to have been herded back into the kitchen and then led out to that putrid-smelling alley.

Hell, he couldn't even imagine Judy shaking Jimmy's not-so-sanitary hand. It wasn't that the women were snobs or anything, just more refined. Different tastes, different backgrounds. They weren't the type to eat in dives, no matter how good the food.

He glanced over at Dallas just as they approached his building. She put them all to shame. Not just the way she looked… God, as if that wasn't enough. His chest and groin tightened just looking at her in those tight white pants that looked like a second skin molding that perfect butt. Nice and round and firm. Made his palms itch to cup her to him. Feel her pearled breasts against his chest.

He forced himself to look away before his jeans got so damn tight his doorman would have to help him to the elevator. Anyway, it wasn't just about the way she looked that turned him on or that set her apart from the other women he knew. It was the way she carried herself with confidence and grace. And more. Much more. Something indefinable that only years of stellar breeding could have produced.

Maybe tonight she'd tell him about herself, about her family. His desire to know about her went beyond curiosity. She fascinated him, occupied his thoughts more than was healthy for him or his career.

He stopped when they got to his apartment building and greeted the new doorman who'd started last week, after Hector had retired and moved to Miami. Eric gestured for her to enter the lobby.

She blinked at him in surprise. "You live here?"

Nodding, he led her to the elevator.

"Nice."

He smiled. "Too bad the lobby's bigger than my entire apartment."

"So is mine, but at least you have a doorman and an elevator."

"You have a walk-up?"

"It is now. The elevator broke and they won't repair it."

"Wow!" He frowned at her. Surely she could afford something better.

"Why are you surprised? It's great exercise. And certainly more affordable."

The elevator door opened, they both stepped inside and he punched the button for the fifth floor. "But having a doorman is more secure."

"True, but fortunately we haven't had any problems."

"We?"

She looked hesitant and his heart plummeted. "I have a roommate."

"Ah." He waited for her to drop the bomb.

"Her name's Wendy."

"Oh." He didn't even bother to hide his relief.

"Did you think—" She squinted at him. "I wouldn't be

here with you if I were living with someone or—heaven forbid—married."

"Unfortunately not everyone shares your conviction. What do you have against marriage?"

"Nothing."

They got to his apartment and he dug in his pocket for his keys. "That's not what it sounded like."

"I know, but I only meant that getting married is the ultimate commitment. Not something I would take lightly." She shrugged, glanced briefly at him. "Nor is it on my 'to do' list. Not soon, anyway."

"I understand." That pretty much summed up his feelings, too. He opened the door. "Jeez, I hope it's clean. I haven't paid much attention lately," he said with a perfectly straight face. "I have a woman who comes in once a week—unfortunately that isn't until tomorrow." That part was true.

Dallas walked in and looked around. "You don't need her. This place is cleaner than mine." She gave him a smile that suggested she knew he'd spent an hour picking up his crap and scrubbing the bathroom just before meeting her.

"I'm not here much. I work pretty long hours. Make yourself at home."

"This is really nice." She trailed her hand along the back of the tan Italian-leather couch he'd spent way too much money for. "Did you decorate it yourself?"

"No, not exactly. But I did pick out the furniture." Ashley, a woman Judy had tried to fix him up with, had done most of the decorating. Not at his request. She'd insisted. He'd seen her occasionally for about three months. Great sex. Lousy conversation. Their split was mutual.

"I really like this." Dallas crouched to study the oval glass coffee table with a black iron base that was supported by four wrought-iron legs in the shape of elephant tusks. "Very unusual."

"Yeah, it grabbed me. Hey, about dinner—I'm sorry about the delay. But I have some mixed nuts, if you're interested." He stepped into the small kitchen where he kept several bottles of wine, a bottle of scotch, a can of nuts, a jar of peanut butter and little else.

A brown-and-cream-colored granite-top counter separated the living room from the kitchen. Since there was no dining room area, he'd meant to get a couple of bar stools so the counter could be used as a table—as it had probably been intended—but he hadn't gotten around to it. He never entertained and rarely ate at home, except for maybe cheese and crackers while he sat in front of the television and watched a ball game.

"And wine. You like white, right?" He got out a bottle of chardonnay from the refrigerator. When he turned around, he found that she'd moved to the counter and, with her forearms resting on the granite, leaned toward him.

His mouth went dry and he exhaled slowly. Her neckline gaped enough to give him an excellent view of the tops of her breasts. He knew she wore a bra, but it had to be really low cut, because another inch and he'd be able to see the rosy crowns.

He realized he'd stared too long and he forced his gaze up to her face. She smiled. He cleared his throat and concentrated on opening the can of nuts.

"How did you and Jimmy Chun get to be such good friends?" she asked.

"We aren't really. I've been getting takeout there for about two years. That's all."

Her eyebrows went up. "He apparently has a different perspective."

"I did him a small favor and now he thinks—" Eric rubbed his jaw "—I don't know what he thinks."

"He thinks you're The Man."

"Knock it off or no wine for you."

She laughed. "There's definitely some hero-worship going on there. What did he mean about having so many customers because of you?"

"Nothing," he mumbled and got down the wine-glasses.

"Come on. Tell me."

"Are you always this nosy?"

She paused for a moment, as if giving the matter serious thought, her lips pursed in a sexy pout. "No, but I am determined." She shifted, giving him a better look down her blouse. "And you will tell me."

He took a deep breath and looked away. "Uh, what were we talking about?"

She laughed and straightened, taking the bottle he'd abandoned and pouring her own wine. "You were about to tell me what you did for Jimmy."

"Determined, you said. As in stubborn?"

"You got it." She gave him a smile that could seduce every last secret out of him. "Are you having white, too?"

"Sure."

She poured another glass of wine and handed it to him. Her fingers casually brushed his, and damn if his gut didn't tighten. "I'm listening."

He sighed and came around the counter to join her. After they'd both settled on the couch he said, "The place never seemed crowded. Even at peak lunch or dinner hour. And I knew firsthand the food was terrific. Then one day I overheard him talking to his daughter—the one who was at the register. He told her he was thinking of closing, that business just wasn't good enough to stay open. She got all upset, and—" he shrugged, uncomfortable talking about this "—I guess I stuck my nose in it."

Her head tilted slightly to the side, and listening intently, she sat facing him with one leg curled under her bottom. "And?"

He took a sip of his wine. "I'm in advertising. I drew up a simple and low-cost game plan to let people know about the place, designed some flyers and a reward system for referrals. The usual. It was nothing."

Her smile lit up her eyes. "You're a very nice man, you know that?"

"I'm telling you it was no big deal. To tell you the truth, if I'd known he was going to act like this, I wouldn't have done it." He focused on his watch. "I can't forget to call him."

Uncomfortable with the conversation, he didn't look up for a long time. She was making too big a thing out of this. What he'd done for Jimmy was remedial stuff he'd learned in college. It had been fun. Not like the work he did now, where the enormous pressure to please the client with his first pitch took all the pleasure out of his job.

"All right, we can change the subject," she said, running the toe of her shoe up his calf and taking a sip of her wine, her gaze fastened on him over the rim.

He smiled, set his glass on the coffee table, and then took hers out of her hand. "Come here."

Her lips curved, and she lifted her chin in challenge. "What do you want with me?"

"I'll show you." He wove a hand through her hair, cupping her scalp, and drew her toward him.

Just as their lips met, the phone rang. Eric ignored it but Dallas leaned back.

"Forget it," he whispered. "I'm not expecting a call." He tried to bring her back to him but she resisted.

"Could it be Jimmy? Does he have your number?"

"If it is, he can leave a message."

"Eric…"

He sighed. The mood had obviously disintegrated so he got to his feet. Before he reached the phone, he heard Jimmy's voice leaving a message on the answering machine. Eric muttered a word he shouldn't have and then picked up the phone.

Dallas watched him pace as he spoke to Jimmy. Even though he was obviously frustrated, his tone never revealed his annoyance. After a brief conversation he hung up and returned to the couch.

He shook his head. "He's delivering dinner."

She laughed. "You have a fan. Get over it."

"Remind me never to do any more good deeds." Sighing, he checked his watch. "He'll be here in ten minutes." He trailed a knuckle along her jaw and then tipped her chin up, brushed his lips across hers. "Any suggestions on how we should use the time?"

"You have Scrabble?"

"Funny."

"I—"

He didn't let her finish but pressed his advantage, slipping his tongue through her parted lips. She sort of fell against him, as if he'd just sucked all the energy out of her. Even if she wanted to refuse him, she couldn't muster the strength to pull away.

Not that she had any intention of retreating. The same musky masculine scent that had taunted her last night filled her every pore. His hand swept down her back, lingered at her waist, cupped the swell of her butt. His touch drugged her. Made her feel helpless. Made her want more.

"Take off your blouse," he whispered as he worked his hand beneath the fabric, his warm palm pressed against her skin, his strong fingers trailing up the muscle on either side of her spine.

"Shouldn't we wait for Jimmy?"

He smiled against her mouth. "You're into three-somes?"

Laughing, she leaned back to glare at him. "You know what I mean."

Eric chuckled and then fell back against the couch and groaned. "Damn that Jimmy."

She placed a hand on his thigh and squeezed a little. "Poor baby."

One of his eyebrows went up. "An inch higher and I'll let Jimmy wait in the lobby all night."

"And what about dinner?"

He looked horrified. "You mean we have to eat first?"

Dallas laughed. "First? Did you have something else in mind?"

His mouth curved in a predatory smile. He caught her arm before she could pull away. "I have lots of things in mind. Want to hear about them?"

She shivered and moistened her suddenly parched lips.

He drew her toward him, leaning forward at the same time. "Or would you rather I show you?"

A buzzing sound startled them.

Eric glanced apologetically at her. "Was that ten minutes? That was not ten minutes," he muttered as he got up and went to the door.

On the right was a small silver panel. He depressed a black button and the doorman's voice came through telling him he had a delivery. Eric spoke into the speaker and told him to let Jimmy come up.

Dallas checked her blouse, smoothed back her hair with a shaky hand and in general made sure there were no telltale signs of their fooling around. She didn't expect Eric would allow Jimmy to stay long. Which would be a very good thing. Her insides hadn't quit tingling. If Eric wanted to skip dinner and resume where they'd left off, that was more than okay with her.

He hovered near the door, with it slightly ajar, waiting for Jimmy. She thought she heard the elevator ding, and then Eric reached into his pocket and brought out some money, reminding her this was supposed to be her turn to buy dinner.

"Hey, I'm getting that," she said and pushed off the couch, looking around for where she'd dropped her purse.

"Please, one argument at a time."

"What?" She had no idea what he was talking about, and then Jimmy showed up at the door, carrying a bag of food big enough to feed five people.

She understood as soon as Eric tried to give him the money.

"No, my friend, this is a gift." Jimmy grinned and tried to shove the bag into Eric's arms.

"No way." Eric stepped back, his arms rigidly at his sides. "Either I pay for this or you take it back."

Jimmy shook his head, a hurt yet stubborn expression on his face.

Eric stuffed some bills in the man's breast pocket. "Take it, okay, Jimmy? Please." Then Eric took the bag from him, cradled it in his left arm and extended his right hand to Jimmy. "I'll see you in a few days."

Jimmy smiled and stepped back. "Okay," he said and left.

Tom had told her Eric was a rising star with Webber and Thornton Advertising. At the time she'd thought it might be an exaggeration to peak her interest, a ploy to get her to the company party. But she'd heard enough from the other guests Saturday night to make her a believer.

She leaned a hip against the counter beside him. "Mmm, smells divine."

He took a couple of white cartons out of the bag and read the black writing on the side. He set them aside and brought out three more cartons.

"Good grief. That's a lot of food. Enough for a party." She stared at the spread.

"Is that so?"

"Come on now. I offered to share my raw fish with you last night."

He winced. "Thank you very much for the reminder."

Grinning, she opened the carton of pot stickers. The tantalizing aroma made her stomach rumble. "These smell way too good. Is there dipping sauce?"

"I'm sure there is. Not that it matters."

At the odd tone in his voice, she looked over at him. "Excuse me?"

He took the carton out of her hand and set it aside. With a sweep of one arm he cleared the counter, sending the cartons of food up against the microwave. "I believe we have some unfinished business," he said, grasping her by the waist and lifting her onto the counter.

CHAPTER EIGHT

SHE COULD BARELY CATCH HER BREATH. Her heart threatened to explode. He'd taken her by surprise. "Hey, you, I'm wearing white. If I get anything on these pants—"

He smiled and kissed the side of her mouth. "You could always take them off."

She let her head fall back and he kissed her throat, continued on to her collarbone, licking the skin just above her neckline. He spread her legs and stepped closer until he was cradled between her thighs. He cupped her bottom and pulled her against him.

She sighed when he put his mouth on her breast, teasing the nipple with his teeth through the fabric. Automatically she tried to squeeze her thighs together, but he was right there, inches away from her core, where the dampness had started.

Clutching two fistfuls of his shirt, she yanked the hem out of his jeans and pushed it up as far as the shirt would go until he gave in and stepped back so she could finish the job. She tossed the T-shirt toward the couch and it landed on the arm.

He grinned. "Nice throw."

"Nice chest." She slid her palms from his shoulders over his nipples and down his belly, feeling it clench as she rested at his waistband. "You're a runner, aren't you?"

"I used to log five miles a day. Lately I only get out about three times a week."

She ran her palms back up, and as she grazed his nipples, he briefly closed his eyes. He didn't have a bulky, heavily muscled weight lifter's body. Simply lean and well defined with a light mat of hair—just the way she liked a man's body to look and feel.

"I know. Getting soft. I probably need to join a gym." He picked up a few strands of her hair and rubbed it between his forefinger and thumb. "It's like silk. I've never felt hair this soft and fine before."

He stared at it as if totally mesmerized, letting the strands sift through his fingers and then starting over. His gaze finally switched to her face and he smiled. He let go of her hair and used the back of his hand to touch her face.

"You're definitely not getting soft," she whispered, making another run up his chest, enjoying the feel of soft, springy hair beneath her palms.

His smile got crooked. "A truer statement was never made."

She realized the double entendre in what she'd said and laughed. "Oh, really? I haven't explored that far yet."

"What's keeping you?" He lowered his hands to grab a hold of her blouse and gently drew it over her head. Without looking, he tossed it in the same direction as his shirt. His gaze stayed fastened to her peach satin demicup bra. Or more accurately what spilled out of it.

Under the heat of his gaze, she shivered. The intensity in his eyes penetrated every bone in her body until she didn't think she could keep herself from sliding to the floor. "Why aren't we in the bedroom?"

He trailed a finger over the top of her bra, occasionally slipping inside the cup and grazing her nipple with his fingertip, creating a nearly unbearable friction. "We'll get there. Eventually."

The teasing in his smile told her he knew exactly what he was doing to her. It called her to action, and she slid her palms to his waist and attacked his belt buckle.

He murmured something indistinct. Sucked in his belly and closed his eyes. She freed the buckle and went for his zipper, but he moved out of reach.

Startled, she returned her gaze to his face.

To her satisfaction, he seemed a little shaken himself. "Oh, man." He exhaled loudly.

"What?"

"Wait. I'll be right back."

She twisted around to see where he was going. He went into the living room and picked up their wineglasses from the coffee table. She swallowed and looked down at herself, suddenly feeling too exposed.

"Bring my blouse, please," she called after him, but it was too late. He'd already entered the kitchen.

Alarm darkened his face. "What's wrong?"

"I thought you—" She shrugged, unwilling to voice her insecurities. "I don't know."

"Here." He handed her the half-empty glass of wine she'd abandoned. "I was abrupt. I'm sorry. No reflection on you, believe me." He got the bottle of chardonnay out of the fridge and then turned back to her with a frown—and one hell of a hard-on. The bulge strained against his fly, and she could barely keep from staring. "I take that back. It's you. You're making me crazy. I need a time-out."

She tried not to smile. "Sorry to hear that."

"Right." Snorting, he poured more wine in each of their glasses. He took a quick sip and then put his glass down beside her on the counter, his hungry gaze drawing to her breasts.

She got that warm, tingly feeling again and prepared herself for his touch. It didn't come. He reached around her and got the carton of pot stickers and a pair of chop-sticks.

Last night proved he was quite adept with the wooden utensils, but tonight he fumbled with them, and finally with a sigh of disgust, he cast them aside, fished out one of the dumplings with his fingers and put it to her lips.

She took a small bite, even though she was no longer interested in dinner, and he finished the rest of it.

That she was sitting here wearing only a bra and ca-pris and he was shirtless with his belt unbuckled eating dinner struck her as incredibly funny and she burst out laughing.

He licked the corner of her mouth. "Come on, admit it. This is the way to eat."

"Trying to steal my pot sticker?"

"I'm after more than that."

She was about to utter a smart retort when her stomach grumbled loudly.

He grinned and picked out another dumpling. "All you had to do was ask."

"I'm not really hungry," she murmured, embarrassed. "I don't know why it did that."

"Hungry or not, you need sustenance." He fed her an-other bite. "We have a long night ahead of us."

She swallowed and moistened her lips, the tingling starting again. "Yeah?"

"Oh, yeah." He locked gazes with her and, after a mo-ment, shoved the carton aside. "The hell with this," he said and scooped her up.

Dallas yelped. At five-nine, she wasn't the type of woman a man easily managed to carry. She tried to ma-neuver herself down, but he held tight and carried her into the bedroom. There he let her down gently, holding on to her until her feet touched the plush white carpet.

He lifted her chin, kissed her briefly and then unclasped the front of her bra. He stopped for a moment to admire his discovery with a fascination that stole her breath, then he tugged the straps off her shoulders. The bra slid down her back and onto the floor.

Lowering his head, he kissed one rosy tip and then the other. She blossomed against his mouth, ached for him to suckle her, but he took his time, finally leaning back to look at her again.

"Do you have any idea how incredibly beautiful you are?" He seemed a little dazed, astonishingly earnest, and she didn't experience the embarrassment she should have. Didn't make the wisecrack she normally would have about the dim lighting. "Tell me this isn't a dream. You are real, aren't you?"

She lifted herself on tiptoes and kissed him before reaching for his zipper. This time he didn't move. He watched her as she slid the zipper down, exposing brown silk boxers, and then shuddered when she touched him.

"Does this feel real?" she whispered, running the back of her fingers over the hard thickness straining against the silky fabric.

He murmured something, his voice too hoarse to understand. Grabbing her wrists, he forced her hands away. Took a couple of deep breaths, his chest heaving.

"Help me," he said, but she didn't understand until he moved back and yanked one side of the rust-colored quilt back from his queen-size bed.

She took the other side but gave up on trying to be neat about it when he shoved everything to the foot of the bed, heedless of the rich textured fabric that spilled to the floor.

When he reached for the lamp, she started to protest, preferring the filtered light coming from the living room.

But he switched it on dim, and the soft glow bathed the coppery tones of the room in a mellow warmth that helped calm her.

"Need help taking those off?" he asked, lowering his gaze to her capris.

She smiled at the nudge. He was already pulling off his jeans. "I think I can manage."

He stepped out of them and then without hesitation he slid off his boxers. She froze and stared. She tried not to. Tried to finish undressing. But she couldn't seem to move. He was truly beautiful. Breathtaking, really.

Swallowing hard, trying to get in motion, she told herself that he wasn't the best-looking guy she'd dated. In fact, she'd dated some real honeys. One of them a famous local model who'd had a terrific sense of humor. But something about Eric appealed to her like none of the others. Something beyond his good looks and generosity and sense of humor. Maybe it was simple chemistry. Maybe it was about this crazy mystery-woman fantasy of hers.

"I guess you do need some help," he said, discarding the boxers and approaching her.

She still couldn't move. Until he was right there. In front of her. And she reached out and touched him. His penis twitched at the contact, and when she circled the glistening tip, he shuddered. She curled her hand around it and stroked down to the base, and he moaned.

A sense of power surged through her, and finding a rhythm, she started to pump him, but he captured her wrist and stilled her hand.

"Wait, Dallas," he said, his breathing irregular.

She smiled. "Whatever for?"

"This." He lowered his head and took control of her mouth, forcing her lips open with his tongue.

She didn't move when he released her wrist and slid

his hands around to her backside, squeezing gently while he kissed her senseless. It took a few moments before she realized he was sliding her capris down her hips, past her thighs.

He broke the kiss to pull them down her legs and stopped to nuzzle her breasts, swirling his tongue around one nipple and then the other. She shuddered and grabbed his shoulder, and he held her steady while she stepped out of the capris.

Standing in only a skimpy pair of cream-colored silk bikini panties, she sucked in a breath when he moved back to look at her. Appreciation gleamed in his eyes as his gaze swept her body, lingering at the small, silky triangle at the juncture of her thighs.

"Take those off," he whispered hoarsely, lowering his hands to his sides, his fists clenching lightly.

She obeyed by slipping her hands beneath the strips of lacy elastic across her hips and then slowly lowering her panties, her palms molding her skin as she slid the silky fabric down her thighs, taking her time, making him wait.

Visibly swallowing, he watched her, his chest rising and falling, his gaze riveted to her little striptease show. His hand went to his straining sex and he touched himself briefly before backing her up so that she fell on the bed. He sprawled over her, hungrily kissing her mouth, her cheek, her eyelids, as if it were impossible for him not to.

She moved her hips and his breathing faltered. He wrapped his arms around her and rolled onto his back, bringing her with him. Her hair fell forward, brushing his chest, and he pushed one side back from her face and rubbed the pad of his thumb across her cheek.

"So soft," he whispered. "So incredibly soft."

She reached between them, stroking his penis. "So hard. So incredibly hard."

He laughed, an abrupt gurgling sound, before rolling her back into position beneath him. "Okay, you asked for it."

She smiled. "Yes, I did."

To her surprise, he turned away. But then she saw that he'd reached into the nightstand and brought out a foil packet. He ripped it open and then handed it to her. She didn't know why it never came up, but she'd never actually done this before. The guy she was with always had.

Carefully she rolled the condom down the hard thickness, smiling when he reacted with a small jerk, his stomach clenching.

"Amused, are we?" he asked, his smile turning feral before he held her hands out wide and touched the tip of his tongue to her nipples ever so lightly. Just enough to make her crazy.

Then before she knew what had happened, he'd spread her thighs. Increasing the pressure of his mouth on her nipples, he explored her with his hand, gently probed her with his fingers until she clenched around them.

She wanted him inside her so badly, she must have somehow communicated it to him. With a guttural groan he positioned himself over her and slid inside with precise aim, as if this were their hundredth time. She bucked at the initial contact, tensing, until she adjusted to the size and feel of him.

He slowly withdrew, never breaking contact, and then thrust deeper. She shuddered and wrapped her legs around his waist, pulling him impossibly closer. Her response ignited him and he thrust faster, deeper, the muscles in his arms and shoulders straining as he held himself poised above her.

She clenched tightly around him and he groaned, started to withdraw, but she wouldn't have it and lifted her hips to stay joined with him. Clearly realizing her intention, he whispered her name and then thrust into her again and again and again until the first wave hit her. She turned her head into the pillow to keep from making too much noise as the convulsions nearly sent her flying off the bed.

He had no such restraint. He cried out as he climaxed, pounding against her, meeting her thrust for thrust until he collapsed on top of her, panting her name and showering her face with kisses.

Dallas lay back, boneless and spent, unable to catch her breath. Eric kissed her a final time on the mouth and then fell onto his back, sounding just as breathless.

"Wow," he said.

"Yeah, wow." She smiled and laid a hand on his thigh. "Double wow."

Chuckling, he rolled over to face her. "What are you doing tomorrow night? I know a great Italian restaurant."

She smiled at his amazing ability to recover. "I can't. I've got something going on tomorrow evening."

"How about Wednesday? Are we still on for my client's reception?"

"Sure."

He lay back with one arm behind his head, looked at her and gave her a smile that made her insides tingle. "Is seven okay with you?"

"Whatever time you think we should be there."

"I'll pick you up at your place around six forty-five."

She shook her head. "I'll meet you there at seven."

He didn't like it, given the sudden frown that drew his brows together.

She snuggled against him and toyed with the hair on his chest. "What's the address?"

"Trying to distract me?" He turned onto his side and curled an arm around her, hauling her against his chest. "You have to do better than that."

She reached between them and found him growing hard again. "Am I getting warmer?"

His laugh was shaky. "I am."

"It's almost midnight. I really should be going," she said, curling her hand around him and feeling him twitch.

"I don't think so."

Before she could reply, he had her on her back, her wrists pinned to the pillows, and she knew she wasn't going anywhere anytime soon.

DALLAS SLOWLY OPENED HER EYES. She blinked at the unfamiliar teak armoire and the valet beside it. The walls were painted a taupe color. Not white. This wasn't her room. Where the hell was she?

She felt movement in the bed. Warm skin brushed her bare back. Remembering where she was and who was curled against her, she smiled. Briefly she closed her eyes again. How could she have fallen asleep? She really had to go home. She still had some work to do for the meeting tomorrow evening. *Just another few minutes,* she decided and slowly turned over to face him.

Eric was still asleep, his lips slightly parted, his chin dark with stubble. She instantly recalled the slightly rough feel on her bare breasts and shivered.

He stirred and she lay quiet, waiting with mixed emotions to see if he'd waken. If he did, they'd probably go a third round. As enticing as that sounded, they both had to get up early tomorrow and he had a big presentation to make to a new client.

Her gaze went to the digital alarm clock and she bit back a curse. It was already after one-thirty. She had to go. No more fooling around. She slowly slipped out of bed and quietly gathered her clothes in the dark. To avoid waking him, she carried everything to the bathroom and dressed there.

When she was finished, she went to the kitchen, where she'd seen a notepad by the phone. She thought for a moment about what she wanted to say and then scribbled him a note.

The obvious place to have left it would be on her vacated pillow, but she dared not wake him. Instead she anchored a corner of the paper under the coffeemaker and then she grabbed her purse. She got to the door, hesitated and then, cursing herself under her breath, snuck back to his room for a final irresistible peek.

He was still sound asleep, his beautiful chest bare, the sheet bunched at his waist. Tempted to crawl back in beside him, she took a deep breath and then backed away from the door. With foolish reluctance, she let herself out.

CHAPTER NINE

DALLAS FILLED TWO PITCHERS WITH WATER and set them next to the coffeepot on the credenza against the wall. She counted the number of chairs at the long conference table and hoped twelve would be enough. Then again, if they weren't, that would still be a good thing. The first meeting had been held at her apartment, but the number of women interested in improving their work conditions had swelled to the point that Dallas could no longer accommodate everyone.

Fortunately her sister had offered the conference room at the law firm where she worked. Like the rest of the family, Dakota thought Dallas was nuts for shunning her MBA and choosing manual labor. But at least she accepted Dallas's choice and was sympathetic to the plight of women who worked in male-dominated jobs. She was also the least snobby of the Shea clan. Although she had her moments.

Dallas checked her watch. The women would start arriving at any minute. She unwrapped the tray of cookies she'd picked up at the corner bakery.

"Hey." Dakota poked her head in. "Everything okay?"

"Perfect." Dallas waved her inside. "Change your mind about staying for the meeting?"

"I can't." She glanced at her watch. "I have a class in forty minutes."

"You're teaching again?"

"Just a couple of summer courses."

"Like you don't have your hands full enough here."

"No lectures." Dakota glared, but she couldn't manage to keep the corners of her mouth from curving slightly. "*I* get paid to give them. That makes me a professional. Don't mess with me."

Dallas grinned at her younger sister. "Glad to see some of the old fire in you again."

"Don't go there."

"What?"

"I like what I'm doing, okay?"

"I'm sure you do."

"God, you know how much I hate that passive-aggressive tone—" Dakota stopped and stared at Dallas in disbelief. "You sounded just like Mom."

"Funny," she said and muttered a curse.

"Seriously. You totally sounded like her."

Dallas bristled and turned away to pour herself a cup of coffee. Of all the insults Dakota could have hurled, that was the lowest.

"No, really. I'm not trying to be obnoxious." She shrugged. "You really sounded like her."

Dallas sighed.

"But only for a second."

They looked at each other and laughed. It felt good. Just like the old days. Before Dakota had gotten so caught up in her career that she forgot to enjoy life. Just like the rest of the family.

"You want a cup of coffee?" Dallas asked.

"Nope. You know I don't drink that nasty stuff. Anyway, I gotta go." Dakota checked her watch again and then abruptly brought her head up. "I almost forgot. Mom wants us all to come to the house for dinner on Saturday."

Great. "What's the occasion?"

Dakota shrugged. "I think she just wants to see every-one."

"I think I can make it. I'll check my calendar."

Dakota hesitated, her serious gray eyes tentative. She obviously wanted to say something. Probably in defense of their mother's dominating edicts. The woman never made requests. They were more like demands. And Andrea Shea expected unconditional compliance.

To her credit, she'd taught her daughters self-sufficiency, the importance of an education and to never trade on their looks. Dakota could have easily made it in modeling. With her honey-colored hair, gray eyes and wide smile, she was perfect for the camera. A real natural. But she'd been a serious and bright student who'd never given her appearance a second thought, much less attempted to parlay her looks into a career.

"Dallas, I'd really like it if you came. We haven't had a family dinner in a while."

A soft knock at the door drew their attention. It was one of the women with whom Dallas worked. Dressed in clean jeans and a white cotton shirt, Nancy smiled shyly. "I guess this is the place."

"Yep. Come in." Dallas motioned her inside. "You're the first one. I'm really glad you came."

"I'll see you later," Dakota said, acknowledged Nancy with a quick smile and then disappeared before Dallas could introduce them.

"How about some coffee?" Dallas set her cup down and picked up a clean mug.

"Sure." Nancy glanced around the conference room, admiring the dark polished wood, the pair of Georgia O'Keeffe paintings on the cream-colored walls. Beyond the expansive windows was a spectacular twilight view of midtown. She walked closer to the glass. "Wow!"

"Do you take cream and sugar?"

"Just sugar," Nancy said absently and then blinked at her. "Oh, I'll get that. You don't have to wait on me."

"I get you the first cup, then you're on your own." Dallas added the sugar and then handed her the mug.

She accepted it, her eyes inquiring as they locked with Dallas's. "Tony said you went to college."

"Yes," she said slowly, not wanting to invite conversation on the subject but not wanting to seem rude either. "So did he."

"Yeah, but he dropped out after two years. He says you even have a graduate degree."

"There are cookies here, too. The chocolate-chunk ones are awesome." She was gonna smack that big-mouth Tony.

Nancy shook her head. Her brown hair, still a little damp, hung down around her shoulders instead of being pulled up in her usual work ponytail. "I don't get it. If I didn't have to do such a dirty job, I sure as heck wouldn't be out there sweating every day. I'd even rather waitress if it weren't for Petey." She shrugged. "When you got a kid and no husband, you gotta make sure the money is steady coming in."

"I understand. But that doesn't mean you have to put up with the kind of abuse those jerks dish out. That's why we're here tonight."

Nancy's face darkened and she hunched her shoulders. "No one knows about the meeting, do they? I can't afford to get fired."

"Number one, they can't fire you for this. That would be illegal. Number two, none of the guys know unless one of the women told them."

"Who opened their friggin' big mouth?" Jan walked in, shrugging off her backpack. She still wore her work jeans and boots. Her short dark hair hadn't been washed but merely slicked back. "I'll take care of 'em."

"No one." Dallas sighed. That's all they needed. Jan was a loose cannon with enough muscle and attitude to cause some damage. Rumor had it that she'd decked one of the forklift drivers and sent him to the hospital. "I was just reassuring Nancy. That's all."

Three other women who Dallas vaguely recognized walked in together. They all worked for Capshaw's Construction, too, but they were part of a crew that worked on the Upper East Side, which meant word was spreading.

Dallas ushered them toward the coffee and cookies and then poked her head out the door to glance down the hall. Another woman had just stepped out of the elevator. Alone. Not good. Apparently word wasn't spreading quickly enough. It was already ten minutes past the time the meeting was supposed to start.

"Hey, are we gonna start soon? I only got a babysitter for three hours," a short, stocky blonde said between bites of cookie. "And I already used up one of them."

"Let's wait five more minutes, okay?" Dallas foolishly checked her watch again. Only seconds had passed. Where the hell was everybody? From the responses she'd received, she'd been so sure of a larger turnout. But that was the basic problem. Their initial enthusiasm always seemed to evaporate into fear.

After ten more minutes of eating and chatting and exploring the conference room, the women began to get restless, and Dallas decided it was best to get started.

They all took seats and went around the table introducing themselves. Even though they all worked for Capshaw's Construction, they worked for different crews and knew each other casually.

"Okay," Dallas said after the room got quiet. "Who wants to volunteer to lead the meeting?"

Six blank faces stared back at her and then they glanced nervously at each other.

Jan spoke first. "I thought this was your party."

Dallas shook her head. "This gender problem doesn't belong to any particular individual. That's the reason for this meeting—to pull together to decide what action we should take. There's strength in numbers."

"We already have a union." Jan snorted. "Not that they give a rat's ass about us."

"Look," Dallas said, "we need to make a stand together. Neither the union nor Capshaw's Construction can ignore us if we make a joint statement."

"But they can fire us." Nancy clasped her hands so tightly that her nails dug into her skin.

"No, they can't." Dallas gave her a reassuring smile. "That would leave them wide open for a lawsuit."

"They'll still give us a bad time," Sally said, her freckled face flushed. She looked twelve and sweet. Amazing what came out of her mouth. "I get enough shit from those pigs as it is."

"Individually, yes, I agree, it's hard to stop the harassment. It's your word against theirs. But what I'm suggesting is that we all sign an informal complaint and give the powers that be an opportunity to talk to the men. Legally, once they know the harassment exists, they have to address the problem and make sure it stops."

"You mean like put our names in writing?" Nancy asked, clearly horrified at the thought.

Dallas hesitated. She didn't want them all running

out of the room. "That's something we have to discuss further."

"I have a question," Yvette said. A quiet woman with sad brown eyes and a heart-shaped face who hadn't said anything since introducing herself, she seemed the most reluctant attendee.

"Yes?" Dallas prompted.

"What if the person giving you trouble is your supervisor?"

"That don't mean nothing. He can't do that." Jan's fists clenched. "Right, Shea?"

"Of course not. It makes the harassment even more despicable. He could be fired for that. Have you discussed the problem with anyone higher up?"

Yvette's eyes widened. "Goodness no. He would have fired *me!*"

"Bullshit! Tell her, Shea." Jan's face reddened with anger. "Tell me who he is. I'll kick his ass."

"Jan," Dallas said softly. "We have the law on our side. There's no need for violence or threats. We just need to stick together to become more effective."

"That's why I'm here," Jan said. "None of them guys bother me." A couple of the women chuckled, and even Jan grinned. "But I see how those pigs act with some of you, and it sucks. It ain't right. I wanna back you up."

"Thank you, Jan." Dallas nodded at her. "We appreciate your courage and support."

"I got a question for you, Shea." Jan studied Dallas for a moment with a hint of suspicion in her eyes and then asked, "Why are you here? Somebody told me you used to model and you went to college. You don't need to do this stinkin' job."

All gazes riveted to Dallas. They all had the same question in their eyes, the same suspicion. Total honesty was required. And owed them.

Dallas cleared her throat. "Yes, I once modeled and I do have a college degree, and in fact, I have a graduate degree in business. But I hated the pressure of modeling and I realized the path I'd taken in school had been to please my parents. To be perfectly honest, I don't know what I want to do." She smiled wryly. "Except that I don't want to work in construction all my life."

They all snorted and glanced at each other.

"I admit this is temporary for me, a way to earn a living until I figure out what I want to do." That her parents considered her choice an act of defiance was merely a bonus. But she didn't want to share that tidbit. "But I still want to help improve the work conditions for women who choose this job."

"Or have no choice," Yvette said miserably.

"It's not a bad job," Jan said, shrugging. "You go home at the end of the day and that's it. No worries."

"Yeah, right," Nancy said irritably.

"I didn't mean nothin'. I get it that the guys give you a hard time." Jan sighed loudly. "I'm just sayin'…"

Dallas slumped in her seat. "How about we try to be a little more constructive?"

The meeting continued for another hour but with little progress. They all agreed on only two things. One was to think about what had been discussed and then meet again the following week. The second was that Dallas should lead the charge. Too bad she had no idea what to do next.

DALLAS LET HERSELF INTO HER apartment and sighed with relief when she realized Wendy wasn't home. They got along great. Rarely disagreed. But tonight had been horrendously draining, and all Dallas wanted to do was stretch out with a glass of wine. And talk to Eric.

No. Bad idea. She'd be likely to spill too much of her frustration with work. Share her disappointment. Let him get too close. That would be totally foolish. Disastrous. A great way to ruin the fantasy.

She kicked off her shoes and poured herself half a glass of wine, when she'd really like to down half the bottle. She stared at the jagged nail on her index finger and gritted her teeth. None of her fingernails were long but she kept them at a decent enough length for an occasional French manicure. Today she'd spent four hours sanding walls. Ever so carefully, with gloves on. Then five minutes before she'd knocked off, there went the nail.

Normally she wouldn't care, but tomorrow evening was the reception with Eric. She looked at the phone. Maybe she should call to confirm. If plans had changed, he couldn't call her. She still hadn't given him her number.

She took a sip of wine, telling herself that was an excuse. She could wait until tomorrow to talk to him. Anyway, he was probably working. Drumming her fingers on the counter, she glanced from the phone to the clock and then back to the phone. Two minutes. That's it. *Just to confirm tomorrow evening,* she told herself and grabbed the receiver.

With her purse slung over her shoulder and carrying the glass of wine in one hand, the phone in the other, she headed for her room. She gave herself a few more minutes to change her mind about calling while she kicked off her shoes and turned down her lemon-yellow comforter.

Her room was too tiny to hold anything more than a twin bed, a nightstand and a small dresser, so she plumped her pillow and positioned it against the wall and then made herself comfortable, sitting cross-legged with her back against the pillow.

After another sip of wine, she took a deep breath and dialed his number. She knew it by heart after a glance. It was an easy one to remember.

She let the phone ring three times and was about to hang up when he answered. His voice sounded hoarse, husky, as if he'd been sleeping, but it was only eight-thirty.

"Hey, Eric."

"Dallas?"

"Yeah, did I wake you?"

"No, of course not. I'm glad you called."

"Yeah?" She smiled, her misgivings dissolving.

"I wish you hadn't disappeared last night."

"I didn't exactly disappear. I just didn't want to wake you. Besides, I left a note."

"You should've woken me."

She smiled at the drop in his voice. "Why?"

"I had something for you."

An image of him standing naked in front of her last night instantly flashed in her mind. "I can't imagine what that could have been."

"Come over now and I'll show you."

Laughing, she put her glass on the nightstand and then slid into a horizontal position. "I bet."

"Where are you?"

"At home."

"What are you wearing?"

"A big, bulky white chenille robe and pink curlers in my hair."

"Ah, my older-woman fantasy come to life."

Dallas smiled and rolled over to her side. "I just got home from my meeting."

"How did it go?"

"Pretty horrible."

"Sorry to hear that. Want to tell me about it?"

She bit her lip, annoyed that she'd allowed the conversation to go in that direction. "No, I want to talk about something more pleasant."

"Okay," he said slowly, "let's get back to what you're really wearing."

"You mean besides the G-string?"

After a long moment of silence he said, "You're kidding, right?"

"It's black. Not that you can see much of it."

After another pause he asked, "What did you say your address was?"

She laughed. "Nice try."

"Yeah," he said, sounding a little put off. "Or you could come here."

"It's late."

"It's only eight-forty."

"I have to get up early."

"So do I."

"We wouldn't get any sleep."

He laughed. "Like I'm going to get any now."

"Good point."

"Tell you what, where are you?"

"At home, really."

"No, I mean right now."

"In my room, lying on my bed."

"Perfect."

She sucked in a breath, suddenly aware of where this was going. "Why?"

"Take off your clothes."

Heat spiraled through her. "And?"

"Take them off and then I'll give you further instructions."

She hesitated, momentarily self-conscious, but excitement at the prospect of what could come moved her to do as he asked, and she unbuttoned her jeans.

"Dallas?"

"Yes?"

"Tell me what you're doing."

"Taking my clothes off as you asked."

"Be specific."

She laughed, a little self-conscious again.

"Tell me," he urged, his voice growing hoarse.

"My jeans," she whispered, her hands starting to tremble. "I'm pulling down the zipper."

"Go on."

"I'm pushing the jeans down past my hips." She cradled the phone between her chin and shoulder as she struggled to free herself of the stubborn denim.

"Are they off yet?"

"Almost." The phone slipped as she shoved the jeans to her ankles. She kicked them off and repositioned the receiver. "Okay."

"Are you wearing panties?"

"Of course." She laughed. It came out shaky.

"Describe them."

"They're black."

"Silk?"

"Yes," she lied. Plain cotton wasn't sexy and she was really getting into the game.

"A thong?"

"Yes."

He moaned, the sound low and raspy and shooting straight down her spine. "Take them off."

"They're already off."

He breathed deeply into the phone. "Now your blouse."

"I'll have to put the phone down."

"Leave it where I can hear you."

She sat up and took a quick sip of wine. "You, too. Take off your clothes."

His laugh was more a low, sexy growl. "Baby, I'm way ahead of you."

"You're naked?"

"Almost. Down to boxers."

She smiled as she unbuttoned her blouse. "What color?"

"Don't ruin the mood."

"Come on. Play fair."

He hesitated. "Black with red chili peppers."

She laughed. "Really?"

"They were a gag gift from a friend."

"Wear them often?"

"Only when I haven't done laundry for two weeks." He sighed. "Can we get back to something more interesting?"

"Such as?"

"Your bra. Take it off."

"You've assumed I'm wearing one."

Silence, and then he said, "You're not?"

She smiled, picturing the way his eyes darkened and his nostrils flared slightly when he was aroused but trying to hold back. Funny how he seemed so clear in her mind, as if they'd shared more than one night together. "It's black, silk and lace, and I'm about to unclasp it."

"Do it."

"Done." She slipped one strap off her shoulder and then the other, and the bra fell away.

"You're naked?"

"Oh, yeah." She lay back down and stretched out, resting her palm on her tummy. "You?"

"Uh-huh," Eric murmured. "God, I close my eyes and

I can see you. Your nipples. They're pink. Not rose or flesh-colored but really pink."

Suddenly so were her cheeks. She was glad he couldn't see them. Curious, she glanced down at herself. Her nipples were rather pink.

"See what I mean?" he asked as if he could see through the phone. "They're so soft, too. Like satin. Touch them."

Dallas sucked in a breath.

"Come on. Touch them and tell me what you feel."

She moistened her lips. Slowly drew the tips of two fingers around the areola and then pinched the hardened nipple between her thumb and forefinger, closing her eyes, imagining Eric's hand on her body. She bit her lower lip.

"Dallas?" Throaty and hoarse, his voice came across the phone line in a whisper. "Tell me."

She couldn't speak at first. The intimacy of what they were doing amazed her. How could she feel so safe with Eric? The idea was absurd, but there it was. "What I'm feeling has nothing to do with my fingertips."

He started to laugh, too, and then gasped and moaned in her ear. A sensual moan that told her he was also pleasing himself.

The idea excited her further and she slipped her other hand between her thighs. "Tell me what you're doing." She closed her eyes, picturing him in her mind's eye.

"Stroking my cock," he said without hesitation. "Pretending it's you lying here touching me."

She shuddered. If he was trying to tempt her into going over to his place, he was doing a damn good job. "Are you hard yet?"

"Oh, baby." His laugh came out shaky, almost a pant. "Where are your hands?"

"I'm touching my nipples."

"That's not your hands. That's my mouth on you. Suckling you, licking you." He moaned softly. "I can taste you."

Her eyes still closed, she bit her lip, squeezed her thighs together.

"Your other hand," he whispered, his voice growing more ragged. "Slide your palm down your belly and spread your legs."

She swallowed, took an uneven breath. Did as he ordered. Her fingers grazed the slick wet folds and a moan escaped her.

"That's it. Push a finger inside. Deep."

She tensed around herself and whimpered.

"Now two fingers."

With a trembling hand she inserted another finger.

"Baby, I'm with you. My cock is in your warm mouth." He groaned. "Damn it, I can't hold out much longer."

Dallas heard the front door open. It was Wendy. "I have to go."

"No. Don't." He groaned louder this time. "Touch your clit. Do you feel my tongue?" And louder still. "Ah, Dallas, I can't wait any longer. Baby, come with me."

She closed her eyes, shut out the kitchen noises Wendy was making and imagined Eric bent over her, his face between her legs. The spasms came instantly. She tried to muffle her moans. Heard Eric's anguished release. Heard him whisper her name. She curled onto her side and buried her face into the pillow.

CHAPTER TEN

ERIC WAITED AT THE DESIGNATED RENDEZVOUS point, a feeling of dread knotting the muscles in his neck and shoulders. It wasn't as if he didn't expect her to show up. She'd promised to go to the reception with him and she'd be here. Dallas wasn't the type to stand him up. He didn't know how he knew that exactly. He just did.

Hell, he didn't know her at all. Only what he'd fantasized about her late at night when he tried like hell to get some sleep or while he sat in his office staring out the window when he should have been working on a new ad campaign for Whompie's Burgers.

He'd made it in time in spite of the fact that traffic had been a bitch. A light drizzle had people lined up along both Columbus Avenue and Seventy-second, trying to hail cabs that were all full and passing them by without slowing down. He hoped Dallas wasn't caught up in the mess or that she'd decided it wasn't worth coming out. Nah, he reminded himself, she wouldn't chump him.

He checked his cell phone in case he'd missed a call but there was no message. Then he checked his watch. Not that he gave a damn about the reception. He just wanted to see her. Touch her hair, her soft skin. For real. Last night had been torture. He'd wanted her so badly, he could taste her. Smell her sweet feminine scent. He closed his eyes. He could taste her now.

That and the thought of their phone play last night made

him shift from foot to foot, willing his arousal to subside. He didn't dare look down. No sense calling attention to the bulge growing behind his fly. He adjusted his suit jacket to hide his juvenile reaction and then squinted to see who was getting out of a yellow cab stopped at the corner.

Dallas jumped out and darted for cover under the eaves of a diner. He cringed at the black stiletto heels she wore and prayed she didn't break anything in her haste. She made it in one piece, her long, slender legs eating up the wet pavement in four long strides.

Amazing that she could look so graceful dashing through the rain like that, her hair all twisted up with flyaway tendrils that brushed her pink cheeks. In fact, she looked stunning. The whole scene was so perfect, it looked staged. As if it had been set up to shoot a commercial.

It wasn't his imagination. He wasn't the only one staring. Three businessmen who'd just left the diner stood gawking at her. Even a young woman with green spiked hair waiting at the bus stop gave her a second look. The slinky black dress alone was enough to turn heads.

He raised a hand to get her attention. She waved back and then darted across the street between cars. Astonishingly no one honked.

"Hey," she said, smiling, a little breathless—a little shy, if he wasn't mistaken. Probably because of their phone sex last night. Hell, thinking about it still shook him up. He'd never done anything like that before. But with her it had felt natural, comfortable, incredibly erotic.

God, he couldn't go there right now and risk another hard-on. He took her hand, drew her under cover and briefly kissed her. Difficult as it was to pull away, he reared back and smiled. "Sorry about the rain."

Her eyebrows went up. "You can control the weather? Who knew?"

Pleased that she hadn't shied away, he drew her close again and whispered, "You'd be surprised at what I can do given the right incentive."

She lifted her chin, excitement sparkling in her eyes. "Maybe we ought to skip the reception."

"I have no problem with that." Actually his boss would kill him. This client was too important.

She lightly punched his arm. "I didn't get all dressed up for nothing."

He snorted. "Hey, I think I'm offended."

"I'm sure you'll get over it." She smiled. "Tell me again what this reception is for."

"A client just bought a small strip mall and this is his way of announcing the deal."

She reared her head back. "In Manhattan?"

"No." He had to laugh. "Suburban New Jersey. Some small town. I can't even remember the name of it." At her look of surprise he added, "I'm not working up any ads for the project. Not yet, anyway. The guy likes to party. Any excuse will do."

She nodded thoughtfully. "His name?"

"Lawrence Horn."

She repeated it and nodded again. "Any other names I should know?"

"Uh, no." The serious look on her face fascinated him—as if she were about to enter a boardroom instead of attend a meaningless party. Of course, this wasn't exactly meaningless for him, and that she obviously was preparing herself on his behalf sent a strange tingle down his spine.

The drizzle turned to a sudden downpour, startling them. He shrugged out of his jacket and draped it over her shoulders.

"No, keep it. You'll get soaked."

He stopped her from returning the jacket. "Better me than you."

"This dress will dry in a flash. See?" She pinched the fabric at her neckline between her thumb and finger. "It's that kind of material."

He stared at the creamy skin briefly exposed by her tugging. The dress was clingy enough. Wet, it would be like a second skin. Shouldn't think about that. Couldn't. Not now. "We don't have far to go. Just two doors down. Come on."

She moved her arm away when he tried to take it, her lips curving in a seductive smile. "We could wait a few moments. See if the rain lets up."

"Yeah, okay, sure," he said as she crowded him, forcing him back so that he ended up with his back against the brick retaining wall that hid the alley.

She grabbed a handful of his shirt and pulled his head down so that their lips met. But only briefly, and then she looked up at him and smiled. "Think they'll miss you if we're a little late?"

His cock had already started to respond enthusiastically, and he didn't give a damn if they showed up at all. The client would survive. Eric might not. He took a deep breath. "What did you have in mind?"

"A little of this..." She brushed her lips across his. "A little of that," she whispered breathily near his ear as she moved her hips against his.

Between the heavy rain and small alcove they'd found, someone would have to try hard to see them. If anyone were that nosy, the hell with them. Maybe they'd get an education.

"Oh, my." She brushed her hand down his fly. "What have we here?"

"You're sadistic." He barely got the words out through

clenched teeth, afraid he was going to lose it right here in public.

She sighed. "Masochistic, actually."

Buoyed with satisfaction from her admission, he lowered his head and gently bit her lower lip. She whimpered, and he sucked the slick flesh into his mouth. She had something that tasted like strawberries on her lip, but it might as well have been a debilitating drug. His head got light and then heavy, and common sense seemed to evaporate like the wintry morning mist hovering over Long Island Sound under the hot sun.

She moaned and pressed closer. He ran his palms down her back and then cupped her round bottom. She plunged her tongue into his mouth, and his fingers dug into her buttocks as he pulled her hard against his erection.

"Eric." With a shaky laugh she straightened and took a step back. "This is crazy. This is—" Her gaze slid past him. "Look, it stopped raining."

He looked over his shoulder. Mostly it had. Doubtful it would get much better than the persistent light drizzle that continued to mess up traffic.

"Guess we should make a run for it," he said, annoyed that he once again had to cool off a horrendous hard-on.

"I guess so."

"Ready?"

She touched the corner of her mouth. "Do I have lipstick all over my face?"

He licked the spot. "Not anymore."

"Oh, God, don't start."

He breathed deeply. "Yeah, I know."

"We're headed that way, right?" she said, pointing toward Amsterdam Avenue.

"Yep. The red door."

"Here's your jacket."

"Keep it until we get inside."

"Okay, and then I'm going straight to the ladies' room." She smoothed her dress over her hips, and he had to look away. "I'll find you after that."

"I'll be waiting right outside. Ready?"

"Let's go."

He took her arm and steered her around a crack in the sidewalk. Selfishly he liked that she wore the sexy shoes, but he didn't want to see her break any limbs. Even a small nick marring those incredible legs would be a crime.

They got to the door, which was promptly opened by a doorman standing discreetly off to the side. With a sweep of his hand he directed them toward the right, and they followed the strip of red carpet that obviously had been laid for the occasion.

Good thing. Or Eric wouldn't have known which way to go. The brownstone had once been a mansion belonging to one of New York's rich and prominent families, but the building had been gutted and divided into several exclusive shops and a pricey art gallery.

"I haven't seen a restroom, have you?" Dallas whispered.

"Nope, but we'll find it."

"This place is huge. You'd never know it from the outside."

"There it is." He heard classical music coming from the end of the hall and figured that's where they were ultimately headed. "I'll wait right outside."

"I won't be long. Unless damage assessment proves otherwise."

He frowned, not getting it at first, and then he grinned and snatched her hand before she got away. "Come here."

"Why?"

He pulled her close enough that she had to tilt her head back to look at him. "You still have some lipstick on that I haven't licked off."

She laughed and started to pull away, but he captured her mouth with his and, taking advantage of her soft gasp, slid his tongue between her lips. Without hesitation she looped her arms around his neck and pressed herself against him.

Ridiculous how quickly and how hard he got. A smart man would back off. He pushed his tongue deeper into her mouth, exploring the soft, wet flesh, her perfect teeth. He drew his palms down each side of her body, outlining her seductive curves.

Voices coming from the hall behind them brought him to his senses. He broke the kiss, his breathing already out of control. "Go," he said. "I'll be here."

She nodded, her lower lip quivering slightly, and then she disappeared inside. The voices got closer and he realized he needed a quick adjustment himself so he ducked into the men's room.

What the hell had happened to his focus? What the hell had happened to him? This was absurd. Acting like a kid at a client's function. He knew better. He should never have brought her here.

After finishing his business, he left the restroom to find her already waiting outside. Her frown immediately turned into a smile when she saw him, and all his misgivings vanished just like that.

"I thought maybe you'd decided to go on inside," she said, her lips tinted peach again, some of the stray tendrils of hair tucked back into place.

He liked the wild look better. Reminded him of the way her hair had fanned out against his sheets. There he went again…shit! "Let's go mingle."

She unnecessarily clutched the tiny black bag that hung from her shoulder, as if unsure what to do with her hands. Wisely he kept his to himself. Obviously he couldn't be trusted to touch her. Once they joined the party it would be easier to get through the evening. Especially since he had no intention of staying long.

They entered the large reception area bordering the art gallery and a well-known jewelry store that sold unique baubles that Eric's annual salary couldn't cover. The room was attractive but staid, furnished with overstuffed chairs and sofas, antique rugs on the floor and rich dark wood paneling on the walls.

In the corner was a humidor with a collection of expensive cigars and floor-to-ceiling racks of wine, probably French and cost prohibitive. At least for Eric. The place looked more like an old gentleman's club from the seventies, when they could still exclude women without ending up in court.

Apparently the rain had either scared some of the guests off or else they were delayed. Less than twenty people stood talking and sipping from martini glasses or champagne flutes. Lawrence's "little" bashes were known to include a hundred or more guests.

"Amazing, isn't it? From the street you'd never know this place existed," Dallas whispered.

"Not really my thing," he whispered back. "But I had to make a showing. I promise we won't stay long."

"I'm not complaining. Really." She looked at him in surprise. "I understand you have to be here. I'm glad you included me."

Eric blinked. It just occurred to him that he'd done exactly what he never did. Never wanted to do. He'd brought a date to a business function. Of course, this was somewhat different from a company party, and Dallas...well, Dallas was certainly different from his other dates.

The thought stopped him. Where had it come from? Why was she different? How? He barely knew her. Yet he felt it deep down in his gut. She was different.

"Eric? What's wrong?"

He stared into her concerned eyes. "Nothing. I was just— Who are you?"

Her face turned guarded. "What do you mean?"

"I know Tom set up Saturday night." He looked closely for her reaction, but she kept her expression neutral. "We saw you in the window."

"What window?"

He smiled. "Come on, Dallas, the joke is over."

"Eric."

At the sound of Lawrence Horn's voice Eric reluctantly broke eye contact with Dallas, and turned to his client—his long-standing, major-revenue-producing client, to whom Eric would do well to be paying attention.

The guy had over a dozen thriving businesses in the New York and New Jersey area and had used Webber and Thornton for two decades, long before Eric had joined the company. It had been an honor for Eric to be entrusted with the account. He wasn't about to blow it.

"Lawrence, good to see you." Eric extended his hand. "Thanks for the invitation."

Short, balding and with a penchant for bright colors, the man had to be older than Eric's father, yet he sported a diamond stud in his left earlobe. "Thanks for the invitation," he mimicked, laughing. "Can you believe this guy?" Lawrence looked over at Dallas. "Modesty doesn't get you anywhere in this city. This man is a publicity genius. A little more arrogance is in order, don't you think?"

Dallas only smiled.

His gaze still fastened on Dallas, Lawrence took her hand. "Who do we have here?"

"This is Dallas." Annoyed that he couldn't even introduce her last name, Eric forced a smile. "And this is our host, Lawrence Horn."

"Pleased to meet you, Mr. Horn."

Lawrence raised her hand to his lips, his gaze staying on her face.

Amusement twinkled in Lawrence's pale blue eyes as he continued to study Dallas with an odd fascination. "Do I know you?" he finally asked.

She blinked and darted a nervous glance at Eric. "I don't believe we've ever met."

Lawrence squinted at her. "I know this face."

Eric didn't say a word. He was enjoying this way too much. Let her try to wiggle out of this one.

She shrugged a shoulder and casually withdrew her hand. "I guess we blondes all look alike."

Lawrence laughed heartily. "No, my dear, not all blondes are created equally."

A waiter appeared with a tray of canapés, and Dallas took an exceptionally long time to choose one of the morsels. Not that it mattered. Eric had faith in Horn. The guy was like a dog with a bone when he wanted something. And Dallas had clearly piqued his curiosity.

"I know." Lawrence nodded knowingly once the waiter had gone. "You're a model in Eric's ads. That's where I've seen you."

"No," Eric promptly offered. "She's never worked for me."

"Come now." Lawrence frowned. "It'll annoy me until I figure this out. You are a model, yes?"

Dallas chewed thoughtfully, and then said, "I used to model, but it's been quite a while."

"Hmm…" Lawrence shook his head, looking confused, and then started to say something further, but Dallas interrupted him.

She put a hand to her throat. "I'm sorry but—Eric, would you mind getting me something to drink?"

"Stay." Lawrence put his hand up to forestall Eric. With his other he snapped his fingers in the air and a waiter came running. That kind of behavior Eric despised. But Lawrence had other good qualities. Besides, he alone was responsible for about twenty percent of Webber and Thornton's revenue. And most of Eric's annual bonus.

They all gave the waiter their orders, and after he left, Lawrence said, "Please forgive my poor manners. I practically ambushed you at the door."

"Oh, please." Dallas put a hand on his arm. "We're flattered that you personally greeted us. But I was wondering if it would be okay to wander into the gallery."

"Yes, of course." Lawrence waved expansively with his hand, the giant ruby he always wore on his ring finger flashing like wildfire under the lights. "No place is off-limits to you, pretty lady." His mouth curving, he inclined his head toward Eric but kept his eyes on Dallas. "Talk him into buying you a piece of art. Always a good investment, in my estimation."

Eric snorted. As if he could afford anything in the building but a cigar.

Dallas laughed and then winked. "Maybe I'll buy *him* a piece of art."

Lawrence chuckled, clasping his hands together. "Such a delightful girl you are." Someone called to him and he briefly turned his head and waved. "Ah, I must go. But I will see you two later. Eric, she's a keeper." He smiled benignly at Dallas but again addressed Eric. "But I can see I don't have to tell you that."

"Odd character," Dallas said when Lawrence was out of earshot.

"Yeah, but he grows on you."

"I didn't mean odd in a bad way. I love interesting characters. People who don't fit the stereotype. Or don't try to mold themselves into an image to meet other people's expectations. I admire them." Her mouth twisted in a wry smile. "Even though he called me a girl."

Eric said nothing but studied her for a moment. Her expression and voice had changed. Subtly but enough that he noticed. Did people stereotype her? Is that why she was so guarded? Because of her looks, he easily saw how she could be misjudged. Truthfully, he'd pretty much done the same at first. But there was so much more depth to her. He'd only been allowed a glimpse so far, but he sensed the well was deep and he intended to dive in. Immerse himself.

The waiter brought their drinks—scotch for him and merlot for her—and then left to take Lawrence his apple martini. Eric recognized only a couple of people, who were busy talking to someone else, so he didn't feel as if he had to hang around and make small talk.

"Did you really want to go see the gallery?" he asked. "Or were you just trying to avoid the conversation?"

She smiled and took his hand. "Let's go see the gallery."

He followed her like a damn puppy dog. Hell, if she'd wanted to go to Siberia, he would've followed.

Like the building, the gallery was larger than it looked from the outside. Still, there were few paintings displayed, along with a ridiculous sculpture of what looked like a worm in the center of the room. As they passed it, he caught a glimpse of the fifty-thousand-dollar price tag and almost spit out his scotch.

She glanced over at him. "What's wrong?"

"Nothing."

"You don't really want to look at these paintings, do you?"

"I don't mind—" Chuckling, he shook his head. "Not even if they paid me."

She grinned. "Want to go back to the party?"

This time he took her hand, and pulled her close. "How about we go back to my place instead?"

Her eyes sparkled with promise. "I thought you'd never ask."

CHAPTER ELEVEN

DALLAS MADE A DECISION. IF THEIR RELATIONSHIP lasted for longer than a week, she'd tell him about herself. Everything. Well, not everything, but the stuff he needed to know. The part most important to him. That she wasn't a model or a socialite or something pretty to put on a pedestal. That she didn't have a power job and wasn't on the fast track at some Fortune 500 company.

The admission would probably end the relationship. No, it was an affair. Fantasy, really. But what did she expect? The whole thing started with a gag. For one night. She was the one who'd wanted to draw out the fantasy. Play dress up and pretend. And the sex. Oh, God, she got heated just thinking about the way he touched her, the way they moved together in perfect rhythm.

How did she know she'd actually start feeling something for him? That was the last thing she'd expected to happen. She didn't go for ambitious exec types. They reminded her too much of her father and brother.

She watched Eric unlock his apartment door, open it, reach inside to turn on a lamp and then stand aside for her to go in first. Yet he wasn't anything like her father or Cody. She doubted either one of them would give up their precious time to help a struggling Chinese immigrant save his restaurant.

Maybe she was judging Eric too harshly. Maybe what she did for a living wouldn't matter to him.

"Hey, what are you thinking so hard about?" He pulled her in his arms as soon as they both got over the threshold.

"Uh, are you going to close the door?"

"First things first." He covered her mouth with his and kissed her so thoroughly, she literally couldn't breathe.

With a light push to his chest she fell back laughing and gasping at the same time. One of her heels caught in the carpet, and when she missed a step, he caught her arm.

"How do you walk in those things?" He frowned at her black stiletto heels, and then closed the door behind him. "They look great but dangerous."

"Oh, they're lethal, all right. I'm lucky I haven't broken my neck."

"Why in the hell do women wear them? Not that I'm complaining."

She shrugged. "It's the style, I guess. Why do you guys wear baggy pants riding halfway down your butts?"

"Um, excuse me, but I don't think you'll ever see me wearing baggy pants riding halfway down my ass."

She laughed. "Okay, and I don't think you'll be seeing me in stilettos much in the future."

Shrugging out of his jacket, he reared his head back, feigning horror. "Wait a minute, I hope that's open for discussion."

Smiling, she walked farther into the room and dropped her purse on a chair. "It used to be easy when I wore them all the time. Now, I have to admit, looking graceful or at least like I'm not teetering takes some maneuvering."

He tossed his jacket next to her purse. "What do you usually wear?"

"Boots."

"In the summer?"

"Yep."

"I've seen some killer heels on women's boots."

"Not the kind I wear," she said, watching him carefully. "Steel-toed work boots."

He laughed. "Really? Trying to start a new trend?"

"No, they're practical." *For work,* she almost added but stopped herself just in time. Perfect time to tell him. But she just couldn't do it. Not yet. It would ruin the evening. Ruin everything, probably.

At the end of the week, she promised herself, she'd explain. No, wrong. It wasn't about an explanation. She owed no such thing to anyone. She'd simply enlighten him. What he chose to do at that point was up to him.

She took a step closer, looking up at him, her smile purposeful as her gaze moved slowly to his mouth. "Why are we wasting time talking about boots?"

That's all it took. His eyes blazing, he pulled her against him, and just when she expected him to steal her breath away, he gently nibbled on the corner of her mouth and then lightly bit her lower lip. She closed her eyes and let her head loll back. With his tongue he traced her jaw to her earlobe, his touch so feathery light, she wasn't totally sure she wasn't imagining it.

"I take it these diamond earrings are real," he whispered, his warm breath penetrating her skin, and her nipples tightened in response.

"Yes." A graduation present from her parents, they were ridiculously expensive.

"Then I suggest you take them off." His tongue swirled around one of the diamonds, his breathing growing ragged. "Take everything off."

She smiled. "Is that an order?"

His mouth slowly curved against her skin. "It can be."

"Honey, if we were going to role-play, I'd be the general and you'd be the private."

"Want me to take my clothes off, ma'am?"

She laughed. "You're so easy."

He straightened and smiled at her. "Disgustingly easy, I know." He cupped her shoulder, wedging his fingers under the slim strap of her dress. Slowly he slid the fabric down and then he did the same with her other strap.

She undid his red silk tie, impatient when she had trouble with the knot, then pulled it from under his collar. He didn't try to help but just stared at her, the desire in his eyes so potent, it seemed to coat her skin like warm honey clinging to a biscuit.

When she tried to unbutton his shirt, he gently shoved her hands aside and reached around to unzip her dress. He pulled the zipper down halfway and then slipped his hands inside and stroked his palms down her bare skin to the curve of her buttocks.

Shivering, she moved closer so that she barely had room to unbutton his shirt. But she managed to free one button and then another. He massaged her lower back, his chest heavily rising and falling, and for a moment her hands stilled, her mind went blank. She closed her eyes.

Standing in his living room under the soft glow of the dimmed lamp, half undressed, his hands molding her back, was so intoxicating she actually felt light-headed and gripped his forearms.

"Dallas?"

Her lids felt so heavy, it was too much a struggle to lift them.

He moved his hand from her back and then tilted her chin up. "I wish you'd trust me," he whispered so huskily, it took her a moment to digest his words.

She opened her eyes. The sensual fog immediately lifted. "Why would you say that?"

"I want to keep seeing you."

She knew where he was going with this but she wasn't ready for that discussion. "I'd like that."

He smiled. "I don't even have your phone number."

"No?" She undid two more buttons, leaving his shirt hanging open. Placing both hands against his chest, she lowered her head and kissed a spot just above his right nipple.

His body tensed beneath her palms.

"All right." She touched the tip of her tongue to his budding nipple.

He sucked in a breath. "All right what?"

"I'll give you my number."

He moved just out of her reach. "And your last name?"

She pushed the shirt off his shoulder. His cuffs were still buttoned. Before she could unfasten them, he slid her dress down to her waist, leaving her breasts bare.

"What's your last name, Dallas?" His gaze stayed on her breasts. He touched one pearled nipple with the tip of his finger.

She got a hold of his cuff and slipped the button free. "Why is that so important?"

"Why is it so important to keep it from me?" He lowered his head and touched the same nipple with the tip of his tongue.

She freed the other cuff and pushed his shirt off. It fell to the floor. She went for his buckle, but he pulled away.

He smiled and slid her zipper the rest of the way down. Her dress joined his shirt on the floor, leaving her in nothing but a black thong and the stilettos.

"Answer me," he said softly, his gaze hungrily taking in her breasts, his nostrils flaring when he got to the small silk triangle at the juncture of her thighs.

Surely he could see her heart pounding. It felt as if it

were going to burst through her skin. She held her breath and willed herself to keep from crying out as he cupped the weight of her breasts in each hand, using his thumbs to tease her nipples.

"Dallas?"

She couldn't blame him for coercing her like this. She'd done the same thing to him trying to avoid the conversation. But it didn't matter. Not really. Her last name wouldn't mean anything to him. She wasn't even listed in the phone book. None of her family was. "It's Shea."

"Dallas Shea. I like it."

He abandoned her breasts to slide his arms around her. Filling his palms with her bottom, his fingers lightly digging into her fleshy cheeks, he drew her against him. The friction of her nipples rubbing his chest hair raised goose bumps on her arms.

"Take off your pants," she said and kicked off one of her heels.

"Leave them on, okay?" One side of his mouth hiked up. "Just until we get in bed."

She tried to hold back a smile. "Is that where we're going?"

"I don't know. This is pretty thick carpet. Might be interesting to stay right here."

She slid her foot back into the shoe. No matter how soft the carpet, the idea of rubbing her bare bottom on it held no appeal.

As if he'd read her mind, he ran his palms down her backside. "Although I'd hate to see anything happen to this. Your skin is so incredibly soft. Like a baby's."

"The bed totally gets my vote." She didn't wait for him but jerked free his buckle.

"Impatient little thing." Grinning, he undid his buttons and fly.

"*Au contraire*. I think I've been very patient." She shoved his slacks down his hips, and he took it from there, yanking them off the rest of the way and throwing them in the direction of the couch.

He wore boxers again, his sex straining so hard against the tan silky fabric that she could see the outline of the head. She touched him there, swirling the tip of her finger until he shuddered. He cupped her shoulders as she hooked her fingers in his elastic waistband and drew the boxers down his legs.

On her way down she flicked her tongue across the velvety tip. He jerked, his fingers digging into her shoulders. But she had him trapped and she took her time ridding him of the boxers as she explored him with her tongue.

Moaning, he closed his eyes and threaded his fingers through her hair. Bobby pins bounced off her bare shoulders as they fell from the French twist she'd painstakingly created earlier. Her hair fell down her back, and he wove his fingers tighter through the strands as she drew the entire tip into her mouth.

His entire body shuddered. She took in more of him, teasing him with her swirling tongue until she reached the base. He moaned loudly, his fingers digging deeper, more painfully into her skin. With a jerk he pushed her back and then pulled her upright, startling her.

"Eric, what's—"

He shook his head, his eyes glassy. He couldn't seem to speak. He guided her backward until she met the couch and gently laid her down. And then not so gently pulled off her thong.

He kissed the top of her foot, worked his way to her knee and then spread her thighs. The reflex to squeeze them together was almost too great, and she balled her fists, closed her eyes and held her breath. Nothing happened for a moment and she knew he was looking at her. There. In the most intimate place.

She opened her eyes just as he lowered his head and kissed her nether lips. Then he spread them and slid his tongue inside. She nearly came off the couch. Realizing she still had her heels on, she struggled to kick them off before she tore the couch.

The movement seemed to arouse him further, and he used his tongue and fingers with such a fever, she knew it would all be over for her in seconds. She fisted his hair, trying to get him to slow down, but he continued, his tongue unrelenting, until the spasms started to rock her body.

Heat seared her and she cried out. Tears seeped from her eyes. She let go of his hair when she realized she was pulling it and then grabbed the armrest behind her head. He reached up to knead her breast, but he wouldn't stop the sensual assault of his mouth until she shifted her hips and squeezed her thighs together.

Without missing a beat he moved up to her breasts, teasing the nipple of one and then moving to the other and sucking it into his mouth. When he tried to slide his hand between her thighs, she pushed him away.

He raised his head in surprise. His face was slightly flushed, his darkened eyes hooded, his moist lips parted in confusion. She wanted to explain that nothing was wrong, that she only wanted to participate, but she could barely breathe. Instead she reached for him, and he smiled, shifting to give her better access.

It wasn't enough. The couch was too narrow to accommodate both of them, and she pushed herself upright to better maneuver. Like a starving man, he cupped her breasts and began suckling them feverishly, almost as if he couldn't get enough of her.

"Eric?"

He raised his head and captured her lips before she could say anything further. His enthusiasm was heady stuff, but she wanted to taste him, too.

She broke away, gasping for air. "Let's go to the bedroom."

He nodded. "Protection," he said unevenly. "In my nightstand."

She sensed he was about to start in again and she quickly left the couch.

He caught her hand, but she snatched it back.

"Oh, no you don't." She laughed at the wounded look he gave her. "Come on, or we'll never make it to the bedroom."

"We will. Eventually."

About to say they didn't have all night, she stopped herself. The truth was she had no intention of spending the night. But she didn't want to get into that conversation either.

"Well, I'm headed that way," she said over her shoulder and caught him staring at her backside. "Come if you want."

A cocky grin curved his mouth. "I have every intention of coming."

"I'm sure you do. So I suggest—" She let out a yelp when he leaped up and sprinted after her.

She ran to the bedroom, barely making it to the doorway when he wrapped his arms around her and dragged her to the bed. They both fell unceremoniously atop the rust-colored quilt.

"Thought you'd start without me, did you?" he murmured against her neck between kisses.

His slightly rough chin tickled, and she giggled. "It never crossed my mind."

"Not once?"

"Not even for a nanosecond."

"I don't know. You sounded like you enjoyed your own company last night."

She gasped and glared at him, hoping like hell she hadn't turned every shade of red. "You—you butthead."

He grinned. "Butthead, huh?"

"As if you didn't get *your* rocks off." She'd really hoped he wouldn't bring up last night. At the time she'd been so turned on, she hadn't cared about the proverbial morning after. But even as she'd gotten dressed earlier for the reception, several flashbacks had had her cringing.

Eric laughed. "Hey, no denying it here. I think we should do that every night. That we're not together, that is," he said, taking a nip at her earlobe.

She bit her lip. Who knew how much longer that would be? A good reason to quit talking and get down to business, she decided and trailed her finger over the tip of his penis, spreading the thick drop of moisture she found there.

That got his attention. He sucked in a breath and leaned back. She lowered her head and drew him into her mouth, flicking her tongue over the ridge she knew was especially sensitive. His thigh muscles tightened beneath her palms and his moan came out a strangled cry.

"Wait," he said, his breathing labored.

She shook her head and sucked him in deeper.

"Dallas. Please."

She smiled and ignored him.

"Dallas."

She had no intention of stopping, and he must have gotten it because he lay back and moaned, his thigh muscles bunching beneath her right hand. He was so big and hard, she had trouble manipulating him with her tongue, but that didn't seem to faze him. He threaded his fingers through her hair as his entire body shuddered and he cried out her name.

Never had she experienced such a rush of power and excitement. And satisfaction. Contentment. The whole thing scared her to death. This was only supposed to be about sex. Fulfilling a fantasy. She wasn't supposed to want to crawl inside him and stay forever.

CHAPTER TWELVE

"YO, DALLAS, YOU READY FOR LUNCH?" Tony stood on the scaffolding two stories above her, clearly not giving a damn that all the other guys heard him cavorting with the enemy. God bless him.

She shaded her eyes to look up at him. "Give me ten minutes, okay?"

"No problem. It'll probably take me that long to clean up Buddy's mess."

"Screw you, St. Angelo." Buddy threw down his work gloves and grabbed his lunch pail.

"Have a nice lunch," Tony called after him. "Don't hurry back."

Several feet away from Dallas the new guy doing the finishing work on the lobby banister started laughing. Nobody else did. At least not out loud. Most of them at one time or another had been the target of Buddy's vicious temper.

Not Tony, though. For some reason Buddy steered clear of him, even though Tony sometimes goaded him mercilessly. No one knew why, and Tony wouldn't say. The funny thing was everyone figured Buddy had some connection to either one of the higher-ups or the union bosses. His work was sloppy and his attendance poor. He should have been fired years ago.

That's the kind of thing that really infuriated Dallas. Most of the women she knew worked twice as hard so they weren't singled out. And then jerks like Buddy skated by for years.

Yesterday and today had been good days. No traffic duty, and Dallas had gotten to work indoors. It helped, too, that she spent most of the time daydreaming of Eric. Twice she'd had to jerk herself back to reality to keep from sanding off the rest of her pathetically short fingernails.

For the first time, she'd forgotten to bring her work gloves. Hardly a surprise considering she hadn't gotten home until four in the morning. Amazing she wasn't a wreck. Sure made concentration difficult.

"Ready?"

She looked up at Tony. "Has it been ten minutes already?"

"Twelve, and I'm starving." He handed her *Aladdin* lunch pail to her and inclined his head toward the unfinished railing she'd been sanding. "This will be here when you get back."

She sighed. "Much to my delight."

"Where are your gloves?"

"I forgot them."

He frowned at her hands. "You should keep a spare in your lunch pail. I have one but it won't fit you. Especially not for this kind of close work."

"Not a big deal," she said, shrugging and heading toward the door that led to the park where they always ate. Well, not really a park—more a triangle of grass with two trees and a couple of benches where mothers stopped with their strollers to chat over a cup of coffee.

Tony followed, saying nothing, until they got to the park and sat on the grass under a pine tree. Then he took one of her hands and inspected it. Lots of skin tears, and two knuckles on her right hand were scraped and bleeding a little.

She winced. Damn it. They looked like hell, and it was a big deal. Eric would… She put the brakes on her wayward thoughts. This wasn't about Eric. If he wanted someone more glamorous, that was his problem. She couldn't mold herself according to someone else's plan.

But her nails and hands did look like hell.

"Hey."

She looked at Tony.

He smiled. "It's okay to be a girl, you know. I actually like them."

"Don't be a wiseass. This isn't about that."

He removed his hard hat and raked his fingers through his dark wavy hair. "I've never asked you questions, right?"

"Oh, God."

"Relax. I'm not gonna get too personal."

"Good." She opened her lunch pail and got out the waterless hand wash.

He stared at her with an amused look on his face. "I had this neighbor in Queens. She moved in next door when I was about ten and she was maybe twelve or thirteen. Jenny was so damn cute. Long blond hair about your color. Blue eyes, too. And dimples…" He shook his head, smiling. "She wore her hair in braids all rolled up and tucked away because her mother wouldn't let her cut it. And she always had a baseball cap on. Never once saw her in a dress. I doubt she owned one."

He paused and stared at two kids playing ball. Tempted to tell him to shut up, Dallas took out a green apple and bit into the tart fruit. Obviously he was using the story as a parable because he thought it somehow applied to her. Which it clearly didn't.

"I wasn't interested in girls yet," he continued, "but some of the other guys in the neighborhood kept sniffing around her. She'd get so mad, she'd call them out to the park and threaten to whip their asses. If you treated her like one of the guys, she was fine. But if—"

"Tony?"

"Yeah?"

"Shut up and eat your lunch."

He laughed. "I'm just saying—"

"Don't, okay. Besides, you got it all wrong."

"Go ahead, straighten me out."

She sighed. "Why do you do this job?"

He snorted. "Why do you think? Number one, I hate wearing a suit and tie. Number two, I don't know how to do anything else."

"Don't give me that. How much money did you make off the last two brownstones you refurbished?"

He grinned, shrugged.

"That was a rhetorical question. I know damn well you had to have made more than five years' salary working here." She sighed and put down her apple.

"So? Why you bustin' my chops all of a sudden? I'm on your side, remember?"

"I know. Really I do." She and Tony were a lot more alike than she'd thought, she just realized. Both restless. Both wanting something a little more but not ready to cave in or sell out.

He was much more ambitious than he'd ever admit. She was probably the only one who knew, but four years ago he'd bought a foreclosed brownstone, lived in it while he'd renovated it and then sold it for a hefty profit before moving on to the next one and starting over.

Shaking his head and frowning, he unwrapped his sandwich. "I think you need to get laid."

A strangled laugh escaped her and she punched his

arm. If he only knew… "Now you sound just like the rest of them."

"That was low, Shea, really low."

"You asked for it." She stared at her half-eaten apple, tempted to tell Tony about Eric. But really, what kind of advice could Tony give her? Besides, then she'd have to confess her lie. No, not a lie. Her *pretense*. She winced. *Fantasy* had a better ring. Either way it sounded awful.

Besides, there was more on her mind than Eric lately. Like how tired she was getting of the job, of having to wash her hair three times every night to get the dust out. She'd made her point with her parents by now. And she'd paid off most of her debts and started saving some money. Maybe it was time to start looking for something else. Possibly even put her business degree to some use.

Of course, her restlessness had nothing to do with Eric and the fact that he most likely came from some upper-crust Philadelphia family who'd expected more of their son than to date a construction worker. Nor did it have anything to do with how much she'd been enjoying the dressing up and evenings out. It was just time to move on. That's all. Nothing more.

Tony grunted. "Quit with the long face. Let's move to neutral ground. Tell me about the meeting."

She looked blankly at him. "That was Tuesday."

"Yeah, so? We didn't talk yesterday. You skipped lunch so you could knock off early. Must have had a hot date or something."

She looked away. Hard to believe is was only Thursday. That meant she'd met Eric five days ago. That didn't seem possible. So much had happened. She felt so much more than she should. Feeling the weight of Tony's stare, she glanced over at him and mentally flinched at the fascinated curiosity in his eyes.

She cleared her throat. "That was only the second meeting. We have a long way to go. We didn't even have that good a turnout."

"They're afraid of losing their jobs. Can't blame them."

"I don't. Believe me."

"Yeah, I know. So what are you gonna do about it?"

"Me?"

He snorted. "Yeah, you. Who else has the smarts and the guts to get changes made?"

"I just want to get them to the point where they don't feel they have to take crap from anybody."

"And then?"

"I'm not their mother."

He smiled. "I'm just saying...you stirred the pot."

"That doesn't put me in charge. What they need to do is unify."

His eyebrows drew together in a thoughtful frown. "They still need a leader."

"God, you look like my father."

"Shit." He gave her a lopsided grin. "You're not gonna be able to walk away from this."

"Who said anything about walking away?" Guilt needled her. She wasn't exactly anxious to carry the torch. She wasn't even sure she wanted to organize another meeting.

"Well, butter my toast. Aren't you getting testy?"

She laughed. "Butter my toast?"

Tony shrugged, looking adorably sheepish. "My mother's from the south," he muttered. "She says stuff like that sometimes."

"Who knew?"

"What?"

She shook her head. "Is she Italian?"

"Nope. Half French and half Irish. Atlanta born and bred."

"Wow! I always pictured you as part of this big Italian family who's been here for three generations."

"Stereotyping, huh?"

"No."

Tony grinned.

Her indignation died a quick death, and she sighed. "That did sound pretty bad."

"Nah, I just wanted to bust your chops. Anyway, you got it half right." Angling his head, he looked past her, the odd expression on his face making her turn to see what had captured his interest.

"Dakota?" She stared as her sister approached from not six feet away, clearly uncomfortable walking in heels on the soft grass. "What are you doing here?"

"Looking for you, obviously," she said, the sarcasm in her tone entirely uncharacteristic. She darted an unsmiling glance at Tony.

"Why?" Dallas pushed to her feet because she knew Dakota wasn't about to sit on the grass. Not that Dallas blamed her. The gorgeously tailored navy blue suit she wore hadn't simply been yanked off the rack. "How did you know I was here?"

"I stopped at your job site." The clipped tone and the annoyance in her gray eyes pretty much said it all. "How can you work with those Neanderthals?"

Tony started laughing, and Dakota gave him a scathing look. "This is when you're supposed to say 'present company excepted,'" he said, dusting his hands together and getting to his feet.

Dakota's perfectly arched eyebrows went up. She wanted to say something. Dallas knew that look. But Dakota was the genteel one of the siblings. She needed harmony even if it meant trying to please everyone.

Tony gave her one of his killer grins. "You have to be the sister."

Dakota didn't seem as susceptible as most women were to Tony's smile, and Dallas quickly made the introduction before Tony did or said something totally annoying. Dakota grudgingly extended her hand, and Tony made a show of wiping his palms down the front of his jeans. Which would've been okay if his jeans were clean.

Dallas sighed. Designer suit, perfect nails, perfect hair, perfect everything, her sister was just the kind of woman Tony liked to give a hard time. At the risk of seeming rude, she gave Tony her back and asked, "So, what's up?"

"I wanted to remind you about dinner at Mother and Dad's Saturday night."

"You came in person for that?"

"Yes, because it's that important."

Dallas glanced over her shoulder at Tony. He'd taken the hint, sat down and returned to his lunch. His gaze, however, stayed on Dakota. Poor guy. That was never going to happen.

"Why is it so important?"

"Because you didn't show up the last two times."

"Wrong terminology. I didn't *not* show up. I declined the invitation. Big difference."

"You know what I mean."

Dallas groaned. She hadn't really thought about dinner yet. "I'll be there, okay?"

"Promise?"

"Yes."

Dakota grinned. "Want me to pick you up?"

"Don't you trust me?" She smiled back. "No, thanks, I

don't need a ride." A wild thought popped into her head. "Hey, are you taking a date?"

Dakota's eyes widened. "To Mother and Dad's? I—I hadn't even considered it." Her gaze narrowed, and she shot a look at Tony. "Are you?"

Dallas bit back a laugh. Her sister could pontificate all she wanted about the importance of family and the duty of children to their parents, but when it came right down to it, she kept her distance, too. Not as blatantly as Dallas, but she wasn't exactly ready to open the door to her life.

"Oh, I don't know," Dallas said slowly. "I'm thinking about it."

Dakota blinked, and her gaze briefly flitted to Tony again.

"Not him. He's just a friend." Dallas smiled. "But I could bring him for you if you like."

"Are you—" Dakota lowered her voice. Fortunately a couple of kids arguing over a ball drowned her out. "Are you insane?"

"Why? He's really a nice guy."

With a haughty lift of her chin, Dakota adjusted her starched white collar. "Dinner will be served at seven. Mother says to come anytime after six. And I suggest you warn her if you do bring someone else."

"Thank you. I never would have thought of that."

Dakota rolled her eyes. "See you Saturday," she said as she turned and headed for the sidewalk.

Dallas idly watched her go, wondering why in the hell she'd even given the idea of taking Eric a passing thought. Of course, she hadn't, really. Mostly she'd wanted to tease Dakota.

"Hey, how come she didn't say goodbye?"

At the sound of Tony's voice behind her, Dallas smiled and went back to join him.

With an exaggerated sigh he put a hand to his heart. "I think I'm in love."

"You said that on Monday about the blonde at the deli."

"Did I?" He frowned. "Hmm."

She shook her head, chuckling as she reclaimed her spot on the grass and unwrapped a piece of Gouda. She probably ought to set him straight. Not that she thought he was really serious. Or not that she wouldn't like to see them hook up. Tony would be good for Dakota. He'd loosen her up. But she'd never go for someone like him. Not in a million years.

Tony grinned suddenly, his gaze focused on something in the distance, and he lifted his hand in a wave.

Dallas twisted around in time to see Dakota snub him and disappear around the corner.

"She turned for a last look," Tony said, still grinning. "She likes me."

"You're too much."

"That's what all the women say."

"Oh, please." Dallas laughed, darted another look in the direction her sister had gone. Dakota was not the type to look back. Interesting.

She was about to take a bite of cheese when her cell phone rang. As she pulled it off the clip on her belt, she checked caller ID. Her heart skipped two beats. It was Eric.

"Hello?"

"Hey. It's me," he said. "Tell me you haven't had lunch yet."

"Just had it." Giving Tony an apologetic look, she struggled to her feet.

Snorting, he tore open a bag of chips. "Nice having lunch with you."

She glared at him before moving out of earshot.

"Uh, sorry." Eric cleared his throat. "Sounds like I've interrupted."

"No, not really. That was one of the guys I work with."

"Ah, well, since you already had lunch, how about a drink after work?"

She glanced down at her miserable-looking nails. "What time?"

"I'm flexible."

"Okay, well..." Her gaze on her watch, she started calculating the time it would take her to dash home and get cleaned up.

Several feet from Dallas one of the kids playing ball let out an ear-piercing scream.

"What was that?"

"Some kid." She walked farther away as the fight between the little boys escalated.

"Where are you?"

"In a park."

"You ate lunch there?"

"Yeah."

Silence stretched and she knew what he was thinking. A park was a strange place to have lunch with a business associate. God, she didn't want Eric to think she was jerking him around.

"Okay, well, if you're busy, no problem," he said, his tone suddenly and achingly indifferent.

"No, really I'm not. I'd met my sister here. She left a minute before you called."

"Ah, I didn't know she worked in the city."

"Yep. Not far from here."

"Where's here?"

Dallas smiled. "Where should we meet for a drink?"

He sighed, his impatience with her evasiveness clear. "Any preference?"

"How about— Oh, no!"

"What?"

"I can't tonight. I'm meeting Wendy and Trudie." How could she have forgotten? "My roommate and another college friend. We get together once a month. Tonight's it." Why did she feel compelled to give him an explanation? She didn't owe him any. "Sorry."

He hesitated for a long tense moment. "Is everything okay with us?"

"Yes. Absolutely."

Tony approached carrying both their lunch pails. He pointed to his watch, she nodded and he headed back toward the job site. They had five minutes to clock back in. She couldn't be late.

"Still there?" she asked, starting after Tony but keeping a safe distance so that he couldn't hear her conversation.

"Yeah, how about tomorrow night then? Have you seen *Aida?* I think I can get decent tickets, and then we could have dinner afterward...."

She cringed. "I can't."

"Okay," he said slowly.

"I promised a friend I'd help her move out of her apartment. Tomorrow evening is the only time we can do it so she can be out by Saturday."

"Need a strong back?"

"Who? You?"

"Very funny."

She stopped several yards outside the door so he couldn't hear the buzz of electric saws and drills as she scrambled for something to say that wouldn't put him off. He couldn't meet Nancy. Tony was going to be there, too. Eric couldn't meet any of them. Not yet.

She swallowed hard, hoping she wasn't about to make the biggest mistake of her life. "How about Saturday? Want to go to dinner at my parents' house?"

CHAPTER THIRTEEN

ERIC HUNG UP THE RECEIVER AND THEN stared at the phone. They'd been going out for one week and he'd agreed to have dinner with her parents. This whole thing with Dallas could hardly get more bizarre. One minute he thought she was brushing him off, and the next she was asking him to meet her family. Not just her parents but her brother and sister—they were all going to be there. Was he ready for this?

"Hey." Tom strolled into his office. "You going out today or eating in?"

"What?"

"Lunch." Tom frowned. "What's the matter with you?"

Eric picked up a paper clip and absently twirled it around his fingers. "She asked me to go to her parents' house for dinner."

"Who?"

Eric blinked at him. "Dallas."

Tom sank into the chair opposite Eric and stared. "You're still seeing her?"

"I took her to Horn's reception last night."

"No shit."

"So?"

Tom snorted. "Unbelievable. This is serious."

"No, it's not."

"Dinner with her parents? Right."

"It's not like that." Eric got up to get a cup of coffee.

"This means you must have boinked her already, right?"

"You asshole. Get out."

"Whoa!" Tom laughed and got up to follow Eric down the hall to the coffee room. "This is serious."

Too late Eric realized he should never have said anything to Tom. Except how would Eric know he'd receive such a juvenile reaction? They'd never had a serious conversation about a woman in his life. Hell, there never had been anyone with whom Eric had considered having a serious relationship.

He made sure no one else was in the coffee room and then turned to Tom and in a low voice said, "Okay, this may be going somewhere, so you gotta lay off."

Tom's eyes met Eric's and the laughter disappeared. Surprise flickered and then genuine concern. "Sure. I get it."

"Good." Eric got his coffee and headed back to his office, hoping like hell Tom didn't follow. He didn't expect his friend to give him a hard time, but he didn't want to field any more questions either. Questions that would expose the embarrassing fact that Dallas had revealed so little about herself.

He got back to his office, and sure enough, right behind him was Tom. Sighing, Eric sat down. "By the way, I'm eating in today. I have a couple of important calls to make."

Tom hovered in the doorway, a dozen questions in his eyes. "Anyone picking up a sandwich for you?"

"I'm having it delivered." Eric picked up his phone receiver for added effect.

"All right, tomorrow maybe."

"Sure. We'll go over to Pete's for a Philly cheese-steak."

"You got it." Tom checked his watch. "Better go. I've got a meeting in an hour."

"See ya later." Watching with relief as Tom headed for the lobby elevators, Eric replaced the receiver. He picked up his coffee and took a sip. Today he'd skip lunch. He wasn't really hungry. If he wanted it later, he had a Snickers stashed in his desk somewhere.

The phone rang, and he muttered a curse when the sound startled him into sloshing coffee onto an expense report. He grabbed the receiver. Before he could greet the caller, Lawrence Horn walked into his office.

"I wanted to give you a heads-up," the receptionist said over the phone line. "Mr. Horn is on his way to your office right now."

"Thanks," Eric muttered and hung up.

"Poor girl, she did try to stop me," Lawrence said as he sank into the chair Tom had vacated.

Eric didn't even try to feign innocence. "What are you doing roaming around this side of town?"

"Oh, I thought I'd slum for a while." Today he wore a royal-blue suit, cream-colored shirt and black tie. "See how the other half lives."

Used to his harmless sense of humor, Eric paid no attention to the obnoxious remark. "Great party last night. Thanks again."

"You left early." Lawrence wagged a finger and grinned. "Although I can certainly understand why. She's exquisite. Truly exquisite. I applaud you."

Eric snorted, glad Dallas wasn't here to hear that. "Wish I could take credit."

"Oh, was I being politically incorrect?" Lawrence frowned thoughtfully, and then a sly smile curved his mouth. "You'll both forgive me when you hear my offer."

"Offer? What offer?"

"I want you to design an ad campaign around her."

"For what?"

"I don't know." Lawrence waved an impatient hand. "Her face haunted me all night. I even dreamed about her. Surely you can use her to link my companies or something. After all, Revlon and L'Oreal have models as spokeswomen or what have you."

"They're cosmetic companies. Of course they would use—"

"Oh, you sound like Bruce." Lawrence muttered an expletive. "You're supposed to be creative. Think of something."

Eric shook his head. "She doesn't model anymore." Actually he didn't even know if that was true. He didn't know anything about her.

"She will." Lawrence stood and daintily dusted off his lapels with his manicured fingertips. "Money always talks. For her and you." He smiled. "I guess I'll stop by the old man's office on my way out. Haven't seen him in ages."

Eric recognized the veiled threat. Lawrence was going to fill Webber in. If Eric didn't produce, Webber would be all over him.

Then again, maybe he was getting worked up for nothing. Maybe Dallas would be open to a modeling contract. Especially if the price was right. It still galled him that he knew so little about her. But that would change. Saturday night. She was finally going to let him into her private sanctum. Suddenly Saturday couldn't come fast enough.

"YOU HAVE A DEATH WISH. YOU know that, right?" Wendy grabbed a handful of peanuts from the glass bowl the cocktail server had set on their table.

Trudie stopped sipping her margarita long enough to make a face at Wendy. "Why are you so negative?"

"Oh, please. Once he meets her parents, you don't think they'll be history?"

Dallas sighed, beginning to wish she hadn't brought up the subject. "I think Wendy's on to something. Maybe I do have a death wish."

Both women looked at her as if she'd just told them she was pregnant. Dallas casually glanced at the guy at the table to the right of her, so close he might as well have been sitting with them. The place was crowded, every table taken, people standing four deep at the bar. Even the poor cocktail servers had trouble squeezing in between the tables bulging with yuppies in suits and loosened ties. She would rather have gone somewhere else, but it had been Trudie's turn to choose the place.

Dallas leaned closer and spoke more softly. "I mean, maybe I want him to find out but I'm too chicken to actually tell him myself. Does that make sense?"

"Yeah, in a creepy Freudian sort of way." Wendy took a thoughtful sip of her club soda. She saved her calories for peanuts or any other snacks the bar offered.

Dallas did the opposite. Her calories generally went toward alcohol when she was out. Trudie, on the other hand, had no boundaries. She simply indulged in everything.

Trudie licked the salted rim of her glass and then put it down near the peanuts. "Well, kiddo, if you want him to find out, this will be one hell of a good way."

"Except I really don't want him to find out." Dallas sighed. "I don't think."

The other two exchanged sympathetic looks.

Wendy spoke first. "Okay, I hate to point out the obvious, but once you take him to meet the parents, it's gonna be out of your hands."

"First, this isn't about meeting my parents. Second, they rarely talk about anything but themselves and whatever research they're currently involved in, and when they don't have the floor, my brother does. Since they dismiss my job out of hand, they never ask about it. In fact, I think they like to pretend it doesn't exist."

Wendy reached for another handful of peanuts. "Yeah, but you don't think they'll be a little more chatty about you with a new face at the table?"

"Not if I warn my mother ahead of time."

They both chuckled, and then Trudie said, "Like she's going to listen to you."

"She will. Otherwise she knows I won't be showing up for any more—" Dallas hooked two sets of fingers in the air "—quote 'family dinners.'"

"Ah, blackmail," Wendy said, nodding. "Good move."

Trudie frowned, clearly not buying the plan. "What about your father or brother? Or even Dakota, for that matter?"

"Dakota will be totally cool. Mother will take care of Cody and my father."

"I still think it's risky." Wendy signaled the waitress for another club soda. "But, of course, I vote you just tell him. If he doesn't like it, screw him. You don't need that. You guys want another one?"

They both nodded, and Wendy took care of it with a few hand signals to the waitress.

"I don't know," Trudie said. "I just don't think she should be hasty. Once he knows her better, he may be more forgiving."

"Oh, jeez," Wendy said loudly enough to earn her a couple of glares. "Like Dallas needs forgiveness. How would you like it if some guy told you he didn't want you working at a department store?"

"That's not what I meant. You always choose to take everything I say wrong." Trudie got that huffy look on her face that meant the silent treatment wasn't far behind. Which also meant it was time to call it a night.

Dallas sighed. "I think Trudie was talking about me playing a mind game with him. The whole mystery thing."

"Exactly." Trudie sat back, her arms folded across her chest.

"Whatever." Wendy fished the lime out of her drink and popped it into her mouth.

Dallas winced. She liked the flavor of lime, but the actual fruit? Eew. "So, what's happening with you, Trudie? Your boss has to love that display window. It really is something."

Trudie's entire expression changed. "They think I'm a genius."

"You are. Wendy, you should go by and see the window. Totally awesome."

The conversation went in a neutral direction and everyone seemed to relax. Pretty typical girls' night out for them, actually. Dallas didn't know why she insisted on throwing Wendy and Trudie together. They were so different. But both dear friends, and maybe she was more like Dakota than she cared to admit.

Dallas liked harmony, the scales perfectly balanced. It was the Libra in her. That's why she couldn't grasp why she'd set herself up as she had. Saturday could be disastrous. And totally avoidable. It wasn't too late to back out.

She had to really think about this. As if she hadn't wrung herself out worrying already.

She took a deep breath, trying to stay focused on the conversation. But something kept niggling at her, something too horrible to admit. There was possibly another reason she wanted to take Eric to dinner at her parents'.

His meeting them, seeing the beautiful white Victorian in which she'd grown up, would legitimize her. Prove she was more than a construction worker. That she was his kind of woman. And no matter how much she rejected the possibility, it sat heavily in her stomach, eating at her, making her sick. Because if it were true, that would make her a snob just like them.

ERIC OPENED THE DOOR TO HIS apartment, his eyes lighting with appreciation. "You look beautiful."

"Thank you." She hadn't even made it over the threshold before he pulled her into his arms and kissed her. She sighed. "Maybe we should stay here."

"Tempting." He smiled and leaned back to look at her. "But I don't want to disappoint your parents. That wouldn't put us off to a very good start."

She stifled a nervous laugh. Start? Tonight could be the finish. "You really don't have to wear a tie, you know."

He stepped back and studied the obscenely expensive red silk blouse she'd received as a Christmas present from her parents but would never have spent the money on herself. With it she wore casual cream-colored slacks and taupe flats.

"Okay." He loosened the conservative gray tie and then pulled it off. "Better?"

"You don't even have to wear a sports jacket."

He looked doubtful. "What will your father and brother be wearing?"

She laughed. "You sound like a twelve-year-old girl."

"What?" One eyebrow went up. "A twelve-year-old girl, huh?"

She backed up. "Yep."

"Better take it back."

"Or else?"

He grabbed her, and she came up against his chest, laughing, struggling for a breath. She tilted her head back, anticipating his kiss, but he only touched the corner of her mouth lightly with the tip of his tongue.

"Hey." She raised herself on her tiptoes.

A cocky grin curved his lips. "Hey, what?"

"You don't want to play this game with me," she said sweetly. "You'll lose."

"What game?" He grunted when she rubbed against his fly and then quickly retreated. "You're a cruel woman."

"Uh-huh."

"Not even going to deny it, huh?"

"Nope." She smiled and rubbed up against him again. He was hard already.

His eyes closed briefly and he moaned. "You're damn lucky the car is going to be here in ten minutes."

"I don't know why you hired one. We could have taken the train."

"I don't understand why you wouldn't let me pick you up at your apartment."

She stiffened and stepped around him to smooth her hair. Her blouse had come loose in the back, and she took her time tucking it in.

"Dallas, I'm not trying to give you a hard time. I figured that going to your parents' meant the mystery stuff was over."

"I was already in the neighborhood." She shrugged, finding it difficult to meet his eyes while she was lying.

"It just seemed easier to meet you here. You still have time to change if you want to wear something more comfortable."

He hesitated, staring at her as if deciding whether to push the issue. Finally he said, "Such as?"

"Jeans, if you want."

"Jeans?"

"Sure."

He cast a skeptical glance at her slacks. "I'll pass on the jeans, but I will lose the jacket."

"That works. Here." She slipped around him to help take off his jacket, and he caught her wrist.

"Anxious to undress me?"

"Always." She smiled, freeing herself so she could stow the jacket on the couch without wrinkling it.

Eric followed her. "The hell with the driver. He can wait."

She put up a restraining hand. "Down boy. Seriously. We need to get through this dinner first."

His gaze narrowed. "That doesn't sound encouraging. Is there something I should know about tonight?"

"Nothing, really." Dallas sighed, wondering how much to say without spooking him. She'd already had a talk with her mother, warning her that playing old tapes would not be welcome. If the conversation went in the direction of her job or personal life, Dallas would promptly leave. "My parents can be a bit trying, though."

"Trying," he repeated warily.

"A couple of pains in the ass, actually." She smiled. "But don't worry. They'll be on their best behavior with you."

He frowned, looking worried, and she was sorry she'd said anything. "Define *pains*," he said.

She took his hand and squeezed it. "You'll probably find them quite charming. It's me. We haven't always seen eye to eye on things. And I haven't been what you call a dutiful daughter."

"Ah, I get it." He seemed to relax. "Will I like your brother and sister?"

"Dakota will charm your socks off. Cody will talk business and about the stock market until your eyes glaze over. They're both lawyers."

"What about your parents?"

"Dad's a judge and Mother is a biology professor."

"Whoa." Eric looked more than a little surprised. "Well-educated family."

"Yep." And then there was her, the black sheep of the family. The thorn in the otherwise perfect rose.

"You should be proud of them."

"I am."

He smiled, disbelief flickering in his eyes, but he wisely kept his own counsel.

The thing was she really was proud of them. They'd all made enormous contributions to society. Well, her father and Dakota particularly. Her sister tirelessly worked pro bono cases on behalf of battered women, and her father had been responsible for groundbreaking legislation protecting abused children.

Her mother and Cody were more mercenary and strived to make the society columns. Social status was important, and they didn't stray from their ivory towers. But they were basically good people and did their jobs well. Dallas had no problem with their choices in life. None of her business, really. She just wished they stayed out of hers.

She sighed. "I know I've given you the wrong impression. I love my family." She shrugged. "We're just different. It's hard to explain."

A thoughtful frown drew his eyebrows together, and

he looked at her as if he weren't really seeing her. "I get it." He blinked. "It's the same with me and my family."

She smiled, doubtful he truly understood, but that was okay.

The buzzer rang from the lobby, signaling that their driver had arrived. This was it. No turning back now. Within forty minutes they'd be in Tarrytown.

Dallas took a deep breath. "Okay. Showtime."

CHAPTER FOURTEEN

ERIC LAUGHED HUMORLESSLY TO HIMSELF as they passed through the double white iron gates that allowed them onto the Shea property. Not considered an estate—at least not by Tarrytown standards—but damn close. About an acre of sloping green lawn, large old pine and oak trees and a curving driveway that led to a stately white Victorian that had to be a hundred years old. Nope, this wasn't the same at all.

If Dallas were to see the place where he grew up, her jaw would hit the ground. His parents still lived there. In a small three-bedroom row house where if you sat on the porch, all you could see was thick black smoke rising from the steel mill where nearly everyone in town worked, including his father and brothers. God, was he glad to be away from there.

When his pop had retired last year, Eric had tried to get them to move, offered to subsidize the cost after they sold the house, but they wouldn't hear of it. That was home. They were happy. Eric couldn't understand that mentality. But he did respect it and had backed off.

He looked over at Dallas. She'd lain her head back against the leather seat, and idly stared out the window. "You grew up here?"

"What?" She brought her head up. "Oh, yeah."

"Nice. Very nice."

"The house has been in the family for four generations.

My father inherited it from my grandparents when I was about three. Before that we lived in the city." She smiled. "Obviously I don't remember. This has always been home to me."

"I don't think I've seen this much grass in two years. You must miss living out here."

She smiled. "How quickly you've forgotten our ride in Central Park."

"Oh, no." He squeezed her hand and their gazes met and held. "I haven't forgotten."

The car came to a stop. The driver had pulled into the circular drive that put them close to the front door. He got out, dressed in a white dress shirt, black slacks, his graying wavy hair slicked back, and opened Dallas's door.

Totally juvenile, he knew, but Eric hoped her family was watching. First impressions were important. He didn't want them to think their daughter had come with some bum from Pittsburgh.

After they both got out, the driver, in accented English, asked what time they wanted to be picked up. Eric looked at Dallas.

She shrugged. "Ten minutes?"

The driver frowned.

Eric laughed. "She's joking." He glanced at his watch. Stupid, since he knew what time it was. Maybe he was a little nervous. "How about nine-thirty? Does that sound about right?"

Dallas nodded. "Fine."

The driver got back in the car, and they started up the front steps. Before they got to the door, it opened. A short dark-haired woman of indeterminate age, dressed all in black, stood at the threshold smiling.

"Tilly." Dallas took the last two steps at once and

hugged the slight woman. "It's been so long since I've seen you."

"That's because you don't come to visit your parents often enough," the woman scolded with gruff affection. She stepped back, holding Dallas by the shoulders to look at her. "You've gained some weight."

"Uh, thanks for pointing that out." Dallas glanced over at him, a touch of pink in her cheeks.

"It's good. You were too thin." The woman squeezed Dallas's upper arm. "Give me another hug."

Dallas obliged her and then turned to Eric. "This is Tilly. She's been with us forever."

Tilly extended her hand. Her palm was slightly rough. "I'm the Sheas' housekeeper."

"I'm Eric," he said when it seemed Dallas had forgotten to finish the introduction.

"Sorry." Dallas briefly covered her mouth with her hand to stifle a giggle. She sounded like a little girl.

Tilly apparently noticed, too, and snorted. "I used to be the children's nanny, as well. Sometimes I think they haven't grown up yet."

"I haven't." Dallas tossed her hair back and shooed Tilly inside. "Where is everyone?"

"On the back patio having drinks and watching the sunset."

Eric sighed. So much for the grand entrance complete with car and driver. He followed the two women through the large foyer, catching glimpses of the dining room on the right and the living room on the left. Lots of polished hardwood floors and Persian rugs, large vases of fresh flowers, an eclectic array of art pieces, no doubt expensive, in unexpected places.

They came to a sunroom, and beyond the French doors he saw them—three women and two men sitting around a

glass table, looking casually chic with drinks in hand—
and he suddenly wished like hell he hadn't let Dallas talk
him out of bringing a bottle of wine.

Dallas abruptly stopped. "Who is that?"

"Clair Sumner." Tilly winked. "Your brother seems
serious about this one."

Dallas crossed her arms and briefly hugged herself. She
seemed unduly annoyed. Almost panicked, which made
no sense. "Mother didn't tell me there would be someone
else here besides family."

Tilly's brows came down in a perplexed frown. "Is that
a problem?"

Dallas blinked at her and then darted a look at Eric. She
turned back to Tilly with a forced smile. "No, of course
not. It's just— Oh, God, please tell me she's not dull as
dishwater."

"Shush." Tilly pinched her wrist. "Behave yourself,
young lady."

"Ouch." She rubbed the assaulted area. "I'm not going
to say anything." She leaned close to Eric and rolled her
eyes. "He's had the most boring girlfriends you could possibly imagine."

Something had clearly spooked her. She'd tried to
cover up her alarm, but he knew the woman's presence
had somehow unnerved Dallas. Tilly seemed to know, as
well.

An older woman with a remarkable resemblance to
Dallas spotted them. She said something that made ev-
eryone turn around and watch him and Dallas go out the
French doors. The two men stood.

"Before you start getting all chatty, tell me what you'd
like to drink," Tilly said.

Eric glanced at the drinks on the table.

"We have just about everything," she said softly, her kind dark eyes putting him at ease.

"Scotch?"

She nodded.

"Thanks."

"He likes it neat," Dallas said. "And I'll have—"

"I know what you want." Laughing, Tilly shook her head and closed the doors.

Dallas cleared her throat and moved toward the others. "Hi, everyone, I'd like you to meet Eric Harmon."

Lean and tall and looking remarkably fit, the older man, who had to be Dallas's father, gave him a warm smile and a firm handshake. His hair was almost entirely white, yet he didn't even look sixty. "Harrison Shea," he said. Dallas's father, of course.

"Pleased to meet you, sir," Eric said, and was mildly amused that the man didn't object to the *sir* part.

"That's my mother, Andrea." Dallas gestured with her hand, and the woman nodded, her smile not as warm as her husband's, her gaze definitely speculative.

"That's Dakota."

No doubt they were sisters. The same high cheekbones and heart-shaped face, but her hair was a darker blond and her eyes were more gray than blue. And like Dallas, she had a great smile.

"And this is my brother, Cody."

The man nodded, his lips barely moving. Eric didn't take it personally. This was the kind of guy who wasn't comfortable smiling. Dallas had warned him her brother was conservative. No kidding. One look said it all—the short haircut, the preppy white oxford shirt and khaki slacks, the serious gray eyes, no laugh lines there.

She looked at the woman next to him and smiled. "I understand you're Clair."

The brunette nodded and stood, petite, maybe five-two, a Lilliputian in a land of giants. Not a single Shea could be under five-eight.

They shook hands all the way around, Andrea the only one not getting to her feet. Which didn't bother him. Feeling like one of her biology experiments being viewed under a microscope did. She was someone he didn't want to end up alone with at any time this evening. She'd be too curious. No telling what she was liable to ask him.

She had to be in her late fifties yet looked more like Dallas and Dakota's sister. And like her two daughters, she was truly beautiful. She sure as hell didn't come off as a biology professor.

Tilly brought out their drinks and then took orders from the others for refills. No one demurred, which suited Eric fine. The more relaxed they all were, the better the evening was likely to go.

While Andrea instructed Tilly on dinner, he checked out the three Shea women. Any one of them easily could have enjoyed a lucrative modeling career. They had that look that brought ad campaigns to life. Horn had seen it in Dallas. That's why he wanted her.

He couldn't think about Horn right now. Or his demands. Later tonight would be soon enough. When they were alone, back at Eric's place. He'd lay the whole thing out for Dallas. The offer was good. She could make a lot of money, and with a three-year contract there'd be security, as well.

He glanced from Dallas to Dakota to Andrea and realized his confidence had slipped the minute he'd seen the three women together. They all looked like models, yet they'd chosen traditional careers rather than trading on their beauty. Maybe modeling was taboo. Too frivolous.

Of course, he still didn't know what Dallas did, which

irked the hell out of him. All he knew is that she'd modeled once. Maybe she was trying to get into acting and was embarrassed to admit it. That would work in his favor. As Horn's spokesperson, she'd be seen all over the tristate area.

"So, Eric, tell us what you do," Andrea said, and Eric had to quickly regroup.

All eyes on him, he smiled. "Advertising. I work for Webber and Thornton."

"Oh." Andrea's lips lifted in approval. "Where?"

"Manhattan."

"What exactly do you do for them?"

"I'm an ad exec. I devise slogans, print ads, commercials, billboards—anything that sells the product."

"How nice. Sounds productive." She slanted Dallas a brief look that made her stiffen. "Have you two known each other long?"

"A few weeks," Dallas said quickly and then stared pointedly out at the pool. "Did you have it tiled again?"

Harrison sighed with a hint of disgust. "Your mother didn't like the dark-blue-and-green combination."

"But you just had it done last year."

Andrea sniffed and picked up her glass. Two lone ice cubes clinked together.

"Touchy subject." Cody gave Dallas a warning look. "Let's drop it." His hair was darker than the rest of the family's, and his eyes were closer to Dakota's color. Good-looking guy but too serious for the camera.

"Got it." Dallas picked up her wine and sipped.

Eric turned to Andrea, almost as if he'd sensed her stare.

She smiled. "What else should we know about you, Eric? Where are you from? Where did you meet our Dallas? Not at work, I'm sure."

"Mother."

"I'm just making conversation, dear." She met Dallas's gaze and held it. "Not to worry."

"Yes, after all, Clair already has gotten the third degree," Harrison said. "I think your mother should have been the one who went to law school."

Eric smiled. No one else did. Apparently Harrison wasn't just teasing, given the tense looks exchanged by his two daughters.

Tilly showed up with a tray, and as everyone busied themselves with claiming their respective drinks and sampling the crab-stuffed mushrooms, the tension quickly passed. Before she left, Tilly informed them that dinner would be served in half an hour.

"Excuse us for a moment, would you?" Dallas said as she rose from the table. "I'd like to show Eric Mother's garden before the sun sets completely."

Eric got up just as Andrea said, "Really, Dallas, we just met the man. Must you drag him away?"

"Good idea. Check out the roses," Dakota said quickly. "The salmon-colored ones are awesome."

"The garden lights will come on at any moment. You can go for a stroll later." Andrea waved a hand as if the matter were closed.

"We won't be long." Dallas took his hand. With her other one she grabbed her glass of wine. Even after their short acquaintance he recognized the stubborn set of her jaw and didn't argue.

He did give the others an apologetic shrug of his shoulders as he was led away. Not that he wouldn't rather be alone with Dallas, but he didn't want to piss off Andrea either. The woman obviously could be a real pain, but she was Dallas's mother and he preferred she be on his side.

Frankly he wasn't sorry Dallas had chosen that moment

to liberate them. He hated the eventual turn Andrea's question would take. Hated admitting he was from Pittsburgh. That his family was a bunch of steelworkers. Hated even more that he felt that way.

As soon as they got past the white gazebo on the other side of the pool, Dallas mumbled under her breath, "God, why did I come here? I should have known better."

"Hey, come on. It's not so bad."

She looked at him with miserable blue eyes. "Plus, I drag you here to suffer, too."

"Fair is fair. I dragged you to Horn's party." He squeezed her hand. "Seriously everything's been fine. I feel totally comfortable."

"Right." She withdrew her hand and sipped her wine, staring out over a sea of yellow and pink roses sheltered by an ivy-covered brick wall separating their property from their neighbor's.

"Look, I don't understand your family dynamics. Obviously there's an undercurrent I don't get. But I am sorry you're annoyed." He decided not to tell her that he thought she was overreacting.

"No, I assure you, you don't get it. Hell, I don't totally get it." She bit her lower lip. "Sorry, I didn't mean to snap."

He remained silent for several moments, not sure what to say. He really didn't know this woman. Not the way he wanted to. All he could do was change the subject. "This garden is something. It's been so damn hot the last couple of weeks, I'm surprised these roses held up."

She smiled as if she knew he had no idea what he was talking about. Maybe roses liked the heat. What the hell did he know about flowers or gardens? Not a Pittsburgh boy like him.

Dallas leaned against him, and they looked out over the

mass of roses and ivy and some other little white flowers he didn't recognize—miniature roses maybe. Clinging to a vine, they climbed over the top layer of a white flagstone fountain nestled in the corner.

She breathed in the heady scent. "They are beautiful. Remind me to snitch a few before we leave. Look, those are the salmon-colored ones Dakota was talking about. I'm definitely swiping one of those."

He slid an arm around her shoulders. "Your mom doesn't seem like the type to garden. Of course, she doesn't seem like a biology teacher either."

"Don't let her hear you refer to her as a 'teacher.'"

"Excuse me. Professor."

Dallas laughed softly. "That woman hasn't seen the inside of a classroom in years. She's the head of research."

"Ah, that I can see."

"As far as gardening, the closest she comes is putting on a hat and sunglasses to come out and supervise their gardener."

He grinned. "Gotta admit, that would be my idea of gardening."

Her lips curved in a grudging smile. "Okay, I'll concede that one."

The lights came on, and Dallas jumped a little. He held her tighter, inhaling the vanilla scent from her hair. Man, what he wouldn't give to lay her down right here, in the middle of all those roses. Naked.

"What are you thinking?" she asked, looking up at him, a smile dancing at the corners of her mouth.

"Why?"

"You started breathing hard."

He laughed. "You don't want to know."

Her eyebrows went up, and she drew the tip of her finger across his lower lip. "Try me."

After glancing over his shoulder, he whispered, "What time do they go to bed?"

That startled a loud laugh out of her, and she quickly covered her mouth with her hand. "Not here. Not in this lifetime. I'd rather run naked around Columbus Circle."

"Hmm, that has possibilities."

She bumped him with her hip. "The lights make the garden look almost magical, don't they?"

"So, you're not going for it, huh?"

"You are crazy." She bumped him again, which wasn't helping to sidetrack him. "Now, can we please enjoy the moment? Eventually we do have to go back to the patio."

"We do?"

She turned to look at him.

"Only kidding."

"No, you're not. But that's okay." Something caught her attention and she squinted. "Looks like there's an opening in the wall."

"An opening?"

"Yeah, see where some of the bricks have crumbled. We could be out of here before they knew we were gone."

He laughed. "You wouldn't do that."

"Bet me."

"No, because then you'll do it." He turned her to face him. "You'd make me look bad to your parents."

"Why would you care?"

Eric brushed the side of her jaw, liking the silky feel of her skin. Remembering how soft her back was, the inside of her thighs, her perfect breasts. "I plan on sticking around for a while. That's why."

"A while, huh?"

"A long while."

"We'll see," she murmured just before he kissed her.

At least, that's what he thought he heard. But it made no sense. Unless she figured he wasn't a commitment kind of guy. The only way she could have arrived at that was by Tom.

He pulled back. The mood was ruined. "What do you mean by that?"

She slowly opened her eyes. "What?"

"You don't think we have something going on here."

"Of course I do."

"What did Tom tell you?"

She looked as if she were about to deny Tom's duplicity, but then she sighed and said, "Just enough for me to feel safe showing up at the party."

"Okay." He smiled. "That's progress. Now I know I'm not crazy."

She didn't return the smile but moved away and drained the rest of her wine. "We'd better go back. The sooner we eat dinner, the sooner we can leave."

He didn't like her attitude. Textbook passive-aggressive behavior. "Sorry if I ruined your fun."

She touched his arm, and when her lips lifted, it was in such a sad smile that he softened. "It was a mistake to bring you here. I'm sorry."

"Why was it a mistake?"

Her brows lifted in surprise, and then she gave a helpless shrug. "My mother— I have too many issues with her. I think each time I come home it will be different, but it never is."

"Turn around."

"Excuse me?"

He took her by the shoulders and prodded her into

giving him her back. "You're tense," he said as he started massaging the tight muscles around her neck.

"No kidding."

Eric smiled. "We'll get you to relax."

"Good luck." She sighed and then moaned a little when he worked on a particularly tight knot. "She irritates me just being in the same vicinity. She could be somewhere in the house and I have no idea what she's doing and she still irritates me."

He chuckled and kept working. She was tight, all right. Tomorrow he'd treat her to a professional massage. The new Hush Hotel had a couples' massage that was supposed to be pretty awesome. He'd have to call and see if you needed to be a registered guest to use the service.

"It's not her fault. In fact, some of it's mine. I totally get that, in spite of all my childish carrying on." She laughed softly. "I'm her daughter and she wants what's best for me. The problem is, what she thinks is best, I don't."

"Gee, never heard that one before."

She hooked her arm around and pinched his waist.

"Hey, no manhandling the masseur."

"Like you'd be so lucky."

"Good point." He hesitated. She was starting to relax, and he didn't want to stir things up. But he'd have to know sooner or later if modeling was one of the issues that polarized them. Selfishly, later was out. Once back at his place, he didn't want to ruin the mood by bringing up Horn. "I have a question."

"Uh-huh."

"Does your mother object to your modeling?"

"No. But, of course, I really don't model anymore. But she's never had a problem with it as long as it's tasteful. Even Dakota did some modeling for a couple of local stores while she was in college."

Relief washed over him.

"Now, if either of us had decided we wanted to model and skip college, that would have been a major problem."

"Understandable. Only a few models make really good money. Unfortunately it isn't as glamorous as it looks, and their shelf life is shorter than a jar of peanut butter."

"Amen. That's why I quit."

Eric had to tamp down his excitement. None of those problems were attached to Horn's contract.

She sighed and covered one of his hands with hers. "As wonderful as this has been, I think it's time to go back."

"To Manhattan?" he joked.

"I wish. To the lion's den."

CHAPTER FIFTEEN

TILLY ANNOUNCED THAT DINNER WAS GOING to be ready in ten minutes. Dallas knew her mother wouldn't be content to stay out of the final preparations, and when, true to form, she headed for the kitchen, Dallas followed.

She'd actually thought tonight might work out. She'd psyched herself up for two days, telling herself it would be okay to bring Eric. The conversation would remain neutral because she'd received her mother's reassurance that she'd make nice.

Clair's presence changed everything. Damn it. It blew all illusion of control.

"Why didn't you tell me Cody was bringing someone?" she asked as soon as they were in private. Tilly was there, of course, standing at the butcher-block island, tossing some field greens in a glass bowl, but Dallas trusted her implicitly.

"I'm not sure I knew when you called." After setting her wineglass on the granite counter, Andrea picked up a fork Tilly had left beside the stove and stuck it in the rib roast. She made a face. "Tilly, are you sure this is done enough? It looks awfully rare."

Tilly grabbed the fork from her and waved her away. "Go back to your guests and let me handle dinner. The meat is still cooking while it rests. In ten minutes it'll be just the way you like it." Tilly winked at Dallas.

They must have had this conversation twenty times in

as many years. But Andrea always had to stick her nose in things.

"Dallas, bring out your grandmother's silver tureen," her mother said. "I think we'll serve the consommé from the table instead of bringing it to the dining room in individual bowls."

"No, we're not. I have everything set out already." Tilly looked at Dallas. "Would you please get your mother out of here?"

"Really, Tilly, I'm only trying to help." Andrea grabbed her drink off the counter and turned to leave in a huff. Amazing how Tilly was the only one who could get away with speaking to her like that. Dallas never could figure it out. Not even her father dared being that high-handed— not overtly, anyway.

"Wait, Mother."

She stopped and looked impatiently at Dallas.

"I want tonight to go smoothly, okay?" Dallas said slowly, enunciating every word.

"Don't be absurd."

"Please, Mother, keep your promise that you won't manipulate the conversation as a means of attacking my job. Am I clear?"

"Everything isn't about you. You're old enough to know that."

Dallas shook her head. "I wish *you* understood that. Why you have to keep—" Dallas stopped herself. This wasn't going anywhere. It never did. "Never mind."

Her mother blinked, and something changed in her expression. Regret flickered in her eyes. "I know you think I ride you too hard, that I meddle too much. But you're so damn smart, Dallas, what kind of mother would I be if I let you slide in life?"

"You're right. I think you push too hard."

"I probably do. Your father and I have always been proud of all three of you kids. But you were always the brightest, the one with the most potential."

Dallas stared in disbelief. For years she'd felt like the runt of the litter. The one who'd always disappointed them.

"Someday when you're a mother maybe you'll understand." She touched Dallas's arm in an uncharacteristic gesture of concern, and Dallas's defenses began to crumble. "I'm glad to see you brought a decent man with you."

Just like that, the forgiving mood was shot to hell. "A man who gets his hands dirty making a living can be just as decent."

Andrea huffed. "You know what I mean. Must you take everything wrong?"

"As long as you keep giving me ammunition." Dallas exhaled and sheepishly met her mother's eyes. "I'm sorry. I really am. I don't want to argue."

Andrea looked at her a long, silent moment and then sighed. "Well, as you've often pointed out, what you do for a living is your business. I am curious, though, what does Eric think about it?"

Dallas hesitated. The question had taken her aback. She swallowed, tried to come up with a flip remark and couldn't.

Her mother stared with open curiosity, and then a slow, amused smile lifted the corners of her mouth. "He doesn't know, does he?"

Dallas stiffened. God, all she wanted to do was leave. Right now. Get back to Manhattan. To Eric's apartment, where anything seemed possible.

The pity that entered her mother's eyes was almost

more than Dallas could take. "If you're too embarrassed to tell him," she said gently, "then, honey, you've got a lot to think about."

DURING DINNER THE CONVERSATION centered mostly on a volatile court case that was in the news but to which none of the Shea legal eagles had any affiliation. Lots of opinions, though. Which made for a lively discussion.

These were the times that Dallas missed. When she was in high school and her friends would come over for dinner, they were always surprised. The expectation was that dinner at the Sheas' would be a quiet, dignified affair. Rarely was that the case.

Since Dallas had little opinion on the subject and wasn't about to get into another debate with Cody over justification of the death penalty, she got up to help Tilly with dessert. Deeply involved in the conversation, Eric glanced at her and smiled before returning another of Cody's volleys. He looked as if he were actually enjoying himself, and even her brother seemed more animated and taking great pleasure in the challenging arguments Eric presented.

This time she didn't have to ask Dakota to babysit Eric in her absence. Not just because the conversational tide was unlikely to change but because she knew her mother would derail any personal talk of Dallas.

Odd, really, that she'd consider her mother an ally. But she'd been more subdued during the meal, sitting quietly and thoughtfully, sometimes glancing at Dallas and giving her an encouraging smile. Weird. Totally weird. But there it was.

She carried two stacks of dirty dinner dishes into the kitchen with her and placed them in the sink. Tilly was making coffee and she turned around when she heard Dallas.

"Leave those," she said. "I'll load the dishwasher while you eat dessert."

"I have a better idea." Dallas turned on the water to rinse the plates. "Eat dessert with us."

"I'm watching my sugar."

"Then have fruit. You're part of the family. You should be eating with us." Dallas looked around, suddenly interested in what Tilly had made, and spotted the apple-caramel pie. Oh, God. Not good. Dallas's favorite. She could eat the whole thing.

"You sound like your mother. Like I've told her many times, I eat my big meal in the middle of the day."

"I sound like my mother?" Dallas said, aware it sounded like an insult when Tilly slid her a disapproving frown.

Snorting, Tilly wiped her hands on her apron and then opened the refrigerator and brought out a stainless-steel bowl of freshly whipped cream. "Yes, your mother. She always insists I eat with her and your father. And one of these days you're going to realize how much you two are alike. No wonder you're always butting heads like two bighorn sheep. I've never encountered two more stubborn women."

"That's not true. Not about me, anyway."

Tilly gave her an amused look.

"Just because I want to live my own life doesn't make me stubborn." Dallas stuck her finger in the bowl of whipped cream and got her hand slapped.

"There's living your own life and then there's rubbing it in everyone's face."

Dallas gasped. "I've never done that."

"No?"

"Of course not."

The older woman smiled.

"Tilly, come on, you're making me feel awful."

"If it's not true, there's nothing to feel awful about." She put an arm around Dallas's waist and hugged her. "I love you. You three kids are like my own. I don't like to see any of you hurting."

"I know, Tilly. I love you, too." Dallas swallowed back the lump forming in her throat. She didn't know what else to say. Tilly had always been fair and a straight talker. She wouldn't purposely needle Dallas. The thought that she'd disappointed the woman made Dallas ill.

"All right." She returned to the freshly brewed coffee and got out a silver carafe. "Get your fanny back into the dining room and take the dessert plates and the pie with you. I don't trust you with the whipped cream. I'll take that out myself, along with the coffee."

Glad to be back on playful ground, Dallas sniffed. "You don't trust me?"

"With my life? Yes. With whipped cream? No." Tilly lightly smacked her on her backside. "Now get."

"All right already," she said and grabbed the stack of plates.

"Use a pot holder. The pie is still warm."

Tilly's caramel-apple pie was to die for. But warm? Dallas sighed in anticipation. "Did I tell you how much I love you?"

Tilly chuckled and winked. "My dear girl, I would bake you a pie anytime you wanted."

"I know." Dallas had to shut up before she got all teary-eyed. It wasn't even that time of the month. Why the hell was she feeling so emotional all of a sudden?

She took a deep breath and then got out a tray, not trusting herself to carry both the pie and plates out to the dining room safely. After she'd carefully balanced her load, she picked up the tray and backed her way through the swinging door.

She used her hip to keep the door open until she made it to the dining room on the other side. Just as she let go, her foot caught on the edge of the door. She stumbled forward and watched in horror as the pie flew off the tray and splattered across the hardwood floor.

ADHERING TO HER WISHES, THE goodbyes were said inside. No more sympathetic looks, no more idiotic jokes, no annoying fanfare as they left the porch. Thank God.

Dallas slid into the backseat of the car Eric had hired, and he climbed in beside her. She'd huddled closer to the opposite door, but he put an arm around her and drew her against him, to which she responded with mixed feelings. Part of her wanted to be left alone to wallow in self-pity, but the other part needed his soothing touch, needed the reassurance that he still wanted her.

It wasn't just about her clumsiness that had her fraying at the seams. Accidents happened. Of course, she wished she hadn't totally ruined dessert, but hey... What bothered her more were the crazy thoughts running through her head. Ideas spawned by her mother and Tilly.

The car left her parents' circular drive and sped off toward Manhattan. Traffic in and around the city was brutal at any given time, but Saturday night had to be the worst. Inbound was horrible. Nearly ten already, and people were just headed in. It felt as if she'd never get home.

Eric kissed her hair. "Hey, are you still sulking?"

"I'm not sulking."

"Wrong word. Stewing."

"Yes, I'm still stewing."

He laughed, hugged her closer. "I knew you were anxious to leave, but that was a bit extreme."

"Are you trying to make me feel better? It's definitely not working."

Sighing, he rested his head on top of hers. "I liked your family."

"That scares me."

"Come on, seriously."

"I am serious."

He straightened to look at her. "What problem could you possibly have with Dakota? It's obvious she adores her older sister."

Dallas leaned back and smiled. She knew that. "We get along great. Of course, we're the most alike."

"And Cody was a little dull at first, but he was great once he warmed up. He isn't all that conservative when it comes to legal issues. He believes in something and he's passionate about it. I admire that."

"I have to admit I did enjoy him tonight. I just wish Clair had a little more personality. He needs someone to give him a jolt once in a while."

"Yeah, I can see that." He started to laugh and then pretended to clear his throat.

She looked at him. "What?"

"Nothing."

She elbowed him in the ribs, and he grunted. "Don't give me that. What were you thinking?"

"About your father. If I were ever hauled into court, I'd want someone like him hearing my case. He seems reasonable and fair. I like him. Part of the dying breed who still watches baseball. Does my heart good."

"Uh-huh." She gave him a "nice try" look.

"And then there's Tilly. What's not to like about her? She's a doll."

She loved that he'd included Tilly as part of the

family. "You still haven't told me why you were laughing. Although I have a good guess."

"You first."

"Chicken."

"But I have my good qualities."

She grinned. "It's about my mother."

"Sort of. I was thinking how she probably gives your dad all the attitude he needs."

"And then some."

"But I liked her," he added quickly.

"Right."

"I did. At first, I admit, she gave me the willies. No offense," he said with a wry smile. "But then later she mellowed. The way she brushed off your dropping the pie and then joking about not needing the calories, well, I thought that was nice."

"Yeah." Dallas had been a little surprised at her laid-back reaction. Maybe she'd figured she'd beaten up on Dallas enough for one evening.

The unfair thought left Dallas uncomfortable. Her mother had given her a lot to think about. Dallas couldn't blame her for that. Nor could she blame her mother for being right. Damn it. The idea chafed.

"Are you stewing again?"

"Now I'm sulking."

"Not allowed." He lifted her chin and brought her around to face him, then brushed her lips with his. "This is a no-sulking zone."

"I could wait until we get home."

He frowned, thinking a moment, and then shook his head. "Better get it out of your system. I have plans."

"Oh? Such as?"

He slid a hand between her thighs.

She jumped. "Oh."

"Need I demonstrate further?" He lowered his voice, prompting the driver to glance in the rearview mirror.

Dallas met his eyes and quickly dropped her gaze. She wagged a scolding finger at Eric, which he grabbed and sucked into his mouth. She got the giggles and couldn't stop until she had to gulp for air.

"Damn." Eric shot a sidelong glance at the driver. "He thinks we're having much more fun than we are."

That started Dallas giggling all over again. Not because that idea was particularly funny but because she needed the release. Needed to laugh or she might start crying.

Tilly's gentle criticism had gotten to her the worst. Tilly had never lied to Dallas. Ever. Tilly had always been supportive, always fair and always available with a shoulder for Dallas to lean on or cry on. In fact, she was that way with everyone in the family. And she thought Dallas had rubbed her rebellion in her parents' faces.

Had she? Certainly when she was younger, just out of college, she'd done her share of flaunting her independence. She'd ended up paying for her own graduate studies as a result. Anyway, she'd backed off since then. The construction job didn't count. That had nothing to do with rebellion. It was good, honest work, and she needed the money.

Her conscience whispered otherwise, and she shifted positions as if the maneuver would ease her emotional discomfort.

Eric obviously misunderstood and pulled her closer. She smelled the cognac lingering on his breath, the musky masculine scent that was all his. "Okay if we go back to my place?" he whispered into her hair and then rubbed his clean-shaven chin there.

She hesitated, unsure what kind of company she'd make. And then he tilted her chin up and kissed her, and she knew she'd be a lot more miserable at home, fretting over what she was missing.

CHAPTER SIXTEEN

ERIC HAD A PROBLEM. HE CLOSED HIS apartment door behind him and watched Dallas sink into the couch and kick off her shoes. She was in a strange mood. Even before she'd splattered the pie on the hardwood dining room floor. The memory brought an involuntary grin to his face, which he promptly stifled.

The thing was, he needed to give Horn an answer on Monday, but Eric didn't think now was the right time. Maybe later, after she'd relaxed. After they'd made love.

Maybe he could even talk her into spending the night. Then over breakfast he'd lay it all out. God, he couldn't even recall the last time he'd let a woman spend the night.

He tossed his keys on the kitchen counter. "How about something to drink?"

She groaned. "I think I've probably had enough."

"You only had two glasses, but I have orange juice, or I can make coffee."

Dallas shook her head and smiled. "I'm good."

"Yes, you are," he said with a suggestive grin, moving in beside her and sliding an arm around her. "Very good, in fact."

She didn't hesitate to snuggle up to him and lay her cheek against his chest. "Tell me something."

He picked up a lock of her honey-colored hair and let the silken strands fall between his fingers. "Anything."

"Tell me about your family."

"Like what?"

"I know you have two brothers and you're the middle one. But that's all."

The subject was bound to come up. He still didn't like it. But he wouldn't lie. Not that he would volunteer more than her curiosity demanded, either. "Well, I think I told you I grew up in Pittsburgh. All of my family is still there. My parents still live in the same house where I grew up."

"Sounds like my family."

"Nope, my family is nothing like yours."

She flinched and moved away, and he knew she'd taken it wrong.

"My family is strictly blue-collar," he quickly clarified. "Our dinner conversation tended to center around who the Steelers were going to cream that weekend."

"That's football, right?"

"See what I mean? That question alone would be considered sacrilege where I come from."

She grinned. "What happens when the Steelers lose?"

"Two days of lamenting what a bum the quarterback is and how the coach has no business coaching in the pros. And then they start getting pumped for the next weekend's game."

"They? You didn't participate?"

Smiling, he ran a hand down her thigh. "You caught me."

She shifted closer again. "Then you went to college?"

"Only one in the family."

"Go back to visit often?"

"Mostly just on holidays. I've got a bunch of nieces and nephews I like to see. And of course, my parents."

"And your bothers?"

"Sometimes there's tension. They think I'm uppity."

"Are you?"

"What do you think?"

She stared down at his fly and gave her head a sorrowful shake. "You're not uppity."

He barked out a laugh.

"But I can take care of that," she said, sliding her hand across his thigh.

That's all it took, and he started getting pretty damn uppity. She undid his belt buckle, and he relaxed his head back against the cushions, his arms stretched out along the back of the couch, and he watched her.

She took her time, unzipping an inch, kissing him through the fabric, unzipping some more. She was making him crazy, just as he was sure she intended. When he lifted his ass so she could pull down his waistband, she ignored him and pushed the front of his slacks aside. She found the opening in his boxers and freed his cock. He sprung up hard and ready.

She touched her tongue to the tip, and he shuddered. She glanced up, took another lick and smiled. "Did you say something?"

"Help."

She laughed. "Don't you worry. A little CPR should take care of the problem." She lowered her head, but fool that he was, he stopped her, and she blinked up in surprise.

"Stay the night."

A small frown drew her brows together. "I don't know."

"We'll get up early, have breakfast and then you can do whatever."

A slow smile curved her lips just as she ran her tongue around the head. "You stopped me for that?"

He groaned and closed his eyes. How could he think straight when she was doing that?

She took him into her mouth, and he forgot about anything besides her warm breath and talented tongue. She went from gentle swirls to assault mode and back again, keeping him off balance, taking him to the brink and then reeling him back in.

Until he couldn't take it anymore. He tried to get up, intent on reciprocating, but she gave it all she had, and the explosion started before he had another coherent thought.

DALLAS AWOKE AROUND DAWN. Bits of dusky light seeped through the blinds. She tried to roll over to see the alarm clock, but Eric had curled around her, his chest pressed to her back, the stubble from his chin tickling her shoulder. Not even her moving around woke him. He snuggled closer, his semihard penis nudging her backside.

Smiling, she thought about waking him. She'd give him two minutes tops to get hard enough to get inside her. The boy certainly had stamina. Last night alone had proved that fact. They'd made love twice before they'd even gotten to bed and then once more sometime between one and three. She'd nodded off after that.

On the nightstand was her watch, and she slowly reached for it. She yawned and blinked at the blurry face until it cleared. Nine-thirty! It couldn't be that late. She blinked a couple more times. Still nine-thirty. That gave her less than two hours to shower, dress and make it home before Nancy and Yvette got there.

Slowly she pushed back the covers and inched away from Eric. His arm came around her waist and he pulled her back against him.

"Morning," he murmured into her hair and then planted a kiss on the back of her neck.

"Go back to sleep," she whispered, knowing that wouldn't happen. Knowing she wasn't going to make it out of bed anytime soon. And not really caring.

"Right." He kissed her again, her neck, each shoulder, then started down her spine.

"Eric, I have to go."

"What time is it?"

"Nine-thirty."

"No kidding." He cupped her breast and teased the already tightened nipple.

She closed her eyes. "Eric..."

"Hmm."

"You promised."

He lightly bit the side of her neck and then rolled onto his back and sighed. "I was a fool, but you're right. I did."

Dallas turned over and laid a hand on his chest. His hair was sticking up on one side and his chin was dark with stubble. He looked adorable. "Of course, I could spare about twenty minutes."

A roguish smile started at the corners of his mouth, but then he frowned, pushed a frustrated hand through his hair and said, "Tell you what, I'll go make coffee while you take a shower."

"Sure." She shrugged a shoulder and turned to get up, but her disappointment must have shown because he caught her arm and pulled her close again.

"I'd like nothing better than to stay in bed with you all day, but you have things to do, and I have something I'd like to discuss with you before you leave."

She didn't like the serious sound of that. "Like what?"

"Nothing bad. Relax."

"Well, let's talk now."

"You sure you don't want to be ready to go."

"Why? Am I going to want to run screaming from the apartment?"

He grinned. "You have quite an imagination."

"It's getting worse by the second."

"Okay." He sat up, letting the sheet bunch at his waist, and she kept her attention on his face, not wanting to be distracted by his yummy chest. Apparently he didn't have the same compunction. His gaze went directly to her breasts. He noisily cleared his throat. "On second thought, I think we'd better get dressed."

She grunted in exasperation, her curiosity about to burst. "I want to know now or I will hurt you."

He smiled. "Sounds promising."

"Damn it, Eric."

"Remember Lawrence Horn?"

"Of course."

"He came to my office on Thursday. He wants you to be his spokesperson."

"His what?"

"That's broad, I know. Basically he wants your face to be associated with his company and he wants me to design ads based on that."

Dumbfounded, she fell back against the pillows.

"The money would be good. I'm thinking six figures over the life of, say, a three-year contract."

She exhaled slowly, her thoughts one big jumble. This was her chance to get out of the construction business. And she wouldn't have to eat crow, either. Not when the job had landed in her lap. But did she want to get back in that crazy business? She was older now and a little out of shape, less tolerant of sadistic photographers who liked to harp on every little flaw.

God, she'd be like Wendy—desperate, chasing after the next gig, pathetically ignoring the fading of youth. She took a deep calming breath and looked at Eric. "I don't think—"

He put a refraining finger to her lips. "I know what you're going to say. But this is different. No cattle calls. No worrying about paying the rent on time. Best of all, no competition. This is a sure thing."

Of course, he knew what she was thinking. They'd had a similar conversation before about why she didn't like modeling. But he didn't know the rest. She already had a job. And it was a far cry from smiling pretty for the camera.

"Look, you'd call the shots on this. We'd work around your schedule. There'd be print ads, commercials, bill-boards—the usual. I haven't done anything on it yet. Not until I talked to you." He gave her a wry smile. "You realize you still haven't told me what you do."

"No?"

He gave her a long-suffering look, and then his gaze narrowed. "You're a lawyer, too, aren't you?"

"God, no." She hesitated. "Three in the family are enough." Now would be the perfect time to tell him. On the other hand, if she accepted the offer, why bother? He wouldn't need to know. What she did for a living now would be irrelevant.

Her mother's words came back to her and she tensed. Not that Dallas was embarrassed. It wasn't as if she were a stripper or made porn movies, for God's sake.

Eric touched her arm, bringing her out of her preoc-cupation. "What are you thinking?"

"Frankly, about how much I have to do today. And now this." She waved a frustrated hand. "Well, I've got a lot of thinking to do."

"Right." He squeezed her arm. "Maybe we could meet for dinner? I'm sure you'll have questions."

"I have one now. How will my decision affect you?"

He leaned his head back and glanced at the ceiling, one side of his mouth lifting slowly. "Horn's an important client and he wants you."

"And your boss has told you to make it happen."

"Of course he wants to keep Horn happy. But this has nothing to do with us. Whatever decision you make has to be what's best for you."

She took a deep breath. Her decision would have more to do with their relationship than he thought. The image he created in Horn's ad campaign would be exactly the kind of woman Eric wanted. At the thought, her defenses started to rise. Stupid, since she couldn't blame him for something he didn't even know was happening.

Besides, she was hardly being fair, having withheld information about herself. Hadn't she also created a certain image? A very wrong image. The idea stung.

"I'll have to let you know later about dinner," she said and started to get up.

"Wait." He tugged on her arm, coaxing her back beside him. He drew the back of his hand down her cheek. "No matter what, we won't let whatever happens affect us, okay?"

She nodded. "Deal."

Their lips met, and she wanted to crawl back under the covers and pretend he was right. That everything would be okay. Only somehow deep down she knew better.

WHEN DALLAS ANSWERED THE DOOR, she was surprised to find not just Nancy and Yvette but also Jan and Sally standing in the corridor.

"Hope you don't mind us tagging along," Jan said,

leading the others into the apartment and then heading for the kitchen with a grocery sack in each hand. She planted both bags on the counter, which pretty much eliminated room for anything else.

"I'll grab a beanbag chair from my room." Dallas hesitated, tamping down her annoyance as she watched Jan take out six-packs of beer and diet cola and a box of cheese crackers.

This wasn't supposed to be a party. They'd said they wanted to talk to her. Fine. But she had other things to do this afternoon. Like mope around the apartment in indecision. Talk to Wendy and Trudie. Let them tell her what an idiot she was for not immediately signing on the dotted line before Horn changed his mind.

Her head hadn't stopped spinning since Eric had told her about Horn's offer. Why she had the slightest hesitation, she couldn't explain. She didn't even get why the idea made her so edgy. A contract would lock her in and give her income and insurance while she figured out what she wanted to do when she grew up. Most people would consider the decision a no-brainer. A normal person would have jumped at the chance.

She brought back the leather beanbag chair—a holdover from her college-dorm days—and placed it under the small window that offered an excellent view of the dirty brick building several yards away.

"You wanna beer or a soda?" Jan asked as she handed a cola to Yvette. Nancy and Sally already had beers in their hands.

"Uh, neither, thanks." Dallas sat on the floor near the beanbag chair. "What's going on?"

Jan grabbed a cola and they all sat down. When the other three looked to Jan, she snorted and said, "We came up with something that the other women might go for."

Dallas let out a slow breath. This was good. Very good. They'd come up with an idea on their own. They were looking to Jan for leadership and not Dallas. This was excellent, in fact. "What's that?"

"We're gonna do the petition thing. Kind of. We're thinkin' maybe more like a letter." Jan shrugged, glanced at the others. "You know, real detailed, like, about the shit that's been going on."

"But no names mentioned," Yvette added, her hands gripping the cola can as if it were life support. "Right?"

Nancy patted her leg. "Right. We just state the stuff we want to see change."

"Or that we won't put up with anymore," Jan said, and everyone nodded.

"Okay. Good." Dallas smiled. This was nothing new, it's what they'd been talking about all along. She didn't bother pointing that out. No need. They'd finally accepted what had to be done. That's all that was important. "Have you talked to the others?"

"Yeah." Jan glanced at Nancy. "They like the idea."

Sally snorted. "I wouldn't say 'like.'"

"Okay, but they'll hang with us." Jan sipped her cola, her gaze on Dallas. "As long as you write the letter."

"No problem. I'll get to work on it right away."

Yvette's sigh was pure relief, and then she smiled. "I might even have a beer."

Nancy elbowed Jan. Subtly, but Dallas caught it.

"Anything else?" she asked, even though she could see trouble in Jan's and Nancy's eyes.

"Yeah." Jan shrugged. "No big deal, though."

Nancy glared at Jan when she hesitated, then turned to Dallas. "We want you to sign the letter."

"By myself?"

Jan wiped her mouth with the back of her hand. "Not

exactly. We'll all sign our names on the next page, like we're supporting you."

Dallas laughed. "What am I? The sacrificial lamb?"

They all stared at her, clearly confused, and then Jan said, "They're gonna know you wrote it." She snorted and glanced at the others. "None of us would know how to write that kind of letter."

Dallas sighed. "That isn't the point."

"You wouldn't get in trouble, right?" Yvette leaned forward, her elbows resting on her thighs, her hands clasped tightly around the can. "You said it would be illegal to fire us."

"Absolutely." Dallas thought a moment. "I could get my sister to write the letter. Some of you met Dakota at our last meeting."

Nancy's eyes widened. "The lawyer?"

Dallas nodded, already knowing it was a bad idea. Too formal. Too threatening.

"That would piss off the suits. Big-time." Jan got up and grabbed the box of cheese crackers. "You're one of us, Dallas. Better it comes from you."

"Better it comes from all of us," Dallas corrected.

"True." Jan passed the crackers around. No one seemed interested. "But I don't think it's gonna fly any other way."

After a long stretch of silence, Nancy said, "This sucks, you guys. We're asking a lot from Dallas. It's not fair to lay this on her."

Sheepish looks were exchanged, and everyone nodded.

"Let's forget it." Yvette stood and squared her slim shoulders. With her brown hair pulled back in a ponytail, she barely looked seventeen. "We can deal."

"Wait a minute." Dallas motioned for her to sit back down. "I didn't say I wouldn't do it."

Their expectant gazes riveted to her.

She took a deep breath, trying to stay calm, trying to stop the crazy thoughts from taking over. Ironic, really, that she was suddenly in such demand. Pulled from opposite ends of the spectrum. But only one side truly needed her.

"I'm saying that I'll think about it." Ludicrous to back-pedal when she knew exactly what she had to do. *I'll do it.*

CHAPTER SEVENTEEN

"To tell you the truth, I don't know what the big deal is. I'd kill for something like this to fall in my lap. I'm jealous as hell." Wendy fished the green olive out of her martini and popped it into her mouth. She looked at Dallas over the rim of her glass. "You'd be silly to pass up an opportunity like this."

Trudie snorted and set down her Fuzzy Navel to glare at Wendy. "Of course it's a big deal. Dallas can't just desert her friends now."

"Did I suggest she desert them?" Wendy looked from Trudie to Dallas. "Anybody hear me say that? I'm just saying there's gotta be a way to work this out so she doesn't lose the contract."

Duh. Is that all? Dallas sighed and briefly closed her eyes. Thank God the neighborhood restaurant wasn't crowded. Only three other booths were occupied. If she screamed, there wouldn't be too many witnesses to her meltdown.

Her friends meant well, but they weren't helping. Besides, she was tired and cranky and feeling guilty for lying to Eric about why she couldn't see him tonight. She'd told him she had a work emergency, which wasn't a total lie. But what she should have done was gone ahead and met with him, explained her dilemma and let the chips fall where they may.

Of course, then he'd probably withdraw the offer, tell

her she didn't have the right image after all. Not for Horn. Not for Eric. They didn't want just a pretty face. They wanted a total package, at least Eric did. And then if that was the case, screw him.

"Dallas?" Wendy waved a hand in front of her face. "What's going on in there?"

She shook her head. "I have never been so confused in my entire life."

"Okay, look. I think I'm missing something here." Wendy shot Trudie a warning glance. "You let me finish before you jump down my throat. This is how I see it. First, you do want the modeling job, right?"

Dallas nodded.

"But you feel an obligation to finish what you started with your buddies on the work crew, which I totally get. But why can't you do both? I mean, wouldn't it be kind of dramatic if you suddenly quit and, hell, lie, tell them you're quitting because of the harassment. That would work in everyone's favor."

"You don't understand. These guys have no conscience, plus they're sneaky and relentless. Those women would have no defense once I left."

Wendy sighed. "Well, Florence Nightingale, maybe your little chicks should just grow up."

"See? That's what I hate." Trudie glared at Wendy. "Do you have to be so snide? This is serious."

Just when Dallas figured the fireworks would start, Wendy gave them a wry smile and said, "I'm just saying—okay, really badly—but I want Dallas to think about herself for a change. She's bailed both of us out many times," she said, glancing at Trudie and then back to Dallas. "You're always there for everyone else. Do this for yourself."

"It's not that simple," Dallas murmured, sorry she'd

involved them. They didn't understand, and she wasn't sure she wanted to let them in on her stupidity. The fantasy had taken over. She'd been Cinderella for several nights. And then it stretched out to a week, and now this.

"It can be."

"I agree with Wendy." Trudie sat back to nurse her Fuzzy Navel. "Eric said he'd work around your schedule. Maybe you're making a bigger deal out of this than it needs to be."

"Maybe." Dallas exhaled sharply. "Let's talk about something else."

"You don't look happy." Trudie sat forward again, concern darkening her heavily made-up eyes. "Was he freaked when you told him what you really do?"

Avoiding their eyes, Dallas grabbed her club soda, and it sloshed onto the table.

"Dallas?" They both said at the same time.

"What?"

"You haven't told him," Trudie said in utter amazement.

Wendy muttered a curse. "Dallas, you're probably more worried about your image than he is."

Dallas clenched her teeth at the stinging words. "Tomorrow night, okay. I'm telling him tomorrow night."

DALLAS HAD JUST CLOCKED OUT for the day when her cell phone rang. It was probably Eric again. He'd already called twice today. She hadn't picked up either time. Not that she was too chicken to talk to him. Well, there was that, too. But each time she'd been working, and the boss was strict about personal calls on company time.

She grabbed her lunch pail and the cell phone off her belt at the same time, hoping to get away from the machinery noise. The project was behind schedule, and half the guys were working overtime. She hadn't been asked if she wanted more hours, of course, nor had Nancy. After all, they weren't heads of households with wives and children to feed. Their attitude made her sick. Made her fighting mad. That's why she couldn't accept Eric's offer.

By the fourth ring she'd freed the phone from her belt and glanced at the caller ID. With a mixture of disappointment and relief she saw that it was Trudie and answered it.

"Dallas, thank God."

"What's wrong?"

"Where are you?"

"I just got off work. Trudie, you're scaring me. What's going on?"

"How fast can you get to the store?"

"Trudie!"

"You've got to do this for me. Starla is sick again, and if I don't have someone in that window in one hour, I'm going to be in serious trouble."

Dallas put a hand to her throat and released a breath. "Damn it. You scared the hell out of me."

"Please, Dallas. I'll owe you big-time."

"You already do," she muttered, thinking about how this whole mess with Eric started. "I just got off work. I've got to shower and wash my hair and—"

"No, come straight here. We'll work all that out, even if we have to use the fitness center next door."

"You know I have to talk to Eric tonight."

"That's tonight?"

Dallas sighed and checked her watch. "Would I have to stay until nine?"

"Would eight work?"

"I'll be right there."

"I love you, kiddo." Trudie paused. "From what you said, Eric sounds like a great guy. Don't underestimate him."

"I know." She started to tell Trudie about her decision but stopped herself. No more discussion was needed. She knew what she had to do. "I've gotta go catch a cab if you want me there soon."

"Go."

They hung up, and Dallas hurried to the corner to catch a Yellow cab that had just dropped someone off. Once she climbed inside, she called Eric's number and got his voice mail. She left a message suggesting they meet later, close to nine, and tried not to dwell on how torturous it was going to be, stuck in that window, thinking about how she had to spill everything to Eric.

She reminded herself that she'd done nothing wrong. She'd never lied about herself. And she wasn't embarrassed, as her mother had hinted. Not really. Her work simply wasn't anything you discussed over dinner. It was boring, really.

Traffic wasn't horrendous yet, at least not by Manhattan standards, and she got to the corner of Lexington and Fifty-seventh in good time. There the bottleneck started, so she got out to walk the rest of the way. Everyone else was dressed in business attire, and she got several second looks and a few blatant stares that really irked her.

Damn, but she should have at least found a mirror. Made a few repairs. She always went straight home after work and changed out of her overalls, even if she was meeting Tony and some of the other guys for a beer. But here she was, in midtown no less, her hard hat in one hand

and her lunch pail in the other. God only knew what her hair and face looked like. Trudie would pay dearly for this.

Dallas spotted her standing outside the store, waiting, with a bag in her hand. She was looking the other way, so Dallas couldn't get her attention. Especially not with all the pedestrians who seemed to have come out of nowhere, as if the recess bell had just rung. Good in a way, because people paid less attention to Dallas.

She narrowly dodged a man too busy talking on a cell phone to see her but then bumped into someone else. "Excuse me," she said and looked up into Eric's stunned eyes. Horrified, she tried to sidestep him. Disappear before his shock wore off. She ended up running into Tom. Literally.

He took her arm to keep her from stumbling, his face a mask of astonished disbelief.

"Dallas?"

She looked back to Eric. "Hi."

He stared at her for one very long, miserable moment. Then his gaze went to the Aladdin lunch pail, to the yellow hard hat, then returned to her face. "What are you doing?"

"I'm late," she said, backing away and bumping into a man who cursed when she smashed his white deli sack. "Sorry," she muttered to him. Then she said to Eric, "I really have to go. I'll talk to you later."

Eric watched her hurry through the crowd and meet up with a short, well-dressed woman who grabbed her arm and hustled her off in the other direction. Half of him wanted to follow them and the other half was too stunned to move.

"What the hell was that about?" Tom stood beside him, the two of them staring after her.

"I have no idea."

"We'd better move before we get trampled."

Eric seemed rooted to the spot. He couldn't get the image of her in dusty overalls and steel-toed boots out of his mind. Not just that. Her smudged face. Her hair a total mess, so dusty, it looked brown. He almost hadn't recognized her.

"Come on, Eric, or I'm going to Pete's without you."

"Yeah, okay," he said, taking a final look, even though she'd already disappeared. He finally turned around. A double shot of scotch sounded damn good about now.

HER HANDS SHAKING, DALLAS reached for the door handle. She'd already seen him through the window, sitting at the bar, staring at the baseball game on the wall-mounted television. The place was dim, not crowded, and for both those reasons she'd asked him to meet her here.

Not that she had to worry anymore about how she looked. She'd been cleaned up, coiffed and made up, thanks to one of the store's stylists. She looked just like the old Dallas. At least, the one Eric was used to.

If only she had told him before he'd seen her, she wouldn't be so nervous. Wouldn't feel guilty, as if she'd done something wrong, which she absolutely hadn't. She just wished her damn hands would stop trembling.

She opened the door and he looked over at her. He smiled, but it wasn't the same excited smile he normally gave her. He looked confused, maybe even apprehensive, and she didn't blame him. Nor did she blame him for the way he sized her up. Head to toe. As if trying to convince himself seeing her earlier had been a bad dream.

Clearing her throat, she took the stool next to him and smiled. "Hey."

"Hey back." He signaled the bartender. "Wine?" he asked her a little too politely, his tone a little distant.

Or was it her imagination? Was she seeing and hearing what she expected to see and hear? "A triple martini would be much better."

He smiled.

She looked at the bartender. "Club soda, please."

"I'll have another," Eric told the man and then turned back toward her but said nothing.

The silence got too maddening, and she pretended interest in the television. "So, who's winning?"

"I have no idea."

"Oh. I thought you were watching."

His gaze stayed on her. "Were you avoiding me today?"

"No." She gave an emphatic shake of her head. "No, really, I was working and couldn't pick up."

"Working?"

"Uh-huh," she said and pounced on the club soda the bartender set in front of her. She hurriedly took a big gulp. Too big. It made her cough.

"You okay?" He touched her arm, and the familiarity was so reassuring, she wanted to melt into him.

"Fine. Now. I was in the window again tonight. For three hours. It was last-minute, and all I could think about was getting something to drink and going to the bathroom."

He nodded knowingly. "I knew you were doing the display window again."

"How?" Had she missed him in the crowd tonight? God knew she'd been looking.

"That ridiculous way you were dressed. Tom and I figured it out." He chuckled. "I can't imagine what kind of display you were doing. I wanted to swing by and have a look, but I had to meet a client for dinner. Besides, I didn't want to embarrass you, either."

She looked down at her tightly clasped hands, wondering what happened to that speech she'd spent two hours rehearsing. Not a speech, really, just a few sentences. She figured she couldn't handle much more.

"Take Horn's offer," Eric said, covering both her hands with one of his. "And you won't have to do any more of those windows or dress like that again. You're better than that, Dallas."

She stiffened, and he leaned forward to lightly kiss her lips. She let him, even though she didn't appreciate what he'd said. After he sat back again, she bit her lip and stared down at her lap. If she looked him in the eyes, she'd get all jumbled up.

"Dallas?"

She looked up into his anxious eyes and swallowed. "Kiss me."

"What?"

"Kiss me again. Please."

He smiled and, leaning toward her, cupped the back of her neck. Their lips met, and she put more enthusiasm into this kiss—enough that his ardent response made her a little dizzy. Made her chicken. But she had no choice. No more fantasy life. This was the end of the line.

She wasn't sure who broke the kiss. They both kind of leaned back at the same time and looked at each other. The only other two sitting at the bar, on the opposite end, let out a howl. Apparently one of the baseball teams had scored. Dallas glanced up at the screen and saw that the game had ended.

"You're not going to accept Horn's offer," he said in a flat voice.

Her gaze went to him. He didn't look happy. "I'm sorry if that screws you up."

"Are you going to tell me why you won't consider it?"

"I did consider it and I've decided it's not the right path for me to take."

"Maybe we should discuss this further. I don't think you realize what kind of opportunity this is. Horn is very influential in the business community. He has deep pockets and he loves to spend money on advertising."

"Look, Eric, I do understand and I'm flattered that you both want me for this position, but I already have a job, and—"

"I told you that working around your schedule is no problem."

She smiled sadly and then looked away. "I don't exactly have the kind of image Horn wants."

"Are you kidding? You're perfect."

Oh, God, this was so hard. "You know how I was dressed earlier?"

He nodded and then laughed, shook his head.

"That wasn't about a window display. That's me. The real me."

"What are you talking about?"

She swallowed. "I had just gotten off work when you saw me."

"No, you were going to work. You did a window display tonight."

"Yes, but that was a favor for a friend. I believe I'd told you I haven't been in modeling for a while now." She hated watching the confusion draw his face into a frown. Hated knowing she was about to end the fantasy forever.

Her stomach was in one big knot, and she swore she was going to be sick if she didn't hurry and get this over with. But all the carefully chosen words she'd practiced wouldn't come to mind. And every bit of it was her fault. She should have told him the moment he'd made the offer. Before he'd seen her dressed in dirty overalls, carrying that stupid Aladdin lunch pail. God, if she could only start over...

Eric could see something was wrong. Seriously wrong. She could have blindfolded him to keep from seeing the anguish on her face and he would know just by the tension cramping the muscles in his shoulders and the back of his neck.

He silently cleared his throat and reached for her hand. It was cold and she immediately drew back. "Dallas, you're obviously upset. Whatever's wrong, I'm sure we can fix it."

She shook her head. "It's not a matter of fixing it. I'm not a model. I don't have a glamorous job. I'm a construction worker. Garden variety. That's it."

"What?" He started to laugh, until he saw that she was serious. "But you have a graduate degree."

"Yes," she said flatly.

He stared, waiting, expecting this to be part of the joke. "You're serious," he said finally.

Her lips twisted in a wry smile. "I wouldn't make up something like this."

"Why?"

"Why have I chosen to work in construction?"

He nodded, not knowing what to say yet juggling a dozen questions in his mind. Hard to reconcile the gorgeous woman sitting in front of him with the one he saw on the street earlier.

"It started out as an accident. After I quit modeling, I signed up with a temporary agency and they sent me on a laborer's job. I have to admit I was somewhat appalled at first, but it was kind of kicky, you know? Doing something so incredibly different. And the pay sure beat typing or answering phones or filling a clerical position."

Another piece of the puzzle fell into place. "And your parents hated it."

Sighing, she briefly looked down at her hands. "Childish, I know."

He took a sip of his scotch, letting silence stretch, trying to figure out where this left them. Personally nothing had to change. After all, what did they have besides sex?

At that undeniable truth, anger gripped him. Anger at her for not being honest with him. Anger with himself for caring.

God, what a mess. He had to hold it together, though. He still had Horn's account to worry about.

"Okay," he said finally, his mind starting to clear. "Frankly I don't see a problem. Horn's offer will mean a lot more money, and you've already had your juvenile fling."

Flinching, she looked at him with such a wounded expression, he immediately regretted his words.

"Look, I didn't mean to sound snide." He pushed a hand through his hair, glanced around for the bartender, but then quickly decided another drink might not be wise. "Let's start over." He smiled.

Dallas didn't. She sighed and shook her head. "Let's save us both the grief. There's nothing you can say to make me change my mind. I can't accept Horn's offer."

"Because of me?"

She laughed softly. "It has nothing to do with you."

"Why then?"

"It's complicated."

"I have time."

She picked up her club soda and took a thoughtful sip.

"I have a question." Avoiding his intense gaze, she paused to put down the glass. And then she looked him directly in the eyes. "Does this change anything between us?"

He cleared his throat, tried to maintain eye contact but ended up briefly looking away. "What do you mean?"

A sad smile slowly curved the corners of her mouth. "That's what I thought."

"Hey—"

She pulled some money out of her purse, laid it on the bar and slid off the stool.

"Dallas, wait, you didn't let me finish."

"Good luck with Horn's account, Eric. I mean it." She leaned over to kiss him briefly on the cheek and then she left.

CHAPTER EIGHTEEN

"YOU'RE OUT OF YOUR MIND." WENDY set down an un-opened box of Kleenex on the floor near the pink fuzzy house slippers Dallas was wearing. "How could you turn down a job like that?"

Dallas sniffed, huddled deeper into the beanbag chair, pointed the remote at the television and turned up the volume. As if she didn't already know every word to *Pretty Woman*. Better than listening to her annoying roommate tell her what a schmuck she was.

Wendy handed her a mug of steaming chamomile tea and grabbed the remote. "Not that I don't admire your loyalty, but you'll probably end up getting fired over this insane crusade and then where will you be?"

"Thank you for your support."

"Hey, kiddo…"

At the sympathy in Wendy's voice, Dallas looked grudgingly at her. Contrary to what Wendy thought, Dallas wasn't crying. In fact, she hadn't shed a single tear. She had got what she wanted out of the fantasy. One week of bliss. The best sex she'd ever had. Now it was over. She was a big girl. She could accept that and move on.

Wendy sighed and curled up on the love seat with her own cup of tea. "I'm on your side, remember? What kind of friend would I be if I didn't tell you that I think you're making a colossal mistake?"

"Okay, you've told me. Thank you. Now, may I please watch this movie in peace?"

"Have you discussed this with Trudie?"

Dallas groaned. "Am I not speaking clearly enough?"

"I bet she thinks you're crazy, too. Those women will be fine. Loyalty has to have a limit. Think about yourself for a change."

Dallas cursed—something she rarely did—tightened the belt to her white terry robe and struggled to her feet. She couldn't listen to Wendy another minute. Sitting alone in her bedroom without a television was better than having the big, fat mess that was her life rubbed in her face.

At the last moment she remembered the small box of Godiva truffles she'd splurged on after knocking off work and scooped it up before plodding down the short hall to her room. Wendy made a comment about Dallas stuffing her face with chocolate not being the solution right before she closed the bedroom door with a deliberate click. Forget about it. She didn't understand. Nobody did.

Even with the air conditioner on, her room was warm and sticky, and she threw off her robe. After carelessly shoving her quilt to the foot of the bed, she stretched out in her bra and panties and stared at the ceiling. Almost as if it magnetically drew her, her gaze went to her cell phone. The message light blinked.

Knowing it was Eric, she forced her gaze away. He'd called three times since last night. She hadn't picked up once. She didn't have anything to say. Anything he wanted to hear, anyway. It was over. She'd seen the look on his face when she'd asked if anything had changed between them. He hadn't needed to say a word after that.

She didn't blame him. In his business, they called what she'd done "false advertising." She'd worn the pretty clothes, the makeup, the whole thing. She'd become exactly the type of woman he wanted. But that wasn't her. Maybe once. Not now. Not for a long time.

Of course, she'd never expected things to go this far. The fantasy was supposed to have been for one night. And then it had stretched into two, and before she knew it, she'd spent over a week with him. He'd even met her parents.

Oh, God. She covered her face and groaned.

What the hell had she been thinking?

It all seemed so complicated. Maybe she needed to see a shrink. Seriously. Because she could deny it all she wanted, but there was still that part of her that wanted to wear the makeup and the dresses and snatch that incredible contract that would put her right back in the game. That didn't put her in the same category as Wendy. Dallas hadn't chased the elusive dream. It had fallen in her lap.

And then there was Eric. She liked him. Really liked him, damn it. Not because of the sex, which was beyond totally awesome. He made her laugh and he'd been a good sport about meeting her family. A lot of guys would have stopped at the sex part. Told her she was crazy for even suggesting dinner with the folks.

Her cell phone rang, startling her, and she bolted up and almost automatically grabbed it. Instead she peered at the caller ID. It was Trudie. Absurdly disappointed, she lay back down. It wasn't as if she wanted to talk to Eric or even wanted him to call again. In fact, she didn't want to talk to anyone. Not even Trudie.

All she wanted to do was wallow in self-pity for a while. Lick her wounds in private. Be alone with her scary thoughts. And wish she'd never met Horn. Or Eric Harmon.

ERIC SAT AT HIS DESK, STARING at his phone. Three days, and she hadn't called. Not once. Hadn't returned his messages. Not even to tell him to go to hell. This was starting to get to him. He wasn't the one who'd orchestrated the charade.

And contrary to what she assumed, he didn't care what she did for a living. He'd been surprised. Okay, shocked. And then confused and hurt. Yeah, they hadn't known each other long, but why couldn't she have told him? Why the big secret?

Granted, he might have been a little turned off if he'd found out when he'd first met her. Curious, certainly, but not seriously interested.

Tom stopped at his office door, glanced over his shoulder and said, "Webber's on the warpath. Horn just called him and wants to know why you're avoiding him."

"Hell, I'm not avoiding him. I told him I didn't have an answer yet."

"Just wanted to give you a heads-up, buddy." Tom slid another look down the hall before frowning at Eric. "You okay?"

"Fine."

"You don't look so good."

"Yeah." Eric scrubbed his face, exhaled slowly. He hadn't slept worth a damn the past two nights. His thoughts were never far from Dallas. How could she possibly prefer her construction job to the opportunity Horn offered? Maybe she simply didn't understand the magnitude of Horn's offer.

If she invested wisely, after her three-year contract expired, she wouldn't have to work for a while. Take time off to figure out what she wanted to do, start her own business, do whatever… So many options would be available to her if she'd only call him back.

"You wanna go to lunch?" Tom studied him with genuine concern. "Might be a good time to get out of here and clear your head before the old man calls you in."

"No, thanks." He got up, grabbed his suit jacket off his credenza.

Tom looked confused, his gaze following Eric's movements as he shrugged on the jacket. "Am I missing something?"

"I need to run an errand."

"Want company?"

Eric shook his head.

"Anything I can do?"

Eric paused. "Stall Horn. Get him off my back. Tell him I'll have a final answer for him by tomorrow."

"Will you?"

"I sure as hell hope so."

ERIC LEFT TRUDIE'S OFFICE feeling less optimistic than when he'd gone in. Just locating her had been a feat in itself. He'd started with the human resource department, who'd claimed no knowledge of Dallas. Nor had customer service. And not the security officer, who, he was pretty sure, had thought Eric was a stalker. By the time he'd gotten a lead on Trudie and convinced her to talk to him, he'd almost given up.

Might as well have done just that. The problem was bigger than he'd thought, and he had no idea how to fix it.

At the intersection he glanced at his watch. Too early to go to Pete's for a drink, which he certainly didn't need anyway, considering the obstacle he faced. But he didn't want to go back to the office, either. Not until he had a chance to think this through.

He headed down Lexington in the direction of his apartment. Normally he'd take a cab, but he figured the walk might help clear his head. Damn it. Any other reason Dallas had for turning down the offer he could poke holes in. But loyalty? He didn't have a chance. Not with this woman.

He smiled at the irony of the situation. Hell, the whole mess was one big irony. The very thing he admired her for doing was going to screw him to the wall. And then there was Capshaw's Construction—biggest outfit in the tristate area and the company who'd built most of Horn's malls. They had her, and Horn wanted her. If Eric could only figure out a way for her to keep her promise to her friends and still accept Horn's contract. Keep her from letting her career go down the damn tubes.

As much as he admired and respected her loyalty, it wasn't going to make a damn bit of difference. The union wouldn't help, and Capshaw's was too big a company to worry about a handful of disgruntled employees. Yeah, they'd make nice, say all the right things because they were obligated to legally, but when it came down to it, on the job, the men wouldn't be admonished for their behavior if it cost production time.

Eric had seen those scenarios back in Pittsburgh. It had always bothered him when his father used to defend these guys—good old boys.

Damn, what the hell was he going to do? He had to think, slow down his spinning thoughts, or he'd be useless. At an intersection he almost stepped off the curb too soon and got plowed down by a green Honda.

This wasn't just about her job. Or his, for that matter. This was about them. It was soon, their relationship was only budding, but he knew there was something there, something they could build on if they both didn't get too prideful or stupid.

He glanced at his watch. Maybe he should catch a cab

the rest of the way. He didn't have a lot of time. As helpful as Trudie had been, she still wouldn't give him information on how to reach Dallas. But Trudie had given him a lead. Dallas would be in the display window tomorrow night. So whatever he came up with, it had better be quick.

DALLAS POSITIONED HERSELF IN the window at the white vanity table that had been preset for the bedroom scene. She was going to kill Trudie. No wonder the coward had had her assistant meet Dallas with wardrobe and instructions. A red negligee. What the hell was she thinking?

Of course, it wasn't too revealing, thanks to flesh-colored tape. They had to keep the window PG rated, after all, but still... What if Eric were to come by again?

The unnerving thought had her furtively scanning the growing crowd. Hell, he probably didn't want to see her, either. The calls had already stopped. She hadn't had a message or even a missed call from him since last night. He sure had given up easily. Even though it wasn't a surprise, it still disappointed her. More than that, depressed her. What a week they'd had. She'd had such hopes....

She couldn't think about him. If she did, her face would show too much expression and movement, and the scene would be ruined. As much as Trudie was going to hear about this particular getup, Dallas didn't want to spoil her high. The windows apparently had been wildly successful resulting in skyrocketing sales, and her boss had given her a promotion and raise. In fact, he was so pleased, he wanted them to continue. Trudie had the idea of a continuing-soap-opera theme and wanted Dallas to consider working for her part-time.

What a joke. Of course, she may need the money after she got fired from Capshaw's Construction.

She almost blinked. Had to force her mind to go blank. Wrong time to think about the letter or anything else that was about to mess up her pathetic life.

For the next two hours she managed to stay on track by mentally reviewing her grocery list, her Christmas list—anything innocuous enough to keep the crazy thoughts away. Even without her watch, she knew it was close to time for a break. She was thirsty and her left leg kept wanting to fall asleep.

Behind her she heard someone at the window door and waited for her cue to move. That's when she saw him. Eric stood at the edge of the small crowd. Her heart threatened to leap from her chest. If she didn't hear her cue in the next three seconds, she was going to take matters into her own hands. She tried like hell to look away, but her gaze stayed on him.

In his right hand he held a briefcase, yet he wore jeans and a white polo shirt. His expression was partially hidden in a shadow, so she couldn't read him. Behind her someone gave her the okay to step back, and when she moved, so did Eric. Straight for the door.

She almost fell on her face in her haste to beat him. Once she got out and made it to the back of the store and through the employees' door, she'd be safe. If he had the nerve to follow, security would stop him. Not that she wanted to make a scene, but she couldn't deal with him right now.

She grabbed the robe offered by Trudie's assistant and then headed for the back of the store without wasting a single second by glancing over her shoulder. She had at least a thirty-second lead and headed the most direct route to the back. Not until she reached the employee door did she turn around. Several people huddled around the customer service desk, and a woman with a yawning toddler browsed the stationery. But no sign of him. Had he given up that easily again?

With equal measures of disappointment and relief she turned back to push through the door. Instead she met a familiar broad chest. "Eric, what are you doing here?"

"You won't answer my calls."

"I can't talk right now." She pulled the robe sash tighter.

"Then when?"

"Later."

"It's important, Dallas. I really have to talk to you tonight. I'll need an answer for Horn right away."

She sighed. If he didn't look so earnest, she'd be angry. "There's nothing more to discuss," she said softly. "My hands are tied."

"I know."

Something in the resignation in his voice made her believe he did. She glanced around and then asked, "What do you know?"

"I talked to Trudie."

"You what?"

He sighed heavily, and for the first time she noticed how exhausted he looked. Lines radiated from the corners of his eyes, and the lines bracketing his mouth were exaggerated. "You wouldn't return my calls. I had to do something."

"What did she tell you?" Anger raised her voice a little, and she had to take a deep breath.

"What you should have. About the letter you're writing."

"Don't you lecture me."

He smiled. "I'm not. I think what you're doing is admirable. But if you don't give me a few minutes to show you the new ad I came up with for Horn, then I will turn you over my knee."

She laughed. She couldn't help it. "Look, I know you mean well, but—"

"I won't lecture you if you don't patronize me. Just listen to what I have to say, damn it."

Dallas grabbed his wrist to look at his watch. "I have only ten minutes left. Let's see if we can use Trudie's office."

She led him through the door, her heart pounding just knowing he was right behind her. He didn't have a solution, she knew. He couldn't possibly, but that he was here, that he was still interested, was something.

Trudie wasn't there, but her door was open and Dallas took the liberty of taking Eric inside and closing the door. He didn't waste any time in propping his briefcase on the desk and snapping it open.

"In the interest of time, I'll cut to the chase. Capshaw's Construction does a lot of Horn's work, mostly malls catering to middle-class families. He's moving more and more outside of the city into the tristate area and he needs to appeal to different kinds of people."

He took out a sketch pad and flipped it open. "What I've done is to incorporate the two companies in the campaign, showing them working together to better the community. I've taken some liberties," he said with a cocky grin as he showed her the first sketch of buildings under construction in the background and a female worker in the forefront.

She stared in surprise. "That's supposed to be me?"

"Nope. One of the others. I understand you have quite a network of women working construction." He flipped to the next page, again featuring a female construction worker at work—a bit more glamorous than was realistic, but still…

"I figure we could use the different women for different billboards, print ads, commercial spots. Capshaw's can't turn it down. Horn is a large part of their bread and butter. Besides, it puts Capshaw's in a better light than they deserve."

"And they'd be forced to play the part of concerned employer," she muttered, still a little dazed by it all.

"Exactly. Interested?"

"Horn's not going to go for this."

"I already pitched it to him."

"What?" She gripped the edge of Trudie's desk. "He wants it?"

"He's thinking about it. But I believe I've made a good case for him to court the suburbs differently than he's courted the city." He paused. "There is a catch. You have to be part of the package."

She'd already figured that out. She'd end up being his rep in the city, doing the glamorous shots. What she didn't know was how much this effort had been about pleasing his client or about smoothing things for them. "You took an awful chance."

He shrugged. "It's a good business idea. Brilliant on my part, really," he said, grinning, but then sobered just as quickly. "And I admire what you're doing for these women. You could walk away and make a bundle." He grinned again. "You're what we call a stand-up guy."

"All right. No butch jokes."

"Not from me. Think your friends will go for it?"

"Oh, yeah. I can't wait to see the guys' faces when they find out." She realized she'd spoken out loud. "The guys we work with who give us a bad time. Their jaws are going to drop."

He nodded. "Want to see the rest of the sketches?"

"Sure." This was terrific. The women would have to

be excited. And so was Dallas. She was grateful, too, but it was dampened by this tiny niggling suspicion that Eric had orchestrated this to get her out of the construction business. No big deal in the larger scheme of things. But it was there.

He flipped through a few more pages and then paused before showing her the last one. "The thing is, you might have to keep your day job. The money won't be as much, since it has to be spread around."

"No problem."

He showed her the final page. "What do you think?"

She stared in disbelief. It was her. In coveralls, carrying the silly Aladdin lunch pail. She started laughing, horribly afraid she might end up crying.

"You okay?"

She nodded. "Kiss me."

He tossed the pad aside and pulled her into his arms. His mouth touched hers and his gentleness made her want to weep.

She didn't have to ask where this turn of events left them. She'd found it in his kiss.

EPILOGUE

"I THINK THIS BLUSH might be too dark. What do you think?" Nancy asked, staring into the mirror with a critical eye.

Before Dallas could answer, the photographer shook his head impatiently and said, "It's perfect. Let's get in place for this shoot."

Dallas stepped back, out of the way, and watched him set up the scene, feeling like a proud mama. Nancy and the rest of the women had really blossomed in the past two months, their confidence and self-esteem soaring. Old man Capshaw treated them like gold, which sure helped.

"Hey."

At the sound of Eric's voice she turned around. "Hey."

He kissed her briefly. "How's it going?"

"Terrific. This afternoon I'll be reviewing the new contracts with Dakota. I'm getting a family discount. I'll owe her dinner."

He smiled. "What a deal. Have you told the rest of your family about your new career direction?"

"Yep. They think I'll make the perfect agent." She knew her mother had hoped for something different, but she was being supportive and Dallas appreciated that. "Of course, right now my job is easy. Everyone's thrilled with being in the spotlight. But I know it won't always be this simple, and I'm looking forward to the challenge."

Eric took her hand and with his thumb, stroked the inside of her wrist. His voice lowered, and he said, "I'm looking forward to tonight."

Holding back a smile, she arched her brows. "And what would that be?"

"Want me to show you?" He tugged at her hand.

She laughed, and shot a glance at the photographer and Nancy. "You wouldn't dare."

"No?"

The simple whispered word, the slightest curve of his mouth was all he needed to turn her to putty. She sighed. Yep, life was perfect.

* * * * *

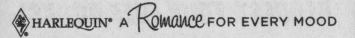

HARLEQUIN® A *Romance* FOR EVERY MOOD

If you enjoyed these passionate reads,
then you will love other stories from

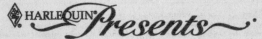

HARLEQUIN® *Presents*

Glamorous international settings...
unforgettable men...passionate romances—
Harlequin Presents promises you the world!

HARLEQUIN® *Blaze™*

Fun, flirtatious and steamy books that tell it
like it is, inside and outside the bedroom.

Silhouette® *Desire*

Always Powerful, Passionate and Provocative

Six new titles are available every month
from each of these lines

Available wherever books are sold

If you enjoyed INTENT TO SEDUCE,
you'll love *Cara Summers's next book,*
TAKE MY BREATH AWAY...
Available February 2011 only from Harlequin Blaze.
Here's a sneak peek...

NICOLA HAD NEARLY protested when he'd moved away.

It wasn't that she wanted him to make love to her again. Although if he tried anything, she was pretty sure she would respond. She didn't seem to be able to stop herself.

But this just wasn't like her. She'd never been so impulsive, so reckless before. She had to break contact with the stranger and get back to being FBI special agent Nicola Guthrie. She just needed another second to think of what she was supposed to do next.

What should she say? How could she explain what had happened, when she didn't understand it herself?

She'd been on duty. She'd been pursuing a thief who'd gotten away, and the man she'd just made love to...twice... might have information that could solve the case.

Back to business, Nicola.

But it was the stranger who began to inch away.

Drawing in a deep breath, she lifted her head and fastened her eyes on him. She felt that punch to the gut again.

"You're awake," he said.

"I have been for a while," she confessed. "I was just trying to figure out what to say to you. Are you all right? I didn't mean to..."

He studied her with those intent eyes of his, and then to her surprise he smiled. "Are you trying to say that you took advantage of me, Curls? I assure you that you didn't."

"Curls?" She stared at him as fragmented images filled

her mind. She was back at the St. Francis Center playing basketball on the small street-side court. With Gabe Wilder.

He took a strand of her hair and tucked it behind her ear. "I miss your curls. Remember when I used to tug on them?"

The widening of his smile transformed the ripples of recognition that had been lapping at the edge of her mind into a full-blown wave. And she did remember. He'd often tugged her hair in congratulations when she'd made an especially good play. And he'd always called her Curls.

"Gabe." She stared at him. "You're Gabe Wilder."

"Guilty."

She closed her eyes. Perhaps when she opened them, she would find that it had all been a dream. "No. No. No. If I'd known you were Gabe Wilder, I never would have…"

At his questioning look, she shook her head. "You don't understand. He…you are my prime suspect."

Find out what happens next in
TAKE MY BREATH AWAY… *by Cara Summers.*
Available February 2011, only from Harlequin Blaze.

HBEXP0211

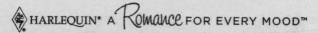

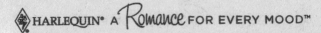

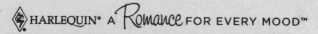
HARLEQUIN® A *Romance* FOR EVERY MOOD™

CLASSICS

Quintessential, modern love stories
that are romance at its finest.

Harlequin Presents®

Glamorous international settings…
unforgettable men…passionate
romances—Harlequin Presents
promises you the world!

Harlequin Presents® Extra

Meet more of your favorite Presents
heroes and travel to glamorous
international locations in our regular
monthly themed collections.

Harlequin® Romance

The anticipation, the thrill of the chase
and the sheer rush of falling in love!